Mary de Laszlo trained as a fashion journalist in the mid sixties, working for *Queen* magazine in London and *Jardin des Modes* in Paris. In recent years she has had various stories published in women's magazines, both in the UK and Paris, and broadcast on BBC Radio Four's 'Morning Story' as well as contributing a short story to an anthology of Christmas writing published by Serpent's Tail. BREAKING THE RULES is her first full-length novel, and her second novel, THE PATCHWORK MARRIAGE, is also available from Headline.

The mother of three children, she is also a director of her husband's travel company. She lives in West London.

G000024630

Also by Mary de Laszlo

The Patchwork Marriage

Breaking the Rules

Mary de Laszlo

KNIGHT

First published in 1995
by HEADLINE BOOK PUBLISHING

First published in paperback 1996
by HEADLINE BOOK PUBLISHING PLC

This edition published 2002 by
Knight an imprint of The Caxton Publishing Group

10 9 8 7 6 5 4 3 2 1

ISBN 1 84067 398 2

Typeset by
Letterpart Limited, Reigate, Surrey

Printed and bound in Great Britain by
Mackays of Chatham plc, Chatham, Kent

Caxton Publishing Group
20 Bloomsbury Street
London WC1B 3JH

For Phebe, John, Margot and Charlotte and in memory of J.R. Also for all the Names, with their courage and tenacity.

I would like to thank these writers for their books and articles which I found invaluable in my research for this book: Jonathan Mantle (*For Whom the Bell Tolls*), Cathy Gunn (*Nightmare on Lime Street*), Adam Raphael (*Ultimate Risk*) and Andrew Jack of the *Financial Times*.

Part I

Part I

Chapter One

Cecily and Linette sat side by side on the stairs listening to Fiona crying. Her sobs were deep, despairing, and the two children huddled together on the wooden step not knowing what to do. If they knocked on her door and asked what was wrong, they knew she wouldn't tell them. She'd sniff, wipe her eyes and keeping her face away from them would say in that calm voice of hers, 'Nothing, it's just a cold . . . hay fever.' And she'd send them away on some errand until she had composed herself.

They were both thirteen years old and had been through a similar scene before. They'd been much younger then and had not picked up the signs until it was too late. Not that there was anything they could have done about it. When Daniel, Cecily's father, tired of a woman, he usually did so because he'd already replaced her with another. Fiona had replaced Zara, Linette's mother, who had replaced Cynthia, Cecily's mother, and the jolting, sick-making shock of displacement that that had caused

3

them thudded back now to haunt them.

There was a sudden sound downstairs, the slam of a door, the scuffle of someone coming in, various objects being dropped on the stone floor.

'Maumm,' Stephen's voice wailed up to them.

The two girls jumped as one and clattered down the stairs to him, maternal feelings to protect him filling their flat chests.

'Caught anything?' Cecily reached him first, tugged at his wet coat, pulling it off.

'Two crabs . . . one got away. It was e-nor-mous.' His eyes, their father Daniel's green eyes, so pale they were almost silver, were round like marbles with his effort to impress them. He made his fingers into a circle to show them the size of the crab that got away, then seeing how small it was, moved them further apart. 'Where's Mum?'

'Resting, she's got a headache,' Linette said quick as anything. She shot a glance at Cecily, who was now pulling off Stephen's jersey, adding it to the pile of damp clothes on the floor.

'She always has a headache these days,' Stephen said with all the wisdom of a five-year-old.

'People do,' Cecily said, the empty feeling inside her yawning large. She couldn't bear this little, trusting boy to suffer as she and Linette had done. 'Why do you get so wet, Stephen? You did stay on the rocks, didn't you?' Her voice was sharper than she meant it to be.

'Yep.' Stephen dodged away from her, running outside in his pants and wet shirt, and fetched his bucket.

4

'Look.' Carefully he picked up a crab, holding it behind its claws, and thrust it out to them.

'Put it back, Stephen.' Linette shuddered. She'd never liked collecting creatures from the rock pools on the beach. It was the one thing in which she differed from Cecily, who still loved to go picking away on the beach when the tide was out, squirreling shells and pretty stones which filled her pockets and drawers and boxes in her room. Now having a small half-brother she had the excuse of watching him on the beach, though this year Daniel had told her to let him go on his own.

'He's nearly six, old enough to go down to the beach at low tide on his own. As long as he tells someone he's going.'

'But, darling, he's only a baby,' Fiona, his mother, had protested, anxiety screwing up her beautiful face.

'He must grow up. When I was five I was—'

'We know, Daddy,' Cecily had broken in quickly. This exchange had been at the beginning of the holiday, here in their castle in Scotland. Daniel had bought the castle when Cecily was three and they had spent every summer here ever since. Cecily loved it. She hated anything to spoil the atmosphere and busied herself fielding any remarks or tensions that might provoke a row. This year Daniel had also sacked Stephen's nanny.

'He's too old for a nanny. Besides, we don't want her moping about up here like a wet weekend,' he'd said.

'You'd like her if she was pretty,' Linette said, laughing and springing away as he pretended to swat her.

Cecily admired Linette's ease with him. She treated

everything he said with a laugh, never caring if he told her she looked scruffy, or needed to wash her hair, or had a terrible school report. But then he wasn't her father, only her ex-stepfather, and she didn't seem to care to impress him, or seek his attention. But she had it anyway because she was so attractive.

Even now at thirteen when Cecily and most of the girls in their form were either too podgy or too gangly as their changing bodies sorted themselves out, Linette was beautiful, slim, tall, her small budding breasts and widening hips perfect in their proportions. Despite loving her, Cecily was pitted with envy. She saw herself like a stick insect, all long limbs jerking from a skinny body that bore little resemblance to a woman's at all.

There was a squeal of brakes on the drive.

'Daddy!' Stephen cried and ran outside again, the water slopping from his bucket. 'Daddy, look!' he called before his father had opened the car door. 'Look, look.'

Daniel got out and came towards him. 'What have you got, ragamuffin?' His voice was rich with pleasure at his welcome. He picked up Stephen and carefully balancing him and the now almost empty bucket on his shoulder came into the castle, bending under the lintel of the door, calling, 'Head down,' to Stephen.

'Hello, girls,' he said, his blond hair tousled by the wind, his eyes clear as glass in his tanned face. 'It's just on lunchtime and this child's filthy. Where's his mother?'

Cecily and Linette exchanged glances at his offhand reference to Fiona. Before, he would have looked for her, whooping up the stairs two at a time calling her name as if he couldn't bear to be another moment without her.

'She has a headache,' Stephen announced cheerfully, pinching Daniel's nose.

Cecily suppressed the small twinge of jealousy she often experienced when Daniel hugged Stephen. Once it was always her he hugged, swept up into his arms and kissed. Since Stephen, his beloved son, had been born, she felt she had taken second place.

Even with Stephen's hand over his face, Cecily could see the annoyance in her father's expression. He wanted his women to be always entertaining, always beautiful.

'Can't stand whingeing women,' he'd say when Cecily grumbled about something. 'You're so lucky, a house in London, castle in Scotland, more than enough to eat and clothe you. Love from me and your mother, and I'm sure your stepmother,' at this he'd wink at Fiona, 'so you have no right at all to moan.'

His words, as he knew they would, always made Cecily feel guilty. Some of the girls at her boarding school came from very meagre or unhappy homes. But she couldn't help feeling things were unfair sometimes. Like now. She and Linette had had this terrible feeling all through the holiday that Daniel was getting tired of Fiona and before long they would be presented with yet another stepmother.

'I'll take him.' Cecily held out her arms to Stephen.

'I can walk,' he said, jumping down from Daniel and

rushing upstairs, his bony little legs flashing like white pistons up the wooden stairs. Cecily followed him, not wanting to be left with Daniel in case he told her with that disarming smile of his that he was moving on.

Linette was stronger. Daniel had married her mother Zara when the two girls were both five – the same age as Stephen was now. They had taken to each other at once, forming a strong defence against the merry-go-round of their parents' lives.

'Daniel,' Linette said now, linking her arm through his, smiling at him with her mother's disarming smile that used to melt his heart, 'why is Fiona so unhappy?'

Cecily, on the last round of the stairs, heard her and gasped. She dreaded yet longed to hear what he said. She wished she was as brave as Linette, could ask him things straight out instead of hiding her fears away in secret places where they woke her in the night, gnawing at her, making her miserable.

'Oh, I don't know, Lin. Ask her yourself.'

Cecily knew that tone of voice, slightly defensive, jocular, hoping to put them off the scent, charm them away from thinking he was in any way to blame. She went on up to the bathroom with Stephen, hoping vainly that it was her imagination. She prayed that whatever it was threatening them would blow over and Fiona would be her happy self again. But all the time the fear tugged at her. How would Daniel deal with it this time?

She and Linette had been eight when Daniel had tired of Zara. They had suddenly to their surprise and horror been sent off to boarding school.

'You'll love it – midnight feasts, masses of friends. I'll write every day and send you enormous boxes of tuck,' Daniel had enthused, his face shining as if he was offering them a marvellous treat. They had hated it. Midnight feasts were severely punished, some of the teachers were petty and bad-tempered, and they didn't much like the other girls.

When they got back for the holidays, Daniel had told them that although he still loved Zara, and of course he loved Linette as his own little girl and she could live with them whenever she wanted, they had a new mother now and a dear little baby brother.

Cecily remembered this now as she went into the bathroom, remembered how Linette had grabbed her hand under the table and held it so tightly she had almost cried out.

'Linette's my sister, you said she could be,' Cecily had protested furiously. 'She must live with me for always and always.'

Daniel had seemed taken aback by her vehemence. Perhaps, she thought now, it had shocked him into feeling guilty at breaking up the family again. Yet he had always been fond of Linette. Sometimes Cecily even thought he preferred Linette to herself. She was so much prettier, after all, and Daniel lay great store by prettiness.

'We'll run away if we can't be together,' Cecily had shouted. She smiled now, remembering the terror on his face.

'Of course she can be with us, or anyway when she's not with her mother. *I* don't want to live without her either.' He'd laughed, pinched Linette's cheek, making her squirm with pleasure, let go of Cecily's hand and smile again.

'I won't need a bath, will I?' Stephen said now, hopefully rubbing at the grass stains on his knees.

'I think you will, you know how Daddy likes you spotless for lunch,' Cecily said, running the water and pulling off the rest of his clothes.

'Ohhh,' he grumbled. 'You don't eat with your knees.' He jerked them up to his lips, pretending he was holding a piece of food between them, making gobbling noises.

Cecily laughed in spite of her misery. After washing him she held him close on her lap wrapped in his towel. She loved him, how she loved him. She had from the moment she'd seen him, his downy head like a baby chick's soft fuzz peeping out from the folds of a shawl, though somehow entwined in that love was a fierce jealousy when she saw how Daniel adored and petted him. Now he was growing out of the roundness of babyhood, his legs and arms skinny and wiry. He looked like Daniel, not like his mother at all.

Suddenly Cecily grabbed him to her, holding him tight against her chest. Would Fiona take him away to live with her? Would she ever see him again?

'Ow! Get off.' Stephen wriggled away. 'You're hurting.'

'I'm sorry.' She tried to smile, the terror of losing him overwhelming her. She had shocked Daniel into

keeping Linette with them; besides, Zara was a
scatty woman, Linette had looked after *her* from the
age of six. She ricocheted from boy friend to boy
friend and although she adored Linette, she was
perfectly happy to let her spend weeks with Cecily
when she was with Daniel, even when she was with
Cynthia, her own mother. Also they were at school
together. But with Stephen it would be different.

Fiona appeared for lunch. Her eyes were red but her
blotched face was defiantly covered with make-up and
her hair was brushed.

'Are you all right?' Linette asked her.

'Fine, thanks, dear.' Fiona glanced at Daniel, her
mouth wobbling slightly.

'What a wonderful steak pie, Thistle,' Daniel boomed
at Mrs Thistlewaite who cooked for them. 'Your pastry
is quite superb, as always.'

'Thank you, sir.' Mrs Thistlewaite, Thistle to them
all, flushed as she always did when Daniel praised her.

'What's for pudding?' Stephen asked with his mouth
full.

'Stephen, don't talk with your mouth full. Empty it
and ask again,' Daniel said.

Stephen gulped his food, then choked, going red in
the face.

'Have some water, dear.' Thistle came over to him,
stroking his back and holding a glass to his lips.

Cecily sneaked a glance at Fiona. She sat tall and
still, her fingers restlessly twisting and tearing at her
linen napkin. Even with her blotched face she was

11

beautiful, Cecily thought, her hair as blonde as Daniel's, framing a perfect oval face with large grey eyes and a long, sensuous mouth. All his women were beautiful, her own mother, Zara and the various others he'd been with from time to time.

'This is Pixie, a good friend,' he'd say smiling calmly at Cecily and Linette if they saw him with one of these absurdly named beauties. His eyes always held defiance, a warning not to make a thing of it, not to mention it when they got home.

'Daniel's a womaniser,' Linette said when they first suspected that he was tiring of Fiona. She was pleased with the word. 'A womaniser, not content with only one woman.'

Cecily looked at him now. He was sitting at the head of the table, tucking in with gusto to Thistle's pie. A stranger coming in would think we were a normal happy family, she thought. Mother, father, three children. Only by looking at us closely would they see how different we are from each other, even Stephen and I, who share a father, don't look alike at all.

Stephen stopped choking and spluttered, 'What's for pudding, Thistle?'

'Greedy boy,' Linette said.

'I want to know.'

Thistle smiled, her smile disappearing into the pink folds on her face. 'Your favourite, chocolate mousse,' she said, 'but only after you've eaten everything on your plate, cabbage and all.' She tapped him affectionately on the shoulder and went out to the kitchen.

Fiona hardly ate, nor did she speak. Cecily felt desperately sorry for her, but she didn't know what to say, how to show that she cared, was on her side. She realised that it was more difficult for Fiona to accept her sympathy because it was *her* father, not Linette's, who was causing all this hurt.

Fiona was an uncomplicated person, happy or sad, pleasant or cross. She didn't employ any of the devious tricks with which so many adults manipulated children. What you saw was what you got. But Daniel, once so in love with her, caressing and praising her, preening himself like a peacock as she laughed and flirted with him, was now bored with her.

As usual, this holiday they'd had various friends and relations staying, but beneath the witty conversation, the picnics, the walks on the moors ran the tensions of a dying relationship, like sinister currents in a clear river.

Watching Stephen, still talking with his mouth full, telling anyone who would listen about his crabs and how he 'would find a hundred and take them all home on the train in the guard's van', Cecily felt like jumping up and snatching him to her to protect him from the pain of Daniel leaving. He adored both his parents. How could Daniel tear his life apart just for another woman?

'Why are you frowning, Cecily? You'll be so ugly with such a crosspatch face, no man will look at you,' Daniel teased, his mouth laughing but his transparent green eyes brittle with disapproval.

'Crosspatch, crosspatch,' Stephen yelled, delighted with his father's description, shrieking with laughter and rocking on his chair. He jabbed his fork at Cecily across the table, caught his glass of water and it fell, throwing its contents all over the white cloth. There was a deadly silence.

'Go to your room, Stephen,' Daniel said coldly. 'You've been behaving badly all through lunch. You will not eat with us unless you can behave.'

'But I want my pudding . . . please.' Stephen rolled his eyes at him, looking the image of Daniel when *he* wanted something.

Fiona began to mop up the water with her napkin. 'It's not too bad,' she said, 'it was only half full, but Stephen, do sit still, there's a good boy.'

Daniel often relented if his children appealed to him, enjoying the feeling of power their request gave him, basking in their gratitude and joy at their reprieve. But perhaps this time Fiona's intervention annoyed him, for he said sternly, 'That's too bad, Stephen. If you'd wanted pudding you should have behaved properly.'

'But . . .' Stephen's lower lip trembled and a huge tear rolled down his cheek. His desolation became worse when Thistle chose that moment to appear carrying the chocolate mousse in its cut-glass bowl, at least an inch of chocolate flakes decorating the top.

The sight of Stephen's despair over the loss of a chocolate pudding and knowing how much more he was to lose later, all because of her father, suddenly enraged Cecily.

Daniel sat there at the head of the table, lording it over them, his eyes hard, determinedly not looking at his wife as though the sight of her stricken face sickened him. Why did they all have to dance to his tune? Why did they all have to be so pretty, so smart, so entertaining just for him? Why were his needs, his likes and dislikes always pandered to before anyone else's?

The anger, the injustice of it all rose like bile in her throat. She sprang up from the table, the force of her movement knocking her chair to the floor. For a split second she felt a surge of power as everyone turned to her, their faces open with amazement, Thistle nearly dropping the chocolate mousse on the carpet.

'How can you be so unfair, Daddy?' she yelled at him, the look of utter surprise on his face goading her on. 'You never stop picking on us, we're never what you want. Stephen couldn't help knocking over his glass, you punish him for nothing.'

'Cecily.' Daniel's voice was like a gunshot, but she didn't care.

'Why do you want us to be so perfect? You're not.'

She heard Linette gasp, felt her hand pull frantically on her skirt.

'*Cecily.*' Daniel's face was set hard, his eyes boring into her.

She felt a surge of fear of his anger, knew with sickness that her outburst had cost her his love. But she didn't care, she didn't care for any of them. She threw down her napkin like a challenge and dashed

15

from the room, running down the stairs and out into the garden. She fled across the lawn, climbed the fence that ran between the end of the garden and the steep drop down to the beach, and scrambled into the ruin of the old castle that was slowly disintegrating into the sea.

It was unsafe and they were forbidden to go there, but she didn't care. She crouched in a corner, every so often kicking at the walls with her foot, hoping that it would fall on her and she would be washed away under the tumbling stones into the sea, away from them all.

It was Linette who came to her, as she knew she would. By then Cecily had calmed down a bit, now feeling sick with the enormity of what she'd done. Daniel would be furious, furious at her rudeness, furious she had shown him up in front of Thistle, and furious because what she'd said was true.

Linette picked her way over the ground knobbly with half-buried stones. She squatted down beside her. Neither spoke for a while then she said, 'Fiona told Daniel it's because you're a teenager. Adolescence, hormones and all.' She glanced at Cecily warily.

'You're the same age. Two months older in fact.'

'She was only trying to excuse you. Daniel is livid.'

'I know. But it's true, what I said, isn't it, Lin?' She turned to her beseechingly, her eyes wide. 'We always have to do what he wants, look how he wants, behave how he wants. He's so selfish.'

'Women love it. They all spoil him so he expects us to

16

as well.' Linette sighed. 'When I grow up I'll only like men who spoil me. Buy me hundreds of presents, take me to fabulous places. But,' she smiled, looked at Cecily from under her lashes, 'he does so love having his own way, it's quite fun giving it to him.'

'I don't think it is,' Cecily retorted, feeling a pang of desolation at Linette's defence of her father. 'What did he say?' Her voice was defiant but her heart hung heavy as she waited for Lin's answer.

'He said . . .' she paused, 'he said he wasn't going to have any teenage tantrums in his house. You could keep them for your mother.'

'I might have guessed,' she said at last, swallowing a huge lump in her throat. 'But I can't bear to think of Stephen being hurt if Daddy is going to leave Fiona. Will we ever see him again if she takes him?'

'Daniel will have him,' Linette said with certainty.

'How do you know? Have you heard something?' Cecily grabbed her arm and shook it.

Linette pulled away in annoyance. 'Hey, lay off. No, of course I haven't heard anything. But he won't let his beloved son out of his sight. What's the betting that this time next year we'll all be here again? Oh, he'll probably have some new woman, but Stephen will be here with us.'

'Do you think so? I feel as if things will never be the same again. I feel . . .' Cecily shrugged, not knowing what to make of the turbulent feelings whirling inside her, fear, hate, love, despair at the way she couldn't control events, couldn't make their life stop, stay as it had always been, like a photograph, a moment frozen for all time.

Linette turned and stared at Cecily in the gloom. 'He might make you stay with your mother.'

Cecily felt as if Linette had slapped her, but she knew she spoke the truth. If she didn't play Daniel's game as he wanted it, he would banish her to her mother's. Even if she was his daughter, she had to be like all the other women in his life, beautiful, entertaining and amusing. Only then would she be rewarded with the full warmth of his love and approval.

Chapter Two

'You and Linette can bring up Stephen on the sleeper. You're old enough now, darling,' Daniel's voice purred down the telephone.

'But Dad, we always go up together.' Cecily felt cheated. It was part of the summer ritual to board the train together in London, have dinner together on the train, be all crammed together in the sleeping compartment until they arrived excited yet chilly with lack of sleep at Inverness.

'I want to go up a week earlier this year and Fiona has to take Stephen to the dentist and things. And you must spend some time with your mother. How is she, by the way?'

'She and Gerald are fine,' Cecily said, 'but, Dad, surely—'

'Listen, darling,' his voice was like warm honey oozing into her ear, 'I have some new friends coming up this year, so I'm going up earlier. You and Linette are sixteen now, you can safely travel alone.'

'Of course we can, that's not the point. I only meant—'

'I know, darling, it is fun to travel together, but now you're older we can change things a little.' He paused, then said cheerfully, 'I expect you'll need some new clothes. Go to Harrods and buy yourself some things, put them on my account. Take Linette too, throw off that horrible school uniform.'

'I'm not wearing it now, Dad,' she laughed.

'Of course not, but go and buy yourselves something pretty.'

Cecily knew he was bribing her, she could picture him lying back on the sofa, his face soft with endearment, putting on his most persuasive voice to hypnotise her into doing what he wanted. Why did she fall for it? What was it about him that made her want to please him, go with his plans even when they upset her own?

The reason this time was purely mercenary on her part. She needed new clothes. She and Linette had felt quite out of it at school this term. For supper they were allowed to change into 'home clothes'. All the other girls in their year, even that mousy Priscilla Wilkins, had outfits from Biba or Mary Quant, while she and Linette were in safe dresses from Harrods.

'OK, Dad, thanks, but we don't want to go to Harrods. We're too old now.'

'Too old for Harrods?' He laughed. 'Where do you want to go to, my darling, Paris?'

'No. Shops you've never heard of. Fashionable places.'

He laughed again. 'I'll send you a cheque then, but mind you buy pretty things, darling.'

'Of course, Daddy, thanks.'

She arranged to go to his office to collect the train tickets, wondering who on earth these new friends were that necessitated his going up to the castle a week early. He had left Fiona as they had suspected he would that summer three years ago, and again it was while they were at school. He waited until the next holidays to tell them.

'Let's go to the Ritz,' he'd said when he collected them off the school train at the end of term. 'It's the only civilised place for lunch as the tables are far enough apart to gossip without being overheard.'

'But we're not properly dressed for the Ritz,' Linette had wailed though they had changed out of their school uniform in the tiny, smelly lavatory on the train. It was strictly forbidden to change out of uniform until one got home. Their headmistress believed that they were safe from evil – by which she meant anything to do with sex – in their uniform. She also considered it extremely immodest to undress anywhere so public as a *train*.

Daniel looked at them dubiously. It was true they were not as elegant as the women he usually took there. But he bundled them into a taxi and they arrived at the Ritz.

Then he'd told them. 'We don't get on any more, that's all there is to it,' he'd said, smiling at them over their table.

'So who are you going to marry instead? Or are you already married with another baby?' Linette asked him candidly, fixing him with her large, grey eyes.

21

Cecily fidgeted uncomfortably. She felt clumsy and large in her creased pencil skirt and her blouse kept coming out of the waistband. Linette looked smart and fresh, her hair behaving itself in heavy folds round her face, while Cecily's stuck out at the side where she'd slept on it.

'No,' he laughed, but Cecily caught a swift look of unease in his eyes. 'I . . . don't want to get married again.'

'Really?' Linette said. 'Why not?'

He laughed, again rather awkward at her question. 'I've done it three times and it hasn't worked out. I'm just not good at marriage. Now, tell me about yourselves. How's the terrifying Miss Trotman?' He shifted the conversation to their headmistress and school and apart from assuring them that they would see Stephen whenever they wanted and that he would spend every summer with them at the castle, he said no more about it.

For the last two years he'd had a succession of girl friends. All pretty, all amusing, all, to Linette and Cecily, instantly forgettable.

Cecily rang Linette and, armed with Daniel's £100, the two girls set off to the boutiques in Carnaby Street, the King's Road and Kensington. Eventually, exhausted but feeling that at last they belonged to the modern, human race, they collapsed back at Cecily's house, both wearing new dresses from Biba.

Gerald, Cecily's stepfather, emerged from behind *The Times* to give them a brief glance.

'They seem to have forgotten to set the sleeves in those dresses,' he said drily. 'I hope they gave you a discount.'

'They're meant to be like this, Gerald,' Cecily said, raising her eyebrows in despair at Linette. The dresses were slim, tight with a polo neck, the armholes cut in a slant to the neck, exposing the whole round of their shoulders.

'I hope my shirts don't turn out like that,' he muttered, going back to the safety of his paper.

'What is all this?' Cynthia glanced at the muddle of carrier bags on the floor as she came into the room with the tea tray. Gerald sprang up from his chair and took it from her, putting it on the table in front of the sofa.

'Clothes we bought – Daddy gave us some money.' Cecily pinched a biscuit off the plate.

'It amazes me how he has so much money to shower on you with all those women in his life, though his own divorces must keep his firm going,' Cynthia said archly. It had always been rather a joke that Daniel's family were partners in a well-known firm of solicitors, dealing mainly with divorce cases. Cynthia maintained that if Daniel spent more time in the office he wouldn't have the energy to exchange wives so often.

She poured out the tea, the aroma of Earl Grey curling into the room. She was an elegant woman, with a pointed thoroughbred face and lustrous brown hair and eyes. 'At least I can stop blaming myself for him leaving us,' she glanced at Cecily, 'now I can see he's quite incapable of staying with any woman for long.'

'Permanently on the move,' Gerald said, taking his teacup behind his newspaper. He was a man of simple emotions. He loved Cynthia, was kind to Cecily, thought himself a jolly lucky chap to have them, and that was it.

'Dull, oh so dull,' Cecily had once described him to Linette. But over the years she had come to value his dependability, the stability of his always being there, just the same, behind his newspaper. She knew it was this side of him that appealed to her mother most.

'Of course it's the women's fault that Daniel is like he is,' Cynthia declared. 'No morals at all these days, just jumping into bed with anyone, married or not.' She glared at Linette, whom in fact she'd grown very fond of over the years, but it was her mother who had usurped her in Daniel's bed.

Linette was used to this and took no notice, cutting herself a huge slice of chocolate cake and consuming it greedily yet at the same time somehow elegantly, quite oblivious of Cynthia's insinuations.

'And as for leaving that Fiona with her little boy . . .'

Cynthia was in full flood now; Cecily sighed, she'd heard it all so often.

'. . . Daniel always wanted a son. God knows I tried. Three miscarriages I had before you.' She nodded at Cecily.

Gerald rustled his paper in embarrassment. Being a typical public school man with no sisters, he felt queasy at any reference to a woman's insides.

'You know, I don't think Daniel can be very potent.

All those women and only two children between them. Not a very good score, I would say.'

'Oh Mum, he did have four with you – counting the miscarriages, I mean,' Cecily said.

Gerald noisily cleared his throat.

Linette giggled.

'They can't have been very strong. His . . .' Cynthia waved her hand as if it would say the word for her. Outspoken she might be, but uttering any technical words concerned with reproduction embarrassed her. When no one helped her she said dismissively, 'You know, his . . . seeds, they can't have been up to much.'

Gerald choked on his tea and she had to jump up and pound him on the back. Cecily and Linette escaped, helpless with giggles.

They were met off the train at Inverness by Angus Gunn the gardener.

'How many people are staying?' Cecily asked him, hoping for a few clues on Daniel's new friends.

'Can't rightly say, but a houseful,' Angus muttered, preferring the silence of plants to the chatter and questions of people, especially children.

'Who is there?' Cecily tried again, but when Angus said he'd been too busy with the vegetables to see, she left it and piled into the back with Linette and Stephen.

They were quiet on the long journey up but when at last they spotted first the ruin then the castle itself in the distance, they stirred and began to chatter excitedly, the joy of being back again after a whole year making them animated.

When Angus carefully stopped the car outside the castle, slowly turning off the engine and pulling up the hand brake, they leapt out and ran for the door, knocking into each other in their eagerness to get inside.

Cecily was the first up the stairs, bursting into the drawing room where Daniel caught her in his arms and kissed her.

'My darling, you're here at last. Let me look at you. How you've grown . . . quite a young lady.' He laughed, hugged her to him again. He hadn't seen her for three months.

'Stephen.' He kissed his son, giving him a playful punch in the arm.' You've grown too. And Linette.' He looked across the room at Linette.

Cecily told herself later that it was her imagination, heightened by the moment of arrival. As Daniel looked at Linette, the first time he'd seen her since last summer, his body stiffened, his eyes widened with pleasure, almost desire. Linette was fully grown now, a beautiful young woman though Cecily knew she was still as immature and childish as she was herself. But in that one split second before the other people in the room greeted them Cecily was certain she saw a surge of excitement pulse between Linette and Daniel.

'Daniel.' Linette kissed him, turning at once to his brother Mark and his wife Jean. 'Hello.' She kissed them too, they were frequent guests here. The

Abbots, Paul and Lavinia, were there too, old friends of Daniel's.

Everyone was talking at once, praising the children on their growth, asking about school, about the journey. Sitting by the fireplace watching this scene was a beautiful, dark-haired woman. A young man, obviously her son, was standing behind her.

Cecily saw them first. They were both dressed as if they were mannequins showing off the sort of clothes a Hollywood director might imagine people wore in a castle of Scotland. The woman wore a red cashmere jumper over red and white tartan trousers with a matching waistcoat. Her skin was very white, her red, made-up mouth vivid. Her hair was black, and for one second she reminded Cecily of the wicked stepmother in *Snow White*. The young man was about twenty, the image of his mother, but somehow on him the looks gave him an almost reptilian air, spivvy with his sleeked-back hair. His flannel trousers and loud tweed jacket were stiff with newness.

Cecily caught Linette's eye and her mouth twitched with amusement from the shared, unspoken jibe that passed between them: 'How nouveau.' Everyone else in the room was dressed in once expensive but now faded cords and tweeds. Daniel's blue jersey even had a hole in the elbow and his shirt collar was frayed. Mark's jacket was so old its sleeves probably stayed curved in the shape of his arms when he took it off.

'Darlings, let me introduce Gail Tetley and her son Ronald.' Daniel jumped forward, his face beaming, his hand lightly caressing Gail's back. 'This is Cecily, Linette and Stephen,' he said proudly, drawing Cecily forward.

'How do you do,' Cecily muttered, a sudden feeling of revulsion coming over her as she glanced up into Ronald's face. His eyes glittered with disdain as he looked her over. He ignored the hand she held out in greeting.

'How do you do. I've heard *so* much about you,' Gail said in a voice that implied that it had all been bad. Imperturbably she moved a little away from them, as if she found them dirty and was afraid of catching something.

'Drink before lunch?' Daniel said smoothly.

Cecily moved away from Gail. She felt sick, empty with disappointment that the longed-for holiday was suddenly blighted by these people. She couldn't be her father's new girl friend, surely she couldn't. She was quite unlike any of the other women they'd met in his life. She was beautiful, yes, no one could deny that, but she was . . . so different. I may be a snob, Cecily thought, but Gail was a different class from his other women. And, she thought, watching her during lunch fawning over Daniel and feeling the supercilious eyes of Ronald on them all, they were members of the worst class of all, the go-getters, the social climbers.

'I see this room with white pillars,' Gail said to Daniel, her manicured hand fluttering over his like a restless insect. 'Of course I understood your point about not having an interior decorator in as you hardly live here, but everywhere is just the teeniest bit faded, don't you think?'

'We love it faded,' Linette said, glancing at Cecily. 'Over-done-up houses are so vulgar, don't you think, Daniel?' She smiled at him and Cecily was certain that yet again she caught a frisson of desire in his eyes before he answered.

'We're not talking about over-done-up houses, Linette, but I must agree with Gail that this place is getting a little shabby. Perhaps next year we'll do it up.' He smiled at Gail. Cecily felt sick.

After lunch, which despite it being one of Thistle's famous pies she hardly ate, Cecily escaped with Linette to the tower-shaped garden shed set in the wall of the vegetable garden.

'He won't marry her,' Linette said picking at the lichen on a pile of flower pots.

'God, I hope not. And that boy – he hates us. Have you seen his eyes, sort of sneering at us. What does he think he looks like in those awful new clothes?' Cecily pounded her toe into the floor. 'How long are they staying? Have you found out?'

'No. I hope not the entire holiday.'

'We'll have to leave. But then there's Stephen, we can't leave him here on his own.'

'Where can we go? Mum's away with some lover and your mother and Gerald have gone to their villa in France. They won't want all of us.' Linette slumped down beside her. 'Look, I vote we stay, just enjoy ourselves and ignore them. After all, we can escape them – most of the time anyway.'

In fact it was hard to escape them, and their remarks. Gail seemed to take delight in belittling them.

'What a pity to wear black with that young skin. So draining,' she said, one evening when they came down, both feeling rather self-conscious in their new Mary Quant dresses, Linette in black, Cecily in black and rust.

'Better than wearing a picnic rug,' Linette muttered loud enough for Gail to hear, but not Daniel. Gail was in a long tartan skirt and a fluffy jumper with a swirl of sequins over the front.

Daniel didn't like their dresses either. 'Hardly pretty, darlings,' he said. 'Rather like a uniform. I'd have thought you'd have had enough of that at school.'

'But Daddy, it's fashionable. You are so old-fashioned,' Cecily protested, stung by his reaction to dresses they thought were wonderful.

'They're hardly flattering,' he said, turning away and fawning over Gail, making them hate her even more.

Daniel did his best to push Ronald on to them, though Ronald preferred to avoid them.

'I have books to read,' he said importantly, as if his time was too valuable to be wasted with them.

'So do we,' Linette retorted. 'What are you reading?' She went over to the pile of books he'd been carrying about and had put down on the table.

'*The Language of Money*?' She laughed derisively.

30

'Heavens, I thought you meant real books.'

He flushed, looked away from her scornful gaze. For a second Cecily felt sorry for him.

'Oh, Lin,' she said, 'don't be mean, there's nothing wrong in wanting to make money.'

Linette shrugged and went out of the room. Cecily made to follow her.

'You don't know what it's like to be poor, really poor, do you?' Ronald said bitterly as she sidled away.

'I . . . I suppose not.' Reluctantly Cecily turned to look at him.

He was standing by the window, his hands clenched so hard his knuckles gleamed white, his face creased with tension. 'My father left us when I was thirteen, I'd just started public school. My mother fell behind with the fees. Can you imagine the humiliation of that?' His voice was agonised, his dark eyes bored into her, his mouth stiffened in defiance as if waiting for her to mock him.

'No, I can't. It must have been terrible for you.' Cecily wanted to go, leave him with his pain. It made her feel uncomfortable.

'You cannot imagine what it is like to be sneered at for having no money. Oh, your lot,' he flicked his hand at her as if she was contaminated, 'are so bloody sanctimonious. If you can't meet the fees, the school waits because your father and your grandfather and God knows who else from the family went there. I will not be put through that again.' He glared at her, came forward until he was close enough for her to feel his breath on her cheek. She willed herself not to move away, afraid to hurt his feelings more.

'How dreadful,' she said weakly, knowing that whatever she said would be inadequate.

He laughed harshly. 'Dreadful,' he mocked. 'Huh, you don't know the half of it. Now run off and tell Linette all about it. Leave me alone.' He turned his back on her and stared out at the grey sea. Relieved to escape and feeling rather sick, Cecily left.

The following afternoon Daniel insisted that, despite the rain, they all walk by Dunnet Point to see if they could spot any puffins.

It was after 12 August and Ronald insisted on taking a gun, 'in case I see any grouse on the moor on the way back'.

Cecily and Linette didn't bother to inform him that it was highly unlikely, and when they all piled out into the rain to start their walk, he carried the gun with him.

'Dangerous to leave it in the car,' was all he said.

Stephen hopped and skipped in front of them, unconcerned by the rain. The adults – with the exception of Gail, who said she'd be happy to wait in the car – straggled out across to the sea and the sheer drop of the cliffs that housed the puffins. Cecily and Linette linked arms and walked close together, gossiping and giggling, hunched against the wind and rain. Apart from Stephen and Ronald, the rest of the party trailed behind them.

'Look, seals,' Stephen called back, pointing out to sea. 'Look, I can see one, no three . . . I'm sure that's one. Look.'

The girls reached him and looked down into the sea. Three dark noses poked out. There was another lying on the rocks below them.

'Let's go down to them, do let's,' Stephen said, running ahead, not waiting for their reply.

Ronald joined them and looked down. 'Where are the blighters?' he said.

'Down there.' Cecily moved away from him, determined now to follow Stephen down to the beach and get away from him. She wanted to show him up, climb down the steep path to the beach as they had so often done before and hope to see him floundering and slipping if he followed them.

Linette had the same idea and soon they were all three on the beach watching the seals, smiling at Stephen's excitement as he pointed them out as if they would not see them for themselves.

Suddenly there was a shot. It was raw and brutal in the wind. They jumped, spun round and saw Ronald was walking towards them, a proud smirk on his face.

'Got it in one,' he said.

They turned in horror to the rock and saw the bleeding body of the seal.

'No!' Stephen cried, hurling himself at Ronald.

'How could you? You monster!' Linette screamed at him.

Cecily caught Stephen and held his sobbing, shaking

body tightly to her. She felt stunned, as if someone had punched her, deep inside.

Ronald just smiled at them. 'How many would you need to make a coat, Linette?'

'You are a bastard,' Cecily screamed at him, 'a real bastard!' She had never hated someone so much in her life.

Linette leapt at him and grabbed the gun. She wrestled with it, shouting at him, 'You bastard, killer, murderer. How could you?'

'Stop, stop.' Daniel was struggling down the slope towards them as quickly as he could. He slipped, swore, came on.

'Daddy, Daddy, he killed the seal.' Stephen ran to him, almost falling over in his grief.

'I wish I could shoot you,' Cecily snarled at Ronald, feeling raw with shock.

'Don't be so melodramatic, Cecily. God, you are all the most theatrical lot.' Ronald's voice was bored, infuriatingly, languidly in control now that Linette had stopped pulling at the gun.

Ronald walked away over the rocks to the body of the seal. Cecily couldn't look at him and watched Stephen struggling to reach Daniel, knowing how he longed for him, how he was certain he would put this foul deed right.

But Daniel just caught his hand and pulled him along with him. 'Stop making such a fuss, Stephen,' he said irritably. 'It's no worse than shooting a pheasant and he probably didn't know you can't shoot them.'

'Daddy!' Cecily was furious at his remarks.

'He's a cruel, wicked lout. Why did you have to invite them here?' She stood there, her eyes blazing at him.

Years later she thought of this as the time Daniel started to destroy Stephen.

'I will not tolerate rudeness to my guests, Cecily. Do you understand?' Daniel's voice was cold, his expression like a sulky adolescent. He stood in the middle of the playroom glowering at them.

'But Ronald shot—'

'Enough,' Daniel broke in impatiently.

'They don't fit here at all, Daniel,' Linette took over. 'Horrid nouveau people. What do you see in them?'

'Girls,' Daniel barked, 'I will not have such bad manners. You can leave tomorrow.'

Cecily gasped. How could he put these people before them? Stephen whimpered, but Linette stood firm.

'We would like to leave while they are here, but we have nowhere to go. So we are going to stay,' she said firmly and turned away from him, making a great show of choosing a book from the shelf.

Spurred on by her courage, Cecily found her own. 'This is our holiday and our castle, we are going to stay,' she said.

'It is my castle and I will invite whom I like and you will learn to be polite.' He glared at her.

Cecily stared back unflinching. Stephen crept close to her, she could feel his body trembling against her. She had never felt so betrayed in her life.

Throwing the cringing Stephen a contemptuous look, Daniel marched to the door. 'If you children can't behave, you will stay with your mothers.' Then he strode from the room, his stiff back like a solid wall against them.

'They are vile, hideous, vulgar people!' Linette burst out almost before Daniel had shut the door behind him. 'Why should we be polite to *them?*'

Cecily shrank into herself, terrified Daniel would hear and demand that they leave at once. But when he didn't come back and they heard his steps going downstairs, she relaxed, screwed up her face and said 'I can't think why Daddy has asked them up here. He's never had such friends before. Do you think she's a witch and has put a spell on him?'

'She's put something on him,' Linette agreed.

'Don't you feel,' Cecily paused, searching for the right words, 'a sort of . . . fascination between them?'

'Sex,' Linette said. They were reading *Lady Chatterley's Lover*, hiding it from Stephen, and Mrs Thistlewaite for that matter, under the mattress. 'It must be sex, powerful, mysterious. I do hope it doesn't hit us like that.'

'How do you mean, Lin?'

'You know, some terrible, wicked man, a maniac perhaps, enslaving us with his sexual magnetism.'

Cecily shivered. She, both of them, knew so little of what really went on in an adult's love life. Not that her father had ever flaunted his, or made crude jokes or remarks about sex. In fact he never discussed it, had never once made any reference to the sexual act to her at all. But sex must be one of the reasons that made him change his women so often, she assumed. But it was frightening if it meant being caught by a woman like Gail.

'Ronald is vile,' Linette almost spat. 'Imagine having to do it with *him*.'

'Ughh. I'd rather not.' Cecily shuddered. What about romance, she thought? Where was that? Could you have it without sex?

Stephen flung himself into the room.

'I hate that Ronald. I shall kill him when I'm older. Shoot him like he did that seal.' He kicked the wall, his small face bunched in anger. 'I hate him.' He kicked the wall again as if it was Ronald.

'So do we,' Linette said. 'But we'll have to pretend not to in front of Daniel, or he'll send us away.'

'I want to go away, back to Mum,' Stephen said, throwing himself down by Cecily, accidentally catching her with his thick-soled sandal.

'Ow! Be careful.' She pushed him away.

'Sorry.' He crept nearer Linette, craving comfort.

'I know. I vote we have a sort of code.' Linette giggled suddenly, sitting up straight, her eyes shining.

'Code?' Stephen perked up. 'You mean with a torch?'

'No, words. We'll think up a code name for Gail and Ronald, something no one will guess.'

'Toad. Smelly, rotten, ugly, disgusting toad,' Stephen spat, scrunching up his face to add emphasis to his words.

37

'Too obvious,' Cecily said. 'It must be something like . . .' She frowned, trying to think.

'Toadstool,' Linette said. 'If we want to talk about Ronald we could say toadstool. I stepped on a poisonous toadstool.'

'Yes. A disgusting puffball one like we had at home once. All brown like poo with yellow dust stuff.' Stephen rolled on his back with delight. 'Filthy, disgusting poo!' he shrieked.

'Pipe down, Stephen, you'll give it away,' Linette hushed him. 'We must be more discreet. Right, toadstool for him, what for her?'

'Wicked witch,' Cecily said.

'Yes. Wicked, wicked, wicked witch with horrid spells,' Stephen yelled.

'Shh! They'll hear,' Cecily warned, half expecting Daniel to burst in and insist they pack and leave at once. Though where they would go, she wasn't sure.

'Witch hazel?' Linette suggested.

'Too nice,' Cecily said. 'How about sorcerer?'

'Poisonous, disgusting apple,' Stephen cried excitedly. 'Dead worm, smelly—'

'Stephen, it has to be something not too obvious,' Linette said again, rather wishing that he wasn't with them. He was bound to get carried away.

'Slime . . . that's better for him. Toadstool for her,' Cecily said.

'Slime. Urgh, slime,' Stephen gagged.

'OK. But we must be careful that Daniel doesn't twig. Just use the words in a normal sentence like,' Linette paused, 'like, there was slime on my chair.'

'Or a toadstool on the bog,' Stephen shrieked, sticking his sandalled feet in the air and screeching with laughter. 'A toadstool on the bog,' he shrieked over and over again until Linette finally smacked him and said if he couldn't control himself they wouldn't let him join in.

Friends were coming to dinner that night and anyway Stephen was not allowed to stay up, so they promised him they wouldn't start until the next day.

At lunchtime Daniel, as usual, held forth. He talked earnestly to Gail who sat on his right, as if she meant everything to him. Jean sat on his left and Linette, Cecily and Stephen sat at the other end of the table, not daring to look at each other, yet each waiting for one of them to say something.

'I saw a poisonous toadstool on the lawn this morning, just before lunch,' Linette threw into a momentary silence. Everyone, including Gail, had gone onto the front lawn to decide whether to have another flowerbed dug in the shelter of the wall.

'It was like . . .' Stephen was overcome with giggles. Daniel glared at him.

'Have you seen any toadstools – poisonous ones, I mean, Daniel?' Linette asked him innocently.

'Toadstools? I don't know. Why should I see any?' Daniel said impatiently.

Stephen, whose face was crimson in his effort to stop laughing, lost the battle, and carrots and laughter burst from his mouth.

Gail winced. She put her napkin to her face as if to shield herself from a shower of his half-chewed lunch.

'Stephen!' Daniel thundered. 'Take your plate and eat in the kitchen. I will not have such manners in the dining room.'

The laughter bubbling through Stephen turned quickly to tears. As he got up, miserably picking up his plate, Cecily tried to cheer him up by saying, 'I saw the toadstool too. It was covered in slime. It was quite, quite disgusting. I wonder if you saw it, Ronald?' She fixed her eyes on him, but he only shrugged and turned away.

'As you children have nothing whatever of interest to say, I suggest you keep quiet,' Daniel said firmly.

Cecily shot a glance at Linette and saw her gazing into Daniel's face with defiance, a tiny smile on her lips.

Steeling herself for his wrath, Cecily was surprised to see his face soften. A gleam of . . . she wasn't quite sure what, but she'd seen it before when he looked at his girl friends, in his eyes. It made her feel uncomfortable and she glanced away for an instant. When she looked back he was talking to Aunt Jean and she told herself that she'd imagined it.

The following day Daniel suggested a ping pong tournament. They all trooped upstairs to the long, dusty attics where the two tables stood. Gail preferred to stay downstairs, but Ronald joined in, playing quite well. When it was over, with Daniel as usual the winner, the adults went downstairs, leaving the children to tidy up.

Stephen had hit one of the balls wide and they hadn't been able to find it, but as Cecily turned to put out the light she saw it lying under a chair in one of the other rooms.

'Just a minute, I've found that missing ball,' she said and went back and retrieved it, putting it in the box with the others. There was a movement behind her and Ronald, his teeth flashing in his face, smirked at her. 'I thought you'd gone on with the others,' she said dismissively, walking firmly towards the door, knowing she'd have to pass him to get out. Her flesh tingled with revulsion, but she kept going.

'You're longing for it, aren't you?' His voice was silky. He moved slowly in front of her, barring her exit.

'What do you mean? Move away.' She fought to hide the fear that was creeping into her.

'You know what I mean.' He smiled. 'You girls are both ripe for it. I'd be doing you a favour.' He grabbed her suddenly, pulling her to him, pushing his mouth on hers, jabbing his body against her.

Cecily just had time to jerk her head away and his mouth landed on her ear. She screamed, kicked out, screamed again.

'What's that noise? What's going on?' Uncle Mark called up from the landing below.

Ronald dropped her, pushed her from him. 'You little baby,' he spat.

Cecily rushed past him and almost fell down the stairs into Mark's arms.

'Hey, what is it? Have you seen a ghost?' He held her

from him, looking into her face.

'It's nothing.' Ronald came down behind her, his voice oily.

'H-He tried to . . . kiss me . . .' Cecily gasped.

'My dear Cecily, what a preposterous idea. Why ever would I want to do that? You're only a child.' He smiled knowingly at Mark, as if to imply that teenage girls were fanciful creatures, and walked away, whistling.

'Are you all right?' Mark, who had no children, was rather out of his depth. 'Look, come and find your father. Or Jean. She'll know what to do,' he said to reassure himself as well as her.

'No. I . . .' Cecily felt defiled. 'I will later.' She ran off and locked herself in the bathroom. Not until she had scrubbed her body, especially her ear which had been touched by Ronald's revolting lips, did she feel better. Then she went and told Linette.

'The creep.' Linette squirmed. 'Rapist, that's what he is. A pervert. We're not safe in our beds. We'll have to tell Daniel.'

'No,' Cecily said quietly. 'I'd rather not. He . . . well, he might encourage it.' She looked at Linette in horror. 'You know, somehow make me out to be in the wrong because he's so besotted by that woman.'

'Oh, Cecily, I'm sure he wouldn't. He adores you, would be horrified if he thought—'

'Would he?' Cecily looked at her gravely. 'Oh, he'd be furious if another man had tried it on, but Ronald, son of the woman he's mad about?' She shook her head sadly, the truth of it making her eyes smart with tears.

Linette hugged her. 'She *is* a witch. Somehow she's got her claws into him and is blinding him to the rest of us. Thank goodness Mark was there or . . . well, we won't think about it. But can't he tell Daniel what a pervert Ronald is?'

'No, because Ronald will deny it.' Cecily sighed, laid her head against Linette's. 'I'll never forget it, or forgive him, but it's better not to say any more.'

'We'll just ignore him for the creep he is,' Linette said. 'We'll see if we can't get back at him somehow.'

But when they went down for dinner, determined to freeze him with their indifference, he was not there.

'He had to get back,' Daniel said airily. 'Gunn is dropping him at the station.'

Gail fixed them both with her gimlet eyes. 'He has a very important party to go to,' she said with a superior smile. '*Tatler*, *Queen*, all the top social journalists will be there.'

'Maybe they'll photograph him, put him on the cover,' Linette said. 'They'd probably sell out the magazine if they did,' she added sarcastically, turning away from Gail towards Daniel, who seemed not to have heard the remark, leaving Cecily floundering in embarrassment and awkwardness, hating Gail, hating her father for bringing her here, and somehow, though she didn't quite know why, angry with Linette as well.

'I have different plans for you this coming term, Cecily,' Daniel said two days later. By then, Gail, too, had left. 'Just going on to my dear friends Sir Paul and Lady

43

Giles,' she said. 'They live near Edinburgh, in the most beautiful house. Such taste.' She glanced disdainfully round the faded drawing room.

'All gold and glitter no doubt,' Linette whispered to Cecily, making her giggle.

Now the castle felt comfortable again, the atmosphere shaken down into the cosy intimacy Cecily loved best.

'Different plans, Daddy? What?' Cecily put her arm round his neck. She was expecting him to say that she must take up another language, or do a secretarial course as well as her A levels.

They had taken their O levels last term. She had passed six, Linette had done better with eight. They both assumed that they would stay on and do A levels, if only to fill in the time before childhood, in Daniel's eyes anyway, ended and they were considered 'old enough' to join the outside world.

'I'm sending you to Paris, to a family I know there. You'll go to school every day.'

'Paris?' If he'd said the moon Cecily couldn't have been more surprised. 'Paris!' He couldn't mean it. Not the city of lovers, where romance danced on every corner.

'Yes, Paris. You've been at St Catherine's long enough. I think it's a great asset to be able to speak another language fluently and the only way to do that is to live in the country.'

'And me? Can I go too? You know St Catherine's is a nuthouse, full of loonies.' Linette turned eagerly to

Daniel, her face shining, the soft lips of her mouth slightly open showing the tips of her teeth.

Cecily was struck suddenly by how very beautiful she looked, her hair falling about her face, her clear eyes looking up at Daniel.

'No, Linette.' He turned away from her. It was almost as if he couldn't bear her beauty, Cecily thought watching him. Then again it might be that he couldn't bear her disappointment.

'I can't make the same decisions for you. That's up to your mother – and of course your father,' he added as an afterthought.

'Oh, Mummy will let me go, and you know my father won't care either way. That woman he married has forced him to forget I even exist. He's hardly going to make decisions for me now,' Linette said brightly. Then seeing Daniel was silent she rushed on, 'Mummy doesn't think much of school anyhow. I don't think she went herself.' She turned her shining face to Cecily. Cecily could see the thoughts tumbling in her eyes: 'Paris! What luck, what joy. Think of all the fun we'll have!'

Daniel's voice was decisive. 'No, Linette. I don't think it will be a good idea if you go just now. You did much better in your exams than Cecily and should go on to do A levels. You can go to Paris later.' He grinned. 'It won't run away.'

'I don't care about A levels. What use are they to me? It would be far better to speak French . . . You said you couldn't make the decisions for me, so Mummy will. I'll go to Paris with Cecily.'

'No, Linette. You can't both go together. You'll get up to all sorts of mischief and you certainly won't learn French. You have to be on your own for that.'

'We will. We promise, *nous parlerons Français tout les temps ensemble*,' Cecily said.

'*Oui. Nous promise*,' Linette said.

Daniel got up and put his hand gently on Linette's head, caressing her hair, letting it run through his fingers like gold threads.

'No, Linette.' His voice was soft yet insistent. 'No, not yet. You have so many talents, my dear, you must recognise them first.' He left them.

Linette called after him, 'Let me go, oh please let me go. Let me leave that dreadful school and go to Paris. I will go, Mummy will let me. I know she will.'

Daniel did not turn back or answer her.

'Why? Why doesn't he want me to go, Cecily? It's not fair. Mummy's so weak he's sure to persuade her not to let me go,' she wailed at Cecily who sat motionless, in shock at the thought of her new life. She was also seized with a feeling of unease which she couldn't understand. It was not caused by her fear of going somewhere new; it was as if something familiar and safe was in danger and it frightened her.

Chapter Three

'But, Lin, I thought it was all settled. That we were going to share a flat together when I got back.' Cecily knew she sounded like a whining, spoilt child, but she felt so disappointed.

She'd come back to London after over two years abroad – not counting coming home for the holidays – expecting Linette to be eager to share her flat. They'd planned it ages ago, talked about it, written about it in their long rambling letters to each other.

'I know I did, and I'd like to later, but . . .' Linette wouldn't look directly at her. She was different, Cecily thought, distant, not exactly unfriendly, but awkward with her. Unable to meet her gaze, be easy and giggly with her as she had always been before.

'I want to travel too,' Linette went on. 'You've been lucky going to Paris and Florence, I was stuck here. I know I left St Catherine's and studied here in London, but that's not abroad, is it?'

'No, but—'

'I want to get away.' She sounded more desperate

than someone just longing for a dream. 'I want to go to America. You remember Podge – you know, Lavinia Stead? She left St C's too and was at the same college as me in London.'

'Yes, I remember her.'

'She's in America, her parents have moved there and she's asked me to stay. I want to go.' She stared at Cecily, almost with defiance.

'I understand that, but when you come back . . .' Cecily didn't know how to handle this. She'd hardly seen Linette this last year. Just as she'd been about to leave her school in Paris at the end of the summer term and come home, Daniel had rung her and told her he was sending her to Florence to a family for three months.

'But I want to come home, go to Scotland with you all,' she said.

'My darling, what a goose you are. Scotland will always be there and you won't have such a chance in your life again. Once you start work, get married, you won't have the opportunity to spend so long abroad. You must go, darling, the art is extraordinary. And now you can speak French, why not try Italian too?'

'Daddy, I'd love to go but can't I come home first?'

'There's no point, my darling. I've found such a charming woman for you to stay with. A widow with a daughter about your age. I'll send you money to buy some Italian clothes. Their style is exquisite, almost better than the French, to my mind.'

She had protested, but only mildly. She'd loved Paris,

its dove-grey buildings jewelled with wrought-iron balconies, the smell of it, the pace of it, the tiny romantic corners, the magnificent sweep of the Place de la Concorde and the Champs Elysées. She'd loved Florence too and the holiday villa at the sea, but she'd been happy to come back, imagining the fun of being 'grown up' and keeping house with Linette in the minute flat Daniel had bought for his daughter in Kensington.

Cecily knew she'd changed. She'd grown up, lived in another culture, but she hadn't expected Linette to change so much, to be so secretive as if she knew something she didn't. Linette had a sophistication, a sort of glow about her she hadn't had before.

'Your mother's all right, isn't she?' Cecily asked, wondering for a moment if fey Zara had done something shameful. She knew Linette found her rather an embarrassment with her 'little girl' clothes and her startling hair and make-up.

'Mum, yeah. She's OK. Got a new boy friend, quite young.' She gave Cecily a slightly ashamed smile.

'You don't mean ... well,' Cecily felt embarrassed herself now, 'he's not one of your boy friends, is he?'

'Goodness no. Too young for me.' The words slipped out and Linette coloured.

'What do you mean, too young for you, Lin?' Cecily laughed. 'He's not some spotty schoolboy, is he?'

"Course not. It's just, well, he's immature, got no style.'

'I see. That's not like your mother though,' Cecily

said, remembering some of the very glamorous men she'd had. 'But . . . when will you go to America?'

'Just as soon as I can.' Again Linette didn't look at her, just picked away at the binding on a cushion beside her.

'There's nothing wrong, is there, Lin?' Cecily tried again, wishing she could find a reason for this change in Linette.

'Wrong?' The word snapped out of her. Her eyes became fearful a moment, flashing at Cecily as if to scour out any information she might have.

'Yes, wrong. You're so unforthcoming. Is there something wrong, Lin? You can tell me.'

'No, of course there isn't. I just want to get out of here for a while. See somewhere new.' With an obvious effort she grinned and said, 'Tell me about your love life. How many French and Italian counts seduced you?'

Cecily laughed. 'None, more's the pity. I told you I had a vague fling with a Frenchman, but it didn't last. He's off to do his military service now. But I met a wildly attractive English man at the vicar's tea party.'

'Vicar's tea party? Don't tell me you've gone religious?' Linette exclaimed with mock horror.

'No, silly. In Paris the vicar of the English church gives tea parties for all the Brits to meet each other. I met this fabulous man, Edmund Mendelson. He was studying at the Sorbonne. We talked and laughed a lot but he's in love with Lucy Gaskell, a girl at my school.' She sighed. 'Everyone's in love with her.'

'Will you see him again?'

'I don't know. We swapped addresses. If I hadn't gone to Florence I was going to invite him to Scotland. He adores it, apparently.'

'Next year,' Linette said.

'Who was there this year? Did Toadstool and Slime go?' she giggled.

'I don't know.' Linette put on her distant face again. 'I only went up for three weeks. Stephen was there with a very noisy friend.'

'And Uncle Mark and Aunt Jean? The Abbots?'

'They were up, I think.'

'But when you were there, who else was with you?' Cecily longed to know, just to get the picture again, to see in her mind all the familiar figures in their well-worn tweeds.

'Oh, just me, Daniel of course, and the boys. But,' she suddenly became animated, 'the boys were terrible together. Crabs in the beds, ghostly noises in the night. Daniel was on the point of sending them home ten times a day.'

'What a pity Toadstool and Slime weren't there. It might have scared them off for good. Is she still around, do you know? Or has he found someone else?' Cecily was half afraid to hear that Gail had moved into his London house with him.

'I think she's still with him. She's a social climber, likes his life style,' Linette said vaguely.

'You haven't seen them?'

'I see Ronald at the odd party. He's apparently making oodles of money in the property business. I'm sure he pulls down the streets where poor people live, chucking them out first,' Linette said.

'Beastly of him. Does he have any girl friends?'

Linette shrugged. 'Sometimes I've seen him with some flash girl. You know, the sort that has beads and tinsel sewn all over her clothes. They're very beautiful, in a tarty sort of way.'

'I can't think who'd invite him to their parties,' Cecily said disdainfully.

'I don't think anyone does, but he tries to worm his way in with the "right" people. He goes to openings of galleries and things too, tries to catch the eye of the photographer. He name-drops like mad.' She giggled. 'Last time I met him at something, he said dreadfully loudly, "I must go, I'm having dinner with the Honourable Patrick Howard." '

Cecily giggled too. 'I can just see him.'

'He always has that terrible supercilious look to him when he sees me. I steer clear, I can tell you. Especially knowing what a pervert he is.'

Cynthia came in, catching their last remark. 'Who's a pervert, dear? Hope no one you know.'

'That awful Ronald I told you about who tried to rape me in Scotland,' Cecily said.

'I don't know what Daniel's coming to inviting people like that.' Cynthia busied herself plumping up the cushions, hitting them fiercely as if they were Daniel. 'Of course those sort of men always lose their charm as they get older, so they get a bit desperate,' she said dismissively. 'But if your father does have to go after a lower class of woman he might at least have the decency to keep them and their offspring away from his own children.'

Cecily did not think her father had lost any of his charm. His hair was greying now, his face a little bit more lined, but she thought it gave him a distinguished air. They were lunching, just the two of them, at the Ritz, and she was aware of the covetous glances shot at him by the other women in the room.

'So, my darling,' he smiled at her, 'I must say you've grown very pretty. I like your clothes too. Paris has transformed you. Every English girl should be sent there to learn their style.'

Cecily flushed with happiness at his praise. 'I loved it,' she said. 'I really did.'

'I knew you would.' He beamed proudly. 'So now what? Have you thought of what you'll do now?' Then before she could answer he said, 'I think you must do a secretarial course so you can get a good job. Get a list of places that run them and find out which is the best.'

'I will.'

'Are you going to live with your mother or in your flat? You could let it, bring you in some money.'

'I wanted to share the flat with Linette but . . .'

'She's living in her mother's house, almost alone since Zara's so often away,' Daniel said. 'She mightn't want to pay the bills.'

'I know. But she wants to go to America, stay with Podge.' Seeing him frown, she laughed and said, 'Just

53

an old school friend. Of course I know she should travel, she's been here all the time, after all, but I'm a bit disappointed we're not going to share the flat together straightaway. We've been talking about it for ever.'

'America?' Daniel said in surprise. 'When is she going?'

'I don't know. But with any luck,' she brightened, 'she'll be back soon. Then we can start sharing.'

'Mmm.' Daniel concentrated hard on buttering his bread.

'So what about you?' Cecily asked to get his attention again. 'You haven't brought me here to tell me I have a new stepmother and more baby brothers and sisters, have you?' She was half smiling, hoping it sounded like a joke, but deep inside her was the nagging fear that it might be true.

'What?' He looked startled, then smiled. 'Of course not, darling.' His patted her hand. 'I told you, marriage is not for me. I've made a mess of it three times. I shall not be doing it again. Far too expensive anyway.'

'That's a relief.' She smiled happily. 'I thought for some dreadful moment you were going to marry that odious Gail. I couldn't possibly have Ronald as my stepbrother.'

'Don't be so unkind, Cecily.' Daniel withdrew his hand and scowled at her.

'But Daddy, she's terrible. A complete social climber. As for him, he's a pervert. He tried to kiss me and worse that summer in Scotland, two years ago.' She was angry, stung by his rebuke.

'Oh my dear, you're not a baby. What's wrong in a young man trying to kiss a pretty girl? You should be grateful, flattered. Don't tell me you're a prude.' He frowned at her, his silver-green eyes scanning her face as if afraid to find she wasn't 'normal'.

'Of course I'm not.' She was hurt by his reaction. She'd been innocent then, and Ronald's action had disgusted her, frightened her. Having since been kissed by men who desired her, who cared for her, she now knew the difference between a man being attracted to her, loving her, and a man wanting to use her and humiliate her.

'You're dangerously close to sounding like it,' he said.

'There's a huge difference between being kissed by a man who respects you and one who just wants to use you then throw you away.'

'Is there, my dear?' Daniel said gravely, looking at her intently. 'Or do some men just have better manners, manage to act the considerate lover more convincingly?'

'How cynical you are,' Cecily retorted, hating him suddenly. She wanted to leave.

'Darling.' His smile was contrite, charming again. He took her hand, held it in both his own. 'Don't let's quarrel, we haven't seen each other for so long. Tell me all about Florence. How did you like the Uffizi? And Michelangelo's David? Isn't it just the most extraordinary statue?'

Cecily sighed, feeling as if she was being fobbed off about the truth of his relationship with Gail. But she knew that if she pursued it, Daniel would become petulant, difficult, make her feel as if she was boring him. Make him wish he had never asked her out to lunch. So she played his game, being the pretty, entertaining companion, talking about safe, amusing things. All the time she scolded herself for falling back so easily into his manipulative trap.

'Cecily,' Linette's voice crackled down the telephone the next day, 'why did you tell Daniel I wanted to go to America? He won't let me go now, says I've got to go to Paris.'

'I didn't . . .' Then her conversation with Daniel slapped her hard. 'Well, I just mentioned you wanted to go so we couldn't share a flat for the moment.'

'I wish you hadn't.'

'But you never told me not to. I'm sorry, Lin, I just said it – you know. But it's nothing to do with him. Surely you can do what you like.'

'I know, but it makes it difficult.' There was a pause. 'He . . . he wants me to go to Paris first, to the Sorbonne. I just don't feel like learning French. I've had enough of schools and colleges. I want to live, get a job, not go on studying.'

'So, tell him that.'

'I have. But you know Daniel. He wants his own way.'

Cecily was silent for a moment. She did not know or care whether her father financed Linette. She was not, after all, his responsibility. But if he paid the bills, he called the tune. Close as she was to Linette, she didn't like to say this. Instead she said, 'You can break away, Lin, and do what you want. Can you afford to go to America?'

'Mum will help me and I can stay free with Podge. I could get a job over there.'

'Then you must go. You're nineteen now, Lin, you don't have to do what Daddy says any more.' She was surprised that Linette of all people should dance to Daniel's tune. She'd had him round her little finger ever since she was a child.

'I know. Well, must go now. See you soon.' Linette rang off.

For the next fortnight Cecily was busy visiting friends, finding out about secretarial courses and doing up her flat, planning to let it for six months and live with her mother. This would bring her in an income and hopefully by then Linette would be back from her travelling and they could move in together.

When she next rang Linette, Zara her mother answered.

'Hello, Zara, it's Cecily. Is Linette there?'

'Hello, my dear. You've just caught me, I'm about to fly to New York.'

'Oh, are you going to see Linette?'

'Linette? Oh no, I'm going with a friend. A special friend.' Her voice was coy. 'Linette's in Paris. She'll be there some months, I believe. Now goodbye, dear. I simply must rush.'

Cecily put the receiver down slowly. Paris? Why was Linette in Paris when she'd said she was dying to go to Podge in America? And if she was in Paris why hadn't she rung her first to tell her? At the very least she'd have surely wanted some addresses, people to see, places to visit. Cecily couldn't understand it at all.

Chapter Four

'But, Daddy, you said you were never going to marry again!' Cecily gasped in shock and horror. Her body felt as if the blood was draining out of it. 'And Gail of all people. You can't, Daddy. You just can't,' she shouted at him as the pain of it hit her, clenching her hands as if to wring Gail's elegant neck.

'Stop being so childish, Cecily,' Daniel retorted, but his eyes slid away from her. He got up and paced the room, going to the window and staring out at the street beyond.

'We won't stand for it, will we, Stephen? He just can't marry that odious woman.' Stephen was slumped with adolescent exhaustion in a chair and did not reply. 'Can't you see,' she appealed again to her father, 'she's just after your money, your castle, your house here. You'll have a terrible time if you do marry her, everything will be done up, fussy and vulgar. You'll get no peace.' She thought suddenly of Linette and her contempt for Gail's taste. If only she wasn't in Paris. Her scorn would surely pull Daniel back to his senses.

'That's enough, Cecily.' Daniel wheeled round to face her.

'You don't even seem to be in love with her. At least the others – well, Fiona anyway, you were mad about.'

Stephen, pale, went paler and hunched into himself. Cecily was worried about him, but then as Linette often said, when had she ever not been? The old worry had come thundering back the minute Daniel had asked them both to come here to his house in Wellington Square.

'You go without me,' Stephen had said. 'He'll only pick on me, ask me why I'm not in the cricket team or president of Pop like he used to be.'

'Nonsense. You must come, he said it was important.' Stephen was now at Eton, a tall, gangling youth who had none of his father's grace and, according to Daniel, none of his talents either. Cecily had often turned on Daniel, accusing him of being unfair to Stephen, expecting too much.

'He must pull himself together. Get that hair cut, stand up, work harder. When I was his age—'

'We can't all be like you,' she'd jump in, recognising in herself that feeling of inadequacy, that she wasn't quite amusing enough, pretty enough for him. 'At least try and encourage him. Be proud of what he does achieve.'

'What does he achieve? Just a huge overdraft,' Daniel would retort, but he would at least stop criticising Stephen, for a while. The moments of intimacy between them that could stir the old feelings of envy she'd experienced when Stephen was a child were rare these days.

'Why must you marry her? Her of all people?' Cecily said vehemently. 'You've so often said you're no good at marriage and won't do it again.'

'Companionship,' Daniel said after a moment. 'Love is . . .' he shrugged, waved his hands in the air, the great lover suddenly unable to explain love. 'Well, you don't get love very often. But there are other reasons why people marry.'

'For money, for position, for power – for greed,' Cecily said, ticking them off angrily on her fingers.

'You're being very melodramatic, Cecily.'

Cecily looked at him critically. His face was a little puffy. He looked bothered, distracted, not in command of himself at all. Certainly not the happy, confident lover. Why *was* her father marrying this awful woman?

'Don't tell me she's pregnant,' Cecily said incredulously.

Stephen shot a look of horror towards his father. He was at the age when the very thought of one of his parents having sex was abhorrent to him.

'Of course not, Cecily. Do stop all this speculating. We're getting married in the Chelsea Town Hall on the fourteenth of April,' he said firmly, as if stating a fact of life that could not be dodged. 'I do hope you'll both come.'

'No fear.' Stephen uncurled himself and walked to the door. He turned back to face them, his pale face clenched in anger. Cecily could see the gleam of tears in his eyes. 'That bastard Ronald shot a seal, and you want to marry his mother!' he spat, his face dark with hatred.

'Grow up, Stephen, do!' Daniel shouted, his eyes blazing. 'That was just an accident. As I said at the time, you don't seem to mind when someone shoots a pheasant.'

'It was *not* an accident. He did it to hurt us. He hates us and all we stand for, or are you too blind to see that?' Stephen yanked open the door and stormed out. He slammed the front door behind him. The house shook.

Cecily got up too. She felt empty and sick. Stephen's words ricocheted round the room, damning in their truth. She could see Daniel was rattled too, but she felt too hurt to care, to attempt her old trick of smoothing it over.

At twenty-four her childhood was long over, but she felt at that moment as if Daniel had truly abandoned her. *Gail*. Of all the women in the world, how could he choose her?

'Daddy,' she said in the voice of an old, weary woman, 'please don't marry her. Marry anyone else if you must, but please don't marry her.'

His lips tightened. She saw his hands were clenched by his side. Still he didn't really look at her.

'There must be a reason why you're marrying her. After all, you've known her . . .' she paused, guessed, 'seven years. Why, if you wanted to marry her, didn't you do so before? Or was there a husband lurking somewhere?' She stared at him, watching his face shift, clench, soften as he fought to summon the old defiant charm. She felt very cold and very afraid. She had never seen him so unsure of himself, even when his beloved mother had died.

'I think you and Stephen are being very selfish and not a little snobbish over this,' he said at last, but there was no fire to his voice. 'Not everyone has had your upbringing, comfortable homes, good education, and although I am hardly a millionaire, you have never wanted for anything. It is not surprising that other people want to be part of our lives too.' He stood a little taller now, and the old gleam of defiance came back into his eyes. Cecily experienced the familiar feeling of him distancing himself from her, isolating himself as he prepared to go his own way, telling her to like it or lump it. He would do what he pleased.

Anger and hurt rose in her. 'Then adopt someone, a child, a young person who needs a chance, if you feel so charitable,' she snapped and ran out of the house, slamming the door as Stephen had done, ignoring his cry of 'Cecily, wait!'

She ran down to her car which she'd parked in the King's Road and threw herself into it. She was shaking with fury and despair. Hot tears ran down her face and she brushed them off impatiently. What use were tears now? Then she wondered where Stephen was and, starting the car, drove towards his mother's mews house off the Fulham Road, looking for him as she went.

Then she saw him, sitting on a bench. She hooted

madly, causing the man behind her to hoot back in return. She wound down the window and called to him. 'Stephen, get in.'

He looked so drawn, so haunted, sitting there. Her heart wept. Would she ever stop having to protect him? He got up slowly and dragged himself to the car. When he got in he was crying.

'Oh, Stephen,' she put her hand on his knee, 'I know it's the most dreadful thing but—'

'How could he? How could he?' Stephen moaned, his tears running through his fingers and splashing on his jeans. 'He hates us, that's why. He just hates us.'

'No, he doesn't. He really doesn't,' Cecily said wildly. She couldn't bear to think that Daniel cared for them so little. But then he had always put himself first, not thinking how his habit of changing wives affected them. 'She's a witch – you know we said she was when we were children. She must have tricked him into it somehow. Maybe,' she said with a sudden surge of hope, 'now that he's seen our reaction to it, he'll call it off.'

'Do you think he will? Oh, Cecily, do you?' He turned to her with such hope in his eyes.

'I don't know,' she said slowly. 'But let's see tomorrow. It's all been such a shock. He might think differently about it tomorrow. Now, shall I drive you home or do you want a pizza somewhere?'

'I'll go home,' he said dejectedly.

'Oh hell,' Cecily exclaimed suddenly. 'I've quite forgotten, I promised to go to a friend's drinks party tonight. I just can't face it now.'

'Everyone's breaking their promises,' Stephen said. 'Don't worry about it.'

'But I do. Penny's a good friend and we all persuaded her to give a party for her birthday. I'll have to go,' she decided, thinking she couldn't bear to go back and sit alone in her flat anyway.

'What will Linny say? She hated Gail too.' Stephen stared morosely out at the darkening street.

'I don't know. She's back from Paris next month. But think, it might be off by then.'

'Or he'll be married. I won't go, though,' Stephen said as they stopped outside his house. 'In fact I'll probably never see him again if he does marry her.'

Cecily hugged him. 'Wait and see,' she said with a confidence she didn't feel. 'I'll come round tomorrow before you go back to Eton, or anyway ring you. Don't let it get you down.'

He didn't answer her but got wearily out of the car and rang the bell to his house.

Cecily rushed back to her flat, changed, picked up Penny's present and walked down the road to the party. She did not feel in the least like a party, but maybe a drink and amusing friends would help deaden the pain of Daniel's news.

Waiting on Penny's doorstep was a young man who was oddly familiar.

'Edmund? It is you, isn't it?' Cecily said hesitantly.

'That's me. Wait a minute.' He faced her, brows furrowed, a slight smile on his lips. 'Paris,' he said triumphantly. 'Vicar's tea party.'

'That's right.' She felt ridiculously pleased that he'd remembered. After all, it had been almost five years ago.

'But,' he grinned, 'that's as clever as I can get. I don't remember your name. I'm awfully sorry.'

'Cecily. Cecily Forester.'

'Of course,' he said a little too obviously. 'Now I remember. Are you coming to this party?'

'Yes. Are you? I didn't know you were a friend of Penny's.' She felt almost breathless with happiness at seeing him again. Of course, she warned herself firmly, he was sure to be heavily involved with someone else.

'I'm not. But my sister begged me to come. Penny works with her and apparently there's a shortage of men. So,' he grinned again, 'never too many girls for me.'

Cecily smiled in spite of a tiny feeling of envy of those other girls. She looked at him covetously as they waited for the door to open. He was tall with thick hair, a rich colour of chestnut that most girls would kill for, his face lean, with a full mouth that smiled readily. She stood as close to him as she dared on the doorstep, enjoying his being so near.

The door was opened and they were whisked into the hot, noisy room. Cecily felt suddenly lost as Edmund was borne away by a large blonde, her breasts in imminent danger of spilling out from her dress.

'Cecily,' Penny said, kissing her. 'I'm so glad you've come. I feel terrified,' she said happily.

Cecily knew quite a few people there and talked and

drank eagerly to hide the frightening pain of Daniel's impending marriage. For a few minutes she'd forget it, then like knocking a wound it sprang up again to hurt her.

Every so often she caught sight of Edmund through the noisy throng. He seemed to be watching her, sometimes he smiled, once he waved. As the alcohol took hold of her, the faces became a blur, a chattering fleshy blur, mouths open, teeth glistening.

Suddenly she felt a firm hand on her arm. It was Edmund.

'Feel like some dinner, or are you doing something?'

'I'd love to. It's so hot in here and—'

'Come on then.' He led her firmly to the front door.

The cold slap of the night air sobered her. He took her arm and she snuggled close to him, her inhibitions dulled by alcohol. She felt a burst of happiness pushing through her pain. Damn her father, she would not let his marriage spoil her life.

'But, Lin, you never said Michael was married.' Cecily couldn't help feeling shocked. Linette laughed.

'Oh, Cecily, you are old-fashioned. He's getting a divorce. He's never been happy with his wife.'

'Why did he marry her then?' Cecily asked, slightly annoyed to be called old-fashioned. 'How do you know it will be any better with you?'

'Of course it will. We love each other, we really do. Don't look so cynical. If you and Edmund weren't so in love I'd accuse you of being a jealous, dried-up old bag, like Miss Trotman.' Linette giggled, thinking of their headmistress, a terrifying woman who could kill a man with a glance at ten paces.

'But we . . .' Cecily pulled herself up short. She was going to say that she and Edmund trusted each other, and for them marriage would be a lifelong commitment, but she realised it might sound a trifle pious. Besides, she had never seen Linette look so happy, so absolutely glowing. She prayed their love would work out. Maybe Michael really did have a terrible wife.

'I know it's different with you and Edmund. But imagine if he was married and very unhappy and you just fell in love. You can't choose who you love,' Linette said reasonably.

'I know. After all, look at Daddy.' Cecily sighed, 'Though his last choice was a disaster. Perhaps Michael's wife is like Gail.'

'No one could be as bad as Gail,' Linette said fiercely. 'What a fool your father turned out to be. God knows why he ended up with her,' she said derisively, not looking at Cecily.

'So what will happen between you and Michael? Will he marry you?' Cecily didn't want to talk about her father's marriage, it upset her too much. Thank God she was so absorbed in Edmund.

'Yes. Maybe we'll be grandmothers together, you and I.' Linette giggled. 'Our children might even marry each other.'

'That would be fun. Think how crotchety we'll be, picking away at the younger generation,' Cecily laughed. They spent a few minutes describing their fictitious children and married bliss.

They were in Cecily's flat in Palace Gate. It had one or two nice pieces of furniture that Daniel had given her, the rest were bits and pieces she'd picked up here and there. Her mother had brought her some pretty lamps from the General Trading Company, and with its soft colours and cheerful framed posters on the wall, the flat had an atmosphere of jumbled comfort.

The bell rang and Michael appeared. It was the first time Cecily had seen him. He had met Linette in Paris on his frequent business trips where they had had plenty of time to build up their relationship away from the prying eyes of the London social scene – and his wife.

Linette, looking as proud and pleased as if she had manufactured him with her own hands, introduced him, 'Michael Gilgrist, Cecily Forester, my ex-stepsister.'

Cecily smiled politely and took his outstretched hand, aware that Linette was watching for her reaction. He was at least ten years older than they were. A tall, blond man with very pale blue eyes that seemed to skim over her body as if he was peeling off her clothes. He had a slightly sardonic smile, but his voice almost caressed her with its warmth.

'Cecily, I've been longing to meet you. I've so loved hearing about your childhood together in that castle in Scotland.'

'You must come up, perhaps this summer,' Cecily said. She motioned him to a chair, offered a drink, using the play of social niceties to hide her discomfiture. The tone in his voice was tantalising yet he puzzled her. He was quite different from what she'd imagined, but then at the moment she could only see men in relation to Edmund.

Edmund. She smiled to herself, glancing at the clock to see how much longer she would have to wait until he came.

Their affair had started like a flash fire. After Penny's party he had taken her out to dinner, apologising for the simple bistro but it was the end of the month and his allowance was low. They had talked for so long, laughing over the same jokes, that they had been swept out by the exhausted-looking management.

He had kissed her goodnight. A friendly, calm sort of a kiss. Then suddenly he had kissed her again and she had kissed him back, igniting a passion that neither had known they possessed. She had taken him into her flat and there half on the bed and half on the floor they had consummated their unexpected passion, laughing with the pleasure they created together.

There had been a sober moment a while later when Cecily had said in a terrified voice, 'Do you think I'll get pregnant?'

'Oh Lord, I hope not.' He'd looked nervous. 'We'd better . . . well, I'll come equipped next time.'

Cecily felt more pleased with his saying that there'd be a next time than his assurance of taking precautions.

Now, two years on, they were still so besotted with

each other they were talking of marriage. Not that Edmund had made any formal offer, but he often talked of their continuing life together and the children he wanted.

Edmund arrived at last. They kissed hungrily, holding on to each other as if they had been apart for weeks instead of hours. She introduced him to Michael – Linette he already knew – and leant back happily against him on the sofa, feeling warm and expansive towards everyone.

The evening went as well as any evening could when people are so in love with their partners that other people are superfluous.

'So what did you think of Linette's great love?' Cecily said to Edmund later as they lay together in bed.

'OK.'

'Just OK?'

'Surely you don't want me to declare a passion for him?' He tweaked her ear playfully.

'Of course not, but don't you think he's nice? He's a bit older than I expected but very good-looking, and very fond of Lin.' There was a silence and she said, 'What is it, darling? Didn't you like him?'

'He's very nice, as you say. But my opinion, for what it's worth, is that she's in love with him but he's in lust with her.'

'In lust.' Cecily sat up. 'You mean he doesn't love her? We love each other *and* lust,' she giggled. 'If you didn't lust after the person you loved it would be terrible.'

'Of course it would, but you can lust without love.'

'But he seems so fond of her. You don't think . . . Oh Edmund, you don't think he'll hurt her, do you?'

'He reminds me a little of your father. I wonder if Daniel ever loved anyone.' He looked at her. 'I don't mean his children, I mean his women. Did he ever love, really love, any of them?'

'Not Gail – no one could love Gail. Goodness knows why he married her, but he loved the others, or gave a good impression of it. Only he fell out of love as often as he fell in,' she said slowly. 'But he doesn't look like Michael, apart from being blond. So what made you say that?'

'There are some men, like your father and, I suspect, Michael, who love being with women, lust after them, but somehow never love them. Perhaps they can't love, or love only themselves. Oh Cecily,' he frowned, 'what a deep conversation for this time of night. Let's go to sleep.'

His words made her feel cold. A moment ago she'd felt sated with love, with belonging to him. Now she felt worried that no man was capable of truly loving one woman, of wanting to stay with her for life. There would always be a prettier, more sexy, more amusing woman round the corner. Daniel had always found it so. If Michael was the same, wouldn't Edmund be too?'

'Do you love me – more than you lust after me?' she said in a small voice, antenna quivering to catch the slightest hint that he didn't, to find a crack in their love.

'About both equally,' he said, stroking her breast and

72

running his hand down her body.

'Be serious,' she said. 'When we are old, wrinkly and ugly, will you still love me? Love lasts longer than lust after all, so it must be the stronger emotion in a relationship.'

'I'll always love you, silly,' he kissed her, 'but I'm going to lust after you for a very long time.'

Gail hated Scotland and managed to persuade Daniel to take her abroad in July. Cecily, Edmund and Stephen travelled up together, Stephen and Edmund boring Cecily terribly with their talk of life at Eton, Edmund having been there too.

'If ever I have sons they'll go up the road to the local school,' she said. 'I have never understood this preoccupation of public school men with their schooldays. Nothing else in life ever seems to measure up to them. Even Daddy still goes on about them.'

'He only goes on because I'm at the same school and not doing as well as he did when he was there,' Stephen said, dragging on a cigarette.

'Any life Linette and I have will be far, far better than our school. I wouldn't dream of going back, or doing anything else but commiserate with someone stuck there. You Etonians latch on to each other for life just because you went to the same school.'

Edmund laughed. 'Do I detect a hint of jealousy, darling? Surely you want me and Stephen to get on.'

'Of course, but can't you talk about anything else but Eton?'

'I like to know that someone survived it,' Stephen said. 'Anyway, you and Lin often talk about school. Is she coming up, her and her bloke?'

'She wants to, she wants to bring him, but . . .' She trailed off, not knowing how much Stephen knew.

'His wife wants him,' Stephen said, puffing again on his cigarette. 'I've asked Miles up. Miles Gardener. Thought we'd look out the local talent.'

Cecily laughed. 'The local talent is scattered all over the place. You'll have to wait until you can drive.'

Stephen shrugged and stared out at the passing scenery.

Cecily laid her head on Edmund's shoulder. She wished Stephen was happier. It was hard to believe that that laughing, boisterous little boy had turned into this morose, apathetic youth. Had Daniel turned him into this? His many marriages, his taking Ronald's side instead of Stephen's over the seal, his criticisms. Or was it Stephen's apathy and untidy appearance that spawned Daniel's disappointment in him?

They arrived at the castle to hear that Linette and Michael would be arriving in two days.

'I understand that Mr and Mrs Forester will be up the week after,' Thistle said.

'You know more than I do,' Cecily replied, wishing that Gail would not come. She hated it so, made cutting remarks about the place and the people. Why couldn't Gail just stay in London and let Daniel come up on his own?

'I hope that Ronald isn't coming,' Stephen said

angrily. 'I'll get the gun loaded, just in case.'

'Now don't you talk like that.' Thistle rushed at him like a bustling hen.' It's talk like that that gets people into trouble.'

'Then you must poison him, Thistle, and her too while you're about it,' Stephen said mildly, smiling up at her.

'You're a wicked boy. I don't know where you get these ideas from,' she admonished him, not knowing if he was joking or not and shocked either way.

Linette and Michael arrived. The four slept in separate rooms, but anyone up in the night would have seen fleeting forms disappearing into each other's bedrooms, only to re-emerge early in the morning before Thistle came up with cups of tea.

Miles, Stephen's friend, arrived, a dark-haired youth with merry eyes and a raucous laugh. They got hold of two motorbikes and sped off into the wilds to look out the local talent.

'He used to show that sort of enthusiasm for crabs,' Cecily laughed to Edmund, 'but I suppose at sixteen girls are more interesting. I hope he doesn't get into trouble,' she said, wondering if he would be like Daniel.

'Spoilsport,' Edmund teased.

'I just hope he won't be like Daddy, never able to settle with one girl.'

'Poor little Cecily. He's mucked you all up, hasn't he? I always thought my parents dull in the extreme, constipated with convention, but perhaps it does make one feel more stable.' He caressed her hair. 'We'll break the mould, don't worry.'

She kissed him gratefully, so happy to have him.

Cecily found herself watching Linette and Michael carefully to see if Edmund's description of him was right. Michael threw himself into their activities with gusto. He walked the moors, spotted the puffin way down in their niches in the rocks and knew a great deal about Celtic history.

Linette was cheerful and fun, but sometimes Cecily thought she was a little edgy, a little thoughtful. But one couldn't probe further – there was no time for the two girls to be alone what with being with their lovers, or listening to Miles and Stephen's boasting about their conquests, real or imagined, in the Highlands.

'I hope we're not exhausting you, Thistle,' Linette said one evening as they helped her clear up. She and Cecily had worried that she was looking rather frail.

'Nonsense, my dears. It does me good seeing all you young enjoying yourselves. There hasn't been so much laughter here for years.' She smiled. 'I said to Angus Gunn, it's good to have the young here, seeing them having such fun.'

On Thursday evening Daniel rang and spoke to Cecily. She'd been laughing with the others at Stephen and Miles's impression of trying to woo a couple of girls at the bus stop.

'Gail and I are taking the sleeper tomorrow night. We'll be with you Saturday,' he said in the defensive tone he used when he knew Cecily would object.

'Can't you come alone?' she said. 'We so want you on your own.'

'Of course not. Now mind you all behave, or you can leave.' His voice was sharp. 'You're not children any more. You must behave politely.'

'So should Gail,' Cecily retorted, stung by his tone of voice. She hadn't seen him for three months, had been so pleased to hear his voice on the end of the telephone, had hoped, stupidly, she knew, that he would come on his own. But hearing him standing up for Gail instead of them filled her again with despair and jealousy.

When she went back into the drawing room, just the expression on her face cut their laughter and their jokes. 'Daddy and Gail will be here on Saturday,' she said. 'I did so hope he'd come alone.'

There was a silence, each person affected in their own way. The three outsiders, Edmund, Michael and Miles, exchanged uneasy glances. Stephen slumped into himself as if already his father had found fault in him. Linette went very white and clung closer to Michael.

'At least we have tomorrow,' Miles said with his raucous laugh. Stephen gave a ghost of a smile.

'I'd better leave on Saturday,' Michael said suddenly. 'Time I was going back anyway.' He gave Linette a swift, contrite smile.

'I'll come too,' she said.

'No, you must stay here, finish your holiday. It's so lovely and you're with your family. After all,' he smiled, squeezing her arm, 'your . . . father,' he looked at Cecily, 'might not approve of me.'

'Rubbish!' Linette said hotly. 'It's none of his business

77

anyway. His morals are nothing. You're not leaving because of his disapproval, are you?' She was almost shouting, surprising Michael, surprising the rest of them with her sudden burst of anger.

'Lin,' Cecily started, making a move towards her.

'Linette,' Michael's voice was stern, 'don't be so absurd. You know I have to go back to the office, that I'm playing truant by being up here anyway.' He got up, crossed the room to the large window and stood looking moodily out at the sea.

'You could stay until Sunday, fly back that evening,' Linette snapped, seemingly oblivious of the rest of them.

Cecily, watching her with concern, saw how she clenched her hands into tight, white balls, noticed the creases of anxiety, almost panic, on her face. She had the feeling that this exchange was an old sore, festering beneath the face they showed the world.

'It is best I go on Saturday.' He did not turn round.

'Daddy won't mind. I mean, he's very broad-minded,' Cecily, yearning to help Linette, put in and instantly knew she shouldn't have.

Michael turned to her. 'I have to go back to work.' His mouth was tight with white lines of tension above his lips, as if he was allowing only certain words out, afraid that if he relaxed, his anger would overflow. Looking at his face, his eyes narrow, a thin menace of blue, she felt a sudden fear, not for herself but for Linette.

Edmund got up, went over to him. 'Whisky, old chap? Let's drink a drop of the malt and calm down. It's always sad when holidays come to an end.'

There was a pause. It seemed to Cecily that Michael was fighting himself to remain calm, adopt Edmund's mood. Then Linette said, 'I think you should at least stay until Daniel arrives. After all, he is your host.' It was the way she said it that surprised Cecily. Bitchy, determined, as if she wanted the two men to meet and would enjoy the outcome.

'I think I should leave now,' Michael said coldly. 'I think I have already outstayed my welcome.'

'Nonsense.'

'Of course you haven't,' Cecily and Edmund chorused.

'Can't see what all the fuss is, can you, Miles?' Stephen said.

'Women,' Miles said, forgetting he'd been chasing some all day. Then seeing Linette's glance he coughed and blushed and let out one of his raucous laughs in embarrassment.

'Dinner's served.' Thistle came in beaming, oblivious of the atmosphere.

'I'm starving. What is it, Thistle?' Stephen sprang up and put his arm round her. She laughed.

'Your favourite. Chocolate mousse.'

'Oh good,' Linette said and went into the dining room, leaving Michael standing by the window.

There was an uneasy truce over dinner, but when they got up in the morning, Michael had gone and Linette seemed curiously brittle. She refused to talk about it, announced she was dying to read her book and disappeared up to the attics with it.

'Leave her,' Edmund advised. 'Things will work out.'

Gail and Daniel arrived mid-morning. Stephen and Miles had gone out. Cecily kissed her father warmly, noticing his hair had become almost totally grey. Seeing his sharp look, she made a token of greeting Gail, but saw by her cold gaze she was not pleased to see her either. Edmund she glowed over.

'How nice to meet you. Are you enjoying it up here? So cold, isn't it?' She shivered, still holding his hand.

To her relief Cecily saw that Edmund was not fooled. 'I simply love it up here. I find the climate so refreshing,' he said heartily, withdrawing his hand and walking away from her.

'Hello, hello.' Linette spun in. She threw her arms round Daniel and hugged him. 'Darling Daniel, how good to see you. Michael has left, slipped away because he thought you'd disapprove, he being married and all.'

'Was he here?' Daniel's brow darkened.

Linette smiled, keeping her eyes firmly on his face. 'Of course. You said I could ask my friends here, any time.'

'But not him,' Daniel said, his eyes dangerously pale with anger.

'Don't be so stuffy, Daniel,' Gail sang out in a little-girl voice that maddened Cecily.

Daniel turned away. 'Any mail, Cecily?'

'On your desk.'

'Oh, this room. It really does need a coat of paint,' Gail said, looking round the drawing room. 'Let me see to it while I'm here, Daniel. It needs lifting.' She clasped her hands together and sighed. 'I think gold would look nice on that moulding.' She looked up at the thick tangle of moulded leaves and thistles now painted off-white on the ceiling. 'Gold,' she said, 'picked out in white. What do you think, Daniel?'

'Very vulgar. This is not Versailles,' Linette said sharply and marched out of the room, ignoring Daniel's protests.

Chapter Five

'You don't want me to go down on one knee, do you, darling?' Edmund said seriously, a slight crease between his eyes.

'Course not.' Cecily laughed, pulled him to her and hugged him. 'We'll be so happy, have lots of children and bring them here every summer.'

He smiled, disentangled himself from her for a moment, then fumbled in his pockets. 'Like all true romantics I have the ring somewhere on my person.' He grinned. 'Ah, here it is.' He pulled a small battered box from his inside pocket. He looked apprehensive. 'I . . . I hope you like it. It was my grandmother's, but if you don't, I'll buy you one.' He thrust the box into her hand as if it was burning him.

They were down on the beach. The ruin of the old castle was above them, flowers waving like flags growing between the stones.

Cecily opened the small box carefully. The diamond set in a circle of sapphires glowed and winked at her in the sun. The sea pounded beside them, the sea gulls crying out mournfully as they swooped and dipped over the waves.

'It's beautiful,' she breathed, looking up shyly at him, quite overcome.

He grinned, pleased at her reaction. He took it from her and put it on her finger.

'Faithful for ever,' he said and kissed her.

'For ever.' She smiled back, the sea and wind surging as if they were powerful witnesses to their love.

'I'll have to ask your father,' he said with a little pout. 'What do you think he'll say?'

'He'll be relieved.' She smiled. 'He doesn't want his daughter to follow in his footsteps.'

'I should hope not. I refuse to be the first of your many husbands,' Edmund said, but under his bantering voice Cecily detected a tinge of unease.

'You will be the only one, always and for ever,' she said dramatically, pulling him into her arms and holding him tightly to her, as if someone else was already pulling him away.

'Well, I must say I'm delighted,' Daniel announced later. 'I'll get some champagne up from the cellar and we'll drink to your future, my darling.' He beamed at Cecily.

She felt a surge of happiness, standing there in the drawing room with them, warm and secure with the two men she loved best in the world. Stephen sloped in to complete her contentment, his long hair looped back behind his ears.

'Stephen,' Cecily broke in quickly before Daniel could break her mood by going for him, 'Edmund and I are getting married.'

'About time,' Stephen said, but he was smiling. He gave Edmund a playful punch. 'Glad it's you and not some git.'

'I'm glad it's me,' Edmund said.

Gail wafted in, all fringed tartan and gold chains. She took one look at them and said in her maddening voice, 'What am I missing? I *feel* something in the air.'

'Edmund and Cecily are engaged,' Daniel said proudly, 'and I couldn't be more pleased.'

'Congratulations, darlings,' Gail said flatly. She went over to Cecily who braced herself for a kiss. Instead Gail took her hand and said, 'Let's see the ring then.'

'Wow, some bauble!' Stephen gave an admiring whistle.

'It really is beautiful. Such a lovely old setting,' Daniel said warmly.

'Never trusted old settings myself, bound to lose the stones,' Gail said dismissively. Cecily thought she saw a sliver of envy in her eyes. Gail felt undressed if she wasn't glittering like a Christmas tree.

'It belonged to my grandmother,' Edmund said quickly to cover the awkward atmosphere. 'Her own parents made her wait eight years before she could marry my grandfather. They hoped for a duke or anyway a viscount.' He looked at Daniel warily, as if wondering if he had wanted someone better for his daughter. 'Finally they relented and they were married only three years before he was killed in the First World War, leaving her with two babies.'

'How tragic,' Cecily cried. 'How terrible to have wasted all those years. Did she marry again?'

'No, she remained faithful to his memory until she died at nearly ninety. But she was one of the happiest, most contented people I've ever known,' Edmund said.

'Terrible, that war,' Daniel said, then glared at Stephen who'd thrown himself into a chair with his legs hanging over the arm. 'Go down to the cellar and bring up some champagne, Stephen,' he barked as if he was a sergeant major giving orders.

Stephen, knowing his father was wishing there was a war he could be sent to to toughen him up, slowly got up and went to get the wine.

'I wish Lin was here,' Cecily said to Edmund later. 'It would have been perfect – well, perfect if Gail hadn't been here.'

'Where is Linette? Is she coming up later?'

'She said she wouldn't this year. Not after all those rows she had with Daddy and Gail last summer.'

'She did behave rather badly. She was very rude to Gail. I mean, I know Gail's difficult, but—'

'She was cross about Michael.'

'I think it was more than that,' Edmund said slowly.

'More? What do you mean?' Cecily looked at him sharply.

'Oh, nothing, just Linette.' He kissed her, took her hand and gazed at the ring. 'You don't feel superstitious

86

about it? I mean now you know my grandmother's story.'

'Not if she was happy,' she said, ignoring a sudden shiver that passed through her heart.

'Stephen, I really must insist you have a haircut,' Daniel thundered. 'You look like a . . .'

'A poof, you were going to say,' Stephen shouted. 'That would frighten you, wouldn't it?' he said defiantly, his voice quieter now.

'What do you mean? No son of mine is going to be queer.' Daniel's voice was like a whiplash. 'Don't you ever even hint at it. If I find you are one, I'll have you at a psychiatrist before you can blink.' His voice was almost desperate now. 'You're not, are you? Are you, Stephen? Answer me, damn you!'

Cecily, who'd heard their raised voices in the hall as she came in, ran up the stairs two at a time. 'Daddy, do leave him alone. Everyone can hear. We don't want Thistle—'

'Leave us, Cecily. This is none of your business,' Daniel said icily. His face was white, he was fighting to control himself.

'You're making it everyone's business by shouting so loudly.' She looked at Stephen who was equally white, slumped on the sofa. He couldn't be gay, she thought, remembering him and Miles chasing the girls last summer.

'I'm going to ring your housemaster this evening,' Daniel hissed. 'It all points to it, your attitude of lying around, long hair, not being good at games. And girl friends – you're nearly eighteen and I haven't seen you with one girl, only that . . . that pretty boy, Miles.'

Stephen blanched. He seemed to diminish, shrink into the sofa as Daniel continued to shout. Cecily felt terrified, out of her depth. If only Edmund was here, but he'd had to leave to go back to work. She wondered if Stephen really was gay, and if he was, how much she minded.

There was a step at the door and Ronald walked in. He was smiling, rather as a black, shiny beetle might smile, Cecily thought when she'd got over the shock of seeing him.

Gail came in on his heels. 'Here's my darling boy,' she enthused, 'just come up for a day or two.' She gave Cecily and Stephen a glittering smile. She ran her thin hand up and down Daniel's back. 'Did I hear you shouting, Daniel? Do be careful, you might have a heart attack,' she purred.

'Hello, everyone,' Ronald said.

Stephen got slowly up from the sofa and walked out, passing everyone as if they were only shadows.

'Hello,' Cecily said vaguely, her skin prickling at seeing Ronald. Why was he here? No one had told her he was coming. She felt sick, as if he was violating the place – he and his mother. She followed Stephen out, muttering an excuse about going to wash her hands.

She knew Stephen would be up in the attics and she gave him a moment before she went after him. She glanced behind her to make sure that Ronald was not coming too.

She found Stephen sitting in a corner, hugging his knees to his chest, his chin on his knees. He was weeping.

'Oh Stephen,' she said and squeezed down beside him, putting her arms round him and holding him close to her. 'He didn't mean it,' she said after a while.

'He did. He's terrified that I'm gay. He thinks that would be the ultimate disgrace, a slur on *his* manhood,' he said sourly between sniffs. 'Imagine, the great lover's only son, gay.' His laugh was bitter.

Cecily didn't know how to ask him if he was gay. Or what her reaction would be if he admitted that he was.

He guessed her thoughts. 'You're afraid to ask me, aren't you?'

'Yes. I . . . don't want you to be gay, Stephen. I don't really know why. Well, probably because everyone is so unkind about them. I wouldn't want you hurt. But I don't think you are. I mean, last summer you and Miles were chasing after all those girls . . .' she said hopefully.

'I don't know what I am,' Stephen said. 'I've . . .' he paused, went even paler. 'I've never exactly slept with a girl, only . . . you know, fumbled about. But also at school two years ago, there was this boy . . .'

Cecily felt cold. She took a deep breath. She'd heard that sexual incidents sometimes occurred between boys at public school. But most of them preferred girls when they had a choice.

'I don't think you are,' she said firmly, as if just saying it would convince him he was not gay. 'Now you've left school, you'll have more time for girls.'

'I'm going away,' he said as if he hadn't heard her. 'I shall leave this country. I don't belong here.'

'Of course you do,' she cried, holding him closer.

'I don't.' He looked at her seriously with Daniel's silver-green eyes. 'Dad's married Gail, so there's no home for me there. You're with Edmund, Linette with Michael, and my mother is so obsessed with her picture restoring she doesn't notice if I'm there or not.'

'You probably should travel, see the world a bit before you go to Cambridge,' Cecily said, relieved they'd got off the gay bit.

'I'm not going to Cambridge.'

'But you are, Stephen!' She was shocked. 'You got marvellous A level results, and you should love it there. So much to do, people to meet.'

'Don't you see, I shall never do as well as Dad. I'm not bad at work, but games – well, I've never been good enough for the teams. I am not much good at rowing, nothing like Dad.' He sounded despairing.

'But you have other talents. We can't all be the same.'

'Tell that to our father,' he said angrily. 'I've had enough of these comparisons, always falling short. I put up with it at Eton. I enjoyed the school, made lots of friends—'

'So you will at Cambridge.'

'He can get at me more there.'

'He might not. Look, just wait. Give it a try.' She tried to sound encouraging, wishing yet again that Edmund was here. He would understand much better than she did.

'I really do mean it,' he said.

'You must stay for the wedding.' She felt a pang of guilt. Did Stephen feel she was deserting him getting married? 'You can come and stay whenever you want,' she added.

He sighed, stretched out his legs. 'Why, oh why, did that bastard Ronald have to come?'

Stephen did not have dinner with them. He went down to Thistle's flat and sat with her there as he used to when he was a child. Cecily was left juggling with Daniel, Gail and Ronald.

Ronald eyed her maliciously. 'I understand congratulations are in order,' he said with a sneering smile.

'I am so pleased,' Daniel said. 'We must have the most wonderful wedding. I'll have to ring your mother up, I suppose.'

Gail looked pained. 'I'm sure Cecily doesn't want to overdo it. You know how she hates extravagance.'

'She is my only daughter,' Daniel said.

'I don't mind, just a simple wedding,' Cecily put in hastily, knowing from some veiled hints from Edmund that Daniel was alarmed at the rate Gail was spending money.

Daniel had taken to carrying about an old battered briefcase. Cecily hadn't seen it for years, but this year it had appeared again, with a new lock. He kept it about himself, opening it and studying the papers inside with care.

'What are you hiding in there, Dad, love letters?'

Cecily teased him, coming upon him one morning with it open on his knee.

He shut it quickly, gave an awkward laugh. 'Oh . . . it's you, darling.' Cecily thought he sounded relieved.

'Of course it's me. Goodness, that case brings back memories of my childhood. I'd forgotten all about it. Bet it's full of love letters. Or perhaps war secrets?' she laughed. 'Can I look?'

He locked it with a small key that he put instantly in his pocket. 'It's full of dull papers, nothing that would interest you, my darling.' He flashed her his charming smile. He got up and opened the flap of his desk, laid the briefcase in it and locked that. His action made Cecily feel uneasy, and sad, as if it was the action of an old man, beset with imagined fears.

She told Edmund about it, knowing that now Daniel had accepted him as his future son-in-law, he had taken to asking his advice in financial matters, Edmund being a merchant banker.

'What do you think he hides in there?' she asked.

He shrugged. 'I haven't seen. Maybe his accounts. He's beginning to worry about his expenses. Men of his age often do. Money doesn't go as far as it did when they were younger, after all. I've suggested a few things, possibly joining Lloyd's, if he has enough free capital.'

'It must be Gail's tented effects in his house,' Cecily said scornfully, 'thank goodness he's never let her loose here.' Daniel had allowed Gail to do up his simple, elegant house in London. It now resembled a sheikh's tent. Endless swathes of hideous and expensive material were pleated round the walls and from a centre rosette in the ceiling, giving the place a claustrophobic feel.

Edmund had laughed. 'So far he's been able to fob her off by complaining of the huge expense it would involve. But I bet it's really because he's afraid of what she'll do with her pillars and gold leaf everywhere.'

'Your wedding will be wonderful, darling,' Daniel said now, holding up his glass to Cecily. 'After all, I hope it will be your only one.' For a split second she had the feeling he was sending her a warning, a secret agreement that he had made one mistake too many.

'I'll never want anyone else but Edmund,' she said.

'How do you know?' Ronald's question oozed across the table. His eyes sneered at her. She felt a shiver run through her.

'I know who I don't want,' she said icily and got up to clear the plates for Thistle.

Edmund rang after dinner, but as the only telephone was on the landing outside the drawing room where everyone could hear the conversation, she dared not say anything about Stephen.

'Something is wrong, darling, I can feel it,' Edmund said.

'I'll try and ring you tomorrow. I can't now.' Despite longing to confide in him she didn't feel like driving a mile to the call box, which might anyway be out of order.

'It's nothing to do with us, is it?' He sounded apprehensive.

'No, darling, of course not.'

'Stephen?'

'Yes.'

'Another row with Daniel?'

'Yes.'

'Serious?'

'Very . . . I think. I wish you were here,' she said longingly.

'So do I. My bed's so cold and empty.'

They exchanged more endearments, and finally she rang off. When she looked up, she saw Ronald watching her from the shadows.

'All alone tonight,' he said and went along the passage to the bathroom.

Cecily felt sick. She went into her room, fetched her night things and her book and went along to Stephen's room.

'Can I sleep in the spare bed in here?' she said looking at the bed piled with his clothes, records, books, a pair of shoes. 'I'm afraid of Ronald.'

'Perverted bastard. Why don't we put a trap in your bed, a mousetrap.' He laughed wildly. 'That should castrate him. Mousetrap in the balls.'

Cecily couldn't help laughing, though she felt Stephen's laughter was bordering on the manic.

The telephone rang again.

She went to the door. Daniel had picked it up.

'Linette, what is it? Pull yourself together, what's happened?'

Cecily ran down the stairs. 'Let me talk to her,' she

said, pulling at the receiver in his hand.

'I can't make head or tail of it, here you are.' He thrust it at her and hovered beside her, his breath coming fast, stepping restlessly this way and that as if impatient to know what was wrong.

'Lin, what's happened?' She could almost hear Linette struggling with herself, willing herself to be coherent.

'Thank God you're still there. I don't know what to do. I'm pregnant and Michael has left me.'

Chapter Six

'It was the only solution, Cecily,' Daniel said, his voice weary, as if it had been working so hard it was almost gone. His eyes were hollow in his gaunt face and it seemed to Cecily as if he had become suddenly old.

'She could have had it and we could have looked after it together.' Cecily felt so empty with shock, with misery, she had hardly any strength left to argue.

'Babies are not dolls, my darling, as you'll find out when you have your own. When Michael heard, he just walked out on Linette. I don't know if you know, but he already has two children, one born only a few months ago.'

'Children! He never said . . . he said his wife was difficult and he would leave her, marry Linette.' Cecily spoke wildly, as if by explaining it would all come right. 'So,' she went on as the thought struck her, 'he was sleeping with his wife after all. He told Linette he hadn't for years.'

'That was the sort of man he was,' Daniel said shortly.

'I can't believe it. I never thought he'd behave like that,' Cecily said, horrified. Then Edmund's words came back: *He's in lust with her.* 'Does Linette know . . . about his children?'

'Yes. Now she does.'

'Oh God, she must feel . . . Oh, why can't I go to her? I wish she'd hadn't agreed to this abortion, she didn't really want it. You know she didn't. I wish I'd been here.' She felt so tired, so confused.

She herself had had a false, as it turned out, pregnancy alarm with Edmund. They'd been worried, agreed to marry if it was true, but he'd been with her, accepted it would be his child, his responsibility, as much as hers. But Michael had dumped Linette and fled.

Daniel took her hands and held them in his own. They were in a small waiting room in a private nursing home in London.

'I know this seems like hell now but, my darling, it was for the best. One can't afford to be sentimental about babies in this situation. Babies need two loving parents. If she'd kept it, she'd have struggled alone, possibly never finding anyone else decent to marry her.'

'But I would have helped.'

'You have Edmund now. Would he want to take on someone else's child? And as for having it adopted, imagine wondering all your life if it was happy, well cared for. Believe me, darling, hard though this is, it's the best choice in the circumstances.'

They sat there together miserably, holding hands.

Ever since Linette's wild call in Scotland, Daniel had been marvellous.

'Keep this strictly between ourselves, Cecily,' he'd said when Linette had rung off. He had stood so close to Cecily, listening to every gasping word Linette had said. She was glad he had heard, it was too great a burden for them to cope with on their own.

Cecily had looked quickly round in case Ronald was lurking somewhere in the darkness, ready to slither in with some malicious remark.

'We'll go down tomorrow,' Daniel said, 'just you and I.'

'But what about G—'

'Leave it to me,' he said abruptly. 'Now go to bed, I have to think.'

Cecily had told Stephen. She was so shocked and upset she'd have died if she hadn't confided in someone. Stephen wouldn't tell anyone, and it was a family crisis after all.

'How could he leave her? Leave Linny!' Stephen cried out in anger and disbelief. His fists balled as if he would strike him. 'I thought he wanted to marry her, divorce his wife.'

'Apparently not. I'll learn more tomorrow.'

'I'm not staying here alone with Toadstool and Slime,' Stephen said suddenly, getting out of bed and rummaging for his bag. 'I'll come and find that creep Michael, make him go back to her.' His face was hard with determination.

'Stephen, you must stay here. You must keep an eye

on them. We don't want to come back next year and find the whole place dripping in gold paint and swathes of material.'

Stephen smiled in spite of his agitation. 'But to stay here alone with *them*.'

But he had, and Daniel and Cecily had flown down to London. Cecily never asked what explanation Daniel had given Gail and Ronald.

They'd found Linette alone in her mother's house, wildly buoyant.

'I'm going to bring it up by myself. I shall tell it about Michael and maybe when he sees it he'll love it and come back. I expect he's just in a state of panic,' she said, a desperate look in her face.

Apart from being rather dishevelled, Cecily thought Linette looked wonderful.

'Yes, you can,' Cecily said, a bubble of hope rising through the mire of misery that had sat in her since Linette's news. 'That might well happen. He's sure to love it. I'll help you look after it.'

Daniel said, 'Where's your mother? What does she think about all this?' He looked round the cream and light green room of his ex-wife's house. The room, like Zara, was pale and delicate with fragile porcelain figures on glass shelves and fine-limbed furniture.

'She's away in the south of France. She doesn't know yet. But she won't mind,' Linette said breathlessly.

Daniel had let them talk, make their plans, but a few days later he insisted that Cecily went with Edmund to his parents' house near Oxford. It was his father's sixtieth birthday and they were having a huge party.

'I needn't go – well, not until the day itself,' she protested. 'Edmund will understand.'

'You must go, Cecily. You belong to Edmund's family too, you know. Besides, we don't want too many people to know about this, and his family will ask why you weren't there. This party's been planned for ages,' he said firmly. 'Linette is fine, I'll look after her.'

It was impossible to keep in touch with Linette at the Mendelsons' house. Nancy, Edmund's mother, really preferred horses and dogs to people and when she first met Cecily she had looked her over as she might a piece of livestock. She was rather offhand about the catering arrangements, as indeed she was about food generally.

'I think she'd rather we went into the stables and ate the hay with the horses,' Edmund remarked.

His sister Amanda and his Aunt Polly were struggling with a local caterer, and Cecily had no alternative but to pitch in too. She found it a relief from the emotional trauma at Linette's and enjoyed chatting about her coming wedding and Amanda's love affair with a polo player from the Argentine.

When she and Edmund had got back to London late on Sunday night, she'd asked him to drop her round at Linette's. The house was in darkness and there was no answer, nor could she find Daniel.

'They're probably fine somewhere, don't worry so, darling,' Edmund said. He was longing to make love to her, as the house had been so full of guests and prying relatives that they had hardly had a chance to kiss, let alone anything else.

'I suppose you're right, but I feel uneasy. Where is everyone?'

'Forget everyone but me. I need you,' he said, making her feel a little guilty that she'd hardly thought of him all weekend.

Daniel had been in his office early in the morning and explained to a distraught Cecily that Linette had agreed to the operation. There was nothing Cecily could do – it was Linette's choice after all. Now they sat here together in this impersonal room.

'Where's Zara, does she know?' she asked bleakly.

'Not yet.' Daniel looked uncomfortable. 'You know how hysterical she gets, which is hardly helpful for Linette.'

'She ought to be here,' Cecily said, hating this small room and the way her imagination was throwing up lurid pictures of Linette's baby being killed.

The door opened and a nurse came in. She smiled, tight, professional. 'It's all over,' she said briskly. 'You can come and see her.'

'You go, Cecily.' Daniel got up, then sat heavily down again. He was looking very green.

'But . . . well, all right.'

Linette looked very white lying on the bed. She lay completely still, her eyes closed.

'Lin, it's me,' Cecily said, tiptoeing over to her as if any sound might upset her. She took her hand and Linette opened her eyes and stared at her.

'My baby,' she screamed suddenly. 'I want my baby.' The agony in her voice devastated Cecily.

'Oh Lin.' She felt the tears pouring down her face. She felt utterly useless standing there, the words 'my baby' echoing on and on inside her head. Why hadn't she fought harder for Linette to keep the child? Why had she been away and unable to prevent it?

A sudden unbidden thought grasped her and held on. Daniel had forced Linette to get rid of the child. Getting her alone, he'd managed to persuade her. Cecily remembered now how he had said nothing, added nothing to their discussion about how they would keep it.

'Hush,' said the nurse, and came forward with a syringe. Linette drifted back into sleep.

The nurse smiled at Cecily. 'She'll be all right,' she said. 'Come back later.'

That day took something from Cecily, a bit of innocence, frivolity. She remembered how they had joked and giggled their way through their life before, giving Gail and Ronald code names, thinking up tricks to play on them to relieve their unhappiness at Daniel's marriage. This was something you could not joke about. It lay like a murder, between them all, Cecily said later to Edmund. She could not speak to her father about it, or look him in the eye.

'I feel he's betrayed us,' she said to Edmund as she sat hunched up in her chair.

'You've got to stop letting this get to you,' he said. 'I don't like the idea of abortion either, but in some cases it may be for the best.' He looked worried. Cecily knew he didn't like thinking about it. This was, he agreed, the first time he'd been confronted with it close to. Before, he wouldn't have given it much thought, but now he saw the devastation it could bring, he felt disturbed by it.

Linette recovered physically very quickly. It had been an early termination and there had been no complications.

'I want to go to New York for a while, stay with Podge,' she said to Cecily. 'I just want to get away from here, go somewhere quite different.'

Since that terrible, desolate cry, she had said nothing about it, just behaved as if she'd been ill, needed protection from anything unpleasant or difficult. She wouldn't talk about Michael either.

'Come back for my wedding,' Cecily said, then felt guilty that she was planning her wonderful day with Edmund when Linette had no one.

'I will. When is it?'

'The first of December.'

'I'll be there.' She smiled, but it was an empty smile. There was nothing they could say to each other, words seemed too trite. Cecily sometimes felt that Linette didn't want to see her because she brought back memories of times past, when she thought Michael loved her. Cecily also felt guilty that she hadn't done more to prevent an abortion, and that Linette thought she had let her down.

Daniel seemed preoccupied too. In the whirl of her wedding arrangements she hardly ever saw him, or

Stephen. Stephen had joined a band with other floppy-haired, black-clad mates and after another almighty row with Daniel had disappeared on a gig with them.

'Come back for my wedding,' Cecily said, having called round two days after the row and heard Stephen's side of it. Neither of them had mentioned homosexuality again. Nor had she liked to discuss it with Edmund. She felt if it wasn't talked about it would disappear and just be a figment of Stephen's imagination, not a reality.

Daniel paid Cynthia a visit and sat in her drawing room drinking Gerald's gin, Gerald watching him warily, as if he might suddenly whisk Cynthia off again. But Cynthia was more preoccupied with the wedding arrangements than her ex- and, to her, bed-soiled husband.

'You cope with it, send me the bill. Remember, it must be a marvellous day,' he said to her, 'so no cutting corners.'

'Don't be absurd, Daniel, of course we won't cut corners,' Cynthia said. She'd already ordered Searcy's to do the catering and taken Cecily to Belville for her dress.

There was a lot to do in the weeks before her wedding. Sometimes Cecily wished she and Edmund could just slip away on their own and get married far away from everyone. There seemed to be so much palaver, wedding lists to complete at the General Trading Company and Peter Jones. Should they also have one at Harrods? Then there was the question of choosing bridesmaids and pages without causing offence to some long lost relation.

'We hardly have any time or energy for each other,' Cecily gasped one evening as they slumped among the boxes and tissue paper that had encased some newly delivered wedding presents. It had not helped that Cynthia had insisted that Cecily move back with her and Gerald as if she was somehow recalling her daughter's virginity.

'We certainly don't have the opportunity,' Edmund grumbled. Cecily had sold her flat and he shared a house with three friends. It was never empty for long and making love quickly with half one's attention on the click of the front door was hardly erotic. They had tramped miles looking for a new home to buy.

'Shall we elope?'

'Or just live in sin.'

'Now, Edmund,' Cynthia bustled in, 'have you got your ushers organised? Can you give me their names?'

'Oh Mum, not now,' Cecily said, seeing the blank look of panic cross Edmund's face.

'We haven't much time,' Cynthia said.

Cecily's idea of it being very romantic to be married in the winter with a dark church lit by scores of candles proved to be true. 'It always rains in the summer anyway and those marquees leak and are icy cold, so having a reception indoors is much safer,' she said. 'We might as well have it in the winter when we know it will be cold and dark anyway, and make the most of it.' And she did.

She looked wonderful in her dress, complete with tiny children straggling up behind her dressed in blue and white. Daniel looked very distinguished and proud as he led her up the aisle then took his place beside Cynthia in the front pew. Gail had made a great fuss about this, but Gerald had calmed her down.

'We're second fiddle in this event, my dear,' he'd said firmly. 'Etiquette decrees we sit behind the parents of the bride.'

At last it was over and, dressed in an apricot wool coat, Cecily, holding Edmund's hand, ran down the steps to leave. She turned and threw her bouquet straight into Linette's arms and blew her a kiss.

'You next time,' she smiled, thinking how lovely she looked, though there was a faraway sadness in her eyes.

"Bye, my darling, be happy.' Daniel swept her into his arms and held her close. For a second she felt tears prick her eyes, feeling a sudden pang that now she really was leaving home. He released her and she saw Stephen looking at her in that vulnerable, little-boy way he still had.

"Bye, Stephen, come and see us,' she said, hugging him too, feeling stupidly that she was letting him down.

In a moment she was in the car that was to take them to the airport.

'Alone at last,' Edmund said, winding his arm through hers.

She snuggled against him, then turned round to

wave one last time. Daniel, Linette and Stephen stood together waving, and she felt a sudden wrench at leaving them. It was Edmund's and her turn to create a family, and however much she felt her own family needed her, they must take second place now.

Part II

Chapter Seven

'Jamie, do come down, you're giving me a heart attack.' Cecily reached out a restraining hand, pleased, despite her fear, that he was so carefree again.

'Whooops.' Jamie lunged his small, bony body out over the turrets, screaming with laughter as she pulled him back.

'You should take no notice, Mum. He does it every time we come up here,' Miranda said leaning against her father, half asleep in the sun.

'I know he does, but one day he might slip.' Cecily pulled Jamie to her and hugged him. Tomorrow they'd be leaving the castle, her castle now, or at least half of it was hers since Daniel's death, and head on back south to London, and school.

She was haunted suddenly with a feeling of *déjà vu*, of holding Stephen to her when they were children and being afraid she'd lose him. She had lost him in the end. He had run away to America instead of going to Cambridge. Apart from the occasional card, always without an address, she never heard from him. She sighed now, thinking of him. They were always there, those ghosts from childhood, the children they once were still hiding in the shadows.

It had been a ritual, since her childhood, to eat their last lunch up here if the weather permitted.

Cecily leant back, lifting her face to the sun, remembering her father complaining about eating up here on the roof.

'Rather a palaver, just for a sandwich,' he'd grumble as they trailed through the warren of dusty attics to climb the tight spiral staircase to the small portion of flat roof on the tower, Thistle, dear Thistle, who had died two years ago peacefully of old age, puffing up behind them with the food heavily wrapped in grease-proof paper.

'It's been a marvellous holiday, hasn't it.' Cecily said it more as a statement than a question. She looked contentedly at her family, all sprawled on the castle roof, high above the moors and the sea. Edmund, a little fleshy round the face now but still good-looking, with hardly any grey in his chestnut hair, Miranda, just eleven, all legs and arms, and Jamie a year and a half younger, his usually pale face just tinged with colour after the wind and the sun, and time spent away from school.

'What time shall we leave tomorrow, darling?' she asked Edmund, knowing with leaden laziness that she'd better start packing.

Edmund, who a second ago had seemed comatose, snapped open his eyes. He sat up, gently pushed

112

Miranda from him and got to his feet.

'I . . . I don't know.' He stood with his back to her, looking out over the sea.

Cecily frowned, half laughed. 'But you do know. It's either six in the morning if you want to stop off at the Crawfords or eight if you want to see Aunt Polly. Which have you decided we'll do?' He looked good in jeans, she thought, noting his lean hips, tight buttocks. Few middle-aged men did.

'I . . . haven't decided yet.' He gave her an awkward, almost an apologetic smile and left them, squeezing himself through the tiny door of the tower and disappearing from view.

'Wait, Dad, you said we'd go fishing.' Jamie scurried after him.

Cecily busied herself collecting up the picnic. She felt a sudden chill, as if Edmund's departure had taken the sun with him. He was probably fed up with her asking when they were leaving. No doubt he, too, felt sad that their holiday was coming to an end, though this time he hadn't relaxed with his usual abandon, playing foolish games and jokes that reduced the children, and often herself, to helpless giggles. She sighed. It must be the office. He'd had so many telephone calls, and a few times she'd found him muttering into the receiver. They still had the same single telephone in the thoroughfare of the landing outside the drawing room, which made privacy impossible.

'Work,' he'd say shortly if she came across him with the receiver clamped to his ear. 'You'd think they'd leave you alone when you're on holiday.' And when she'd asked him if there was a crisis or something, he'd looked impatient, told her he wanted to forget about the office now he was here.

When the children had at last gone to bed, Cecily sat in the drawing room looking out at the glittering sea. The light was soft, silver and pearl with milky, diaphanous clouds bunched across the sky. The ruin stood dark and mysterious against the sea. She was curled up, her legs under her, on the chaise longue by the tall window that rattled in the wind. She drank in this beauty, to nourish her in the year to come.

'Cecily.' Edmund, who was slumped in a chair by the fireplace, broke into her reverie.

'Mmm.' She turned to smile at him, half stretching out her hand to pull him to her, so they could absorb the beauty together.

'I . . .' He got up, paced the floor. Went over to the drinks tray, poured himself a neat whisky and gulped at it. 'I . . . well, it's awfully difficult to say this but . . .' He looked at her helplessly, as if she knew what he was finding so difficult to say and would say it for him.

'What?' She watched him flailing about, a tiny chill starting somewhere deep inside her.

'You know Rowena . . . Rowena Morrison?'

'Of course, we were in Verbier, skiing with them at Christmas. How is she?' She smiled, relaxed again.

'I'm . . . we're in love and I—'

'In love?' Cecily almost laughed. Rowena was plain, rather bossy and red-faced, always in a fuss with her children. Besides, she had a perfectly good husband of her own.

'Yes.' Edmund stood tall, looking red and defiant, as if determined that she would not laugh at him. 'And we want to get married and live together.'

'What?' A sickening, hollow pain began to grip inside her.

'B-but when?' The words croaked from her. It was a joke, surely it was some terrible joke. Edmund would never do this to her, to them. Not Edmund.

'Tonight . . . I mean I thought, now the holiday was over, I'd . . . leave tonight. I'm so . . . sorry,' he blustered again.

'Is she somewhere here?' Cecily looked wildly towards the door, as if expecting Rowena suddenly to materialise, as Ronald used to do. She felt faint, empty, as if all her happiness was draining out of her body.

'Of course not, but I thought it better if I left now.' He looked away from her, his mouth tight.

'So all this holiday you knew you were going to leave us?' Cecily cried out, the pain, the injustice of it, gathering force, tearing at her. 'Why didn't you tell us at the beginning instead of letting us think everything was wonderful – as it always has been.' She felt panicky now. It wasn't happening, not Edmund. Why, only last night he'd made love to her. It had been . . . well, they'd been married so long, but it had been fine. Perhaps that was it, he wanted it more than fine.

'Why?' she said, thinking fast, her thoughts jumbling up in their haste to get sorted in her mind. 'Is it sex? Is there something I – we can do? Is it just an affair? Hundreds of people have affairs and a good marriage pulls through.' Her voice was racing now as she tried frantically to find a way round this so he would stay with them.

'No.' His voice barked out too loudly as if he was frantic for her to understand. 'No, Cecily. It's more than that. I'm sorry, really I'm sorry. You're not at fault. We just fell in love and we want to be together.'

'But Peter—'

'She's told Peter. She told him at the beginning of the summer. They hadn't been happy for ages so . . .' He gave a shrug as if that somehow made it all right.

'But we were.' Her voice shook. 'Edmund, we were happy. Ask anyone. Look at us today, picnicking in the sun. We're a family, a happy family. You can't just throw it all away. Not now, the day before we have to go back to London, the children back to school. That is too cruel.'

'There is no good time,' he said defiantly. His face was clenched, she could see how he was hating this, hating the feelings of guilt her words were breeding in him. He wanted to leave, just walk away from this scene. Cecily closed her eyes to stop the past thudding back. She'd been here before with her father. She'd thought it was over, now he was dead.

'How long have you thought that you loved her?' She felt as if she was falling, as if her life was crumbling like the ruined castle into the sea.

'We only decided in June . . . that we wanted to spend

the rest of our lives together.' His voice was half ashamed.

'We wanted to spend our lives together too.' She looked coldly at him. 'Did I live too long?'

'Cecily . . .'

'You should have told me before, and the children . . .' Tears rushed into her eyes, her throat, as the truth bit deeper. 'The children, how can you leave them like this, without explaining?'

The image of Stephen haunted her. Little Stephen whom she and Linette had wanted to protect from the pain of divorce. She swallowed the lump in her throat.

'Dear God, don't tell me history's repeating itself,' she wailed.

For the first time Edmund looked contrite, then he said weakly, 'Cecily, I just don't know how to tell them.' He bit his lip savagely. 'It's such a mess . . . I want to see them, keep in constant touch with them. I'm not leaving them.'

'But you're leaving *me*?'

'Well . . . I . . .' He raked his fingers through his hair, took a few steps away from her, then back again, as if he was doing a foolish dance. If she hadn't been so shattered, she'd have laughed at how ridiculous he looked, stepping in and out of his responsibilities.

'Darling, I . . .' The word slipped out from habit. Cecily turned on him.

'Don't call me darling, not any more. You can't leave a person you still think of as darling.' The pain bit deeper, chafing like a vice. How often he'd called her darling in a soft, warm way, looking at her, his eyes suffused with love, with desire. She shook her head as if to rid herself of his words but they stuck to her like burrs. He could not mean this, this madness of loving Rowena. Surely, he could not.

'I do care for you, Cecily, very deeply. I always will, but it's just that Rowena and I . . . it's different. We love each other and . . .'

'And we don't?'

'Not . . . as we did. Admit it,' he pleaded desperately with her. 'Things are not as they were. We've moved on. I'll always be fond of you, and I'll never desert the children. I'll pay their school fees as I always have. After all,' he said in a bracing voice as if it was the solution to the situation, 'we were selling the London house anyway. You choose one you like, smaller of course, but I'll pay for it.'

'You can't buy me off!' she cried. Then as if to haunt her she heard Daniel's gentle voice with its undercurrent of insistence: *You'll still come and stay with me, Cecily, and we'll have such treats together, you and I.* He, too, had offered presents each time he'd left her.

'I'm not buying you off, Cecily.' Edmund looked hurt. 'I'm just trying to be fair, to explain that you won't be short of money.'

'Why do you men always think you can buy your way out of your responsibilities?' she spat suddenly, angry with Edmund, angry with Daniel whose voice had held the same persuasive charm as he made his farewells, as if he was doing those he left behind a favour.

'Can't you see, it's you I want, you and our family to stay as it was. I don't want money, I just want us, as we were.' She looked up at him imploringly, her whole body stretching towards him, begging him to stay.

'But Cecily . . .' He looked fearful now, as if she would suddenly have hysterics and add to his guilt. He took a few steps nearer the door. 'I . . . I've explained. It's over. It's not your fault . . . I feel dreadful, I know I'm to blame, but it's happened. I fell in love and . . .'

'Did you never love me? Was it just an illusion?'

'Of course I loved you, still do, but this is different.'

'How? Has she three sets of breasts, three—'

'Don't be crude, Cecily, it's not like you.' He looked embarrassed, imploring, as if he expected her to behave differently. Make it easy for him.

'You're not like you.'

'Look, Cecily, I'm going now. It's better before we say things we regret.'

'Oh Edmund, please, think of the children if not of me. Think of Jamie, so unhappy at school, trying so hard to do well for you.' She got up, holding out her hands. 'Why didn't you tell me before? Why did you let me think we were a perfect family, having a perfect holiday?'

'There's no more I can say, Cecily. I'll see you and the children are all right, always. I promise you that. I'll ring them tomorrow.' He ran out of the room and down the stairs.

Cecily moved to follow him, to catch him and beg him to stay one more night. Then she saw Daniel's photograph on the piano, the heavy, sleepy lids half closed over his silver-green, indolent eyes, his sensuous mouth smiling at her, charming anyone who saw it.

Don't make a scene, she heard him say. *I detest scenes, so undignified.*

She heard Edmund's car start and leave. He must have packed up and got it ready before supper, she realised. The thought of him planning this, secretly packing and tiptoeing downstairs to hide his things in the car, sickened her. And Rowena, red, round face, shiny as a currant bun, what could she have to offer him?

Suddenly the large drawing room seemed to close in on her. She longed to scream, to howl in anguish and anger at the searing pain in her. She ran from the room, down the stairs and out across the lawn. Her breath came fast, she had a stitch in her side, but on she ran. Down the path to the beach, her slim figure bent slightly on one side to relieve the stitch. She didn't stop until she felt the knobbly shingle beneath her feet, misshaping her thin shoes. Then she gave way to huge, gasping sobs.

'Why,' she called out to the pounding sea, black and sinuous as oil under the moon. 'Why did he go? How could he destroy our family?'

After a while she calmed. What could she say to the children? She thought of Jamie, only now after seven weeks of holiday relaxed and happy after his ordeal at prep school. Edmund was determined that he would go to Eton despite the fact that Jamie was probably not clever enough. He was under enormous strain, worrying himself into a pale, skinny shadow. Miranda was happy at her boarding school, although she grumbled, telling unbelievable stories that, if true, would have the school closed down immediately by health inspectors. They both adored Edmund, and whatever he said to them they would feel that he had abandoned them, preferred Rowena's simpering, pretty little girls to them.

Cecily walked up and down the beach, trying out various ways to tell them. Perhaps Edmund didn't really mean it, would have his fling with Rowena and then come crawling back. She felt brighter at this, and decided just to tell them that Daddy loved them very much but he wanted to go and live with Rowena for a while.

But her hope soon plummeted again as she remembered the vague suspicions, which she'd hastily squashed, that Edmund had had affairs before.

If she'd been honest with herself she would have admitted that their marriage had not been as carefree and idyllic as their time before they married. But then surely that was how marriage often was. They'd bought a huge dilapidated house and spent years restoring it, both working hard to pay for it, Edmund striving even harder to get on in his firm. Then the children had been born, wanted, loved by both of them. But babies, as Daniel had told her on that terrible day with Linette in the hospital, were not dolls. Among other things, they were killers of passion and energy. But they had been happy, she told herself defiantly. The romantic spark may have wavered a little, but they'd had a deeper, richer relationship. Or so she'd thought.

She must have been wrong, she thought with despair. What had happened to make him leave them?

She looked back at the castle, dark with pinpoints of light at some windows. It stood strong and dependable against the winds and storms hurled from the sea. It was hers, or as good as, since Ronald never came here now, hating it as much as his mother had done.

Two years ago Daniel had died, killed instantly in a car crash at five in the morning coming back from spending the night with another woman. Cecily had thought he'd leave the castle to her, or to her and Stephen, though after the last quarrel Stephen had disappeared from their lives. Inexplicably he'd left half to Gail. Not that it did her much good. She'd died three months ago, choking on a piece of steak. Her dinner companions had thought she was having a heart attack and hadn't known they could have saved her with a swift blow to release the blockage.

The pain of Edmund's leaving hit hard, bringing back all the times she'd been abandoned as a child. She fell onto the beach, writhing in agony in the wet sand. She had no one now. Daniel was dead and Edmund had deserted her. The loneliness yawned ahead, filling her with despair. How would she cope without them?

She felt the desolation of Edmund's betrayal, the

agony of telling the children, of making their lives without him. Daniel's death had devastated her, but she'd learnt to live round the pain of his loss, knowing deep inside that he would have hated to live with old age. She must learn to cope with this. And, unlike death, there was a hope that Edmund might come back.

At last the pain and panic receded enough to make her realise she was cold and damp. She dragged herself up, shook the clinging sand from her clothes.

She trudged back up the path to the castle. 'Surely nothing will ever be so bad again,' she muttered to herself like a mantra, searching desperately for comfort. At the top she paused to get her breath. 'I must be strong for the children's sake,' she told herself feebly. 'At least I have the castle. That will be my strength.'

Chapter Eight

'**O**h, Cecily, I'm so sorry. Look, come down next . . . no, the weekend after. Do come.' Linette had sounded genuinely upset. 'I don't know how Edmund could leave you, but then . . .'

'Then what?' Cecily asked sharply, the old feeling of inferiority to Linette, of her knowing something she didn't, welling up inside her.

'Men . . . just men,' Linette had said flatly.

The two women now lolled in a sea of Sunday papers in Linette's house in Sussex.

'I'm afraid Richard's away this weekend,' Linette said with exaggerated casualness when Cecily arrived.

'Are you hiding Richard from me, in case I'm desperate?' Cecily joked, knowing she'd rather take a vow of celibacy than touch Richard.

Cecily and Linette hadn't met much over the years; Linette had married a man Cecily didn't like.

Richard Symonds was the sort of man who thought he was irresistible to women. Whenever he met one he seemed to feel it was his duty to flirt with them. He made remarks about their bodies as if he was some sort of expert and had superior knowledge, unknown to other men. That a female might have a brain he totally dismissed. He was not bad looking, had an influential job in the City and materially Linette lived a very comfortable life.

Cecily had begged her not to marry him, but Linette, completely crushed after Michael's betrayal and the abortion, refused to listen. She became quite angry with Cecily and that was one of the reasons they didn't meet very often.

'There is not a perfect man anywhere, Cecily,' she'd said bitterly. 'I'm sick of my job. Besides I want children and I want someone . . .' she paused, looked defiant. 'I know you'll say I'm a weed, but I want to be looked after. I'm tired of being on my own, going out with this man and that and after a romp in bed being back where I started, on my own.'

'But do you love him? In the end that's the only important thing,' Cecily said. Disappointing though it was, her not liking Richard was not as important as Linette loving him, and he her.

Linette had looked sceptical. 'I love him enough,' she said shortly. 'Love is mostly an illusion anyway.'

But when Edmund had left her, and she'd struggled through the first weeks of agony, the first person Cecily had rung was Linette.

'I should have expected it. After all, Daddy kept leaving us, along with his wives. But I never thought Edmund was like that,' Cecily said sadly.

'Daniel was . . . different,' Linette said vaguely. She sat, her knees hunched up, staring out at the trees in the garden.

'Different?'

'You know.' Linette fiddled earnestly with a loose button on her jersey. 'Daniel really liked women. Unlike most public school boys, he was neither afraid of them nor treated the seducing of them like a sport alongside shooting and fishing.'

'But Edmund liked women,' Cecily protested.

'Of course, but he . . . well, he should have stayed with you,' she finished weakly. Then she quickly changed the tone of her voice and said, 'Not that I know what goes on in London these days, being stuck down here.'

'You know you can always come up and stay.'

'I know, thanks.' She sounded distant, then as if pulling herself back to the situation she said, 'Look at it in a positive light, Cecily. You're free. You've got a little money, two children, a new house. You've got freedom while you're still young and attractive enough to have another chance at love, or a career, should you want it.'

'I only want Edmund.'

Linette sighed. 'You say that now, Cecily. It's only been a few months, and you wasted two of them holed up in misery.'

'I mean it. I know I didn't get in touch for a while, but I just wanted to hide in my pain. Also we had a good offer on the house and I found another one immediately. I had all that to cope with.' Cecily was still suffering from the exhaustion of it all.

'He wasn't good enough for you. No man who leaves a woman and his children is good enough,' Linette said suddenly, her mouth hard. 'Let Rowena have him and good riddance. You can make a new life.'

Cecily was hurt by her remark. She was about to protest when she stopped. She knew Linette had never got over Michael leaving her, so she said instead, 'Rowena had a perfectly nice husband. I didn't know Peter very well, but he seemed all right.'

'He was nice, but pretty dreary. Preferred his smelly old Labrador to her. I could see that when they came shooting here.'

'I'd forgotten you knew them better than I did.'

'Not really. I keep out of much of that hearty male stuff. Besides, I hate all that beating business. Tramping about in the wet and cold to send up a few birds for them to slaughter.' She got up and picked up some rose petals that had fallen from a vase, and tossed them in the fireplace. 'Funny, isn't it, it's always the wives and girl friends who march through the brambles, hitting at the undergrowth so the birds will fly up and be shot by their men.' A flicker of tension passed over her face. 'Keep the boys happy.'

'I bet Rowena's good at beating,' Cecily said savagely.

'Oh yes. Hearty and bossy to the core. She probably ordered Edmund into her bed, and then to live with her. Some of those nanny-reared men love a bit of that.'

'But Edmund wasn't like that,' Cecily wailed.

'No, he never seemed it anyway. Though would you

know? Do any of us ever really know the men in our lives?' she said seriously. 'All those judges and MPs who are meant to like weird things before they can perform in the bedroom. Their families never seem to suspect a thing, do they?'

'But not Edmund.'

'No, not Edmund.' Linette smiled at her, then said quietly, 'You were lucky with Edmund, even though he left you. You did, after all, marry the man you loved and have his children.'

'You said you loved Richard, enough anyway,' Cecily said gently.

A line tightened each side of Linette's mouth, as if a string had been pulled. It relaxed almost immediately. 'Yes, of course.'

'But you're thinking of Michael. Oh Lin, it wouldn't have worked, you know.'

'If he hadn't been married it would.' A wistful, sad look crossed her face. 'I often think of that baby. I love my girls, but I think of that baby, torn out before it had a chance.'

'You mustn't think like that, Lin. You mustn't.' Cecily went over and hugged her. She felt her tremble a moment, before Linette gave her a tight hug back and released her, laughing, though it was a brittle sound.

'I know. Now tell me about your job in the gift shop and your fearful boss.'

Although it was some time since Edmund had left her, Cecily still felt lopsided, as if half of her had been torn savagely away. She'd forced herself through each day, trying to persuade herself and the children that Edmund's betrayal was just an aberration, an act of male menopause. That he would come back, surely he would. But she found it hard. So often she found herself thinking of Daniel, wishing more than ever he was here. Once, when she'd moaned about something, he'd said to her, 'You can tell your problems once to someone then shut up. There's nothing worse than having people's problems dished up again and again like cold rice pudding.'

He'd kept his own advice. When Uncle Mark, his adored brother, had died painfully and slowly, she remembered the suffering in his face, the grim pain in his eyes. But he wouldn't discuss it. 'Everyone has tragedies,' he'd told her, 'but shoving them down everyone else's throats doesn't make them any easier.'

But it was hard to be so stoic, Cecily thought. She found herself wallowing in Edmund's betrayal, more than once, to a sympathetic friend. One day she felt better, then a chance remark would throw her back again.

'I think Dad loves that Rowena,' Miranda said after coming back from spending a weekend with them. 'They never stop touching and kissing. Uurgh, it's disgusting. Old people kissing like that.'

Jamie had said nothing, but he'd shot Cecily a glance of fear, as if the news would send her off into screaming hysterics again. It hadn't, but Miranda's words caused her pain for days.

'I wish,' she said now to Linette, 'that I could have the

children home with me, send them to day schools.'

'Why don't you? You're lucky living in London, there are lots of good ones.'

'Edmund wants Jamie to go to Eton. He thinks that his prep school, which sends so many boys there, is the only place.' She sighed, looked out of the window. 'I don't want to lean on them. They seem pretty resilient over all this, but they do see Edmund quite often and I suppose so many of their friends are in the same boat. And I feel I must get through this on my own.'

'You will. You'll find someone else. Just see if you don't.' Linette stretched across and squeezed her hand.

'I don't want anyone else.'

'At least you have a new house, and your job's still there.'

Cecily nodded. 'I know.' She smiled self-mockingly. 'It might not look like it, but I am trying to count my blessings.'

'You're better off than either your mother or mine were when Daniel left them. I know he gave them money, but basically they had to fend for themselves. Jobs for ladies like them were quite out of the question. Nobody would have employed either of our mothers anyway, would they?'

Cecily laughed. 'No.'

'Luckily Cynthia married Gerald, and my mother, well, Zara always seemed to find a man to look after her,' Linette said sourly. 'But you must be different,' she said suddenly to Cecily. 'You must stand alone, unless you find a man you really love and who loves you. Don't prostitute yourself into someone's care just because you think you can't cope alone.'

'I won't but . . .' Cecily had a sudden insight into what Linette was saying. She seemed to be warning her against doing what she had done herself when she married Richard.

'If you're alone but have somewhere to live and a job, you are not beholden to anyone. I bet you'll get used to that freedom. Don't throw it away.' Linette's mouth went tight again and her eyes took on the lost look Cecily remembered seeing there after Michael had left her. Feeling they were now on very rocky ground, she changed the subject quickly.

'Strange, Gail dying like that.'

'And in a smart New York restaurant too. She must have been livid,' Linette said, looking suddenly relieved as if she, too, had seen that rocky ground and was glad to arrive safe on the other side. 'It's surely not done to die in public.'

Cecily giggled. 'Do you remember that time when we thought we looked marvellous in those dresses? "Such a pity to wear black, so draining," ' she parroted in Gail's imperious voice.

Linette laughed, mimicked the voice too. ' "Not much can be done with you, but you might do well to cut your hair, make a bit of an effort." '

Cecily giggled again. 'She was ghastly. I still have no idea why Daddy married her. Do you?'

'No,' Linette said stiffly, looking awkward again.

'I wish,' Cecily now felt near tears, 'I do so wish I

could contact Dad, ask him all these questions.' She sniffed fiercely. 'Don't you ever feel like that, Lin? About dead people?'

Linette began to fold up the newspapers. 'I think it's sometimes better not to know all the answers,' she said, keeping her eyes firmly on her task, folding each paper exactly in the middle, then over once again. 'I mean, some things that seemed right at the time might not sound so good later. Some things you just can't explain.'

Cecily sighed. 'I think he was mad, had some sort of brainstorm. Perhaps he panicked, thinking he was getting old or something.'

'Daniel never got old. After all, he was racing away from the bed of another woman when he was killed in his car,' Linette said.

Cecily shuddered. She had a sudden vision of Daniel's mangled body. They hadn't seen it after the accident, and her imagination often threw up lurid images.

It had been Edmund who had told her about her father's death, Edmund who had held her as she collapsed in grief, Edmund who had shielded her from the outside world, especially from Gail and Ronald who seemed like circling vultures waiting to grab the flesh of his estate.

Cecily resolutely pushed this from her mind. She must cope without Edmund, and the knowledge yawned painfully before her. 'I never told you,' she said to chase away her memories of Edmund, 'one of the reasons Ronald is as vile as he is is because his father

left them with no money, and Gail couldn't pay the
school fees. It must have hurt him terribly, the humiliation of it. You know,' she smiled awkwardly, 'how
beastly us smart little kids can be at school if someone's
different.'

'They were different all right,' Linette said sourly.
'It's pathetic really how some people long to belong
somewhere different from where they are. Most of
them end up fitting nowhere and spend the rest of their
lives taking it out on everyone else.'

'But we don't exactly welcome them, do we?'

'Your father did, and look where it got him,' Linette
said tartly. 'Don't tell me you feel sorry for Ronald just
because he was humiliated at school.'

'He was awfully hurt.' Cecily remembered his
anguished face.

'Don't lose any sleep over it, he'll bleed you dry if he
can, just like his mother did Daniel,' she said warningly.

'I'll take care,' she smiled, then stretched and got up.
'I must go home before the traffic builds up too much.
Thanks for having me here, Lin. It's cheered me up a
lot.'

But although her weekend with Linette and her
daughters had, indeed, cheered her, Cecily was disappointed in how little support Linette had given her over
Edmund's betrayal. It was no doubt selfish of her to
expect more. After all, Linette was busy with a demanding husband, the children, the house and grounds. But
she'd expected more sympathy than bracing remarks
about how lucky she was to be free again.

Cecily knew, through other people's handling of problems and her father's advice all those years ago, that if she went on too much about her troubles she'd become a bore, and friends might start to avoid her. Besides, she felt embarrassed about Edmund's defection, as if it was shaming that Edmund preferred red-faced Rowena to her. It became easier to hide in her new little house and put on a brave front when she faced the world. But she did feel hurt that Linette, of all people, had not rushed to her aid.

'It's been a lovely weekend,' she said brightly as she got into the car. 'Do come up and see my new house. You never come now, Lin. I don't know when I last saw you.'

'There's so much to do here.' Linette, away from the intimacy of the drawing room, now wouldn't look at her. She glanced at her watch, then at the gate. She seemed agitated.

'What is it?' Cecily said. She'd noticed this agitated tension when she'd arrived, but had soon forgotten it as they fell back into their familiar mode of gossiping and giggling.

'N-nothing. Take care.' Linette stood back from the car and waved.

'You too. Love to Richard.'

'Ric . . . yes, of course.' Her face worked again. She pushed a smile through the tense lines. Her eyes swivelled out to the gate again, almost as if something fearful was coming up the drive. "Bye. Hurry, or you'll get caught in the traffic,' she said firmly, as if she wanted to get rid of Cecily as fast as she could.

The children, Harriet and Chloe, came running round the side of the house.

'We're back. We're back,' they chorused, their faces rosy and hot from running. Two other small girls followed them, then a woman.

'Here we are,' she said. 'We had a lovely afternoon.'

'Thank you, Philippa, your two must come over next weekend.'

Cecily kissed the girls goodbye, and then Linette again. Despite the cheerful muddle of boisterous children chasing each other round the flowerbed she felt apprehensive, as if things were not as idyllic as they seemed here at this lovely period house with its pretty garden. Something was missing.

Was it Richard? Why wasn't he here? Linette had not given her any explanation. Why had Linette become so anxious for her to leave? Was it because she expected him back any minute and he had told Linette not to invite her here? All the way back to London Cecily wondered about it. She'd been relieved that he had not been there, but she'd felt that Linette had also, and was now dreading his return.

Cecily arrived home in good time. She was pleased with her new house. It had been the one thing that had gone smoothly in the last, horrendous months. The sellers had been about to move when their sale had unexpectedly fallen through. Cecily had seen it and liked it straightaway, and bought it.

It was small, one in a terrace of ice-cream coloured houses, off the New King's Road in Fulham. She had decorated it in clear, subtle colours, finding as she selected the curtain material and wall coverings an unexpected pleasure in being able to have her own choice, apart from the children's bedrooms which they chose themselves, and not to have to compromise with Edmund. She'd spent rather too much on it, digging deep into her own store of money. But it had been a comfort to her, a treat, a wobbly bravado to start her new life in style.

As she opened the front door, the smell of a closed-up, unoccupied house hit her. A wave of loneliness engulfed her. If only the children were here with their squabbling chatter, pushing and shoving as they fell over themselves to get in first, warm and alive. She bit back her unhappiness, tried to push her thoughts onto something else. She picked up the mail on the doormat, poured herself a glass of wine and sat down to read letters.

She opened the white envelope from Lloyd's in anticipation. Edmund had suggested a few years ago that becoming a Name in Lloyd's was a good investment. He was careful with their money, searching round to find the best ways to get the most from it. With two children to educate, even his well-paid job in the City was not enough.

Her underwriting agent had hinted some months back of a hefty cheque this year. She'd use it to spoil the children after the traumatic effects of Edmund leaving them; she'd take them to Euro Disney at half-term.

The figure £90,000 leapt out at her. For a split second

she assumed that was the amount they were paying her. Then she saw they were demanding it, for her underwriting losses. The figure, like a ghastly monster, embedded itself in her stomach, sucking at her, making her feel sick, dizzy. There was a rushing sound in her ears.

'Calm down,' she told herself firmly. 'You always were hopeless at maths. It's probably ninety pounds, or nine hundred.' But however she looked at it, the sum shot out, stark and clear. She owed Lloyd's £90,000 and she didn't even possess it.

She tried to push it out of her mind, read her other mail, but she couldn't concentrate. The figure thudded in her brain, sending waves of panic through her, hanging over her like a terrible guillotine threatening to smash down on the remains of her security and happiness.

Being Sunday night, Cecily could not get in touch with her underwriting agent at Lloyd's.

'Blast you, Edmund, why did you leave me?' she cried out in panic and despair to the empty room. If only she could ring him, hear his voice, reassuring her, laughing at her fears. 'Perhaps this once,' she thought, hand out to pick up the receiver. She dithered a moment then forced herself not to give in to the longing to lean on him. She must not go bleating to him every time she had a problem. Or irritate him by making him think she wanted more money from him. She sighed. Deep inside herself, though she'd rather die than admit it, she felt that if she behaved well towards him, he would come back to her.

She curled up in a tight ball in her chair, the letter still in her hand, as if she was cowering from its strident demand. It couldn't really be £90,000. The amount must be a typing error. Or the computer had muddled its figures. The letter stated coldly that there had been catastrophic losses, and of course the agency was very sorry about it. She grimaced at their attempt at an apology, it seemed more like an insult. But this letter couldn't possibly mean it had lost her that amount, Cecily told herself bravely. The thought lifted the leaden apathy of shock for a moment, gave her a surge of energy.

She'd ring her underwriting agent at home. After all, he'd almost wooed her to get her into the place, nothing had been too much trouble then. She remembered the time he'd invited Edmund and her to a barbecue at his large Tudor-style house in Surrey.

'I think, darling,' Edmund had begun in the ponderous voice he used when talking of business, 'that it might be a good idea if we joined Lloyd's. This agent has asked us over this weekend, to talk about it.'

'Can't you talk about it in the office?' Cecily had said, not really wanting to waste her weekend talking business.

But they'd gone. The house had been opulent, and overdone, the garden stuffed with ready-bought plants, all standing to attention as if their paper wrappers had just been taken off. Cecily thought the whole place had a phony air, as if it was a television set.

'Obviously,' Edmund whispered back to her giggled remarks, 'it's all laid on to impress people and make them long to join Lloyd's too. Hope the decor isn't compulsory.'

'Gail would have loved it,' Cecily said.

The agent, large and opulent himself, his red hair oiled down, his fat neck bulging over his check 'weekend' shirt, was very positive about joining Lloyd's.

'Makes your money work twice for you, on the stock market and on the insurance market.'

'But if there was a disaster, like an earthquake in San Francisco, you could lose everything,' Edmund pointed out.

'Nonsense, my dear chap.' He'd clapped him on the back, poured him out more Pimms. 'If you have sensible advice, you can't possibly lose in Lloyd's.'

'If it's that certain, why aren't people clamouring to join?' Cecily said, looking round at the other guests, obviously people like her and Edmund, brought here to be persuaded.

He threw back his head and laughed uproariously. It sounded very false to Cecily. He gave her a pitying look as if she couldn't help being stupid.

'My dear,' he said patronisingly, the pseudo-American twang to his voice more apparent than before, 'Lloyd's is a club, we can't open it to everyone. Keep it for one's chums.'

'But . . .' Cecily was about to say they weren't his 'chums', nor did she think she ever wanted to be. But he'd moved on, grabbing another man by the elbow, talking to him intently as he walked him away, down the garden.

'I don't like it, Edmund,' she'd said then, but he had smiled and kissed her and she'd left it to him.

This demand for £90,000 must be the computer going batty, Cecily said to herself with more courage than she felt. She took a deep breath, tried to control the trembling in her limbs. What a fright it had given her all the same. She'd complain about that. They had no business sending out such letters without any warning. It could kill off some of their more frail members.

She dialled the agent's home number, but was answered by an answerphone. She did not leave a message.

The next morning before she went to work she rang the underwriting agency.

A harassed woman could only tell her her agent wasn't there. 'Can anyone else help you?' she asked.

'I've got a ridiculous misprint on a letter. The computer must have—'

'Oh, yes . . . well, who is it again?'

'Cecily Mendelson.'

'One minute.' There was the rushing sound of a hand being held over the mouthpiece. Then a man's voice clipped in.

'Mrs Mendelson, good morning, how can I help you?'

'This letter, it must be a mistake. I mean ninety thousand pounds!'

'No, I'm afraid it's not a mistake. It's been a bad time.

141

You must have read about it in the newspapers. Piper Alpha, the—'

'You mean,' she broke in, feeling the terror bite her again, her stomach sinking like a stone, 'that it's true?'

'The losses have been very heavy for eighty-seven, I'm afraid.' Cecily thought she detected a note of panic in his voice. 'If you want to come in to discuss—'

'I want my agent to ring me today. He got me into this. And why were we not warned? As the results go back three years, you've had plenty of time. To just send out a letter like this, with no warning, is disgraceful. Tell him to ring me, today without fail,' she burst out, furious with fear, with the cavalier way she felt she was being treated. Ninety thousand pounds! How could she find such a sum?

'I'm afraid . . . well, he's unavailable.'

'I bet he is. Make him ring me, please.' Anger surged through her, pushing away the panic for a moment.

'I . . . why don't you discuss it with your husband and—'

'I no longer have a husband,' she snapped. She was trembling, she had difficulty breathing, her limbs felt like jelly. There must be a mistake. Was she the only one to lose so much, or had other Names been hit as well?

She put down the receiver as if it was contaminated and lay back in her chair. She felt cold, distant with shock. She had never really been without money in her life. Oh, she'd had a few tough months when she'd been younger, but she'd always known Daniel would bail her out if she asked him. Ninety thousand pounds would more than clean her out. How would she ever get hold of that sort of money? How would she feed and house the children?

Then a thought nearly made her vomit. What if she couldn't look after them? Would Edmund, with his well-paid job in the City, take them in instead? She wondered if he'd lost money and again longed to ring him. Then she caught sight of the clock and pulled herself to her feet.

She'd be late for work if she didn't leave now. Automatically she went through the motions of leaving the house – putting on the alarm, locking the door. She walked to the gift shop where she worked, but she didn't notice the weather or the traffic, and suddenly she realised she was there, outside the shop.

It was rather a Sloany shop. She'd been working here since Jamie had started boarding school. Before the children were born she'd had various secretarial jobs, but finding her office skills were sadly inadequate in these computer days, she'd taken this job more to fill in her day without the children than because she needed the money. But now it would be essential to her. She began to see it in a new light.

It was near her house so there were no fares to pay. It was not badly paid, for the hours. She was conscious suddenly of acting a part, moving carefully, like a drunk determined to walk straight. All the time she was fighting to quell the terrible fear inside her, that she had lost all her money, and without it she could lose her children.

'You all right, Cecily? You look . . . a bit spaced out, as my daughter would say.' Daphne, her boss, a voluptuous blonde woman always dressed in beige clothes and gold chains, looked at her critically as she came in, shutting the door with extra care behind her.

'Yes, I'm fine . . . late night.' Cecily forced a smile. Telling people Edmund had left her had been a nightmare. It made her feel a failure, an outcast in society, even though spouses leaving each other was epidemic these days. But admitting she'd lost all her money too would be almost worse, making her a double victim.

She was too proud to ask other people for help or throw herself on their pity; but she knew her status with other people would change yet again. When Edmund had left her, some women had drawn away as if she might steal their husbands. Now, even more people might shy away, afraid she would ask to borrow money.

Edmund rang at the end of the morning. By sheer chance both Daphne and Gilly, the other assistant, had popped out, leaving her alone in the shop, so she could speak freely. Despite her resolutions not to show any weakness to him, she found herself blurting out the contents of her letter hysterically.

'Calm down, Cecily. I've had a letter too. There have been horrendous losses right through the agency, right through the market, as far as I can gather. But we'll weather it, Lloyd's won't let its Names down.' He sounded brave.

'How much have you lost?' Cecily asked.

'A bit.' He sounded cagey. Cecily knew that voice. She could imagine his mouth tightening, making a tiny white mark under his lip. Once she would have kissed it until his lips were soft again. She wondered with a pang of jealousy how often Rowena kissed him.

'But don't worry about it,' he went on more defiantly. 'I can still pay the school fees.'

'I didn't mean that. I just want to know if it's . . . legal. I thought—'

'Look, Cecily, leave it with me. I'll look into it for you. But don't worry, Lloyd's is bound to sort it out. A respectable institution like that won't let their Names down.'

'Don't be too sure,' she said, not feeling much cheered by his words.

Edmund ignored her remark. 'I think you better pay what you can. You don't want to be stuck with interest.'

'But darl—' she bit back the word; if only she didn't still think of him with endearment. 'Edmund, that will leave me with nothing.'

'I could lend—'

'No,' she said firmly. She could imagine the gossip – 'Poor Edmund, he's still paying off Cecily's debts.'

'Pay off what you can. I know they'll be understanding. There's a good chance you'll make some of it back next year.'

'I don't feel as confident as you,' she said, seeing Daphne coming up the street. 'Must go, ring again. 'Bye.' She put down the telephone. She remembered

Daniel's attitude to money: 'Never owe money. It's a great weakness and an embarrassment.'

The newspaper quickly screamed the huge losses across their pages, naming celebrities who'd been caught in the biggest losses for years. But there was a general feeling that the Names were rich enough to cope with it. They were portrayed as people with at least two houses, fat pay cheques and fleets of cars. There was little sympathy for them.

The Chairman, looking sleek and rich, appeared on television, scolding the Names for grumbling about paying their debts. He did not mention that very few had made enough to cover the enormous and, to them, completely unexpected losses. He did not mention that many were not rich at all.

Cecily was irritated with herself to discover that she felt ashamed, as if she was suffering from some unmentionable disease, or was personally responsible for losing so much.

She paid off £30,000 of her debt, with a sickening fear in her. She explained that she could not manage the rest at the moment. She felt so agitated, so unsure what to do in the face of such an enormous debt. Should she take in lodgers? Or find a second job? She felt embarrassed and afraid that she still owed so much. The shock had also made her feel lethargic; as each day ended, she still had not made a decision what to do. At night she woke suddenly in panic, wondering what had frightened her. And at once it hit her again. She had no money, less than no money if any more huge demands came in. How would she get by?

One evening after staying late at the shop, she bought some pâté and some pasta salad from the delicatessen for her old schoolfriend, Penny Young, who was coming to supper. Remembering how Penny had a passion for Bendicks Mints, she added a box to the packets on the counter. Something about the way the assistant eyed her made her feel that she was wondering if she could pay. Cecily thrust a £10 note at her, scooped up her shopping and fled, mortified.

Apart from doing up her new house, Cecily rarely spent money lavishly. She enjoyed cooking, and whenever possible cooked fresh food for the children, spoiling them in the holidays with their favourite pizza and Häagen-Dazs ice cream. She had never paid much attention to the bills. Now she found herself scrutinising each item, weighing up which would be cheaper. She economised on small things for herself, cheaper loo paper, make-up and tights, walking instead of using the car or public transport. She felt quite useless floundering about making these paltry economies in the face of her terrifying debts.

In her low moments she visualised large men coming round to repossess her house, or assess her furniture with cold, disdainful eyes. But when no more money was demanded, and the only news of Lloyd's was in the newspapers, she let her life slide by, hoping, as one might with a frightening symptom, that if ignored, it would go away.

'Bloody thing, this Lloyd's business,' Felix Mayle

greeted her in the shop one Saturday morning. He was
a brash man, she'd known him and his wife some time.

'Have you been done?' he asked.

Taken aback by his directness, Cecily glanced awkwardly round as if afraid to admit it and be isolated like
a leper. She'd mentioned to Daphne and Gilly that
she'd had losses in case they found out anyway and it
became an embarrassment. She had not told them all
the details.

'It's a scandal, you know, unloading all their incompetence and trickery onto a few outside Names. Well, I
won't stand for it. None of this shut up and pay up
nonsense for me.' His heavy face was flushed with
indignation. Cecily edged closer to him, whispering to
him to keep his voice down. He ignored her.

'I've been to see a solicitor, and he says question the
buggers. Don't pay until they send a writ, then counter-
act it by sending one back. Sue them for negligence,
incompetence, underhand dealing and see what they
say to that.'

'But that will be expensive too,' Cecily broke in, her
eyes swivelling in Daphne's direction.

'Carry on living, that's what my solicitor said. If you
spend it, the buggers can't get it.' He grinned, pointed
to a pair of expensive porcelain lamps. 'So to hell with
it, I'll buy those for Serena's birthday, enjoy life before
the balloon goes up.'

Cecily felt a sudden urge to laugh. Her spirits lifted.
She picked up one of the lamps and began to wrap it in
layers of tissue paper.

'I felt it couldn't be right. Edmund says they won't let us down, but—'

'Don't you believe it. They've got themselves in one hell of a mess, scuttling money into offshore accounts, re-insuring everything in a bloody spiral, like pass the parcel only we've been caught with the parcel. You must fight, Cecily. Don't lie down and pay.' He handed her his credit card.

'But how . . .?' She saw Daphne glaring at her. She hated her assistants to gossip with their friends. But when she caught sight of the pair of expensive lamps that had sat for weeks in the shop disappearing under sheets of paper, her face relaxed.

'Join action groups. There's a lot of anger, you know. Not everyone is going to pay up and shut up. It may have been thought bad form to whinge about one's debts, and no doubt that is what they're banking on, people paying because they think they have to. You haven't paid up, have you?' he demanded, seeing her expression.

'A bit of it,' she admitted, feeling guilty and foolish under his fierce gaze.

'Don't pay any more. The whole thing stinks.' He laughed at her startled face. 'Not all of us, dear Cecily, went to smart public schools. You need the likes of us to shout out that the Emperor is bloody naked.' He winked. 'I'll bet you that before long a lot of those who graced the dormitories of those exclusive establishments will be shouting the loudest!'

Cecily saw some of the people in the shop give Felix

disapproving looks. One man gave him a thumbs-up and a grin. Daphne, caught up with a customer, threw Cecily a glance as if to say, 'Hurry up and get rid of him, he's too loud for us.'

Cecily felt the huge weight of her terror and bewilderment shift a little. If she could do something about these horrendous losses, fight back, then she'd feel more positive, more able to cope.

'How?' she hissed, stalling for more time by being slow to check his credit card and give him his receipt.

'I'll put you in touch with the action groups. Where are you living now? Dreadful about Edmund, leaving like that.' He leered at her. 'Must say though, always fancied you myself. So if Serena's away and you want a bit of dinner and a chat . . .' he chortled. 'New chat-up line, what! Come up and see my syndicates.'

'No thank you, Felix,' Cecily said firmly, but unable to stop a smile. 'But I would like to know about the groups. Please drop the addresses in here.' She handed him his parcel. 'Say happy birthday to Serena for me.' She felt pleased that she had seen him and he had given her a weapon, however slight, to fight back. His brash way of talking about it so openly crashed into her isolation, giving her courage.

But when Edmund heard about Felix's advice, he contradicted it.

'It's mad to go to court, Cecily. The lawyers are jumping on the bandwagon, grabbing at every chance to make money. Even if there was a case and it got to court, it would take years and cost even more than your losses.'

'But surely we have a case.'

'These things are very difficult to prove.'

'The people I've met don't think so. If half what is reported in the papers is true about Lloyd's, I'd say we have a case, many cases. I'd rather put what money I have left into fighting through the courts,' she said firmly.

'You're a fool, Cec—'

She rang off. Every time Edmund rang, it hurt dreadfully. She wanted him back. She ached for his arms round her, his warm body next to her at night. Apart from Felix, no other man had shown any real interest in her.

Cecily didn't go to the AGM of Lloyd's members. 'I can't bear any more of their smooth talk,' she said to Daphne who offered her the day off. 'It's as if nothing is their responsibility at all. I can't be doing with it.'

'There have been some dreadful stories in the press,' Daphne said. 'Some people barely had enough to join, and now they've lost everything. I do hope that hasn't happened to you, Cecily?' She looked at her keenly.

'Not yet,' Cecily said with feeling, having just received another letter from Lloyd's demanding money. These days just the sight of a white envelope with Lloyd's written in black on it put her into a panic. 'If only they'd refuse to pay until the courts have looked into it. They may never get it back, and if they do, they'll probably be dead.'

★ ★ ★

'Don't join the Hardship, they'll have a hold on you for life, then take your house when you're dead,' Felix said, taking Cecily for a drink in the local pub one evening. She'd bumped into him on her way home from work and in her desperation had asked him what to do.

'Edmund wants me to pay,' she said. 'He says I can this year and if it's found to be wrong they are bound to pay us back.'

'There will be no money left out of this mess to pay anyone back.' Felix leant rather too close to her. She could smell the whisky on his breath. 'Anyway, there are worse losses forecast for next year. Then what will you do?'

'But if they draw down on my bank guarantee, I'll have to pay the bank back. I still don't have it, and the interest will mount up and . . .' She ground her hands in despair.

Felix covered her restless hands with his large red one. 'It's the devil, I know. I can pay off my bank then that's it. I sit tight. Lloyd's won't get another penny from me unless they come for it, and then they'll have to find it. Anyway, if there's lots of us to come for, it will take them years. Look, love,' he leant closer still, 'is there nothing you can sell, so you can pay off the bank? Then you, too, can sit tight. You'll win in the end, you know, if you – if we all – hold out against them. They might even go into liquidation.'

Cecily moved away from him. What sort of payment did Felix expect for his advice? She wondered if Serena was away. 'I don't have anything. I have my house, but

I have to live somewhere with the children.' She paused, thinking how she, but more importantly, the children, had taken to the house, thought of it as home now. 'I suppose I could sell it, move into something even smaller, in a cheaper district. But the housing market is bad at the moment.' She sighed in anguish. The idea of moving again so soon, especially after she'd spent so much on doing this one up, sickened her.

'No jewellery, holiday house?' Felix's face was sweating, his large hand sticky on hers.

'Not much jewellery, nothing worth that much and . . .' She stopped, gasped, as if someone had punched her in the stomach.

'What is it, sweetie?' Felix leered over her.

Cecily couldn't breathe. She jumped up, pushed her way out of the hot beer- and tobacco-laden air. The castle. They'd take the castle. She stumbled outside and Felix rushed after her. He took hold of her arms.

'What is it? Are you ill?' He looked alarmed, as if she might throw up all over him.

'The castle,' she said piteously, her eyes begging him to tell her it could not happen. 'They can't take my castle!'

Chapter Nine

'So I'll offer you sixty thousand pounds for your share of the castle. I think that's very generous of me, Cecily. It needs a fortune spending on it.' Ronald towered over Cecily in her small drawing room. With his sleek black hair, now feathered with grey, and reptilian eyes, Cecily almost expected a forked tongue to dart out from between his thin lips.

'I don't want to sell it. It's part of my life, the happy times I spent with Daddy. The children adore it too. Anyway, you don't even like it, Ronald,' she accused him angrily. 'Nor did your mother, so God knows what Daddy was thinking of, leaving half of it to her. Whatever will you do with it?'

She couldn't look at him without feeling sick, any sympathy she might have felt for him over his start in life now forgotten. She couldn't help remembering with revulsion that moment years ago when he'd pressed his body against her and tried to kiss her. He seemed now to pervade every corner of the room, octopus like, stretching his tentacles into every nook and cranny, as

155

well as herself, sucking everything out.

The image of the happy summers she'd spent in the castle flashed into her mind. Ronald of all people could not have it.

His sinewy voice had oozed down the line last week. He had telephoned her out of the blue. She hadn't seen him since Daniel's death, except photographed at some social event in the free glossy magazines delivered through her door. He'd brought a cat-like woman with long painted nails and black-rimmed eyes to Daniel's funeral, much to their disgust. Cecily could not bear to be near him. In his black suit and tie he'd been like a beetle, slipping here and there, always by her elbow as if it was he who was Daniel's son.

They had tried to contact Stephen, but no one could find him. Even his mother didn't know where he was. This had added to Cecily's heartbreak, but she was also angry that he was not there to claim his place at his father's funeral, leaving the role open for Ronald.

'Edmund suggested that I come and see you,' he'd said with a touch of smugness. 'I can help you out of your present difficulties. I believe I'm the only one that can.'

'No,' she had cried to Edmund. 'No, I cannot, will not sell it to him.' But now he was here, in her house with his monstrous offer.

'You have no choice, Cecily,' Ronald said impatiently, 'unless you sell this house, take the children and go up and live in the castle. Whatever happens with Lloyd's, even if eventually the courts do find in your favour, you have to pay back the bank once they draw down, which they will very soon. Or face ever-increasing interest. Anyway,' he sneered as if she was a fool and deserved to lose her money, 'you know the rules with Lloyd's, pay now, sue later.'

Cecily felt defeated, cornered like a rabbit with a stoat, but she wouldn't let Ronald see that. She still could not understand why Daniel had left half the castle to Gail. If only she hadn't been so shattered, so stupid in her grief, she'd have enquired into it more fully.

Perhaps, Cecily thought, with bitter humour, Daniel had left it to her as a last joke. Gail had managed, by fair means or foul, to hang on to him far longer than his other wives. But now the joke had rebounded on her.

Edmund had reminded her, when she'd rung and shouted down the line at him, afraid and angry at his suggestion, that she had no other way of raising the money. He doubted that anyone else would come forward to buy it, and certainly not at Ronald's price.

'I could borrow the money,' Cecily said defiantly to Ronald.

'Who from? You have to put something up as security. And think of the interest. You don't have a job to speak of and without Edmund . . .'

'How you hate us,' she said, her eyes flashing.

'Don't be so dramatic. Keep to the issue,' he snapped. 'Take it or leave it, but don't blame me if you're left with huge interest charges from the bank. Lloyd's will take your money any day now, so you haven't much time. I'd

157

have thought,' he flashed her a reproachful look, 'that you would have been grateful. After all, Edmund thinks it's a good idea.'

Cecily said nothing. She remembered Edmund's voice as he described Ronald's 'extraordinarily kind offer'.

'I know it will be hard for you, Cecily,' he'd said sitting here in this room with her, after dropping the children back. 'But there is nothing else you can do. Everyone has had to make enormous sacrifices over this Lloyd's business, and after all, Ronald is your stepbrother. He's sure to let you and the children go on spending the summer there.' He'd smiled, lifted his hand to put it on her shoulder but thought better of it, and used it to scratch his neck awkwardly instead.

'You know what a swine he is. He won't let us near it again,' Cecily snapped. Tears of anger and frustration at the very horror of Ronald, of all people, taking her castle stung her eyes. She wanted to howl, to throw herself on Edmund, to feel his arms round her again, holding her close, safe against this nightmare.

Edmund moved slightly away from her, as if guessing her thoughts. 'You can't afford the luxury of liking the purchaser of your property, Cecily. I know there's a lot of resentment seething under the surface, but he is family of a sort. Besides,' he smiled encouragingly, 'you may make the money back in Lloyd's and buy it back.'

'Huh! If I *must* sell it, then I will put it on the open market,' Cecily said fiercely, jumping up and holding her arms tightly by her sides as if afraid they would shoot out and cling to him of their own accord. Or, worse, hit him in her anger.

'You can't without his permission. He's the co-owner,' Edmund said quietly.

'I can't believe the castle is his. Really I can't, Edmund!' she cried out in fury. 'I'd suspect him of changing the will, though I can't think why he'd want it. He and Gail hated it so.'

'Dear Cecily,' Edmund laughed. In the old days he'd have kissed her. 'What an imagination. Who knows what devilry Daniel was plotting when he made that will. It's hard, I know, but that castle is an expensive white elephant. It needs so many repairs done. You'd be hard pushed to keep it up, even without Lloyd's.'

She was thinking of Edmund now while Ronald paced about the room, watching her. Deep inside herself she knew that she'd have to give in. If I hadn't got the children, she thought, I'd sell this and go up there. But it's too far from their schools, and from Edmund. She closed her eyes. If only she could let Edmund go. Tortured though their few meetings were, when he picked up or dropped off the children, she longed for them. She studied him carefully, praying to see a crack in his love for Rowena, a sign that he wanted to come back to her. If she moved to the castle in Scotland, she might never see him again.

'I want this last summer up there please,' she said, not able to bear the gleam of satisfaction in Ronald's eyes. 'But tell me why you want it so badly when you were never happy there.' She stared at him now, seeking in that face some weakness, some clue as to why he wanted it.

'I want to shoot and fish,' he said, his mouth defiant. 'Why shouldn't I? You all made fun of Mother and me, you and the people up there, just like they did at school. You sneered because we didn't know the rules. But I've as much right to it as you.' For a moment she saw the desperation in his eyes, before it changed to determination.

'Why are you taking what happened to you at school out on me?' she cried. 'Surely it was your father's fault, leaving you with no money.' Even as the words left her mouth she saw how they wounded him. Despite her hatred for him, she felt a pang of sympathy.

'I got into one of the top schools by my own sheer hard work.' His voice was cold. 'I was cleverer than most of the boys in my class, yet when we couldn't pay I had to go to some unheard-of little dump. It's almost worse to have to leave a good school in the middle of one's education than never go there at all.' The angry pain in his face made her afraid. She realised that he would never get over what had been done to him all those years ago.

'So you're doing this just to get your own back,' she said quietly.

'I've talked enough about it, Cecily. I'll get my solicitor to cope with it all. Sixty thousand pounds. That's it.' He put down his glass with a thud and walked to the door. 'I want it on the first of September. That will give you six weeks to take what belongs to you – pictures of

your father and such. I want the furniture, that's
included in the price.'

'But—'

'No buts, Cecily. It's not particularly valuable furniture and it certainly won't fit in here.' He cast his eyes
disparagingly round the small room.

He stalked out and left her, slamming the front door
behind him as if he was cutting her off from her past,
taking away the last of her security, leaving her feeling
violated once again.

It was the last day of August. The castle was silent.
Cecily stood in the drawing room looking out at the sea
under the wide, luminous sky. How could she survive
without coming back here?

'Oh, Daddy!' Her mouth twisted in bitterness. 'Why
did you leave half of this to Gail?' She could almost feel
the woman smirking at her from her chair close to the
fire. She always insisted on a fire, even when the sun
was shining. She'd sit in her woolly tartan outfits in the
green silk-covered chair, one side of which was now
singed by being pulled too close to it.

Cecily left the room hurriedly. It was no good letting
her feelings eat away at her like this. It was done.
Ronald had paid her the money. She'd paid off the
bank. Her only debts now, increased to a further
£30,000 with more cash calls, were to Lloyd's and they
must take her to court before she'd pay those.

She must leave, she knew it. Better to do it quickly.

She paused on the stairs to look out of the large

window. The bull had been put in with the cows. Cecily had supposed he would run at them, mount them and discard them. To her surprise the courtship was longer. He'd choose a cow, edge up to her, eat from the same piece of grass, getting closer all the time. But that was all he seemed to do. Another cow had finally mounted her friend as if to show him what was expected of him, but he had taken no notice, continuing to eat. Cecily wondered how many calves this gentle courtship would produce, and if they would be enough for Ronald.

She went on up to her room wishing the children were here with her. They had left yesterday with Penny and David and their children to drive down to Edmund. Penny had begged her to come too, but she'd refused saying she'd rather say goodbye to the castle alone, to slip away and not look back, hoping the ghosts of happier times would come with her. But now she yearned for the children's squabbling laughter, their vitality in this gloom of departure.

Resolutely, Cecily picked up her cases and went downstairs, forcing herself to think only of the last-minute things she must do, trying desperately to kid herself that she was leaving as she did every summer, and that she would be back again next year.

She dumped her cases on the stone floor of the hall, went to the overladen pegs behind the door and took down her Barbour jacket and hat. An outgrown duffel coat of Jamie's hung dusty in the corner. She snatched it off the peg, held it to her a moment, remembering when they'd bought it in Wick. It had been a size too big for the tiny child who was just on his feet. She saw him staggering, fair-headed, across the lawn down to the sea, his small body bundled in the coat, one hand from the turned-up sleeves holding a bucket, the other a spade as he ran after Miranda to hunt for crabs on the beach. She could almost feel Edmund beside her, his arm round her, his laughter in her ear. How happy they had been, how mercifully oblivious of the pain to come. Biting back her tears, she picked up her luggage and carried it and the coat out to the car.

She must go now, she thought, before she broke down completely. She walked back into the house to say goodbye to Jane Drew, the housekeeper who had taken over from Thistle. As she reached the first landing she heard a car speed up the drive and stop with a spray of gravel. She looked out and saw it was Ronald.

She stayed there on the stairs, staring out of the long window until he found her.

'I thought you'd be gone,' he said in greeting.

'It's mine until tomorrow.'

He pushed past her, taking the stairs two at a time. 'Is Jane Drew in?'

'I'm just going to say goodbye to her.'

'I want her to make up the beds. I've some people coming tonight. She must cook dinner too.'

'Have you warned her?' Cecily asked, knowing from many years' experience that housekeepers liked advance warning of domestic plans. She felt sick and angry that, tonight, when it was really still her castle, Ronald would be filling it with his friends.

163

'She is paid to housekeep and housekeep she must. It's not as if she has to work all year,' he said, marching through to Mrs Drew's quarters, calling her loudly as he went.

Cecily sat down on one of the broad wooden steps in fury and despair. They never spoke to Jane Drew like that.

Mrs Drew came onto the landing with Ronald. Her mouth was tight, her face pink with suppressed annoyance. She kept nodding and saying through clenched lips, 'Yes, Mr Ronald, very good, Mr Ronald,' in answer to his imperious orders.

'I shall sleep in the big room overlooking the sea. I want the double room and that single one made up too, dinner for four at eight sharp. Get some lamb, smoked salmon perhaps. Clear?' He glared at Jane Drew as if he was addressing someone mentally deficient.

'I think you could have waited until tomorrow, Ronald.' Cecily sprang up from her step. 'Given Mrs Drew more notice. After all, I might have been staying here tonight.'

'Well, you're not, are you?' Ronald said rudely. 'You'd better get going, you've got a long drive ahead.' He turned away from her, striding into the drawing room.

Cecily felt as if he'd struck her. How he detests us, she thought. Or was it fear she'd seen in his eyes as he turned away. Was he afraid that she'd see his friends?

'I . . . I hope you have a good journey,' Jane Drew said hesitantly, visibly shocked by Ronald's behaviour. Her eyes filled with tears and Cecily saw written there as if they were printed words, 'Why is he the master here? What will happen now you're gone?'

'Goodbye, Jane.' Cecily took her hand, then quickly dropped it and moved away before she either collapsed weeping on Mrs Drew's thin bosom or killed Ronald.

'Come and visit us,' Jane Drew said bravely.

'I . . . I will.' But Cecily knew she would not. While Ronald was here, she would not return. She looked once more up the wide, carved staircase, then out of the window to the drive and the fields leading to the moors beyond. She felt so angry with Ronald, with herself for selling the castle to him and leaving Jane Drew in his hands.

'I wish . . .' Jane followed Cecily down a step. Her pink, dry-skinned face under her dyed brown hair was twitching. She licked her lips, as if to oil the words she wanted to say. 'I wish things had not worked out as they have. Wouldn't Lloyd's understand, let you pay them off in instalments?' Her face was eager, hopeful in the way of people who believe in honour.

'No, Jane.' Cecily tried to smile. 'No, they will not. Besides, it's my bank guarantee I had to pay back, there's no way out of that. There are so many of us,' she said gently into Jane's perplexed and sorrowful face, 'who have to sell their homes. I'm lucky to have somewhere else to live.'

'But surely a big, respectable—'

Cecily shook her head. 'It's all changed, Jane. It's all changed.'

'Get a move on with those beds, my guests should be

here within the hour.' Ronald came out on the landing and glared at them.

Cecily, quivering with anger, ignored him. 'Goodbye, Jane, thank you for all you've done for us over the years.' Impulsively she hugged her. Jane clung to her as if she could stop her from leaving, then, looking ashamed, as if she too had to show courage, she let her go.

'I'll keep in touch. Let me know if you need anything.' Cecily managed a wobbly smile. She walked resolutely down the stairs and out of the castle, holding herself stiff and taut to keep in the tears.

Chapter Ten

'So I'm afraid, Mrs Mendelson, Miranda is just not working hard enough.' Miss Bealy, the principal of Quinton Hall, glared at Cecily, her half-lensed glasses glinting ferociously on her nose.

Cecily felt the familiar sinking in her stomach that she'd experienced as a child at school. Why, she wondered, did some headmistresses have such a gleam of satisfaction in their eyes when they criticised your child?

Despite having Linette with her, Cecily had hated school. Hated the petty niggling of the teachers, the utterly predictable dreary days, plodding on like weary footsteps, seemingly going nowhere.

She and Linette had spent much of their time in the headmistress's study, being reprimanded for some failing or other. Sitting here now in front of the grim Miss Bealy, her grey-suited body built like a bulwark against the world, was like a rerun of her own school days. It brought back all the feelings of misery, frustration and terror that Miss Trotman had wrought in her all those years ago.

'I know you've had your problems,' Miss Bealy continued with the smug look that shrieked that if *she'd* ever been bothered with a husband, *he* wouldn't have left her, 'but we have other girls in similar situations and they just buckle down and get on with it.'

Cecily didn't say that Miranda, dreamy, artistic Miranda, was not the buckling down type. She'd always had a horror of the bossy, rosy-faced jolly girls who'd buckled down to life with a frenzy, sweeping such tiresome things as men out of their way, or if they were like Rowena grabbing the men they wanted regardless of whom they belonged to. She knew this was a frivolous notion and that Miss Bealy knew she thought like this and despised her for it.

'I'll talk to her,' Cecily said lamely, hating herself for not being more forceful and saying, 'You obviously don't see Miranda's talents and potential and make an effort to nurture them. You want her to be a clone of all the conforming children who keep your place high in the league tables. Miranda's not like the girls that are happy to slot straight into the mould you've set for them and like blinkered horses look neither right nor left in life.' But she didn't. She didn't because she didn't dare, part of her feeling she'd be set a thousand lines and banned from the few miserable weekend treats and partly because she knew a dozen other, uncomplicated girls destined for university were said to be queuing up to fill each space. Miss Bealy would much rather have one of them here than her Miranda.

'You really will have to take a stand, Mrs Mendelson.

Get her father to talk to her perhaps.'

'*I* will talk to her,' Cecily said firmly, sitting up straighter, hoping to give the impression that she was an independent woman who fought her own battles and did not need to keep on bleating back to Edmund.

'I shall expect a definite improvement after this exeat then,' Miss Bealy said doubtfully, standing up to dismiss her. Cecily did her best to leave the room as a tough, sophisticated woman, not as a cringing child in awe and fear of her headmistress.

'So, darling,' she said later to Miranda in the glaring, fat-smelling café where Miranda was filling up on hamburgers and Coca-Cola, 'please try and work harder. Is anything bothering you? Do you find it difficult or—'

'It's just so boring,' Miranda said, sinking her teeth into the flaccid bun and greasy meat with relish. 'Boring. I mean, Miss Hampton's voice puts you to sleep and as for Mrs Gates, she speaks French with such an accent,' she made choking, guttural noises, much to the consternation of the people at the next table, 'and uses words that no French person has ever heard of.'

Cecily laughed, then looked guiltily round as if Miss Bealy was hiding somewhere and spying on them. She couldn't help agreeing with Miranda, though she didn't say so. She'd felt the same way when she was young. It seemed that it was never the teacher's fault if a child was bored or not making progress.

'I know, darling, but it can't all be boring. Perhaps if you listened more, made a real effort to take more interest, you'd find it more fun,' she tried valiantly.

'Fun!' Miranda shrieked, 'Oh Mum, you don't know anything.'

'Parents never do,' Cecily said with a sigh, remembering Daniel cutting off her headmistress's string of complaints against her with, 'My poor Miss Trotman, but I'm sure there's nothing you can't handle', and giving her a smile that almost melted her cold heart.

'Just try and do better, or they might chuck you out,' Cecily finished.

'Doubt it, they need the cash,' Miranda said mildly.

'There are dozens of other girls waiting to take your place, so—'

'Want to bet?' Miranda said. 'No one with any sense wants to go to a dump like that.'

Cecily left it, not wanting to spoil the few days they had together by arguing.

Selling her half of the castle to Ronald had completely drained her. Without that prop in her life, the feeling that there were only a few months before she'd be back there, under those luminous skies, she'd found it harder to cope with Edmund's betrayal and her Lloyd's losses. She found herself stepping gingerly through life's minefields as if the slightest jolt would injure her raw emotions. She preferred to leave things alone if they were likely to erupt in her face, to tiptoe round them, especially where the children were concerned, though she recognised there could be problems if she became too weak with them. But she so wanted Miranda to be happy and good-tempered this weekend, wanted her to see that she could enjoy herself, even if Edmund wasn't there. Talking about her school work would be guaranteed to make her sulky and resentful. Cecily sighed, sipping at the dubious beige liquid that masqueraded as coffee. She wished she could have the children at home with her, going to day school, but Edmund still would not agree.

Cecily had hoped, after Edmund had left her, that she could have them both at home. She and the children had clung together like storm-blasted survivors. She felt that they, as well as herself, needed that extra security of home. She'd even tried to use Edmund's guilt to get her own way, but he'd succeeded in making her feel selfish, saying that instead of making them happy, the change would disrupt them further.

'They enjoy it really and it's such good discipline for life,' he'd said. 'You learn to be self-reliant.'

'Other nationalities manage to be self-reliant without boarding school.'

'That's debatable,' he said dismissively. 'Look, Cecily, don't let's go into this again. They're settled, let's leave them where they are.'

'You have no right to talk of unsettling them,' she retorted. 'You who've broken up their home for . . .' she floundered for an apt word to describe Rowena.

'That's enough, Cecily.' Edmund had got up from the sofa at once and walked out of her house. She'd known, with bitter tears, that he would always win, for he could keep away from her if she irritated him. If only she wasn't still cursed with loving him, still wanting him. She would do almost anything to safeguard his meagre visits to her.

So here they were, Jamie at a nice little country prep school that got boys into Eton, and Miranda at Quinton Hall. It had been unfortunate that the previous headmistress, an energetic, positive woman, had been taken seriously ill and that Miss Bealy had succeeded her in Miranda's second term. Cecily missed the two of them dreadfully and once said to Susan, her boisterous neighbour whose four boys had been through Eton, 'that now they had joined the EC, surely they should try and have the same education. All other European countries seemed to produce well-adjusted, bright people without sending them away from home.'

'That's a matter of opinion,' Susan said firmly, convinced, as Cecily was not, that British public school men were the most level-headed in the world. 'Just because you're so sad and lonely doesn't mean the children are too. It might be selfish to tear them away from their routine and their friends.' Susan laid great store by 'friends'. They could only be of a certain kind, of course, same class, same school.

Despite the changing social fashions and financial situations, Susan's views were shared by the majority of the parents at Jamie and Miranda's schools. Cecily felt depressed by them. But as she knew too well, if you voiced different opinions to them they labelled you an oddball. Parents, too, expected conformity among their ranks, buttoning up their own fears as they'd been taught to do when they were children. The new thinking of some English families that keeping their children at home was beneficial had bypassed a whole load of boarding school parents. 'You must not be possessive, you must let them go,' Susan and her kind chorused. Cecily thought it could also be called 'opting out' of parenthood.

Cecily and Miranda had a good weekend together. Edmund was away on business so Cecily had her daughter to herself. This time she didn't have the nightmare of dropping her at some convenient meeting place with Edmund and making herself scarce until it was time to collect her again. Cecily kept away from the house in Kent that Rowena and Edmund had bought together. To see the home they shared would be too intimate. It was bad enough imagining them in bed together, without being confronted by the concrete evidence of their happiness. So they would meet at a hotel halfway. 'At least I shall be well-read by the time the children are old enough to travel on their own,' she'd joked sourly to Edmund. 'I've read a Dickens and a Trollope already. It's Jane Austen's turn next week.'

All too soon it was the dreaded Sunday night. It seemed darker and damper, as if not just the weekend but the world was sliding towards a close. Miranda became grumpy then petulant in the car as they left London and headed down the A3 towards the school.

'I can't see why you let the castle go to Ronald so easily. Surely the bank could have waited, they must have millions,' Miranda began fiercely, pinpointing that as her grievance instead of admitting she didn't want to go back to school.

'I know, darling, but I've explained it all to you. The longer I don't pay the bank, the more interest I have to fork out,' Cecily said patiently, struggling to control the hopeless pain of her loss. Two images were a nightmare to her. Edmund and Rowena locked in a passionate embrace and Ronald play-acting as the laird of Daniel's castle.

'Caroline Massy may have to leave school because of Lloyd's and go to a state one. She cries all the time 'cos she thinks it will be like Grange Hill. Will I have to leave?' Miranda turned her pointed little face towards Cecily. Although she didn't want to go back, she didn't want to leave either.

'Daddy is coping with your school fees, darling. You know that.'

'But he's lost money too. I heard him talking about it to Rowena.'

'I don't think he's lost much,' Cecily said, wondering what Miranda had heard. She hated hearing about their weekends with Edmund and Rowena, so afraid that Rowena in her jolly, bossy way would win them away from her, just as she'd taken Edmund.

'Rowena is worried. I heard her say, "It can't be so much, it must be a mistake." Then Daddy said something under his breath and they shut the door.'

'He told me his losses weren't too bad,' Cecily said with more conviction than she felt. 'Anyway for years we've paid into a school insurance scheme, so you should both be all right.'

'Jamie wouldn't mind, then he wouldn't have to go to Eton.'

Cecily stole a look at Miranda. She was sucking a strand of her long auburn hair, gazing ahead at the dark road.

'Doesn't he want to go to Eton?' she said with as much nonchalance as she could muster. That he didn't really like boarding school and was struggling with the work she knew, but Edmund kept reassuring her that he was fine, and it was only because the school kept them so busy that he looked so tired.

'No. He knows he's not clever enough, and if he did get there he'd probably get chucked out like Emma Delvin's brother who passed the exam but was too thick when he got there.'

Cecily had worried about this. She knew the Delvins. Their children were older than hers and Robert Delvin was determined that his son should follow in his footsteps to his old school. The child had been force fed with extra coaching and had passed Common Entrance. Robert was ecstatic, brought him a new computer, bicycle, goodness knows what, but the boy couldn't keep up and was asked to leave after his first year. The family were devastated and Cecily, among others, thought the boy would never get over it.

She'd had many rows with Edmund over this. It brought back unpleasant memories of her father and Stephen. Stephen had got to Eton, done quite well academically, but in sports he'd been a failure. Why, she kept thinking, does history keep repeating itself?

She didn't want Jamie to go to Eton unless he could easily keep up. She was sure in her heart he could not, and the thought of the damage failure would do to him terrified her. He had just over a year before the dreaded Common Entrance and already Edmund was getting him extra coaching and making 'study plans' for the holidays. Rowena had two small daughters, and though Cecily was sure she supported Edmund in this fiasco, she did not take it so seriously, not having sons.

'We'll have to see what happens,' Cecily said lamely, deciding to go behind Edmund's back and try and talk to Jamie's headmaster about it. They were nearing Quinton Hall now and she felt sick and dizzy, a feeling reminiscent of her own school days that came upon her each time she took her children back. She always fought to hide it. They were so brave about it, she must be too.

She hated saying goodbye to Miranda, leaving her here, especially on these dark, gloomy winter evenings. The agony of knowing there was nothing for Miranda but a tasteless snack, followed by bed in the dormitory, all done up in dull pinks and greys, depressed her. Cecily remembered with sickening clarity the same evenings at her school, the empty, leaden feeling that you were stuck for another few weeks with people who, on the whole, you didn't much like, certainly wouldn't choose to live with, and food and lessons of such dreariness that you felt inert with tedium.

'Here we are,' she said with false jollity.

'Don't sound so pleased,' Miranda said.

'I'm not, darling, I'm not. I'll miss you, we had such fun.' Cecily bit her tongue. How impossible it was to strike the right note. It would not help if Miranda knew how much she missed her, how much she longed to turn the car round and speed them both back home, to have her and Jamie living every day with her in London.

''Bye then,' Miranda said resignedly, sounding much older than her twelve years. She got out of the car as if her limbs were heavy and disjointed.

Cecily got out too. Miranda's mood threw more gloom like a wet mist over her. She longed to say, 'Let's go, darling, escape. Dash off somewhere on up the motorway, miles from here.' Instead she pottered with the luggage, struggling to hide her true feelings. It's mad, she thought. In wartime children have to leave their families, but here we are in peacetime sending them away from us, making us feel like proxy parents when we could just as easily keep them at home and send them to day school.

'Hi, Squige, had a good time?' Miranda yelled cheerfully as a large, amiable-looking girl passed them, her arms filled with belongings.

'Brill. How about you?'

'Brill. Wait for me . . .' Miranda looked young and happy again. She yanked out her case. Cecily pulled out some bulging carrier bags stuffed with endless last-minute things. She grinned awkwardly at Squige, feeling suddenly shy and out of it.

'Shall I help you carry all this up to the dormitory?' she asked tentatively, aware now that she was an outsider in this part of Miranda's life.

'Don't worry, Mum, we'll manage. 'Bye.' Miranda gave her a fleeting kiss, grabbed the straining bags. 'See you soon, thanks for a great time.' She attempted to wave, bags dangling from her hands.

''Bye, darling, have fun,' Cecily said, stretching her mouth into an enormous smile. She used an old trick that she and Linette had perfected for awkward moments, pretending she was an actress, the cameras full on her, playing someone happy, not a mother longing to snatch back her child and run off with her. Too late she remembered she hadn't had a serious talk about Miranda's work. Miss Bealy would not be pleased nor, she supposed, the least bit surprised.

She turned slowly to get into the car, not looking at Miranda's retreating back. She felt utterly bereft. It was so much worse leaving them at school now she hadn't got Edmund to cheer her up on the way home.

Next weekend she'd have to go through the same thing with Jamie and the thought poleaxed her. It was worse with him. He bottled things up and would sit in the car, his whole body clenched on the edge of the seat, going greener and greener the nearer to the school they got. But whenever she asked him if he was happy he said he was fine. 'He's a popular boy,' his headmaster said when she'd asked how he was getting on, a description which seemed to please him and Edmund and seemed rather ambiguous to her. She suspected that if Jamie didn't feel he had to make it to Eton, he would enjoy school more.

''Bye, Uncle Jerome. Thanks for bringing me back. See you.' A tall girl turning round to wave at someone almost knocked Cecily down. 'Gosh, I'm sorry,' she said cheerfully and dashed inside.

'Clarissa, you've forgotten your coat.' A man sprang out of a car and called after her. He walked a few steps towards the door of the school.

'Oh thanks. I never wear it if I can help it, but I'll get killed if I don't have it. ''Bye.'

''Bye.' The man handed it to her and as he turned round he saw Cecily standing dejectedly by her car.

'Are you all right?' The warm concern in his voice made tears spring to her eyes. Just when she was fighting to face the lonely drive back, letting herself into the empty house with Miranda's things still flung around, making her feel somehow lonelier, this kind voice was chiselling through her reserves.

'You're not all right, you're crying,' he said gently.

'I'm not really,' she sniffed hurriedly, wiping her eyes with the back of her hand.

'It's hell, brings back the days when we had to go back, doesn't it?' He took a handkerchief from his pocket and handed it to her. She wiped her eyes gratefully.

'Yes.' She looked up at him, defiant in her grief. 'Yes, it does. It's selfish of me I know, but I'd much rather she was at day school, my son too.'

'Ah, the old British system of toughening them up.'

He smiled. He had a nice smile, she thought, it lit up his whole face, and he looked at her, not somewhere over her left shoulder as many men were apt to do.

'Are you on your own? Or is your – I was going to say husband, but nowadays you never know if it's boy friend, partner . . .'

'I'm divorced.'

'Me too.' He paused. Cecily said nothing, she just stood there, under the lights – 'searchlights so we can't escape or meet men in the garden' was how Miranda described them.

She felt warmer, less desolate just standing beside this kind stranger. Now that she was alone, without Edmund, she'd found herself in moments of stress responding to even the slightest hint of friendliness, spreading it as balm over the pain of his leaving.

'How about having a drink to cheer you up, if you've time, that is? The only place I know nearby is that large white hotel just up the road. Hardly a cheerful place, all dark wood and dull red pseudo cosiness.' His voice held a laugh. She wondered if he was just being kind.

Cecily looked more carefully at him. He was tall with dark hair which curled close to his head, giving him a boyish look, almost Italian, she thought, though his accent was pure English. The thought of putting off the dreary drive and the cold homecoming was tempting. He seemed nice enough. Safe enough, is what she really meant. She felt so vulnerable meeting strange men now, afraid that in her hope to be loved again she would be taken in by a maniac. This fear had taken away much of her spontaneity, turning herself inwards in her determination not to appear eager or, as she would have put it with a brave laugh to a girl friend, 'desperate'.

But this was something different, a kind offer from a kind person. 'Thank you, that would be lovely. I . . . I won't blub all over you, I promise. I just felt . . .' She shrugged, attempted a smile.

'I understand exactly. My sister's the same, so I offered to take Clarissa back for her. Actually she loves it here, says there's always someone to gossip to, things going on.'

'I think Miranda likes it too, it's just me being selfish, and reliving my hatred of boarding school.' Cecily felt better, stronger, having someone to talk to, as if she was, after all, part of the human race.

'I understand exactly,' he laughed. 'Come on, follow me down the drive and we'll meet at that hotel. I can't remember its name. Red Hart? White Hart?' He shrugged. 'Meet me there.'

'OK. Thanks.'

'Oh, I should introduce myself,' he grinned. 'Jerome Clifford.'

'Cecily Mendelson.'

'Right, Cecily, get to know you better in a minute.' He opened the door of her car for her, then waited until she had started the engine before going to his own and weaving his way slowly down the drive, past the Volvos, the Range Rovers and the chattering mass of girls, parents and dogs.

Chapter Eleven

The shrill call of the telephone stopped Cecily in her rush to leave for work. She cursed, dropped her bag and snatched up the receiver.

'Hello.'

Her voice must have sounded impatient as the person on the other end said timidly, 'Is that you, Cecily?'

'Yes . . . Oh, Linette?' It sounded like Linette, and yet . . . 'Is it you? Sorry if I sounded cross but I'm running late for work and I'm just – oh, you know, nothing's gone right so far this morning,' she grumbled cheerfully, hastily dismissing her initial feeling of disquiet at Linette's timid voice. Linette was never timid. Normally she'd have met her irritation with a joke about disturbing her with a lover or some such nonsense.

But then again, the easy familiarity they'd shared as children had somehow evaporated with adulthood. Cecily was not one to analyse emotions. She'd been so caught up with Edmund and her children, and Linette with her family, that it was hardly surprising they'd lost touch. But something about Linette's voice snagged on her feelings of pleasure at hearing from her.

'How are you, Lin? I haven't seen or heard from you in ages. What have you been up to?' Cecily said into the silence that greeted her ramblings.

'Fine.' The word sounded brittle with brightness. 'I'm coming up to London today, I have an appointment, but I suddenly thought, well, I wondered . . .' Her voice petered out.

'If you can stay? Of course you can. The children's beds are free. Will Richard be with you?'

'No.' There was another silence. Cecily waited for Linette to make an amusing remark about why he couldn't come. But all she could hear was Linette's breathing.

Cecily registered this as her mind spun on through her plans for the day. 'What time will you be here?' She was having lunch with Jerome, she couldn't bear to miss that. The feeling of joy at seeing Linette again was quickly dashed by a sense of desperation. If only she could have come another day. She was about to say so when an instinct that Linette needed to see her crept into her whirling thoughts. 'Are you all right, Lin?' she asked, feeling a prickling of insecurity.

'Of course, I'm fine,' Linette answered too quickly. 'I'll be with you about four. Will you be working then?' Again there was that hesitant tone to her voice.

'That's great,' Cecily said with relief. That would leave her time for Jerome, but what if he suggested they meet again in the evening. She pushed the thought from her mind; she was rushing things. 'I'll be at work. Come to the shop. You remember it, don't you? I'll try and get off early. I'm *longing* to see you.' She put extra warmth into her voice, feeling that Linette needed her reassurance though that was quite unlike her.

She was probably imagining it, Cecily thought. Weighed down as she was with her own problems, she'd found herself looking for problems in other people. Her mind shot back to that weekend they'd spent together in Linette's house. Linette had been edgy then, especially when she mentioned Richard. Was he playing around? Cecily wondered. But there was no time to talk about it now. She tried to think of something funny to make Linette laugh before she rushed to work, but Linette broke in before she could.

'Sparrows or Magpies, isn't it? The name of the shop.'

'Magpies, dark green paint, gold lettering. Just up the road past the bus stop. Longing to see you, Lin, but I must rush or I won't have a job, and I need it more than ever now.'

'See you then.' Linette rang off quickly, making Cecily feel uncomfortable, as if she'd offended her in some way. But Linette was not like that. If she'd offended her she'd retaliate, throw something back at her. But she seemed to have lost that energy, that laugh in her voice.

Cecily pushed these thoughts from her head and concentrated on getting to work. She grabbed her bag, checked for her keys, put on the alarm and dashed out. As she flew up the road she realised she felt happy. One of the reasons was Jerome, though her sense of excitement concerning him was mixed with apprehension. She liked him, she was attracted to him, but she was afraid of fantasising it into a lasting romance. She hadn't clicked like this with any other man since Edmund had gone. Friends had invited her to dinner with various 'spare' men. Deep down, she knew she was really waiting for Edmund to come back, or she was looking for a clone of him. She dismissed the few men paraded before her by caring girl friends, finding them wanting. Briefly she wondered if these men were produced out of kindness or as a foil to keep her away from their husbands.

She experienced one awkward night with a perfectly nice and very good-looking man called Jonathan. She'd ended up faking an orgasm to spare his feelings, and to get him to finish his tedious love-making. She vowed not to go to bed again with anyone just because they were nice and she was lonely. But Jerome was different. He had been so kind that night he'd found her crying at Quinton Hall. When he'd said goodbye, he'd cupped her cheek gently in his hand and said, 'I hope I'm there next time. I'll ring you, we'll meet again soon.' And she had spent the night ricocheting between hope that he had meant what he said and despair that he had not.

And now Linette was coming and without the tiresome Richard. They could curl up in the drawing room with a bottle of wine and gossip half the night, offloading their worries and fears, supporting each other with humour and affection.

But something nagged at Cecily about Linette. She had not sounded like herself at all. She hadn't made one joke, or even laughed. Usually when they were together, or just on the phone, one always reduced the other to laughter. Edmund used to accuse them of never growing up and being no better than a couple of giggling schoolgirls. Something had changed.

Cecily was late for Jerome. Rushing in, hair and scarf flying, coat undone, she saw him before he saw her. He was sitting in the corner of the restaurant, intently studying the menu. Her heart gave a little lurch. He looked vulnerable but at the same time quite content to be alone, not expecting a companion at all.

'I'm so sorry,' she said shyly, feeling a sudden rush of pleasure when his eyes lit up, his face becoming suddenly alive at seeing her. 'I . . . I had a difficult customer in the shop, a horrid old lady . . .' She rattled on, thrown by being so close to him.

'Take off your coat, sit down and tell me,' he laughed, his hands on her shoulders as he eased off her coat. A waiter appeared and took it from him. She sat down opposite him feeling like a teenager on her first date.

'Drink?'

'I'll just have Perrier,' she said, knowing wine would go straight to her head.

'How are you?' He leant forward, his eyes warm,

amused, searching her face, his hands almost touching hers.

'Fine.' She looked across the table at him. He looked older than he had the other night. She judged him to be in his late forties. He had on a dark suit, blue shirt and blue tie with a discreet pattern of yellow knots. She liked what she saw, relieved suddenly that she did still like him and hadn't built up a false picture of him after his life-saving offer of a drink the other night.

She smiled at him. Then, disconcerted by the warmth in his dark eyes that made her body stir as if he was touching her, she said awkwardly, 'Th-thank you again for taking me for a drink the other night. I hope I wasn't too dreary. I just hate taking the children back to school, especially on a dark winter's night. I've brought your handkerchief.' She searched in her bag, pleased to have something to do, but it wasn't there. 'At least, I thought I had it.'

He laughed at her embarrassed face. 'Don't worry, I have plenty more. My aunt gives them to me every Christmas and birthday, best Irish linen. Keep it.' His smile was easy.

'I will find it. It was just that this morning someone rang and I was late for work.' She wished she wouldn't witter on so. Why couldn't she just stay silent, smile enigmatically, be in control of the situation?

'Really, don't worry. Have you heard from your daughter?'

'Not yet. She doesn't write very often and only rings when she wants something. But I'm sure she's fine. I was only being over-emotional. It's just those dark evenings make it worse somehow.'

'They go on for so long, don't they? When you're alone.' He smiled self-mockingly, as if ashamed to admit to loneliness. 'As far as I'm concerned,' he continued in a brighter voice, 'the one good reason for not putting the clocks back is to cheer up people on their own. Daylight is much more positive.'

'I hate getting up in the dark though. But in Caithness at this time of the year there are hardly any hours of daylight. Though we more than make up for it in the summer.' Still she rambled on, feeling that if she could cram words, any safe words, into the space between them, it would hide the sudden restlessness in her body at being with him again, the wish she had to feel his hands, firm and secure, on her shoulders. She wondered what it would be like to be held in his arms.

Cecily often forgot that she could no longer return to Caithness. Now the truth suddenly struck her hard like a blow and she winced, bit her lip.

Seeing it, Jerome said, 'Is that where you lived before you divorced?' This time he stretched out his hand and touched hers.

'No.' Her mouth wobbled with a smile. A tear rolled down her cheek, she sniffed fiercely. 'I'm sorry, here I go again.' She tried to laugh, took her hand from under his and fumbled in her bag for a handkerchief, taking a Kleenex from a packet and dabbing her eyes. 'Sorry,' she said again. 'But every time I think of it, it makes me cry. It's like some awful bereavement. You know, you suddenly think of the dead person, think of something you must tell them, then it hits you that they're no longer here.'

'What happened?' His voice was very still. His eyes studied her face with understanding as if he really cared, felt more than a polite concern. She took a deep breath, conscious that she was about to pour out all the injustices, all the agony of her feelings over the past months. Then she checked herself. She didn't know him well enough and she didn't want to chase him off with a tirade of self-pity and misfortunes.

To her relief, the waiter came to take their order, giving her time to compose herself. She ordered an avocado salad and lamb in fig sauce, and another bottle of Perrier and began to feel quite strong again. It was Jerome's genuine kindness that was making her feel so vulnerable. It was a long time since a man had taken such an interest in her. She told him a potted version of her Lloyd's history and Ronald, even managing a few jokes.

He listened intently, occasionally frowning, a bunch of furrows drawing his eyes together.

'I never went near the place,' he said when she'd finished. 'I'm sorry, hell for you. Might you be able to buy your share of the castle back?'

'I'd do anything to get it back. I feel I let it go too easily, but I didn't know where else to get the money.' She sighed. 'Some people have had to sell their only homes, homes they've worked for all their lives that they hoped to pass on to their children.' She looked up at him, anguish in her eyes. 'There are so many decent people who have been hurt by it.'

'I know. I've even heard of elderly people being hounded with writs in nursing homes, some even having heart attacks over it.'

'When the demands went out like that with no advance warning at all, most of us went into shock. We were too honest, stupidly honest really, feeling we ought to pay our debts as soon as they were asked for. I couldn't pay it all, so they drew down on my deposit. I had no choice but to pay back the bank at once. I won't pay any more, not that I have any more money left to pay with.' She smiled wanly.

'What about the Hardship Committee?'

She sighed. 'If you join that you're in hock to Lloyd's for ever. They want to know everything you own, even what you might inherit. You can keep nothing to pass on to the children until your debts, as yet unproved, are paid.' She paused, then said with a rueful smile, 'Some of us felt if we could settle things straightaway, somehow the nightmare would go away. That if we took extra jobs, did anything to get more cash, we'd be all right. But now it looks like it will never get better. It's said the losses will be even worse next year.'

'It must be a dreadful curse hanging over you. I can see no solution, unless they settle out of court.'

'So there's no end to it?'

'Who can say? Lloyd's might even fold. But what will you do? Can you keep your children on at school?' He poured some more water into her glass. Unconsciously she'd almost emptied it in nervous gulps.

'Edmund . . .' Even as she said his name, Cecily felt the old pain of losing him. For a moment it spoilt being here with Jerome. It should be Edmund sitting opposite her, Edmund watching her with such concern in his eyes, as he used to do, long ago. But now he couldn't even look straight at her, his eyes were always veering off, suffused with guilt. The few times they'd met since the divorce made her feel she was with a stranger, a familiar stranger but a different man to the one she'd known and loved.

'Your ex-husband?'

'Yes. He pays for that. He's lost money too but he says he hasn't lost a lot.' She remembered the tight, closed look on Edmund's face when she'd questioned him, and Miranda's description of Rowena saying 'it can't be so much'. But, unlike her, Edmund trusted the great institution of Lloyd's. He was certain it would not let him, or the other stricken Names, down.

'So many people, judges, MPs, even members of the royal family, a lot of powerful people have been hit. But how will you cope, Cecily? It must be difficult for you.'

'I will somehow.' Her mouth went firm. 'As long as I can keep my house for the children and get them through school, I'll cope.'

'These school fees are the devil,' Jerome said. 'I don't see our children being able to pay them. Still, maybe that will improve the standard of the state schools. My daughter's fees rise constantly. I can't help feeling she's not getting enough out of it.'

At the mention of his daughter Cecily felt a pang of jealousy. She dropped her eyes onto her bread and began to pull out the soft centre. 'How old is she?' she asked as nonchalantly as she could, feeling annoyed with herself that she should mind that he had a child. After all, she had two children. Was Jerome jealous of hers?

'Almost fourteen. A difficult age, so my ex-wife says.' He sighed. 'But Emily's fine with me. I suspect she gets in the way of her mother's love life.' There was a bitter twist to his mouth.

Cecily looked at him with sympathy. She said gently, 'Is she at boarding school?'

'Yes, but she's not happy. Her mother lives in Wales. Emily's at a school near her, she could be a day girl, but Sophia hasn't much time for her.' A look of impatience crossed his face. 'It might be best if Emily came to live with me and went to day school in London.' He sighed. 'But that would mean a housekeeper. She'd die if I got anyone approaching a nanny.' He grinned sourly. 'Divorce makes the most dreadful complications.'

'I know,' Cecily agreed. 'I'd love my children home with me, though some people think I'd lean on them too much. But whatever you do as a parent, someone finds fault with it.'

'That's true. Most of us flounder about at it. It was easier when they were small.' He looked wistful. Cecily thought he was remembering the good times, with a wife who loved him. She wondered if he still loved her.

'Have you been divorced long?' she asked, wanting to

curl her hand over his as it lay on the tablecloth.

'Two years now. And you?'

'Three months, though he left last September.'

'Still so new.'

'Yes.' She looked down at the tablecloth, feeling shy suddenly at his intense gaze. She wondered why, or if, he was still alone. Surely he had a collection of girl friends hovering close by. She wondered if she would join them. It was with a sudden shock that she saw it was three o'clock. She leapt up.

'It's so late, I must rush. Oh Jerome,' she clutched impulsively at his hands, 'I'm sorry, but I promised I'd be back by two thirty and I'd hoped to leave early as my ex-stepsister . . . Oh,' she laughed, seeing his perplexed face, 'my family is too complicated, my father had four wives.'

'Heavens, I hope it's not contagious,' Jerome laughed, holding her hands firmly in his as if she had given him a present and he was treasuring it. He bent forward, kissing her on her cheek, holding his face close against hers for a moment. 'When can I see you?' His eyes searched her face as if he was looking for confirmation that she would see him again.

'I don't know.' She felt suddenly agitated, fearful of being so late back to the shop, fearful she might be dismissed, torn between wanting to see Linette and not wanting her to encroach on her being with Jerome. Oh, why couldn't Linette have come last week, before Jerome had come into her life?

'Ring me,' she said desperately, feeling too frantic to

make plans now. She saw a flash of disappointment in his eyes.

'What about dinner?' He kept her hands in his.

'I would love to . . . some time. I must go.' She felt a surge of panic. How long would it take her to get back to the shop? Should she ring, pretend the traffic was bad? Jerome saw it and mistaking it for panic about seeing him again said coldly, 'Look, you ring me when you're free.'

'I will, thanks so much for lunch. Sorry, I must rush. 'Bye.' His look stabbed her with insecurity. Perhaps he didn't want to see her after all but was only saying it out of politeness. Afraid to go on confronting him, and of her lateness for work, she turned and rushed out into the street, the waiter calling her back, waving her coat. She saw a taxi and jumped in. Throwing herself back on the dark seat, she wished for the hundredth time that Edmund had not left her and she didn't have to flail around in these relationships, with all the worry and insecurities they brought.

She felt comfortable when she was with Jerome, though she was unsure of him because she knew so little about him. He was divorced with a child, but surely a man as kind, as attractive as he was had any amount of girl friends. She did not want to share him. Would he put her number in his Filofax or electronic organiser, if he had one, as just another woman to take out, to lighten a dark evening? She found him attractive and would like him as a lover, a proper lover that her body responded to, not a fiasco like that disastrous night with Jonathan. But . . . and here the whole tide of emotions engulfed her. If she allowed it to progress to the bedroom, would she fall in love with him and be hurt again if he left her? And the children? How would they feel if she brought a new man into their lives? They had barely known Rowena when they'd shared the same chalet with mutual friends but since she had taken their father from them, they'd hated her. Or so they said. Would they hate Jerome on sight? Could she put him on ice when they were home in the holidays, see him only when they were at school?

The complications tormented her. Oh, Edmund, her heart cried out in despair, how could you wreak such havoc on us all? Why can't we still be together, secure in each other's love as we once were?

Chapter Twelve

'There you are, at last, Cecily,' Daphne said icily, her gold chains quivering on her large bosom.

Cecily, torn between thinking up an apology and concealing her shock at Linette's haggard appearance by greeting her, hovered humbly between the two. 'I-I'm sorry,' she stuttered. 'Really I am, Daphne.' She glanced guiltily at Linette who, transparent as a ghost, stood, or rather supported herself by leaning on a table, in the small shop.

'You cannot have such long lunch hours.' Daphne glared at Cecily through her over-made-up eyes.

'I know, I'm sorry, I couldn't get a taxi.' Cecily knew she was in the wrong but resented Daphne's scolding her here, in the middle of the shop. It wasn't as if she was in the habit of having long lunch hours. She hadn't had a lover, or rather a man, to lunch with before.

She went over to Linette and kissed her, embarrassed in front of Daphne's bristling annoyance. A sliver of fear at this new, subdued Linette edged into her. Before, she would have giggled at Daphne.

Instantly she and Cecily would have been transported back to their school days when Miss Trotman had them trapped like mesmerised rabbits in her study, going on at them in her fog-horn voice about their disobedience, displaying pained amazement at their being in trouble yet again.

'You won't be able to leave early,' Daphne said as if Cecily had just asked her if she could. 'There's far too much to do. For a start, that table looks a mess. People touch things so, leave them in such a muddle.' She gestured towards a table covered with small objects – little porcelain boxes and dishes, amusing and not so amusing devices to open bottles with, keyrings, silver animals and so forth. They did not look particularly untidy to Cecily, but she knew Daphne in this mood. It usually came after the month's balance sheets had been studied and she'd seen a drop in them.

'I'll do it at once.' Cecily went to the back of the shop to leave her coat, motioning Linette to come with her. To her relief, Lady Fox, a friend of Daphne's, came in with her Christmas shopping list. Her voice was loud as if she was in a huge emporium instead of a tiny gift shop. She complained, as she always did, that she couldn't think what to get for all her godchildren, nephews and nieces, 'the young being *so* difficult to please these days'.

Cecily giggled, caught Linette's eye, expecting to see the answering gleam of amusement, but her face was blank. Cecily felt disturbed. She wanted Linette to be the strong one, as she used to be, someone she could rely on. Cecily didn't feel she had the inner strength to help her at this moment. Cancer, she thought suddenly. God, don't tell me she's got cancer.

'How are you, Lin? Sorry about . . .' She gestured behind her where Daphne and Lady Fox were in full voice.

Linette gave her a hint of a smile. 'I'm fine. Shall I come back later? I'm early.'

'You can go to the house. I'll give you the key. But, Lin,' she laid her hand on her arm, 'you don't look well. Is anything wrong?' She looked into that faded, defeated face with concern and not a little fear. Linette was well dressed in an expensive navy suit with a cream silk shirt and a string of pearls. She always dressed well, but usually with more flair than these safe clothes. She wore lipstick, but no other make-up. Her hair was clean but not styled. It was as if she had dressed herself up to go to London but taken no pleasure from it, not bothered with the extra touches that she usually excelled in.

'No . . . nothing.'

Cecily knew she lied.

'Cecily,' Daphne called, 'can you fetch some more of the silver clothes pegs? There should be some in the stockroom.'

'OK.' Cecily dropped her voice, leant closer to Linette. 'Look, I should be back just past six. Do you want to stay here or go to the house?' Looking at her pale shadow, Cecily didn't feel she should go out in the street alone, in case she collapsed.

Linette, as if guessing this, said with more energy, 'I've a few things to do. I'll see you at six.'

'Here's the key.' Cecily fumbled in her bag. 'The alarm is under the stairs. Key in 2949 to turn it off.'

'Cecily!' Daphne sounded agitated.

'Coming.' Cecily patted Linette on the arm then fled downstairs to the stockroom. When she returned, to her relief she saw that Gilly, the other assistant, a plain, jolly woman, had returned from her dentist's appointment and was gift wrapping Lady Fox's pile of presents.

The shop door opened and Mrs Grant, whom Daphne described as their best customer, came in.

'Hello, we haven't seen you for ages. Been away?' Gilly said, smiling at her. Mrs Grant was a rich widow with married children and grandchildren, nephews and nieces. She was always buying presents for someone's birthday or because they were going back to school or deserved a prize. She hadn't been into the shop for some time.

'I know . . . I've . . .' Her eyes flickered distractedly round the shop. 'I've been so busy.'

'Cecily will look after you.' Gilly was still doing up Lady Fox's packages.

'Of course, what are you looking for today? Christmas things?' Cecily came forward willingly. She liked Mrs Grant, enjoyed helping her choose and her pleasure as she described each member of her family and what they were interested in at that moment.

Mrs Grant looked embarrassed. Cecily noticed that

her usually immaculately brown-tinted hair was letting through the grey quite badly, and her make-up was streaked and not the subtle shade she normally wore.

'I just need something for Anna's birthday. Something small,' she said hesitantly.

'Ah, Mrs Grant, I've got just the thing, only unpacked yesterday.' Daphne beamed at her. She picked up an exquisite glass paperweight and handed it to her. 'These are French, you said your son collects them.'

'I-It's lovely, but not today.' Mrs Grant barely looked at it. She picked up a dark green china box with a gold A on it, checked the price and thrust it at Cecily. 'I'll have that, thank you.'

'I'll wrap it,' Cecily said, trying not to sound surprised. Before, Mrs Grant never asked the price, would be quite happy to be piled high with purchases, saying laughingly that she always had someone to give things to and she liked to have a few spare presents in her cupboard, just in case.

'They're so lovely,' Daphne said flatly, as surprised as Cecily at Mrs Grant's reaction.

Mrs Grant said nothing. She stood, waiting awkwardly for her china box to be wrapped, not looking round the shop as she usually did. When Cecily handed the parcel to her, she said goodbye and left.

'I wonder what's happened to her? I hope she's not ill,' Daphne said.

'Poor thing, she's lost masses of money.' Lady Fox, who had been seemingly engrossed in some books covered in marbled papers, spoke in a stage whisper.

'Not Lloyd's?' Cecily said, looking with distress at the door that Mrs Grant had gone through, thinking of how generous she had been with her money and how it must hurt her now to be only able to buy a small gift. She wondered what else she was going without.

'Yes. Really, that place. It never used to be like that. It's the people they let in there these days. No longer gentlemen.' Lady Fox's tone was dismissive. 'Could bring the government down, you know. Quite a few Tory MPs have lost a packet too. The Prime Minister may have to intervene.'

'It's dreadful. Quite dreadful. Poor Mrs Grant,' Daphne said, pointedly not looking at Cecily.

Cecily went down to the stockroom on the pretence of fetching more stock. She didn't feel she could bear to hear Lady Fox's assumptions that only 'gentlemen', by which she meant men from the top families, public schools and Oxbridge, were suited to run Lloyd's.

The house was warm with light and the smell of coffee when Cecily got back from work. For a moment she stood in the hall and savoured it. She'd forgotten the pleasure of coming back to a lived-in house. Usually it was echoing with emptiness; the kind that knew that no one else was living in it. She had to bring it to life with light and music.

Linette came out of the drawing room, her hands curled round a mug. She was so thin and white, with blue-grey smudges under her eyes, yet she looked better than she had in the shop.

'Shall I make you some coffee?'

'Thanks. Would you rather have wine? There's some white in the fridge.' Cecily took off her coat.

'No, not wine.'

They went together into the kitchen. Cecily put the supper she'd bought from the all-night shop in the fridge and Linette made her some coffee. Cecily watched her covetously, steeling herself to cope with Linette's problems. If it was cancer or some other terrible disease she would fight it with her, though she felt sick at the thought of it. She wanted to hug Linette, hold her, tell her whatever it was they'd get through it together. She turned, arms moving to take her, mouth half open to question her.

'You seem to be coping well alone,' Linette said as if to stop her. 'I must say you look better than I thought you would, and with all this terrible Lloyd's thing too.'

Cecily picked up her coffee and walked into the drawing room, saying as she went, 'It's pretty hellish, but I'm managing. Sometimes, though, I wake in the night, terrified at what might happen when they come for the money. It's draining from my account at such an alarming rate, cash calls, action groups, with their fees for the legal costs, and so forth. Not to mention every-day living.' She sighed. 'But it's the children I miss so much, I wish they were here.'

'You should have them back. I told you before, there are plenty of good day schools in London.'

'I know, but Edmund won't have it.' She sat down,

smiled wanly at Linette. 'I hope Jamie won't turn out like Stephen and run away from us all.'

'I'm sure he won't. Daniel was terrible to Stephen, wasn't he? Do you remember how he used to shake?'

'Yes, and that hounded look he had. Oh Lin, how we had to fight for him, and now he's gone.' Cecily looked sad.

'But he writes at Christmas and birthdays.'

'But never with an address. It's as if he never wants to see us again. It was terrible not being able to contact him about Daddy's funeral.' Cecily sighed. 'I adored Daddy, he was too good, too spoiling to us really, wasn't he?'

'We were girls, and old chauvinist that Daniel was, he thought we only had to look good and be entertaining,' Linette said slowly. 'He loved Stephen, I know he did, but he couldn't show it. Strange, when he could show such love to us, to the women in his life, but not to his own son.' Linette stared into the distance as if she was seeing that tortured boy who never stood up to his full height or looked his father directly in his eye. Then she said suddenly, 'Do you mind being alone? I mean, in the house at night. Do you hear burglars and rapists all the time?' Her voice was light but Cecily sensed she meant it seriously. Linette leaned forward a little in her chair, gazing at Cecily with intent eyes as if her answer was the most important thing in the world.

'I have heard odd noises, and when I wake up in a fright about Lloyd's I'd love to have someone here to talk to.' She gave a hollow laugh. 'And – well, I know this sounds mad, especially as we never lived in this house together, but sometimes I still expect to hear Edmund's key in the lock, the clunk as he drops his briefcase in the hall. Crazy, isn't it?'

'You still love him, don't you?'

'I wish I didn't. I feel ashamed about it. Little ex-wife, still pining. It would be easier to hate him, get on with my life. I've met . . . well,' she grinned, 'I'll probably never see him again, but I've met a really special man. But I can't let Edmund go enough to care for him.'

'Would you take Edmund back?'

Cecily moved restlessly in her chair. 'I often dream he'll come back, say he's been mistaken over Rowena, that it was just a sex thing. But it would be impossible, wouldn't it? I've lost all trust in him. But I love him, so I probably would stupidly take him back, knowing it wouldn't work. Every time he went out I'd imagine him with another woman, another Rowena waiting to grab him.' She smiled sadly. 'Who was it who said love makes fools of us all?'

'Lots of people probably said it. It's so true. But I agree, it would be hard to take him back, build up that trust again.' Linette gave Cecily a quick smile. Then she let her eyes drift away into some sad place of her own.

Shocked by the misery in her expression, Cecily said impulsively, 'Has something happened between you and Richard?'

'Richard . . .' She said the name as if the word was

alien. Cecily saw her make a great effort to relax the tight lines that clenched in her face. 'He's fine.'

'What's wrong then, Lin? You're not ill, are you?'

Linette shot her a quick glance, forced a smile. 'No, why?'

'You don't look well, so thin, so unhappy. Are you and Richard really all right, and the children?' Perhaps one of the girls was seriously ill, Cecily thought suddenly with fear. That would be worse than being ill oneself.

'Why shouldn't we be?' Linette looked wary, her eyes seeming to close down. Then she took hold of herself.

'You should see Chloe riding,' she said with a smile. 'She's so good, fearless. I can't think where she got the talent from. I was always hopeless on those ponies Daniel hired for us.'

'They were usually such bad-tempered creatures,' Cecily said, thinking it safer not to ask if Richard was a talented horseman, 'and Daddy was hardly the most patient of teachers.'

Linette smiled almost ruefully. 'No,' she said, 'he wasn't always.'

Cecily fumbled her way to the bathroom the next morning, drugged with sleep. She pushed open the door and Linette gave a little scream and tried vainly to hide her body as she got out of the bath.

'Sorry, Lin,' Cecily mumbled, her befuddled brain slow to notice this unusual act of modesty. Waking up a little, she tried to make a joke about their school days, when the strict religious rules encouraged them to undress completely under a dressing gown. There was a story that one girl had changed from her riding gear into a ball dress without showing so much as an inch of bare flesh. But then she saw Linette's body and all jokes fled.

'Lin, oh Lin.' She put her arms out, then couldn't touch her for the revulsion she felt.

Lin scrabbled for her towel, trying at the same time to cover herself with her other arm.

Cecily picked up her towel and wrapped her in it, hugged her to her, carefully as if she was afraid of hurting her. She felt Linette stiffen, then relax. Then the tears came. She held her a long time, not knowing what to say or do.

At last it was Linette who lifted her wet face from Cecily's shoulder.

'I don't know what to do,' she said. She turned away and began to pick up her nightdress and wash things.

'How long has he been doing this to you?' Cecily felt a flash of anger burning in her. If Richard had walked in at this moment she'd have beaten him.

Linette pulled her towel tighter round her and methodically began to pack away her toothbrush, facecloth and shampoo into her sponge bag. 'He . . . he first did it after Chloe's christening. He'd drunk too much and someone had made a joke about fathering sons – you know he always wanted a boy. He was very upset about what he did, and things were all right for about three years. Then he did it again.' She paused, looked ashamed as if she was to blame for his act of violence.

'Was he drunk again? The bastard, oh Lin, the bastard.'

'It's not—'

'Don't tell me it's not his fault, Lin,' Cecily burst out. 'How could he? He's sick, dangerous, I don't know which, but you can't go back. You can't.'

'I must.' Linette suddenly looked very strong. 'I must, for the children's sake.'

All Cecily's worry at having to cope with yet another disaster was swept away with her anger at Richard. She felt a firm resolve rise in her. 'You must bring the children here. Does he hit you in front of them?'

'No. He doesn't do it very often, and only when he's drunk.' Her towel slipped down and she bent to pick it up. Cecily stamped her foot on it and stared at her friend's body.

'He did that recently,' she said, gazing in horror at the yellow, red and blue bruises and weals on her body. There were none near her neck and face; they were only visible to someone seeing her naked. 'Lin,' she said, her anger sinking with her disgust, 'you can't go back. He can't get away with doing that to you. He simply can't.'

Linette said nothing, but pulled on her nightdress.

'I'll come with you and pick up the children. Then you must all stay here. You must see a doctor, a solicitor. Oh, I wish Daddy was still alive,' she sighed. 'Richard would never have dared do it if he was, would he?'

Linette smiled wanly. 'No, he wouldn't.' She paused, then said, 'I didn't want you to know and yet . . . well, I wanted someone to know. I can't leave him,' she held up her hand to stave off Cecily's protests, 'not just yet. Look, let's get some coffee and I'll tell you.' She led the way out of the bathroom. 'I don't want you to be late for work though.'

'Work's not important after this,' Cecily said.

'It is, you can't lose your job.'

'I've a good hour before I need go, but I can't leave you like this, Lin.'

'I'll be fine. I feel better now you know.' She smiled a thin, brave smile that almost made Cecily weep. 'But you see I have no money and—'

'But you had lots of money. Your mother left you everything. You didn't join Lloyd's too, did you?'

'No. I . . .' She looked awkward, then taking a deep breath said quickly, 'I lent it to Richard for some venture or other.'

'I suppose he made you give it to him and now it's gone.'

'Yes.' Linette looked ashamed. Cecily recognised that shame. She felt it over her Lloyd's losses.

'So the girls and I are dependent on him at the moment. They're at good schools and Chloe so loves her riding . . .'

'If he can pay for all that, he can pay you back. A solicitor would find a way. But you can't go on hiding this from the children. One day he'll do it in front of them, or go for them. You must leave him, Lin, you must.'

'I will one day.' She looked defeated now, wan and ill.

'You can live here with us, get a job. I'm sure a solicitor would get money out of Richard for you. He makes a packet, doesn't he? You can't let him hold you like this.' Even as she spoke, Cecily saw her words were falling off Linette like blunt arrows. No doubt she couldn't take any more. She hadn't the strength to get up and leave him, to strike out on her own.

'I'll help you, Lin,' Cecily said gently. 'Please try and leave him. Or just stay here and I'll go and get the girls.'

'I can't. I can't leave the girls any longer and he comes back today.' Her voice was almost a whisper.

'Surely you can stay with me? After all, we're sisters really.'

'That's just the reason why I can't.' She looked at Cecily, then away. 'He doesn't know I'm here. He,' she paused, then said quietly, 'he doesn't like me visiting my old friends, or you.'

'The bastard. That's just because he knows that I or your friends would take you away from him. Expose him for his cruelty. And I will too – no, don't worry,' she said less vehemently, seeing the terror in Linette's eyes, 'I'll wait until you're safely away. But I'll get you away, Lin, somehow I will. That I promise you.'

Linette said nothing, then moved along the passage to Cecily's bedroom.

'I . . . I must tell you something else, Cecily,' she said in a voice so low Cecily wondered for a moment if she'd imagined it.

'What? Something else?' She slipped her arm round

Linette's shoulders. 'Tell me anything, you know I'll do what I can to help.' She smiled encouragingly, supposing yet dreading Linette was about to tell her of some perversion Richard insisted upon.

'I'd like some coffee first, or rather a stiff drink,' Linette said.

'We'll have both.' Cecily led her downstairs to the kitchen. She made two mugs of coffee and poured in a generous dash of brandy.

'OK, tell me. Take your time,' she added unnecessarily seeing Linette take a breath, expel it, look frantically round the kitchen as if calling on some other object to speak for her.

'It's about Daniel,' she said at last, examining her coffee with deliberate intensity.

'Daddy?' Cecily said stupidly.

'H-he was my first lover,' Linette said with a great rush. Then seeing the horror on Cecily's face hurried on, 'Oh, it wasn't how you think, some dirty old man seducing a young girl. It was beautiful, it seemed so right. But the trouble was he was so good, so kind and considerate, I've never met anyone like him since. I suppose I'll be looking for someone like him for ever.'

'But how . . . when . . . oh, Lin, I can't believe it. Not you and Daddy.' The revelation had knocked the breath from her. She felt herself picking round the emotions of it, trying to keep it at arm's length in case it grabbed her and suffocated her.

'You had gone to Paris. He took me out a few times. We became very close. He was such fun. Oh, Cecily, you know how terrific he was when he wanted to be.' She smiled. 'Then . . . well, I was almost eighteen. Cecily, don't think of it as some grubby act, but something beautiful and good. It was, I promise you. But,' she paused, now looked guilty, 'Gail found out.'

'Gail?'

Linette nodded. 'She blackmailed Daniel into marrying her and leaving her most of his estate. She even hinted that he'd seduced me under age.'

'Oh, Lin, he didn't . . .' Cecily thought she'd faint.

'No, of course he didn't. He wasn't like that, but she wove it into some sordid little story, threatened she would put it in the papers, pass it round to you, his friends, his office, making people believe it was far worse than it was.'

'And he believed her?'

'She could have made it very difficult for him. You know how often one sees cases in the papers of men accused of sexual crimes. Even if they're proved innocent, people still wonder about them. Daniel hated to lose face.' She smiled wryly. 'It wasn't difficult for her to frighten him enough to agree to her demands.'

'So that was why he married her,' Cecily said slowly. 'Oh, Lin, why didn't you tell me this before?'

'I couldn't, I tried . . . after he died, but you were so upset I just couldn't.'

'Why are you telling me now?' Cecily looked at her intently, wondering if she hated Linette. Wondering why she should hate her. She remembered now the way Daniel had looked at her. *Droit du seigneur*, she thought suddenly; no doubt he could not bear someone else to deflower her. And Linette had had to live with the consequences. They all had.

Linette sat silent for a moment, then she said, 'You've seen what Richard has done to me and are horrified and expect me to leave him. I want to, that's why I was asking you about living alone, but I know I can't because in a way your father was responsible for it, and so am I.'

'How?'

'In a moment of weakness on our honeymoon I told Richard. I'd never told anyone before, not even Michael. It was in the middle of the night, we'd just made love and I felt we should be one in every way, that I should tell my husband about the most important times in my life.'

'What did he say?' Cecily felt exhausted now, drained by this surprising – yet if she thought rationally about it, not surprising – revelation.

'He has never forgiven me,' she said simply. 'He knows I search for Daniel in him and will never find him.'

Chapter Thirteen

'I have a Herr Jurgen Brehme, a Swiss-German, looking for a room for one month,' a woman from the Mayflower School of English informed Cecily over the telephone early one morning.

'Does he want it now, at once?' With her financial situation worsening, Cecily had, a few days ago, rung various schools of English to ask if they had any students that needed a room. With the children home for half-terms and holidays she couldn't have a full-time lodger. A student, in London for a short time, would be ideal. The schools had told her that they had more rooms than students, but would keep her name on their books. She had not expected a response so soon.

'Yes, please. Today if possible, just for a month.'

'Oh . . . I . . .' Instinct warned her to refuse, but the looming bills that lay unpaid on her desk haunted her. How could the telephone, gas and electricity cost so much? She had to get more money, and quickly. Here was one solution being offered to her.

'All right,' she said reluctantly, 'but he can't come

until this evening as I'll be at work. I don't have to cook dinner too, do I?' she added ungraciously.

'No, just provide a continental breakfast. That is dreadfully kind of you, Mrs Mendelson.'

The woman sounded so relieved, Cecily said sharply, 'I thought you had more people offering rooms than students to fill them. He is all right, isn't he?' Images of a wife beater like Richard swam into her mind, not to mention her father's seduction of Linette.

'Of course, all our students are vetted,' the woman said as if they were personally neutered by her. 'Herr Brehme is a married man. He's in the textile business and lives near Zurich.'

Her description did not altogether reassure Cecily. 'If you're sure, only I do live alone and the house is not very big.'

'I understand. You'll have no problems with him,' she said hurriedly as if she didn't wish to discuss what other problems she might have. 'Now, I haven't seen your house, usually we send someone round first to see everything is comfortable – you know.' She laughed awkwardly. 'But we haven't time for that today. Could you tell me something about it? Will he have his own bathroom?'

'Yes, he will.' She would use the children's bathroom. Her own, though next to her bedroom, had another door from the landing. But which bedroom would she put him in? There were four bedrooms, one each for the children and herself, and a fourth that was used as a play cum storage room, though it did contain a bed. She wouldn't have time to sort it out by tonight.

Cecily described her house, her heart sinking more and more at the thought of this stranger, and a man too, living at such close quarters. Having a lodger had seemed the easiest way for her to make extra money but now suddenly faced with it, she had cold feet. But she forced herself to accept him, knowing with growing panic that she couldn't afford to be fussy; the rent would pay some of her outstanding bills.

She put down the telephone feeling already as if her house was invaded by a stranger. But perhaps Herr Brehme was nice, would be a pleasant companion for her. He might suggest they went out to the theatre, concerts together. She felt a little better. Why must she always think the worst? Just because she had had so many mortal blows lately, it didn't mean there would be one at every turn. He might be charming, sweep her off her feet.

Jerome rang her at the shop later that morning and asked her to come out with him that evening.

'I can't, I've got a lodger coming,' she said reluctantly, her heart soaring at his voice, swearing inwardly that she had to turn him down. It was the first time he'd called her since their lunch together. She had sent him a card thanking him for lunch, but had not found the confidence to ring him. She knew he'd told her to, but in her insecure state she'd been afraid she'd ring at the wrong time, worst of all when he was with another woman, and annoy him. Now, here he was, asking her out and she had to turn him down.

'A lodger? You mean a lodger lodger, or a friend?' He sounded incredulous.

'A lodger lodger. A Herr Brehme.'

'Is he nice?'

'I've no idea. He's coming this evening so I must be there, sort of hovering around. I don't like to leave him his first evening.' She suddenly had a fear of leaving him alone in her house at all. What if he took things? Would she have to stay in every evening for four weeks?

'Cecily, do you have to have someone? I mean, you alone and . . . well, do you want me to be there, to see him with you?'

Daphne walked past Cecily and glared at her. Personal calls were frowned upon. Cecily felt a little bubble of euphoria. Jerome cared enough about her to be worried. He wanted to be with her when she faced this stranger. 'I can't talk now, Jerome, but it will be fine. I've masses of friends who put up people and nothing's happened to them,' she said with more bravado than she felt.

'But why must . . . No, I'll talk about it with you later. Do you want me to come round?'

She did, how she did, but she didn't think having Jerome and Herr Brehme facing each other in her drawing room was the best way to begin a relationship with either man. She wanted Jerome on his own, to build up their friendship carefully, without having him witness her playing the role of landlady.

'I shall be fine, but thanks for thinking of it,' she said warmly. Daphne glared at her even harder.

'I must go.' She wished she didn't have to be beholden to so many people. Having no money, needing every penny she could get, she had to fall in with those who paid her. She hated feeling like this. She had barely thought of the importance of money before, but now she saw it as a source of confidence, of independence, of being able to throw one's cap to the winds and be free.

'I'll ring you in a day or so,' Jerome said.

'Please do,' she said fervently, wondering if she detected relief or disappointment in his voice. Damn Herr Brehme, she thought. Damn Lloyd's.

Cecily rushed home in her lunch hour and cleaned round the house, making up the bed in Jamie's room and putting his toys and clothes in the fourth bedroom to give Herr Brehme space. She whisked round with vacuum cleaner and duster, spraying a little furniture polish into the air to give the illusion of a spotless house. Outwardly it was, still gleaming new with the expensive furnishings and fresh paint she'd lavished upon it. Surely no one was going to look behind the sofa or in the corners of the kitchen cupboards.

Daphne was out that afternoon when Cecily sneaked back a few minutes late; she'd had to buy some croissants and fresh orange juice for breakfast, one-time necessities but lately luxuries she now did without.

'I'm sorry, Gilly, I've a lodger coming this evening and I had to clean the place a bit, get the breakfast.'

'Don't worry. I doubt we'll get many people this afternoon, it looks as if it will pour any minute. What sort of lodger?' She put down the book she was reading.

'A Herr Brehme from Zurich, over here studying English.'

'Have you met him yet?' Gilly lived on romances. She had never married, never, as far as Cecily knew, had a boy friend. No real person had ever lived up to the fictional heroes that filled her dreams.

'No. But the language school seemed quite desperate to find somewhere for him to go, after telling me there was little hope of having one at all, so I do hope he's all right.' She laughed to hide her fear. If only she hadn't found out about Richard beating Linette just the other day, seen the bruises on her body, she might not feel so uneasy.

Since Linette had told her about Daniel she'd felt even more betrayed, her confidence more shaken. Strange that one could never see one's parents as people. The more she thought of it, the more obvious it was that it was in Daniel's nature to have seduced Linette. She could understand the man, but not the father.

Gilly broke into her thoughts. 'Some of that race can be so good-looking. Tall and tanned, icy-blue eyes, blond hair.'

'I'll let you know if he is. You can come and cook him breakfast,' Cecily said hurriedly, turning away to hide her real thoughts.

She felt positively sick that evening when she got home. She hated having strangers in her house, had even found it difficult to share the house with an au pair when the children were babies. 'You have to do it, think of the money, tiny drop that it is, compared to what you owe,' she told herself firmly, as if she was selling her body, not letting out a room.

The bell rang, loud and strident.

'Good evening.' A short, square man stood on the doorstep blinking through thick glasses.

Well, he's not tall and tanned, she thought slightly hysterically, wishing Linette was with her, knowing she would reduce her to giggles, and his eyes don't look very blue.

'Mrs . . . Mendel?' He glanced at a piece of paper in his hand.

'Mendelson, yes. Herr Brehme, come in.'

He had a huge suitcase neatly secured with a polished leather strap. He wiped his feet then bent to take off his shoes. Cecily looked horrified.

'You needn't—'

'My vife always takes off the shoes. Put on the soft ones,' he said, looking round the floor of her tiny hall intently. 'Where are the soft ones please?' He glared at her through his glasses. His mouth set in a line as if it did not know how to smile.

'Soft . . . Oh, you mean slippers. I don't have any in the hall.' She tried not to giggle.

'My vife keeps many . . . slippers in the hall. So the carpet is clean,' he said severely.

'A good idea, but I don't. Please come in.' She tried to smile, to appear friendly, but she felt her body pricking in revulsion. He smelt heavily of cologne.

221

He followed her into the drawing room, looking round disdainfully as if he was a health inspector.

'My vife does not have curtains so pale coloured. Dirt goes to them.'

'I like pale colours. Can I get you some coffee?'

'No thank you. I will make my own tisane soon. The kitchen?' He left the room and went into the dining room and then the kitchen.

'Do you clean every day?' he asked abruptly, looking round her almost tidy kitchen in horror. 'My vife—'

'I do clean every day. Now, let me show you your room.' Cecily was beginning to feel paranoid. How could she cope with four weeks of this man? He made her feel as if her whole house was infested with rats and cockroaches. She rather wished it was, to frighten him away.

She took him upstairs to Jamie's room. The wallpaper was royal blue with a pattern of white sailing boats. The bedcover and curtains were blue.

'Here you are,' she forced herself to smile. 'This is my son's room. He is away at school.'

'Have you no other? This one is too busy. It hurt my eyes.' Herr Brehme shielded his eyes from the wallpaper.

'Only my daughter's room and that is not suitable,' she said firmly, thinking of all the tatty posters stuck haphazardly round the walls. They would surely ruin his eyes for ever. She knew now why the language school had been so relieved she'd take him in.

'I vill see it,' he said.

Cecily walked upstairs passing her own room. He went into it.

'I like this one.' He looked round the pale green and cream chintz room, stared a long moment at the double bed.

'That is my room, and you cannot have that,' she said, feeling as if he had violated her.

'I am paying good money.'

Money. The word made her retch. What other agonising things would she have to do for money?

'I do not let out my room,' she said firmly, shutting the door and going on upstairs.

'Vat is this one?' He opened the door of the fourth room in which she had piled all Jamie's things on top of everything else. She had not decorated this room, leaving the plain terracotta coloured curtains and brown carpet until she decided what she wanted to do with it. Now she had so little money, it would never get done.

'I vill have this. It is peaceful coloured,' he said.

'But I haven't . . . it's got . . .' She gestured helplessly at all the things heaped in it.

'I vill vait downstairs while you make it for me.' He gave her a little nod, might almost have clicked his heels, and went downstairs.

Cecily was too appalled by his suggestion to say anything. Then she rallied. She would not be treated like this in her own house. Jamie's room was much nicer than this one and perfectly all right. She whirled round and began to go downstairs. He could sleep in Jamie's room or go, she didn't care. But the terrible sick feeling of needing the money came back to haunt her. She had to keep afloat, just day to day, financially. She had no alternative but to put up with it.

Swearing, she set to and cleared the room, putting everything in Jamie's room. She felt worn out. Her arms and back ached from carrying things back and forth. When she had at last made the bed, she looked up exhausted, her hair over her eyes, her clothes sticking to her.

'Thank you,' Herr Brehme said.

She wondered how long he had been standing at the door, and if he had enjoyed watching her work.

He came into the room with his suitcase, looking round critically as if to catch her out with some hidden dust or forgotten cobweb. Cecily fought to stop herself from shouting at him.

'I am tired. I go to sleep. Vhere do I vash?'

'The bathroom is on the next landing.'

'I see.' He looked annoyed. He opened his case and took out a large black bag. 'I have some vashing for tomorrow.'

'I don't do washing. There's a launderette on the corner.'

'My vife does not allow the launderette.'

'Your vife will have to put up with it,' she said, and marched out of his room with as much dignity as she could muster.

She heard him running the water in the bathroom and felt nauseated at the thought of his square, pink body in her bath. Then she heard him cough, splutter, cough, spit and she felt so sick she had to put her hands over her ears to shut out the sound.

'I'll be able to laugh about this with Linette, or perhaps with Jerome, if he ever rings again,' she told herself fiercely. Why couldn't he have been nice or at least civilised?

She felt furious and disgusted that she could find herself in such a situation. The fact that her life would now be filled with such men as Herr Brehme horrified her. She knew she'd have to choke on her pride, ingratiate herself with such people, such situations, indefinitely now.

If Edmund could see me now, wouldn't he be sorry and come back to me? she thought tragically, allowing self-pity to catch her in its grip, whilst knowing guiltily how many people lived with this fear of poverty all their lives. It was the one thing Daniel had never thought to train her for.

'Oh Edmund,' she cried out in the dark for him, feeling physically ill without his reassuring bulk beside her. Then she thought of him entwined in bed with Rowena, her fat limbs twisted through his, and she felt weak with despair.

Chapter Fourteen

'Will you come back with me tonight, Cecily?' Jerome's voice was soft but insistent, his fingers gently stroking little circles on her wrist. He studied his hand, those long, elegant fingers caressing the creamy skin of her wrist, as if he was afraid to see a rebuff in her eyes.

Cecily, too, watched his fingers, enjoying his touch on her skin. It had been a happy evening, a play followed by dinner in this intimate French restaurant, the deep crimson walls womb-like, cosy.

Jerome had been away a lot on business and their meetings had been spasmodic. He had taken her out once to the cinema, but she had been so agitated about leaving Herr Brehme alone in her house – no doubt feeling for dust behind her radiators or under her fridge, so he could scold her and tell her how often his 'vife' spring-cleaned – that Jerome had laughed ruefully and said, 'I won't ask myself in for coffee in case your lodger questions me on my standard of housework.'

'He'll be gone in three days,' she'd replied, 'and I'd rather sell myself than share my house with another one like him. If I hear about his "vife" one more time, I'll kill him.'

The day Herr Brehme left she'd luxuriated in being alone. She scrubbed out the bathroom and his room until all trace of him had gone. 'Even your vife couldn't make it as clean as this,' she'd called out to the empty house.

But she was confused by the raw tumult of her emotions. She couldn't decide how deep her feelings were for Jerome. She still loved Edmund, but that, she knew sadly, was a wasted emotion.

She certainly liked to be close to Jerome, liked the way he guided her to her seat, the way he helped her with her coat, his hands resting a moment on her shoulders then drawing away, down her body, barely touching her, though she could feel them, imagine them. Love, she thought, was probably a luxury. She should be content with what she felt now. Leaning towards each other over the table, she felt little bubbles of warmth rise in her at the admiration and desire in his eyes.

It was foolish to be alone just because Edmund had left her, and just because her last attempt at love-making with the unfortunate Jonathan had been such a failure. She raised her eyes at the same time that Jerome raised his. They caught, locked; they smiled shyly at each other.

'I'll get the bill,' he said, kissing the inside of her

wrist before he let go of her hand.

They both felt rather awkward then, sitting here, waiting for the bill. Waiting for the waiter, Cecily thought hysterically, almost repeating it to Jerome with a giggle. Then she felt a sudden surge of panic. What if her body refused to respond to his, as it had with Jonathan? What if her body could only respond to Edmund?

In the heaving flurry of love-making with Jonathan, she'd thought only of Edmund. Her mind had closed down and rendered her body cold to Jonathan's efforts. She didn't want this to happen with Jerome. She cared for him too much. She wanted to please him, to please herself, not cheat with faked passion. She wanted something to come from their relationship; if she failed him in bed, he might take it as a rebuff and not want to see her again. This fear made her feel gauche, inexperienced, imagining a hundred and two embarrassing disasters.

She'd never dream of voicing her fears to him. She thought love-making should be spontaneous, joyful, natural, as it had been with Edmund from the first moment they'd tumbled, laughing, into bed together. Not something preceded by analytic discussion. She nearly burst into frantic giggles remembering Linette telling her about the night she'd spent with a man whose bedside table groaned with sex manuals.

'I wondered if he was taking a degree in it,' she'd said. 'He certainly performed as if he was. It was terrible, like a robot.'

She felt swimmy with panic. She was happy with Jerome as he was. If she discovered anything strange about his bedroom habits it would ruin the relationship they had. It would be better to postpone it, go away together sometime in the future, when they'd have more time. Frantically she tried to think of something to say to extricate herself.

Then the waiter came with the bill folded over on a plate with two foil-covered chocolates. Jerome put his credit card on the bill, unwrapped a chocolate and held it to her lips, his eyes sensually watching them, his own parting in anticipation.

She took the chocolate between her lips, felt the richness of it against her tongue, then the cool tang of the mint centre. Her heart beat faster as he watched her with such obvious pleasure. Then he got up and gently pulled her to her feet, holding her to him for a second before they walked to the door.

In a moment they were out of the cosy little place into the cold dampness of the street. Lights glowed and danced from other night spots. Neon lights shrieked 'Girls, Girls, Girls' in red, for a second debasing the warmth in her, touching her with melancholy. There were smells of garlic, alcohol and spices coming out onto the street. People jostled on the narrow pavement. Jerome kept his arm firmly under hers and propelled her across the road. In another moment they were in a taxi and he had his fingers laced through hers, his shoulder snug against her own. He did not speak.

Cecily wondered what he was thinking and if he

seduced many women. Seeing in her mind's eye these 'other women', all surely much more glamorous and experienced than she was, she felt the darting panic of lack of confidence again. This fear spawned others. The spectre of Aids rose up to torture her. She remembered the nightmare stories of going to bed with everyone your lover had slept with before you. What if Jerome had slept with someone who'd slept with someone who'd slept with someone with Aids? And why, for goodness sake, was she assuming that Jerome might be a carrier when she hadn't with Jonathan?

She sat up rigid in the taxi. She desperately wanted Jerome to be part of her life. But her self-confidence, so badly cracked since Edmund had left her, and her miserable night with Jonathan, made her throw up all sorts of excuses and fears to escape the possibility of failure. She might have jumped out into the dark street to escape the problem if Jerome hadn't said, 'What is it, Cecily? You're behaving as if you've suddenly remembered you've left the iron on.'

'No . . . it's nothing.' She slumped back into the darkness of the cab, biting her lip, feeling his intense gaze on her, sensing his concern. God, what a fool she was being, she thought. Here she was on the way to a night of love with a man most women would die for, and she was behaving like a paranoid spinster.

'Come on, darling, I know there's something.' He stroked her cheek.

'It's just . . . well, I feel a fool saying it, but I've led such a sheltered sex life . . . It's Aids.' She didn't look at

231

him, feeling now as embarrassed as if she'd asked him when he'd last taken a bath.

He laughed softly in the dark. 'I don't actually have a certificate to prove I'm clear, but I'm pretty sure I am. I'll use something to put your mind at rest.'

'It's just so scary,' she said lamely, looking out of the window at the lighted shops and scurrying people.

'It is if you're stupid,' he said. 'But I'm very selective in the few relationships I've had since my marriage broke up. It's pretty unlikely that we'd get it, in the normal course of events.'

'I suppose so, it's just . . .'

'I know.' He squeezed her hand, then said after a moment, 'Look, Cecily, if you don't feel ready to go further with me yet, I quite understand. I'm in love with you, but I don't want to force you into anything.'

In the darkness of the taxi with the street lights crossing his face, Cecily glimpsed the intensity in his eyes. She felt his loneliness mingled with his desire and knew he wanted her for comfort, as well as for love.

'I know I'm quite dotty, but I feel as if I'm being unfaithful to my husband.' The words were out before she could stop them. She'd never felt this with Jonathan, but then she'd never cared for him.

Jerome kissed her cheek, then her lips, gentle, constrained kisses, but she could sense the passion behind them. 'You don't have a husband any more, my darling,' he said. 'Once you've accepted that, you can start living again.'

232

'Good morning, darling,' Jerome said, taking Cecily in his arms. She felt the smooth warmth of his bare skin against hers. 'You're lovely to wake up to.' He kissed her, then made love to her slowly and sleepily, making her forget that she'd known any other body but his.

He dropped her home in time to change for work, kissing her goodbye with passion. Cecily saw the tweak of curtains at the window of her neighbour Susan, opposite, and felt an illicit thrill. She let herself into her house feeling elated, the embers of their love-making still glowing in her. It had been an exquisite night. Her body had quite forgotten its coldness the moment Jerome had touched her, leaping into passion with the same abandon as he had. It was good to be loved again, she thought happily. It made her whole being zing with life, gave her strength and purpose to carry on.

She picked up the letters scattered on the doormat and skimmed through them. There was one from Jamie. She put down the others and opened it, reading it with as much joy as if it had been from a lover.

It was full of descriptions of a match against another school, further complicated because she didn't know many of the people involved, or couldn't recognise them from the way he'd spelt their names. But she read it three times with as much interest and delight as if it was the most fascinating letter in the world.

When she came back downstairs ready for work she saw the other letters she'd left on the ledge in the hall, and idly skimmed through them. They were mostly catalogues, a bill or two. Then her heart missed a beat, a faintness rose in her. There was one from Lloyd's, the name black on the white envelope, like a summons.

All her feelings of warmth and love vanished in the terror that gripped her. She put it down, then picked it up again. Willing herself to be strong and open it. It was another cash call for £10,000.

She slumped down on a chair feeling dizzy with shock. Her heart beat very fast, she was out of breath. Again Daniel's decree of never owing money scratched at her, filling her with guilt. But after a moment this advice began to conflict with her desire to find out the truth, her determination not to be intimidated by the vast institution of Lloyd's.

'What would you have done?' she said weakly to Daniel's photograph on the bookshelf.

She didn't have £10,000. She was managing with difficulty on her wages, not daring to touch the small sum she had left from Ronald's purchase of the castle. Even filling the house with a dozen Herr Brehmes wouldn't help her in the end. She'd said she wouldn't pay, she must not weaken now. It wasn't as if she was the only Name they were hounding, she must stand strong for them all, but still, to her fury, she felt guilty, that she should pay somehow.

Edmund had told her repeatedly not to worry, that Lloyd's had a duty to its Names and would not let them down, even though various press reports seemed to dispute this. She glanced at her watch. He'd be in the office, she could ring him safely without Rowena answering. She suddenly yearned to hear his voice. Then she remembered her love-making with Jerome and found herself blushing in case he guessed about her night of passion.

Edmund sounded very tired when she got through to him.

'I've got one too,' he said. 'Look, ring that firm who took over from the agent. That chap you spoke to before. No, I'll do it.' There was a long pause. 'You may have to join the Hardship Committee, they allow you about fourteen thousand a year and—'

'And lecture you on sending your children to private schools, having a decent car, a mobile phone, all the things they have as a matter of course, things they tempted you with to join,' Cecily said bitterly.

Edmund's voice sounded infinitely weary. 'Look, Cecily, I'm sure it will work out. I'll ring your agent, and ring you back. Will you be there?'

'No, I'll be at work. Can you ring me tonight?' She felt weak with exhaustion now. Defeated. Just when her life was picking up, this demand had come to whack her down again.

'I . . . I don't know.'

She could picture the awkwardness on his face, see his fingers pulling at his hair in the way they did when he felt uncomfortable. She longed suddenly for him to hold her in his arms, to feel him, smell the scent of him again. For a moment the intensity of her emotion made her feel dizzy, then she said bitterly, 'Surely Rowena

235

doesn't mind. After all, she can hardly pretend the children and I don't exist.'

'No, it's not that.' He instantly jumped to Rowena's defence.

'Then ring me, Edmund, please.' She put down the receiver as if it was a dead weight.

'What can I do about Linette?' Cecily asked Jerome as they sat over dinner in her dining room. She had rung Linette a few times only to have her make a hurried excuse and hang up. When she'd rung back immediately, all she'd got was the engaged tone.

He gave her a cynical smile. 'After the so-called advice I received over my marriage, I'd say keep out of other people's relationships unless specially asked. Even then, people can resent advice.' He took her hand. 'Mm, this venison's good. You're a marvellous cook.'

She beamed, feeling warm with his praise. It was worth her week of near starvation to have been able to buy this good dinner for him.

'Once I found out that cooking can be creative I loved it. But seriously, Jerome,' she frowned, leaned closer to him to emphasise her concern, 'I've got to help her. I've rung her, tried to make her come up, offered to go down, but she says she's fine. I last saw her before Christmas and—'

'Darling, she knows she can come to you. If she says she's fine, then accept it. Things may be all right between them now and she may feel embarrassed at having told you.'

236

'I saw what he did to her, Jerome. No man should be allowed to do that.' Once or twice waking in the night she found she was confusing Linette's bruises inflicted by Richard with the unseen wounds of the abortion. She wondered if her guilt at not helping to prevent the abortion was now being transferred into being doubly anxious over protecting her from Richard.

'Of course they shouldn't, but as you said, afterwards he's very sorry. Maybe he's stopped doing it altogether and they're trying to make a go of it,' Jerome said reasonably.

'I wish I felt convinced. Linette used to be so vital, so full of confidence. I'll never forget the day we first met. My father had left my mother and gone to live with Zara, her mother, and he invited me over to meet my "second mother", as he called her.' She smiled, remembering.

'He sounds quite a one, your father.'

'He was dreadful with women. He loved them all,' she said blithely, then paused, remembering 'all' included Linette.

'Go on,' Jerome said.

'Oh, sorry, I was lost. Well, I went into this huge flat with enormous modern pictures, you know, splodges and bare canvas, covering the walls. Zara came towards me, all scent, pearls and floating garments.'

'Wow!' Jerome laughed.

'She enveloped me in all of this and then said, "And this is my little girl Linette. You're the same age, isn't that lucky?" I'd imagined that I'd hate her. She was dressed in a pale pink jersey with a lace collar, a white pleated skirt and pink shoes. We still laugh about those pale pink shoes.' Cecily giggled, seeing again that beautiful child. 'But she had a mischievous twinkle in her eye that drew me to her. She grabbed my arm and said, "Let's go and listen to my records." We were close from day one, and now . . .' She trailed off, squeezed Jerome's hand, thinking of what life had done to that innocent little girl in pink. 'I *must* help her. She was always more confident, more devil-may-care than I was. I followed her where she led. But now she needs me. I'm the only person who can help her now that Daddy has gone.' Again she felt the lost emptiness of Daniel's passing. How they needed his strength now. Edmund, Lloyd's and Linette, he would have known how to cope with them all.

'Why *should* she be hit, kicked, beaten by this man?' she said vehemently, pounding the table with anger against Richard, and against Daniel for dying, and the price they'd paid for his seduction. 'She must leave him if there's any risk that he's still doing it. You should have seen her bruises.' She shuddered and Jerome held her hand to his cheek, stroking it. 'It's horrible.'

'Don't get so upset, darling. Of course something must be done if it's still going on. They probably both need – anyway he certainly does – professional help.' He kissed the palm of her hand. 'Apart from supporting our friends, there are some problems better left to the experts. And Cecily, you must remember he's the father of her children, and as an estranged father myself I feel very strongly about being able to keep in contact with one's children.'

'I know, but he *beats* her. I'm sure you didn't beat Sophia.'

'No, but I felt like it sometimes after her nights away.' His mouth curled with bitterness.

'But you didn't. What if Richard hurts the children?'

'I really think such problems need professional advice, darling. If he drinks, as you say, he may be able to get cured, solve it that way. Just go on ringing her for friendly chats, invite them to dinner,' he shrugged, 'as you would any of your friends. If she needs you she'll say.' He put his hand in her hair, stroking it gently. 'Now, what shall we do this weekend?' His eyes glowed with desire. 'I want you all to myself. Shall we go away somewhere for a weekend of unbridled passion?'

She smiled, got up and sat on his lap, wanting suddenly to feel the security of his embrace. 'Wherever you like, as long as it's not too far away.' She kissed him, laughing as he caressed her.

'The sofa is far enough,' he said huskily, lifting her up and carrying her into the drawing room, laying her on the sofa still entwined in her arms.

It was so new, their affair. They were both still at the moonstruck stage, amazed that they had found each other and got on so well. Jerome had told her a little about his ex-wife, a beautiful, unstable-sounding woman who'd soon got bored of marriage and now had a string of lovers.

'We must get all our children to meet,' Cecily had said cheerfully one Sunday as they sat over a late breakfast in Jerome's house. She imagined a relationship like hers and Linette's springing up between Miranda and Emily. 'I'm longing to meet Emily.' She poured Jerome some more orange juice, wavering between dreading the intrusion of the children on their love and determination to scoop them all up into one happy family.

'We must.' He smiled at her. 'When are yours back from school again?' He got up and fetched his diary.

'They break up in three weeks, end of March. My two don't have a weekend out together which is maddening. I think it best if they all meet together, don't you?'

'Certainly.' He paused, then said more seriously, 'I think I'm going to have Emily to live with me anyway in the term time. She's not doing well at school, got in with some crowd, always in trouble. She's got a good brain and should do well, but ever since the divorce . . .'

'Won't her mother mind?' Cecily asked, sinking inside at his words. It was one thing being a happy family in the holidays, but the whole time? They could hardly embrace each other, make love when it suited them if a child was in the house. Perhaps later when, or if, this great need to touch each other constantly, to express their love with such physical abandon, cooled, they could all set up house together.

'It wouldn't make any difference, she hardly sees her anyway as she's away at school.' He gave a rueful grin, 'It may sound pompous, but I don't think it's a very good environment for a teenage girl to live in. Sophia's a good mother, but she has too many lovers. I wouldn't be so concerned if she'd settle down with one. But it's very unsettling for Emily, and I wouldn't like her to think it was the way to live.'

'Isn't it a bit late to pretend her mother lives otherwise? Children are very quick to pick up on such things these days. You say she's a good mother . . .'

'She is, but they're not getting on at the moment. Also,' he looked concerned, 'I'm sort of afraid Emily might take after her.'

'I can understand that, but if that sort of promiscuity is hereditary, there's not much you can do.'

'You may be right.' A haggard look clenched at his face. 'But I'm concerned for her academic future too. I think she should change schools, and a day school is worth a try. But it means I'll have to get a housekeeper for the extra cooking and to be there when I go away on business trips.' He sighed. 'It will be quite an upheaval, but I feel I must do it.'

'I'm sure you're right,' Cecily said reluctantly. 'I wish I could have mine home too. I'm sure they'd do better.'

'We'd better get them all home then, set up together in a huge house,' Jerome said lightly, looking at her from the corner of his eye.

'It would be chaos,' Cecily said, that old panicky feeling of taking on more responsibilities pricking at her. Did he mean it as a distinct possibility? Or was he joking? It would certainly solve all his domestic problems if she was there, running everything, she thought.

A chill went through her. Love was one thing; commitment, responsibility for a family, another. She realised with a start that she would prefer to be alone with her children than have Jerome with them. She would feel inhibited in their presence. She wanted to keep them in separate compartments. Jerome, the children, and where would she put Emily? In with her children or with Jerome? Suddenly the jigsaw didn't seem to fit so well.

Chapter Fifteen

Edmund sat tight in the corner of the taxi, as if fearful of any bodily contact with Cecily. They were on their way to the AGM at Lloyd's and Cecily couldn't help thinking how ironic it was that their first date since splitting up should be so uninspiring.

Edmund was grinding his lower lip between his thumb and forefinger. There was a constant furrow between his eyes as he stared out into the traffic. Cecily had a suspicion that his silence covered more than the feelings of embarrassed guilt and awkwardness he still seemed to go through whenever he was alone with her.

'He's suffering badly from an Englishman's fear of emotions,' she'd said to Penny when she went round to supper one night. 'If he was French or Italian he'd be much more sophisticated about it all.'

'I'd call it guilt,' Penny said drily.

Despite the continuing horrors of the Lloyd's situation, loss piling upon loss, with cash demands coming at regular intervals through her letterbox and rumours that this year's losses would be even worse than last year's, Cecily felt curiously buoyant today. She couldn't resist teasing Edmund. 'If your thigh accidentally brushes against mine I don't think it will be counted as adultery,' she said jauntily but he didn't seem to hear her. He was, she thought, altogether too preoccupied. Life with Rowena was turning him into a dull, staid man. Ironic, she thought, that many middle-aged men fled a supposedly boring marriage to have a last rejuvenating fling, while Edmund seemed to have fled what she had thought was a reasonably exciting marriage to become quiet and grey with Rowena.

'You probably can't commit adultery with your ex-wife anyway, Edmund,' she went on. 'Do you remember that play we once saw? I can't even remember who wrote it now, about the married woman who slept with her ex-boy friends, not counting it as adultery as she'd slept with them before she'd married.' She prattled on, to hide her irritation at this new inertia in him.

She looked at him closely. He seemed exhausted, his hair more faded, his face more lined. Yet when they'd talked about the Lloyd's situation half an hour ago with her solicitor he'd been alert and articulate, pushing in points and questions with the powerful vitality that so attracted her. Had that exhausted him so soon in the day? Or was he worried about the meeting ahead?

'I expect the play was written by a woman,' he said vaguely, still staring out of the window.

The tone in his voice annoyed her. 'Edmund, did you leave me because you were as bored with me when we were married as you evidently are now?'

'Of course not, Cecily. And I'm not bored now.' He had the grace to look surprised. 'Wherever did you get that crazy idea from?'

His indignation made her feel ridiculously pleased. She couldn't stop her mouth breaking into a smile. 'It's just . . . you seem so quiet, subdued, after being so animated with the solicitor. I can't help feeling it's something to do with being with me.' Her voice was brisk as if bracing herself for him to admit she did bore him.

'Cecily,' he looked at her gravely, 'I have a lot to think about. This Lloyd's business is very serious. Oh, I'm sure they'll sort it out, produce a settlement to help us, but at the moment it's quite a worry.'

'I do know that, Edmund. I've had enough cash calls to wallpaper a downstairs loo, though they belong inside it,' she said tartly. 'But now they've brought in someone else from outside, a one-time monk, they say, I do feel more confident, though it would be too much to hope, I suppose, that his religious leanings will encourage them to confess and repent.'

He smiled in spite of himself, lifted his hand as if to cover hers, then tucked it sharply away. 'Cecily, will you never be serious?'

'It hurts too much,' she said. There were dark smudges under his eyes as if he hadn't slept properly for weeks. She wondered if Rowena cared enough for him. 'No doubt we'll keep getting their begging letters, demanding Mickey Mouse sums,' she went on hurriedly, to stop herself asking about his relationship with Rowena. 'It's a laugh, though I'm not laughing. However much you and the solicitor try and find ways for me to find the money, I know I can't possibly pay it. I'm only thankful there are so many of us in the same boat and if we all refuse to pay – not that most of us can pay anyway – something will have to be worked out. Lloyd's might even sink for ever, taking all the people responsible for this mess with it.'

'They are trying to be sympathetic, seeing that people have enough money for school fees, nursing homes, things like that,' Edmund said flatly.

'Are they really? What's the catch?' She looked at him, sitting so still in his corner. 'If they were so helpful, how come people have killed themselves with worry?' Edmund didn't reply, he seemed to have stopped listening, so partly to shock him into giving her attention, and partly because she had to tell him sometime, she said, 'I don't know if you've heard but I've got a new man in my life.'

'Oh?' This did wake him up; he turned to her and studied her face as if the revelation had suddenly changed her appearance. 'Do I know him?'

'Do you have to?' she said sourly, wondering what reaction she'd hoped for. A confession that he'd never stopped loving her and that living with Rowena was a mistake? She wished she could let him go and give all of her love to Jerome, instead of just a part of it.

'I didn't mean it like that, Cecily.' He smiled at her as

if he still cared for her and it lifted the grey look on his face for a moment. She felt a sudden lurch of her heart.

'You deserve someone nice,' he said. 'As you know . . .' He looked grave again, stared down at his hands, then blurted. 'I do feel very sorry and guilty for what happened. Rowena and I, well, we just clicked. It had nothing to do with me not caring for you, or any fault on your part. We've had some wonderful times together, and of course we have the children. You will always be very special to me, Cecily. It's just,' he shrugged, a rueful smile on his mouth, reminding her of Daniel smiling at his betrayals, as if they were beyond his control, 'events change. People change, we all do. Sometimes we want different things, different people, not because we dislike the old ones, but we can't always have both. You do know that, don't you?' He looked at her imploringly. 'I never wanted to hurt you and the children. It just went too far and—'

'I wish I could hate you,' Cecily said bitterly. 'I wish I could hurt you as much as you hurt me – us.'

'Oh Cecily, I am sorry, I really am. But these things happen. Look at your father.' His mouth closed in a defiant line, he looked offended as if she was the one being unkind, drawing attention to the fact that he'd hurt her.

'I don't want to look at my father's behaviour, I've been trying to escape it all my life.'

Edmund looked miserable now. 'I really am sorry, I'll always be fond of you.'

'But you wouldn't come back, would you?' She looked

directly at him, watching his expression as her words hit him. The pain of his leaving fossilised into a hard core inside her.

'No. Well, it's too late, Cecily. Rowena and I love each other, and now that you have someone too, well . . .' He smiled awkwardly. 'I'm very pleased for you, really I am. What is his name, what does he do?'

'Jerome Clifford, forty-eight, educated at Marlborough and Cambridge. He's a fund manager with Merrill Lynch. Divorced with a teenage daughter,' she rattled off. 'Suitable enough for you?'

'I want you to be happy, Cecily,' Edmund said, his fingers fluttering out to skim over her hand a second.

Fighting down the surge of warmth that his fleeting touch brought to her she said sadly, 'Then you should have thought of that in that chalet in Verbier.'

'Will you marry him?' he asked as if he hadn't heard her.

'He hasn't asked. Are you going to marry Rowena?'

He shifted in his corner, didn't look at her. 'We might do. She . . .' he hesitated, struggling with some inner turmoil as if he wanted to say something but was debating whether he should.

Cecily bit back her words to urge him on, certain he was on the verge of a confidence. She knew of old that if she pushed him, he would clam up and say nothing.

Edmund stared out of the window as if whatever he wanted to say was emblazoned in lights in the street. 'She wants another child,' he blurted suddenly. 'She wants us to have one together.'

Cecily felt as if she'd been punched in the stomach. She felt faint and sick. How stupid of you to be surprised, she told herself impatiently. If a woman loves a man, she wants his child. It's the normal course of events. But the shock made her say cattily, 'Rowena's almost two years older than I am. We're virtually donor egg age now. We don't have many left of our own, and they'd probably only be the dud ones anyway.'

'You've put it rather crudely,' Edmund said, knowing she meant to be unkind.

'It's true though, isn't it?' Cecily wondered why she minded so much if he had another child. The memory of the sheer elation and pride on his face when she'd told him they were expecting their first baby came back as if it was yesterday. He'd treated her with such care and wonder, as if no other woman had achieved the feat before. She remembered the children's births and how he had almost wept with joy when they'd emerged bloody and wet from her. It was moments like that that held more love, more intimacy than any sexual act. She could not bear him to share such moments with Rowena.

'Time is not on our side, I know. I would like to wait and see how this Lloyd's situation develops. Now is not the time to be taking on the extra expense of another child. But,' he frowned, 'it's difficult for Rowena to accept. After all,' he laughed awkwardly, 'the old body clock goes on working for men, we can father children for ever.'

'I wouldn't be too sure of that,' Cecily said drily. Her

heart was so full of the memories they'd shared, she had to fight with herself not to grab him, hold him, implore him to come back to her. Pull yourself together, she ordered herself desperately. At least she had the memories and had lived with Edmund during the best years of his life. But oh, how she wanted him back. She ground her hands together and stared out at the street, fiercely counting the windows of the tall buildings ahead to keep her tears and entreaties at bay.

They arrived at the Royal Festival Hall to a barrage of press photographers, clicking away at the Names and Lloyd's workers who poured through the doors. A collection of down-and-outs watched them from faded eyes, hunching their grubby clothes round them, some even asking the dapper-suited Names for change, disappointed and incredulous that they had none to spare.

Cecily moved closer to Edmund, slipping her arm through his, the sight of the tramps sending a cold shiver through her. It was not them she feared but they reminded her, like a beggar at a feast, of the looming prospect of poverty that hung over her and the other Names.

They reached the entrance and the cameras turned towards them, as they did to everyone obviously connected to the meeting, in case they missed a celebrity. Cecily held tight to Edmund and smiled into the flashbulb thinking, with a little surge of satisfaction, at least we'll be immortalised for ever in this picture.

She stayed close to Edmund as they went into the meeting together.

After the Chairman had explained why Lloyd's had lost almost three billion pounds, even more than the previous year, people asked questions. They were angry, bewildered yet constrained. When a woman complained that she felt bitter that the trust Lloyd's used to be based on had been betrayed, the Chairman looked hurt, as if being set on by a bully. He told her she was being unkind.

Cecily, stealing a glance at Edmund, saw his shoulders droop, his face tighten, his Adam's apple jerk up and down as he swallowed. She took his hand, felt it lie lifeless in hers. She squeezed it, willing him to respond, to come back to her and tell her that together they would surmount even these shattering new losses.

The meeting rambled on. Cecily felt a surge of anger lick through her. She got up. 'Edmund, I'm going. I can't stand this any more. It's getting us nowhere. Put me down for all the legal actions, I'm going to fight to the death with everyone else. If I'm going to be wiped out, then I'll go fighting.'

'Hear! Hear!' a man behind them grinned at her. 'That's the spirit.'

'I think you're being a bit melodramatic,' Edmund said.

'I don't at all. Oh, Edmund.' Impulsively she put her hand on his arm. 'Don't you understand? Honour and loyalty belong to the fairy stories. The only people left with it are the Names.' She gestured towards a group of elderly people, the men spruce in old but once-expensive suits, the women in well-cut, faded country tweeds. They stood tall and dignified, trying to find some hope in the Chairman's words. The sight of them, so brave, so bewildered, touched Cecily. They were like her mother, her aunts and uncles. Decent, well-meaning people who still believed that the word of an Englishman – their sort of Englishman anyway – was his bond. They were scrupulously honest and they were now bemused and lost, like geriatrics who'd mistakenly dropped into a rave party when they were expecting drinks before Sunday lunch. They, like Edmund, could not, did not, want to believe what had happened. She felt a burning sense of anger. She glared round the crowded room, at the men in their sleek city suits, their expensive shirts and silk ties. But maybe some of them were belea- guered Names too.

'Thank goodness there are some strong, tough fight- ers among the Names, who won't give up before they find out the truth,' she said, 'who know well the people they are fighting. But I'm fighting too, for people like that,' she gestured towards the bewildered group in their country tweeds, 'as well as myself. I shall not pay another penny. If they want it, they must take me to court first.'

'That's very noble, Cecily but—'

'I've had enough here, Edmund.' She glanced again at the little group of elderly people. 'Thank you for your advice and help over this, I really do appreciate it. But I won't be paying out any more, so don't waste time and sleep worrying about how I can find the money. They must come to me and get it. With any luck the queue to the bankruptcy court will be years long.' She kissed him lightly on his cheek, let her face rest against his a moment, then was gone.

Part III

Chapter Sixteen

'Next Sunday the children will be home,' Cecily said, tossing away the newspaper and leaning over Jerome to grab the colour supplement.

'So they will.' He was deep in an article in the business news, his glasses perched on the end of his nose.

Cecily snuggled closer to him. 'More coffee?'

He looked up from his reading, took off his glasses, a new acquisition that he hated, and kissed her. 'No thanks.' He stretched his long legs down the bed, his movement almost knocking off the breakfast tray. She put her arm round him and laid her head on his chest. She felt his arm tighten round her. Neither spoke.

She knew what he was thinking; she was thinking the same thing. Once she'd have been ecstatic about having her children home so soon, but now her joy was tempered with regret and uncertainty. When would she and Jerome be able to sleep together in the same bed again, let alone make love?

The children both knew about him and had met him once. Despite many rehearsals, Cecily had found it difficult telling them about him. She'd been afraid of their reaction. Would they be angry, jealous, even shocked? Would they like him? She didn't want to cause them any more pain. She knew with sickening dread that if they objected to him too strongly she would have to see Jerome only in term time. Amenable and understanding though he was, he'd soon come to resent that. She'd deliberately played down their relationship to the children.

'He's just a very nice person whom I've been going out with,' she said to Miranda.

'Does that mean you're going to bed together?' Miranda demanded archly. They had just been doing reproduction in biology and sex was the big topic at the moment.

'We are very fond of each other,' Cecily had hedged, Miranda's question making her feel like a guilty teenager.

'As long as you don't get AIDS or babies,' Miranda said. 'We think Tania Leaming is having a baby, she's been slimming for ages and she's still so fat.'

Rather despising herself for her cowardice, Cecily feigned an interest in Tania's condition to stave off any more embarrassing questions about Jerome. Miranda would be asking her if she was using contraceptives next.

Jamie had gone a bit whiter when she told him. He seemed to diminish into himself. He looked anxiously at her, as if she was suddenly going to disappear with this 'special person'.

'It's all right, darling, things will be just the same as they are now. I just wanted to tell you about him. He's longing to meet you and Miranda.' Cecily had felt a pang of guilt at the confusion her news was causing him.

'I wish Dad would come back,' was all he said, extricating himself from her arms and turning on the television, flicking from channel to channel, studying the fleeting images with intense interest.

Jerome took them all out to lunch at the Rib Shack in Knightsbridge. He was quite relaxed with them, telling them about his daughter Emily, wishing she could be with them. He was sure they'd all get on so well together. Cecily felt as nervous as if she was introducing the most unsuitable lover to the most exacting and disapproving of relations. Later that evening, when the children were asleep, Jerome said to her, 'Really, darling, you must relax about us. If you send out signals of apprehension, your children will think I'm some sort of monster, someone to be feared, not accepted at all.'

'I'm sorry, Jerome. Did it show? Oh God, I didn't mean it like that.' She clutched at his hands. 'It's just if . . . if for any reason they didn't like you, didn't like us being together, it's going to make life hell.'

'I know,' he kissed her, 'but they'll get used to it. They're great children, even Jamie got quite talkative before we left the restaurant.'

'He's so quiet these days,' she said sadly, thinking of his tight little face. 'If only Edmund would relent and not expect him to try for Eton.'

Now as they lay in bed in Jerome's house, breakfast and newspapers scattered over the bed, Cecily asked as nonchalantly as she could, 'When is Emily coming to live with you?' She didn't want him to know she was anxious about her coming, wanting her so much to like her, afraid she would not.

'I'm not sure. She breaks up this week as you know, then has a school trip, then probably goes to Spain with her mother. I hope to take her to America for ten days or so, about the time you're in France with your mother.'

'That should be fun for her.'

'I hope so. Long Island's a great place, as I've told you. There'll be a lot of young people there, and tennis and swimming. She should enjoy it. But I wish you could come.' He nuzzled her face, kissing her. 'That would make it the perfect holiday. I don't know how I'm going to do without you.' He stroked her breast.

'I wish I could come with you,' she sighed, wondering if he would stay faithful to her with all those long-legged American girls to tempt him.

'Can't you? Really can't you? Change the dates with your mother?'

'You know there's nothing I want to do more, if for no other reason than to keep an eye on you,' she joked. She wasn't going to mention the expense. With things as they were she couldn't possibly afford an air ticket to America for herself, let alone the children. She didn't want to admit this. She didn't want Jerome to offer to pay for them, to feel she was a financial drain on him.

Instead she said, 'I haven't seen my mother for ages, and she loves having the children. I'll come another time.'

'I shall insist the next time.' He continued to stroke her breast abstractedly. 'It's a wonderful place for children. I've got some photographs somewhere. Want to see them?'

'Mmm. Show me.'

He got out of bed, put on his silk dressing gown and went downstairs. In a moment he was back with a thick black envelope. He sat down beside her and began to pull out the shiny pictures. 'There's the pool, and the view. Look at that water.'

'That's a wonderful sunset. Who took it?'

'Me. I love photography, but I only get down to it when I'm on holiday nowadays. At one point I wanted to make a career of it,' he smiled, 'but I gave in to parental pressure and went for a "real job". I'm sometimes tempted to take early retirement and take it up again.'

'You should. These are wonderful. Quite unlike the usual holiday snaps.' Cecily was entranced by the colour, the light. There were various groups of people, in tennis gear, in bathing suits, laughing, mocking the camera. She wondered if his wife was there among the slim, tanned bodies.

Instead she asked, 'Is Emily here?'

'No. She didn't come last year.' There was a slight tightening round his mouth when he said this.

Cecily felt the pain in him, so she didn't ask him if

261

he'd seen her that summer. She laid her head against his shoulder. He'd told her how difficult his ex-wife had been about access to his child. She suspected she was only letting him have her now because it suited her.

'You must come and see it for yourself. We'll have a wonderful time.' He kissed the top of her head.

He was about to put the photographs away when the picture of a young man caught Cecily's eye. He was standing by the water, tanned and laughing. He was the image of her father.

'Who's that?'

'Oh, Stephen . . .'

'Stephen Forester?'

'Yes,' he looked surprised. 'Do you know him?'

'He's my brother.' Cecily felt breathless with shock. She devoured the photograph with her eyes. 'I haven't seen him for seventeen years.'

'Your brother?' Jerome stared at her, incredulous.

'Well, half-brother. He got so tired of the family upheavals, and . . . other things, he dropped out before Cambridge and fled to America. Do you know him, darling I just don't believe it, it's such an extraordinary coincidence.' She couldn't take her eyes off the picture. He could have been Daniel. A younger, tauter Daniel. Her eyes were shining as she begged Jerome, 'Tell me all about him, every single thing.'

Jerome looked at her. 'I . . . I don't know him very well,' he said with a trace of hesitation. 'He works in our office and comes to the island in the summer. He's just one of the crowd – you know.' He scrutinised the photograph. 'He doesn't look much like you.'

'He's the image of my father. When I last saw him he was nineteen, rather gawky and very moody. He slumped about the place rather than walked. He looks wonderful here. Oh, I must get in touch with him.' Her eyes were shining with delight. 'Tell me where he is.'

'You mean you haven't heard from him all these years?'

'Christmas cards, but never with an address. I suppose he kept in touch with his mother.'

'Fiona? Yes, I've never met her. Married to a *diet* doctor, I think he is,' he chuckled. 'He's very rich.'

'So that's where she went. We lost touch when Daddy married Gail, his fourth and most hated wife.' Her mouth clenched angrily. 'God, the damage Dad's love life did to us,' she sighed. Jerome reached out and squeezed her shoulder. 'But how is Stephen, darling? Is he happy? Is he married?'

Jerome's eyes shifted away from her eager ones. 'I . . . I don't know. I think he was married.'

Cecily had the uncomfortable feeling he was hiding something from her. She felt the twist of the familiar sick tension worrying about Stephen gave her. 'There's nothing you're keeping from me, is there, Jerome?'

'Darling,' he touched her cheek, 'I don't know anything for sure. But I heard a few rumours . . .'

'What sort of rumours?' Her voice was sharp.

'Don't panic, he's fine now, but rumour had it that he had a difficult time, a marriage that went wrong, but as

I say, he seems fine now.' He smiled, kissed her. 'Don't worry so much, Cecily. Get in touch with him. You've so much to catch up on.'

'I can't believe it, after all this time.' Cecily stared at the picture as if it would take life and talk to her. A suntan's a good camouflage for emotional trauma, she thought suddenly. Standing there in the picture he was like an advertisement for the man who had everything.

'I'd ring him, but he may not want to see us again. If I write, it will give him a chance to get out of it,' she said a little sadly. Then she added slowly, 'I can't bear Edmund wanting Jamie to go to Eton so much. Seeing this picture of Stephen brings it all back. Edmund's much nicer to Jamie than Daddy was to Stephen, but I wish he'd just let him be himself and go his own way, the right way for him.'

'My father was a bit like that too,' Jerome said. 'I think they'd be horrified if they thought they were being cruel, storing up such damage for later on.'

'When my father realised that it was too late. Stephen ran away and Daddy never saw him again. But he does look happy now,' she said firmly. 'May I ring Linette? She adored him. She'd love to know that we'd found him again. May I, darling? It's such an amazing coincidence.'

'Of course.' Jerome smiled at her. 'Keep the picture. I can't wait to tell him about you. There's another reason why you should be coming with me.' He stroked her hair, looking at her wistfully.

'What a summer to miss. You *and* Stephen.' She

sighed, wishing with all her heart that she could go. But she knew with sickening emptiness there was no way she could, even if she changed the dates with her mother. She just didn't have the money for the tickets and dared not saddle herself with another debt by borrowing. 'I can't disappoint my mother,' she said.

'I understand. Next time I'll organise it better.' He kissed her and left the room to let her phone in peace.

Richard answered. 'Cecily,' he drawled. 'How exciting, haven't heard from you in yonks,' Richard prided himself on his slang, not realising he was usually years out of date. 'How are you?'

'Fine,' she snapped, visualising his fleshy face and thick rubbery lips. Once he had been good-looking; she doubted he was now. 'I want to speak to Linette.'

'Of course, hang on, I'll just see where she is.' His voice was exaggerated, the way it was when he felt important. Cecily bit back a sarcastic remark, her hatred for him and the pain he had caused Linette making her feel sick. She dared not say anything in case he took it out on Linette afterwards.

'She's just coming, having a bit of a lie-in, you know.' He chuckled as if he was being amusing. Cecily forced herself to remain silent.

'Yes . . . hello?' Linette's hesitant voice came over the line. Cecily could still hear Richard's breathing. He was listening in, no wonder Linette sounded scared. She prayed she wouldn't hang up.

'Hi, Lin, it's me,' she said as cheerfully as she could. 'I've got some marvellous news.'

'Oh, what is it?' Linette sounded flat, as if any nuance in her voice would give something away.

Cecily felt the excitement of telling her about Stephen ebb from her. She was certain Richard had beaten her again. Hearing his breathing in the background she did not dare ask Linette how she was, or suggest she escape and come to her. Was he holding onto her? Cruelly digging his nails into her arm? Or was he glaring at her, willing her to say nothing? With difficulty Cecily kept her voice as natural as she could.

'You remember I told you about Jerome, my new man.' Linette didn't say anything so Cecily went on, 'He's just been showing me some photographs taken in America and there's one of Stephen. He's a friend of Jerome's, isn't that extraordinary? I'm going to write to him at once and insist that he tells us where he is.'

'Stephen! I don't believe it. Oh, that's fantastic, can't you ring him at once?' The old Linette flared for a moment.

'I could but, well, you know what happened, Lin. How badly Daddy treated him. He looks so happy, so filled out, and I'm afraid that we may hold too many unhappy memories for him, and I might frighten him away. After all, he would have told us his address if he wanted to see us.'

'But *we* got on with him.' Her voice was pleading.

'I know we did.' Cecily tried to soothe her. 'I'll write to him today. Jerome has the address at his office.'

'OK. Let me know, Cecily. Be sure to let me know,' her voice pleaded.

'Of course I'll let you know. How are the girls?' Cecily felt uneasy. She hoped that Linette would understand she was really asking how she was, could somehow send her a signal to come if she needed her. She could still hear Richard's breathing in the background. She longed to shout at him to go away.

'Well, thanks. I must go now. Let me know.' The receiver was put down abruptly, leaving Cecily in despair. Would Richard hurt her now? She glanced at her watch. Ten past ten. Would he have been drinking already?

'Jerome.' Fear seemed to latch onto her like a web, sticking to her. She sprang out of bed and ran, still naked, downstairs.

He was in the drawing room, looking for something in his desk. 'Wow,' he said. 'What a lovely sight. Come here.' He held out his arms and she went into them, feeling the warmth of his skin through the silk of his dressing gown.

'I know you'll think I'm mad but I've got to go to Linette. Something's wrong, I know it is. I'm sorry, darling, but I must go to her.' She tried to escape from his caresses, anxious to get dressed and be off.

'Wait,' he said gently, leading her over to a large armchair. He sat down and pulled her onto his lap. 'Tell me quietly what's happened before we dash off on a wild-goose chase.' He covered her neck and shoulder with feather-like kisses, his hand stroking her thigh.

She struggled to ignore the stirrings of desire. 'I . . . well, it's complicated. You see,' she took a deep breath, 'my father . . . oh, this sounds awful, but when Linette was much younger he seduced her.'

'What? The old devil. How much younger?' he asked frowning.

'Almost eighteen, not a child. It wasn't – well, Linette says it wasn't like that. But ever since, she's found no one to match him. I feel rather responsible and now Richard beats her . . .'

'Cecily, you can't be responsible for something your father did. Really, you're carrying this concern of yours too far. If Linette really is unhappy with her husband, she must leave him. There are refuges for battered women.' He hugged her close.

'There's a bit more to it,' she said and told him about her guilt at not being able to stop the abortion.

'Good grief. I'm beginning to see why you're carrying the sins of your family on your back, darling.' He looked anxiously at her. 'Your father playing musical chairs with his wives, leaving you to protect the devastated children and the discarded wives. And this too. Forgive me, darling, but your father certainly did his best to cock up your life.'

'I don't think he meant to,' she said wildly. 'You don't always know what your actions are going to do, do you? But don't you see,' she cried, breaking away, 'I must go. I just feel things are wrong. Richard was listening in for a start, and she sounded afraid, subdued.' Reluctantly she moved away from his mouth, and carried on, 'Normally she'd be thrilled to hear about Stephen. She was very fond of him, very upset by the way she felt he was hounded out by my father.'

'Cecily, I'm out of my depth,' Jerome sighed, 'but you know best. Maybe she was afraid Richard would be jealous. Does he know he's her – what is he, half – or stepbrother?'

'Ex-step. But it's more than that. It was what she didn't say.'

He put his hand on her hip, running it over her stomach. 'It's all beyond me. Where do they live?'

'Sussex.' She lay back in his arms.

He laughed, kissed her, outlining her lips with the tip of his tongue. 'At least it's not the depths of Scotland. Come on then, let's have a day in the country. The sun is shining.'

'You don't understand,' she said, moving away from him. 'I just feel she needs me.'

'Or you need her.' He looked serious. 'I'm fascinated by your father. Was no woman safe with him?'

His words made her feel cold, ashamed, as if Daniel was indeed a dangerous lecher. 'Linette was very beautiful. She suddenly grew up and he . . .'

'Fancied her.'

'Yes. But Linette didn't seemed to be harmed by it. It was just what happened afterwards that hurt her. It might have been his fault, it might not have been.' She told him about Michael and the abortion and then her marriage to Richard.

'What an unholy mess,' Jerome said, stroking her back. 'I don't know whose fault it is, but it's certainly not yours. But if you want to dash down there, then I'll come with you.' He smiled, kissing her breast, caressing it gently. 'Are we in a hurry?'

'Oh Jerome, I'm sorry. It was seeing that picture of Stephen. I suppose. I feel that I let him down. I was in love with Edmund, not noticing Stephen was so unhappy, until he escaped from us all. Now I feel Linette needs me.' She was breathless now, her body losing its battle against his desire. 'You needn't come, but I just feel—'

He stopped her mouth with his finger. 'You suffer from too much guilt, my darling. If we're to go to Sussex, we're to go to Sussex.'

'Oh Jerome, I do love you.' She hugged him.

'Show me then, it need only hold us up a few more minutes,' he said laughing, lying back in the chair and closing his eyes.

They arrived in the lane leading to Linette's house at half past twelve.

'What if they're having a lunch party?' Jerome said. 'We might look rather foolish then. Are we just passing or what?'

'I don't know. We'll have to play it by ear.'

Jerome pulled in and stopped the car. 'Right, let's think it out. If, as you say, Richard beats her, us turning up without a plausible excuse, especially as you've just rung her, might make him angry and take it out on her later.' He frowned. 'Cecily, I really wish she'd seek some professional help. We might do more harm than good, blundering in in such an amateur way.'

'A psychiatrist would have a field day with her. My father and all his wives and his seduction of her. Her stepbrother so persecuted by his father he escapes to America. Her own mother having dozens of affairs. They suspected she took an overdose, you know, though they never proved it.'

'Enough to send any psychiatrist raving mad.' Jerome covered his face in mock despair. 'I'm amazed you're so normal.' He took her hand, said half laughing, 'You are, aren't you?'

'Probably not. But don't you see they'd jump to endless conclusions, say she was a victim, that she wished it on herself as she suffered from low self-esteem or some such nonsense. No, she can't go through that. *He* beats *her*, there's something desperately wrong with him, not her.'

'She should go to a marriage guidance agency. Relate, or whatever it's called.'

Cecily looked sharply at him. 'Have you been to them?' But before he could answer she went on, 'I certainly didn't. Agony though it was I had to accept that Edmund loved someone else. He'd rather have died than go somewhere like that anyway, having our marriage laid out and picked over by strangers. I should hate it too. I'm sure if you're not careful, those sort of people pry too deeply into your life, make you say things you'd rather were left unsaid, or didn't mean even.'

'No, I didn't go, but then my problem was fairly straightforward. Sophia likes men – she sounds a bit

271

like a female version of your father.' He laughed. 'Maybe something happened in her childhood to make her constantly look for new excitement, I don't know.' He tossed away such thoughts with a flick of his hand. 'Nor do I care. I ceased loving her years ago, and certainly don't want to live with her again. Besides, now I've got you.' He slipped his hand into her hair and smiled at her.

'But you do see why Linette wouldn't go for help, don't you, Jerome? It's a sort of pride thing too, not wanting to admit one can't cope.'

'Yes, I do.' He sounded doubtful. 'Sometimes, though, one does need help, especially over something like this.' He looked ahead as if Linette was coming up the lane towards them. 'Tell me, did she love your father? Like a lover not a parent, I mean.' He watched her intently.

Cecily was silent for a moment. 'I don't know.' Then the scene of Daniel's funeral came to her, so clear she could have been standing in that church now.

After his death Cecily hadn't been able to bear the idea of seeing Daniel's coffin. Edmund had suggested that they go to the church early before the service.

'Once you've seen it, it won't be so bad again,' he'd said.

He pushed open the door of the church and she'd crept in, not able at first to look towards the altar.

Linette was there by the coffin. She was rearranging the flowers on the lid. For a second Cecily had been tempted to ask her why she was rearranging them, when she had spent such a fortune on them. Then she saw that she was not moving them, just smoothing a petal here, a leaf there, as if everything must be perfect for the final journey. She seemed at ease even with Daniel's death, as she always had been with him in life. Cecily felt a pang of envy. Then she hadn't understood it, but now she did. The expression on Linette's face was one of such love, such grief.

Cecily got out of the car and together she and Jerome walked to Linette's house.

'It looks like no one's here,' Jerome said after ringing the doorbell.

Cecily ran round to the back. It was shut up and silent. 'Where are they?'

'Gone out to lunch, or church, I expect.'

'Oh, Jerome, I'm sorry. All this and no one's here.'

He took her in his arms and held her close. 'A nice day out in the country. We'll go and have lunch at the Black Rabbit in Arundel, just the two of us.'

'But I'm worried about Linette,' she said anxiously, her mind feeling restless with visions of Richard hurting her.

'We'll call back before we return to London if you like. But don't worry so much. Think what fools we'd look if they were perfectly happy together.' He walked back to the car, his hand protectively on her shoulder.

'I know I'm overreacting.'

'That's part of your charm.' He squeezed her shoulder.

'Look at that view.' Cecily stopped a moment.

'How wonderful to wake up to that every morning,' Jerome said standing behind her, encircling her in his arms, marvelling at the sweeping curves of the Downs under the dazzling blue sky. 'Why do we live in London when this is down the road?'

She smiled, thought sadly of another sweep of land, the moors and the sea with a ruin silhouetted against the wide Caithness sky. If only they could be there together.

How happy I feel with him, Cecily thought, leaning against Jerome, wishing there was some way she could preserve this moment. Their relationship was at the perfect pitch. When she was with him, the pain of wanting Edmund lessened. They were still slightly tremulous with insecurities, but they loved each other enough to accept the imperfections in the other. She hoped they'd never reach the stage when disappointments, real or imagined in each other, brought out the niggling criticisms. We may never again be as happy as I feel at this moment, she thought sadly, turning to him and holding him tightly, as if she'd never let him go.

Chapter Seventeen

'**A**t least Jamie looks better, more filled out.'
Cynthia pushed her sunglasses onto the top of
her head and scrutinised him. He was playing with a
ball in the pool, throwing it, diving for it, over and over
again, absorbed in a separate world of his own.
Miranda lolled on the other side of the pool, her nose
deep in one of the new and, to Cecily, disgusting-
looking horror books that targeted the teenage market.

'It's being out all the time in this lovely sun,' Cecily
said slightly defensively, wishing she still didn't feel
she had to justify herself to her mother every time she
said something about one of the children.

When they'd first arrived at Cynthia and Gerald's
villa in the south of France, Jamie had looked skinny
and pale. His eyes, ringed in shadows, were enormous
in his small face. Cynthia had been horrified and
searched in her medicine cupboard for an ancient bottle of Minidex which she insisted on ladling into his
mouth at every opportunity. Even when it was finished,
helped by Miranda pouring some of it down the loo for

him, she went and bought some phials of 'beef's blood' from the pharmacy and forced those down him.

Jamie protested loudly. 'Gross! Blood! I'll get AIDS.'

'Cows don't get AIDS, but you might get mad cow disease,' Miranda teased, pulling a terrible face and acting as if she was mad.

'Don't be silly. It's not blood as such. It's treated, enriched with vitamins.' Cecily sided with her mother over this. For the first couple of weeks of the holidays Jamie had been so withdrawn and listless that, sick with worry, she'd rung Edmund.

'He'll be fine, he's just tired. They work them awfully hard as Common Entrance gets nearer,' Edmund said. But he too had sounded tired, distant, as if he was pulling each word out of a fog. Cecily then found herself worrying about him. Do stop it, she scolded herself impatiently. Just let him go.

She'd so hoped that loving Jerome would cure her love for Edmund but she found she couldn't transfer her feelings like a piece of clothing, pulling off one, putting on the other. Lying with Jerome in the delicious melancholy after love-making, she felt he was the one she loved. But every time she saw Edmund her blood quickened, her heart and body ached for him. She felt confused, miserable about it. When she was with Jerome she felt she was cheating Edmund. When she was with Edmund she felt she was cheating Jerome. It was a relief to be here, away from everything, even though Cynthia could be difficult.

'It's sad it's happened to you too,' Cynthia said. 'The

divorce I mean, though it seems depressingly common these days.'

'It doesn't make it any easier.'

'I know, dear. I was very fond of Edmund. Never thought he'd go. Not like your father.' She gave Cecily a martyred smile. 'Daniel was like a child, always wanting what he didn't have. Once he owned one woman, he turned his interest to someone else. If he hadn't killed himself driving like a maniac, he'd probably be on his sixth or seventh wife by now. Though why he wanted to marry them all, I'll never know.'

'You know Stephen got in touch again?' Cecily wished her mother wouldn't always go on so about Daniel. She'd been happily married to Gerald these last forty-two years, yet whenever she saw Cecily, she went on about Daniel. Cecily was terrified her mother would find out about him and Linette. The waves that would cause would drown them all.

'Yes, you said. Poor boy.' She always referred to Stephen as 'poor boy'. 'He's coming to London next month isn't he?'

'Yes. He sounded so different, yet the same. He's longing to see us again.'

'Why didn't he get in touch before? After all, you said he comes to London sometimes,' Cynthia said. 'Now Daniel's dead, he can't get at him any more.'

'I expect he'll tell me when he sees me. Oh, it's too hot.' Cecily sat up and pulled up the top of her bathing suit. 'I must swim, cool off.' She didn't want to encourage another tirade about Daniel's shortcomings. 'I hate to think we'll be back in London tomorrow. How lucky you are to live here.' Lazily she let her gaze linger on the pink villa with its dark green shutters, standing in the middle of a lawn with its overflowing flowerbeds. Her mother had a constant struggle to keep her English garden green and fresh in the scorching sun. The watering alone took most of the evening, with its complicated tangle of hosepipes dotted with sticky plaster to stop the numerous leaks.

'You could always stay on,' Cynthia said, but both of them knew she didn't mean it. Cynthia loved the idea of seeing her daughter and grandchildren, loved to boast over the bridge tables to her cronies about them. But after they'd been with her a few days she tired of them, professing herself 'quite, quite exhausted'.

Gerald came out onto the patio. He looked quite old now with folding skin like an elephant's. He wore long, faded shorts and an old shirt. A nautical cap was set at a jaunty angle on his head.

'Damn hot, probably be a storm,' he said and came and sat down beside Cecily.

'You said you'd bowl me a few, Gerald.' Jamie jumped out of the pool, water streaming from him, and ran up to him, bobbing about, dripping everywhere.

'Did I, my boy? Damned hot.'

Jamie caught Cecily's warning eye. She'd given them both a long lecture about not being too demanding on their grandparents.

Gerald saw the look. Though past seventy-five, he hated to be thought old. 'Come on then, let's go behind the house, out of this blessed sun.'

'Don't go near the windows, Jamie,' Cynthia said. 'You know the whole of France is on holiday and we won't get a broken window mended until September.'

'I'll be careful, Grandma,' Jamie said. 'I could probably mend it myself. If anything did happen,' he added quickly in case his grandmother decided it might be more advisable for them not to practise his batting.

'But this Lloyd's business . . .' Cynthia's mind skittered from subject to subject these days. Seeing her only child and her grandchildren always made her over-anxious about the pitfalls in life. 'I wish I could help more. But since Gerald was ill last year, I feel I should keep some in reserve.'

'Ma, paying for our tickets was wonderful of you, and I'm really grateful. But you're not to go short. I'm not paying Lloyd's another penny until the courts decide if the claims are legal. I wouldn't have paid at all if they hadn't called down my bank guarantee. I had to pay that back.' She sighed, the niggling headache that she nicknamed her Lloyd's ache beginning to nudge her.

'Paying off that must have cleaned you out,' Cynthia said briskly, trying not to seem prying.

'I sold Ronald my half of the castle,' Cecily said slowly.

'Oh, darling, I wish you'd told me. You loved it up there, though God knows why. I mean, it's a beautiful part of the country, but so cold.' She shot Cecily a glance from her faded eyes. 'I'll never know why your father left you only half, or anyway half with that last woman

279

of his. Why not leave it between Stephen and you?'

'I don't know,' she said as nonchalantly as she could.

'He did it to spite that last wife of his, I suppose. The old fox. You always said she hated it up there.' Cynthia laughed sourly. 'But it's not like him to play a trick on her at your expense. What did it say in the will?'

'I never saw it.' Cecily felt uncomfortable. Before Linette had explained how Gail had blackmailed her father, she too had talked exhaustively about why he'd left half the castle to Gail. But now she didn't want to talk about it with her mother, in case she stumbled on the truth.

'Never saw it? But why?' Cynthia demanded, looking at Cecily as if she was stupid.

Cecily sighed. 'I was so upset, so shocked, I was in a sort of daze. I got quite a bit of money and half the castle . . . I may have queried it, but Ronald said—'

'Ronald. He's a dreadful man, by all accounts,' Cynthia said dismissively. 'I really think,' unconsciously she patted her thick grey hair, 'that Daniel's choice in women got worse and worse. I wouldn't be surprised if Ronald had a hand in cheating you out of it. But then he couldn't possibly have foreseen his mother's death or you being forced to sell out to Lloyd's. Did Edmund see the will?'

'Yes. He thought it was all right. But Ronald,' she sighed heavily, 'now sees himself as the laird.'

'Well, Daniel must have gone senile in his old age, especially knowing how much you hated his last wife,' Cynthia said crisply. 'But getting back to this Lloyd's business, I suppose Edmund made you join.' She glared at Cecily accusingly, as if Edmund's leaving her was surely enough, without his bankrupting her with his financial advice as well.

'It seemed a good idea at the time.'

'Has *he* lost much?'

'He won't tell me the exact amount.' Cecily got up to go for a swim.

'Well, I hope he's got enough to get Jamie through Eton. I suppose that's where he's still going?' Cynthia went on.

'I hope so.' Cecily thought it wiser not to elaborate on her fears that Jamie was not up to passing Common Entrance. Cynthia would never believe that a grandson of hers would not be welcomed with open arms by any public school they chose.

'I hope he's not pushing him like your father did Stephen. Nearly had a breakdown, that poor boy. Funny, Daniel always wanted a son and once he got one he persecuted him.'

'How do you know all this?' Cecily turned on her impatiently.

'Linette told me. When you both used to come and stay. She told me everything. I suppose she couldn't talk to her own mother, not surprising really, she was always bedding another man.' Cynthia pursed her lips in disapproval. 'Poor Stephen, no wonder he ran away as soon as he could.' She pulled her glasses down over her eyes again and lay back under the shade of the umbrella. 'How is Linette? I haven't seen her for ages.'

'She's fine,' Cecily lied. Richard's violence was another thing to keep from Cynthia. She would ring Linette at once and demand that she leave him. She would also accuse Richard of everything from impotence to lunacy. Once she had got Linette and the children safely away from him, Cecily thought, then she might tell Cynthia about it, let her loose on Richard.

She dived into the cool water, feeling sick about Linette. She and Jerome had returned after their lunch in Arundel, but the house was still empty. Cecily had rung her that night and Linette had gasped with disappointment. 'We were sailing,' she said. 'We didn't get back until after supper.' When Cecily had asked her to come and stay with her mother in France, the disappointment in Linette's voice was evident as she'd refused, saying they were staying with business friends of Richard's in Portugal. Then her voice had become louder. 'I'm just coming, Richard . . .'

'Shall I come now and see you?' Cecily said urgently.

Linette's voice changed again. 'No, of course not. I'm fine, really I am.' And she'd rung off abruptly, leaving Cecily agitated. It had taken Jerome a long time to soothe her.

As she swam, Cecily felt the tight knots of tension begin to tie themselves in her. Tomorrow they'd be back. The children would go to Edmund and Emily would soon move in with Jerome. There would probably be another cash call from Lloyd's. Maybe even a writ to demand she pay what she already owed. She lay on her back in the water and looked up at the sky which was almost white in the heat. If only she could stay here, just floating in the sun, leave her problems to fight among themselves.

There was a splash and Miranda joined her.

'Will you take me to the arcade?' she said, 'to play on the games?'

Cecily turned over. 'No, lovey, we can do all that at home. Let's just enjoy this.'

'I'm bored,' Miranda pouted. 'Can't we go to the beach?'

'It will be too crowded, we're staying here today.' She smiled at her, though she didn't feel like it. Her dreamy child who'd always been so happy just to be here or in Scotland, pottering about after her own amusements, now needed constant outside stimulus. Cecily supposed it was her age. The thought saddened her.

Scotland, she thought, seeing those wide, luminous skies with bank upon bank of clouds, and the moors coloured in soft greens and browns, smudged with patches of terracotta. She almost preferred it at this time of year before the heather took over. What was Ronald doing to the castle? What kind of people filled it now? She felt an almost physical longing to be there, a terrible sense of loss that it was no longer hers. For the first time in her memory, she'd gone through a whole year without being there.

'What is it, Mum?' Miranda said. 'Have you swallowed some water? It tastes horrid, doesn't it? Remember when I nearly drowned and swallowed so much I nearly burst?'

'You didn't nearly drown, darling,' Cecily said and

swam to the side. Miranda followed her.

'I could have done. You must have got sunstroke. Grandma said you should wear a hat.'

'It's not that. I was just thinking of Scotland, and feeling sad that we won't be going there this year.'

'Or *ever* if horrid Uncle Ronald's got it. Why won't he invite us?'

'I wouldn't want to go if he did.'

'No, nor would I. But p'raps we could go when he isn't there. Mrs Drew would let us in.'

Cecily smiled sadly and kissed her. 'I don't think we can, darling, Ronald would have us arrested for trespassing or something. Remember, it's not ours any more.'

Cecily opened her front door in answer to the hesitant ring on the bell, and there stood Stephen. They stared at each other for a long moment, both a little embarrassed, unsure how to react. Then she threw herself into his arms.

'Oh Stephen, I can't believe it. After all this time.' She stood back from him and scrutinised his face. He was the image of their father, younger, perhaps a little fairer, but the silver-green eyes with their slightly heavy lids, the wide sensual mouth over the square jaw were just like Daniel's.

'You haven't changed, Cecily.' His voice held a slight twang.

'I have. I'm fatter, greyer, more lined.' She laughed, pulled him in.

He came in through the tiny, cluttered hall into the drawing room, looking round keenly.

'These the children?' He picked up a photograph of Miranda and Jamie in jeans and sweaters against the ruined castle in Scotland. 'Ah, the castle. Do you still go there for your summer vacation?'

'No. Not this year.' She glanced away. 'You know Daddy left it to me and Gail?'

'Yeah. Mum told me.'

'I had to sell my share to Ronald.'

'Not old Slime?' There was a trace of a smile, of the child who'd giggled so over the 'code' name.

She laughed too. 'Yes.'

He frowned at her. 'How come he's got it?'

Cecily told him about Lloyd's, her voice heavy with resignation. Stephen swore under his breath. 'That's too bad. Damnable. But it's funny that Dad,' he gulped over the word, 'should leave half to Gail. She really hated it there. Was it a sick joke on his part?'

'I . . . I don't know.' She couldn't look at him. Suddenly she felt angry, shocked at Daniel's behaviour with Linette. She said quickly, 'It happened. I try not to dwell on it too much. Others have lost far more.'

'I know, I've read about it. Dozens of Americans have been caught. But Lloyd's won't let them sue in the American courts. Oh, but the castle. I loved it there,' he said wistfully. 'I often think of it even now. It was my most favourite place, those lovely summers with all of us there.' He looked again at the picture. 'Great-looking kids. Are they here?'

'No, they're with Edmund. But they come back tomorrow. They're intrigued to meet you.'

'Me too. You with children.' He laughed and dropped down beside her on the sofa. 'I'm sorry about Edmund,' he sighed. 'Your letter was wonderful. I had to read it three times to get to grips with everyone again. It was so good to hear from you, Cecily.'

'I wish we hadn't lost touch,' she said seriously, looking at him intently. 'But first, coffee? Breakfast? I could do you a fry-up, you used to love that.'

'That was before I'd heard of cholesterol. Nothing for the moment, thanks. I'm sorry,' his expression was grave, 'I know I should have kept in touch, or rather let you know where I was. I could have written to you at the castle, I knew that wherever you all were, that was the one place my letters would reach you. But now . . .' He looked at her with sympathy. 'Slime would probably tear up my letters and bin them.'

'You bet he would.'

'So where's Linette? Is she coming?' He looked round the room as if he expected to see her.

A flicker of tension passed over Cecily's face. 'No. She's in Portugal with her husband. She was dying to be here.'

'Is something wrong with her?'

Cecily sighed. 'I couldn't tell you in the letter, but she's had an awful time. Her husband beats her.'

Stephen looked appalled. 'No! She must leave him, get a divorce. What happened?'

'Oh, it's a long story. She married the wrong man.

You remember she was desperately in love with Michael and got pregnant.'

'Yeah. But the baby miscarried, didn't it? Or it was a false alarm or something. Daniel told me. I remember thinking that was lucky. Then forgetting about it.' He smiled wryly. 'I was so tied up in myself then.'

Cecily studied the mantelpiece with its row of Staffordshire houses. She said heavily, 'Daddy insisted we tell everyone that knew that it was a false alarm. But the truth was Daddy persuaded her to get rid of it. He said it would ruin her life. Michael didn't want to know, and wouldn't see her again. His wife was his boss's daughter.' Her face clenched with tension, remembering again Linette's terrible screams calling for her baby.

'I don't believe it!' Stephen's mouth tightened, cutting two furrows in his cheeks. 'And you went along with it?' He looked betrayed. 'You didn't even tell me the truth. Poor Linny, how could he do that to her?'

'He thought it was for the best. Really he did. Children are a great responsibility and at that time Lin wouldn't have been able to cope. We all thought it better forgotten,' she said hurriedly, feeling agitated at the pain she'd disturbed in him.

'It never ends,' he said in despair. 'What havoc that man brought us.'

Seeing the haunted look in Stephen's eyes, Cecily realised with a shock that the defeated, listless youth was still there inside this outwardly confident man. There was an awkward silence as if their quick burst of questions and answers had exhausted their conversation. She wanted to ask him about himself, but that look, like a wounded dog's, made her anxious not to intrude. She said quickly, 'We won't talk of Daniel.' She knew there was no way now she could tell him about Daniel's seduction of Linette. 'Tell me how you know Jerome. I love him so much. I feel so lucky to have met him. He'll be back soon from his holiday, but his daughter's moving in with him, she'll rather cramp our style, I'm afraid.' She knew she was running on, trying to fill in the silences that now loomed between them.

'I don't know him too well, but he seemed nice enough. I'm sorry about Edmund. He was good to me when I was at that awful adolescent stage.' He looked at her gravely, then said, 'You and Linette don't sound too fortunate in the marriage stakes.'

'But you were married too, weren't you?' Almost before the words were out, she knew she'd made a mistake. His face darkened, his eyes skittered round the room, he looked cornered. 'Don't talk about it if you don't want to,' she said quickly, putting her hand on his arm. 'Tell me about your job.'

He was silent a moment then said abruptly, 'It just didn't work, these things often don't.' Then with a supreme effort he smiled, looking just like Daniel about to embark on an amusing anecdote. 'At least it got me a visa, and . . .' His face darkened again, he bit his lip impulsively, his eyes pained.

Cecily felt a pang of fear for him. She searched for a word of comfort, a joke to chase away the tension, but he controlled his feelings again, threw her a wan smile. 'I got a good job in a great firm. I'm really quite rich now you know.'

'Good,' she smiled, trying to shoo away the feelings of disquiet that were worming their way into her. There was another silence. 'Is Fiona with you? Jerome said he met her?'

'Yes, she lives in New Jersey.'

'That's nice.'

He got up and began to pace the room, picking up things, putting them down again, his restlessness filling the room, adding to her agitation.

'Are you sure you're not hungry? Want some coffee?'

'No . . . thanks.' He threw her a smile and went on pacing the small room. 'I like your curtains,' he said, 'blue and yellow.'

'Thanks.' She felt awkward, wondering what she could say to him, how they could get back on a familiar footing, wishing he would sit down, relax.

He went over to the bookcase by the window and her stomach lurched. A photograph of Daniel sat in the centre of it. She should have moved it. Vainly she tried to think of a way to distract him, but he saw it, stared at it a long time, then said quietly, 'I was never the son he wanted. I didn't have the talents he had. I wasted my life trying too hard to be what I wasn't and ended up not knowing who I was. I ended up hating him for not loving me, for not accepting me for who I was.'

'Oh, Stephen, don't torture yourself!' She jumped up and went to him, putting her arm round him. 'He loved you. He may not have shown it but he did love you.'

He gave her a smile as if she was deluded. 'He only loved himself, and perhaps you. He wanted to destroy me, he saw me as a threat.'

'A threat?' She frowned up at him. 'Stephen, what do you mean?'

The closed look came over his eyes again. He attempted to laugh it off. 'Oh, nothing. But I sent the money back that came when he died. Everything I have I've earned for myself.'

'I wish you'd come back before,' she said. 'Daddy looked for you.'

'I know. He nearly found me once.'

'Why didn't you let him? Oh, Stephen, we missed you so much. We all wanted you back.'

'Thanks,' he touched her lightly, 'that means a lot. Only my mother knew where I was.'

'But she disappeared too. I got back from my honeymoon knowing you were away but expecting you back for Cambridge. Then you sent a card saying you weren't coming back. Even then I thought you would, a term or so late. But by the time we started seriously to look for you, Fiona had gone.'

'She came to America a few months after I did.' He paused and she saw the pain in his face again. Cecily kept her arm round him. He continued with difficulty, 'She came for a holiday initially. She tried so hard to appear happy, but she seemed so lost, so vulnerable, so in need of protection.' He stopped then said with a bitter laugh, 'I've always felt guilty about her unhappiness, not being able to do anything about it. She was devastated when Daniel left her. I know I was little but I knew. She would cry all night sometimes. She may even have had a breakdown. Then she threw herself into her picture restoring, but after I left she didn't even seem able to do that.'

'I should have kept up with her, but I was so busy with Edmund. Oh, why is it when you're in love, you have no time for anyone else?' Cecily said.

'You couldn't have done anything. Nor could I, I suspect. But I was selfishly bound up in myself. Anyway, she came out. She's married such a nice man.' He smiled. 'Greg has changed her life.'

'I'm so glad.'

'She told Daniel's lawyers where she was, for my sake really. She didn't want me to be cut out of his will.' He smiled. 'Always practical, my mother.'

'But they didn't tell us where you were.'

'I know, she forbade them to tell anyone. But that's how we heard about his death.'

'Still you never came back for the funeral,' she said quietly. 'We tried so hard to find you then, but it seemed as if you'd disappeared off the face of the earth.'

His face creased in pain. 'I . . . I was busy somewhere,' he said vaguely, then cried out in anguish, 'It was too late. Too late to hope he loved me then.'

'Oh Stephen.' Cecily was almost in tears.

'Let's not talk about him any more,' Stephen said with an effort to swallow his pain. 'Now I'm here I'd like to get to know your and Linette's children. Tell me all about them. And,' he grabbed her hand, his face boyish again, his eyes shining with adventure, 'tell me how we are going to rescue Linette from her brutal husband. We can't let her be terrorised by him. We must get her away.'

Chapter Eighteen

'This is Cecily Mendelson, Emily,' Jerome said, his voice formal, as if he was introducing a maiden aunt instead of his mistress. Cecily could see a slight tremor of nervousness under his smile. It did not help her feelings of insecurity. She remembered him telling her off for being nervous with him in front of her children. Now he knew what it was like.

'Hello, Emily. I've been so looking forward to meeting you.' Cecily gave her a big smile. She had, she hoped successfully, hidden most of her fears over this meeting from Jerome. They were quite irrational anyway, she'd told herself endlessly. It wasn't as if she didn't have children of her own, and didn't know how they ticked. She reminded herself how close she and Linette were. How perfect it would be if Emily and Miranda became as close. But looking at Emily now, forcing herself to smile, she felt as if Emily was ten years older than Miranda instead of barely two.

Emily was beautiful. She was tall and slender, her body perfectly proportioned, quite unlike Miranda who seemed to be all legs and arms. Her dark hair hung to her waist and she had Jerome's eyes. But as they scrutinised Cecily they were as brittle as ice, making her feel as if she was being assessed for a job, and found lacking.

'Hi,' Emily said without interest.

Cecily glanced quickly at Jerome for support. She'd expected a child, a girl with Jason Donovan or Take That posters in her room; who'd run on about *Neighbours* and *Home and Away* as if she knew the characters as intimately as friends, as Miranda did. Instead, she was confronted by a woman, a cold and calculating woman, who wasn't even fifteen.

'Have a drink before we go?' Jerome said and slipped his arm round Cecily's shoulders and guided her to a chair. 'Fetch some ice please, darling.' He smiled at Emily, who glared at Cecily as if she was some sort of weirdo to want ice, before slouching off towards the kitchen as if the exercise demanded the last shred of energy in her body.

Jerome kissed Cecily on her lips, his hand slipped into her hair, gently caressing her neck. 'I've missed you so much,' he said. 'It's so wonderful to be back with you.' He kissed her again, then leant back smiling at her. 'You look great, so brown and well. I wish I'd been with you, lying by the pool, you in a bikini.' He glanced admiringly at her, then, hearing a clatter from the kitchen, he sprang up and went over to the drinks tray, leaving Cecily feeling rejected and curiously guilty, as if Emily was his wife and not his daughter.

They lunched in a hamburger joint owned by some pop star. Emily's eyes seemed to be seeking people in the crowd, her body jerked to the pulsating music. Her whole attitude seemed to shriek, 'I'm not really with these people, but there's nowhere else to sit.'

Cecily leant over to Jerome, putting her hand over his. He turned his hand over and held hers.

'Quite a place,' she mouthed over the din.

'I feel a hundred years old,' he laughed, 'but no doubt I'll get used to this sort of thing. Maybe we can educate her into other places – when she's with us anyway.'

Cecily smiled, though she didn't feel like it. She felt the smell of the place permeating her hair and her clothes. Emily glanced at them, saw their clasped hands. Her mouth tightened.

Seeing this, Cecily shouted at her, 'What are you going to eat, Emily? Can you recommend anything?' She remembered her father flirting with his latest woman in front of her and the sick pang of jealousy and isolation that had gripped her.

'I'm not hungry. I'll have a salad,' Emily said in a bored way. Cecily felt as if she'd been slapped. She reasoned with herself that it was only their first meeting. Emily had to adjust to it, accept that the love she shared with Jerome would not minimise the love he felt for her.

Cecily squeezed Jerome's hand defiantly. She loved him, she'd rise above a petulant, teenage child. It was natural that Emily should feel confused and unhappy over the behaviour and changing partners of her parents. Cecily wondered suddenly if she had seethed with such unbridled antagonism, egged on Linette and Stephen to do the same. Perhaps that was why Gail had hated them so. But Daniel would not have stood for it. He'd have said in his firm voice that warned against disobedience: 'You'll be polite and friendly to all my friends, as I am to yours. If you can't then you can stay with your mother. I will not tolerate bad manners.' He meant it too, as she'd found out on more than one occasion. But despite his women, he'd loved her, and despite some unhappy times when he was cross with her and she had sworn he hated her, she'd known deep down he did not.

Four evenings later Jerome picked Cecily up from her house after work.

'Are you sure you don't want us to go out? You don't need to cook supper for us,' he said when he'd kissed her. He seemed a little distracted, didn't prolong his kissing as he usually did.

'I enjoy cooking. Besides,' she flashed him a smile as she got into his car, 'as you said, we must start living our lives all together. The children must accept us together.'

'It's a great pity yours aren't here too.'

'I know.' She swallowed over the emptiness she felt now they had gone back to school. One minute the house was zinging with their noisy and vital energy, the next it was dead, the very air inert. 'I really envy you having Emily living with you, going to day school. I tried to talk it over with Edmund again, but he refused to discuss it.'

She quashed her feeling of anxiety over Edmund's curt dismissal of her fears. Before he'd always listened to her, reasoned with her gently over her worries. If only, she thought for the millionth time, I could stop caring about what Edmund thinks of me, love Jerome more.

'This was on Saturday when he dropped them back?' Jerome glanced at her as they slowed down at the traffic lights.

'No, over the phone. He didn't come in on Saturday. He waited in the car until I opened the front door and then just drove off. He usually does come in, has a drink. As I told you, we felt it important to be friendly together in front of the children.' Cecily didn't add that she still felt the ache of disappointment when he'd driven away.

'Perhaps he was in a hurry.'

'Hurry's not the word. The children said he was very tired. Like an old, deaf man, Miranda said. Didn't listen to anything they said. Of course,' Cecily smiled, 'he may have put that on. Miranda's got it into her head she wants to be an actress and go to stage school.'

'I'd be deaf on that one too,' Jerome laughed as they pulled up outside his house.

Emily was sitting at the only table in the kitchen/ dining room doing homework. Books, papers and folders covered the whole surface. The television was blaring.

'Hi, Dad,' she said, ignoring Cecily.

'Turn this off,' Jerome snapped off the television, 'you can't work with that on.'

'Oh, Daaad,' Emily said, but not angrily. 'None of this has to be in tomorrow. I was only doing it while I waited for you.' She shut the folder she was working on with a slam, jumped up and kissed him, ruffling his hair with her fingers.

'You need a rinse, Dad, you're going grey.'

'Thanks, I'll think about it.' He shot an amused glance at Cecily who felt about as welcome as a stripper-gram at a funeral.

'Let me pour you a drink, Daddy,' Emily said.

'Good idea. What will you have, darling?' He turned to Cecily. 'White wine, gin?'

'Wine, please.'

'Cecily's brought our dinner, so pour her an extra large glass,' he said to Emily.

'Hope it's not mammal, I've decided not to eat mammals.' Emily poured out two glasses of wine and handed one to her father with a smile. The other she stuck out in front of Cecily as if she was a shelf to dump it on.

'You ate a mammal this morning,' Jerome said with a laugh. 'You had bacon for breakfast.'

'Well, I've decided not to eat them any more,' Emily said defiantly, and turned on the television.

'Turn it off, love,' Jerome said. 'There's nothing worth seeing.'

'You don't normally say that,' she said, her eyes

skimming sulkily over Cecily behind Jerome's back.

'I've brought lots of vegetables, you can eat those,' Cecily said, taking her basket of food into the kitchen. Miranda had been a vegetarian once. She'd decided upon it ten minutes before lunch, but the sight and smell of the roast chicken had soon put paid to that conversion. Cecily unpacked the food and pushed dishes into the oven, put the pudding in the fridge. All the time she felt awkward doing these simple tasks, feeling Emily's resentment in every move she made.

'Dad, do you understand these maths?' Emily slipped her arm through Jerome's and pulled him towards the cluttered table. 'I hate them, I don't understand them at all.'

Jerome sat down at the table and looked at them. Emily pulled a chair up as close to him as she could get, wound her arm round his neck, and pushed her face close to his.

'I'll never get it, without your help,' she said in a little girl voice.

'Of course you will, darling.' Jerome looked pleased. 'Look, you take this figure there . . .'

Emily glanced up at Cecily, a gleam of triumph in her eyes. Cecily chopped the fresh mint with increased vigour, keeping her eyes firmly on the green juice staining her fingers. She cooked lamb chops in the mint, tiny baked potatoes, peas and carrots, followed by red fruit salad and homemade meringues. Emily refused the lamb, but ate the vegetables and the pudding as if she was starving.

'What a wonderful cook you are, darling,' Jerome said. 'Isn't she, Emily? Much better than poor Mrs Tompson.'

'Mrs Tompson only cooks breakfast, her feet hurt too much to stay on for dinner,' Emily said.

Jerome smiled at Cecily. 'Mrs Tompson's my daily. She's been marvellous since Emily's moved in. She cooks us breakfast, cleans, does the washing and the shopping and leaves us something for supper.'

'I'm going to bed,' Emily said, getting up from the table.

'Help clear the table first, darling,' Jerome said.

'Mrs Tompson will do it,' Emily said.

'Help put it in the dishwasher. We need some space to eat breakfast,' Jerome said reasonably. He had fortunately asked her to tidy away her books before dinner. Cecily knew she would not have done it for her.

'OK.' With heavy sighing, Emily flung a few plates into the machine, then stomped off upstairs.

Later, sitting close to Jerome on the sofa, Cecily said, 'I'd better go, love. I'll get a taxi.'

'Go? Of course you're not going. You're staying the night, remember?' He kissed her, pinched her nose gently. 'Have you forgotten you've brought your night things?'

Cecily hadn't forgotten. She just couldn't get into bed with Jerome with Emily here. As for making love, her body felt as tense and cold as a diehard spinster's. 'I just feel . . .' she glanced at the door as if Emily was standing there, criticising her with her icy eyes, 'I just feel that . . . that Emily needs more time to get used to me. No, listen.' She put her fingers over his mouth as he opened it to speak. 'I understand how confused she feels. Remember, I went through it dozens of times with my father. Also, girls of her age are a bit . . .' she was about to say bitchy, spiteful, but she said lamely, 'difficult. You know how one never imagined one's parents made love more times than the amount of children they had, and certainly not with anyone else.' She forced a laugh. 'I just feel Emily needs more time before I spend the night here with you.'

'Darling, we decided that we would live our lives openly. I love you, I want you in my bed. If I had a different woman in my bed every night I'd understand how she'd be confused, but we love each other, we want to stay together. She must accept that.'

'I know, but not now, not tonight. I don't feel the time is right, Jerome. Believe me,' she said a little wildly, knowing he wouldn't agree with her.

'No, Cecily, you're wrong. If we behave as if what we are doing is wrong or shameful then she, and your children, will think it is. We love each other, want to be together, don't we?'

'Of course, but—'

'There are no buts. I can't leave Emily here alone all night, and I'm certainly not getting out of your warm bed at two in the morning to get back here. So for the moment you come here. When your children are back from school and Emily is either with her mother or

friends, I'll come to you. They'll soon accept it. After all,
Emily accepts it with her mother, and no doubt your
children accept it with Edmund and . . . what's her
name?' He frowned.

'Rowena.'

'Rowena. So,' Jerome kissed her impatiently, 'stop
behaving like a disgusted from Brighton, and relax.'

'What about . . . Mrs Tompson and her bad feet?'
Cecily tried desperately to joke. She could feel his
desire for her, knew he would not be fobbed off with any
more excuses.

'Why on earth should it affect Mrs Tompson?' He
kissed her again, this time more urgently, his hands
caressing her breasts, then running down her back to
her thighs.

'Bedtime,' he said huskily.

Her body felt cold, stiff, rejecting his advances as if
he was a stranger and she had not become impassioned
by his body, had never become aroused when his lips
and hands touched her.

'Come on, Emily will be asleep by now. It will be fine
in the morning, you'll see.' He pulled her up. 'Hurry,
darling. I can't wait for you.'

Cecily hid her face, devoid of desire, in his shoulder.
She felt his body hard against her and longed for the
answering leap in her own. She felt nothing. It was as if
she'd been asked to perform this most intimate of acts
in public.

Jerome led her upstairs, carrying her case in one
hand, his other arm round her waist.

'You must leave some clothes here, stupid to bring things each time,' he said.

'I will.' Her mouth felt stiff.

His room with its ensuite bathroom was on the first floor. Emily's room was on the upper floor. He opened the door to his room and clicked on the light. Emily lay across his bed, fast asleep.

Chapter Nineteen

'I cannot absolutely assure you that there'll be no more losses in future years, Mrs . . . er . . . Mendelson, or that any settlement would cap them,' the dapperly dressed man opposite her said smoothly, as if he was advertising a soothing bedtime drink, instead of discussing her complete ruin.

'I will not pay,' she said, looking at him coldly. 'Don't you see,' she leant forward a little as if she was talking to someone who had difficulty in grasping the truth, 'I cannot pay these enormous amounts that you keep asking for, even if I wanted to. Even selling everything I have, destituting my children, even if I worked night and day, I have no way of finding this sort of money.'

'Mrs Mendelson,' his easy smile was somewhat marred by a slight tic in his cheek, 'Lloyd's will not abandon its Names. There is the Hardship Committee. Shall I make an appointment for you?'

'No, thank you,' she said, as polite as he. 'I shall be going bankrupt, then in three years' time I shall be free of Lloyd's. If I join the Hardship they'll have a hold over me for life, even after my death. They'll take my house from my children.' Despite her bravado, she felt sick inside, quivering like a mouse before a stoat. 'Even if I sell everything I have, I won't be able to pay,' she repeated quietly. 'And the demands will keep on coming, won't they?' She felt hollow. She had never minded much about money, though it was true she had never ever been exactly starving. But now, on paper anyway, she possessed nothing, less than nothing, for she still owed Lloyd's a fortune, and with interest and further cash calls, it was rising daily.

Still he smiled, as if he was dealing with a poor deluded fool who didn't understand what she was saying. 'You knew there was a possibility of losses. We've had a horrendous time.' He laid out his thin fingers. 'Hurricane Hugo, Piper Alpha, San Francisco earthquake.' He ticked them off one by one.

His patronising manner, as if he was explaining it to a child of four, infuriated her. She held up her hand. 'I'm not a total idiot, you know,' she said icily. 'What about the LMX spiral, asbestosis. Offshore accounts?'

For a split second alarm showed in his eyes, as if he had misjudged her and there was more to her than just a floundering female. 'I think you're being—'

'Unkind? Unfair? Really. And what do you think all that's happened has been to the Names Lloyd's is meant to represent?' She glared at him.

He looked miserable and a lock of hair fell over his forehead, giving him a boyish, vulnerable look.

'I wish . . .' He clasped his hands and leant forward. 'I wish I *could* do something, Mrs Mendelson, but I can only suggest you write to the Hardship Committee. For a moment, your losses . . .' He hesitated, looking fearful as if the word 'losses' was the pin of a grenade, held in her hand.

'I'm not paying them. The little money I have left has gone to join the action groups. I may have to get legal aid to continue the fight, but I'm going to court before I pay you. I can't afford the stamp to write to the Committee, and I feel doing so would be a waste of time anyway.' She got up from her chair and swept out. She hated him, hated them all with their smooth hair and their smooth tongues.

'L-Let me show you out,' he said, running after her and reaching the outer door of the office only just ahead of her.

'Thank you.' She fought to keep her dignity, longing to throw something through those massive plate-glass windows, feel the crash vibrating through the whole building, the glass shattering out into the autumn sunlight to the pavement below.

Thinking of it, almost hearing the smash, made her smile. She turned as they waited for the lift, her eyes shining. 'Imagine throwing something heavy through that window.' She gestured towards it.

He looked horrified, turned to see if anyone else was coming, had overheard. 'I . . . I expect the glass is toughened,' he said lamely.

She smiled at him sadly. 'You're afraid of emotion,

like most public school men. You must have seen a lot of
it recently.'

'Yes, well . . . Ah, here's the lift.' He held the door for
her. 'Goodbye, Mrs Mendelson. Please come back if
there is anything . . .'

She half entered the lift; there were two other people
in it.

'There's no point in my coming back. I was brought
up not to owe anyone any money, but I cannot pay these
outrageous claims.' She stepped in and let the door
shut out his embarrassed face.

The man and the woman in the lift exchanged
glances and moved fractionally further away from her,
as if she had committed an indecency.

Cecily walked out into the street away from the
gleaming, inside-out building. It was a bright autumn
day, the sky blue above the narrow streets flanked by
other tall office blocks. It made her feel enclosed, like
an ant in a box. She thought fleetingly of the wide open
skies of Scotland.

'Cecily, wait.' She turned and with sinking heart saw
Felix Mayle lurching towards her. His normally red
face was pale and puckered like a cheese. He looked
drunk.

'You haven't been in there, have you?' He waved his
podgy arm vaguely in the direction of the Lloyd's
building.

'Yes, I have. Not that it did me much good.'

'Good? Who cares about goodness any more, my darling?' He leered at her, smacked his lips. 'You look good

though. Very good.' He lurched closer to her, took her arm. 'Any hope of lunch together?'

'Sorry, Felix.' She tried to move away, shocked and distressed by his appearance. His suit was stained and his tie sloppily fastened. 'I'm having lunch with someone already. But how are things?'

'Bloody. You've heard Serena's left me?'

'No! Oh Felix.' His statement hit her in the pit of her stomach, reminding her of her own pain at Edmund's desertion. She touched his arm with sympathy. 'For someone else or . . .'

'I've lost my money, dear. Apparently that's all she loved about me,' he said heavily, putting his hand over hers. It was moist and hot; she steeled herself not to pull hers away.

'That's not true. Serena wasn't like that,' she burst out, then seeing his face and guessing at the truth she said lamely, 'Of course one doesn't really know everyone's secret fears, but it can't have been just the money.' She managed to extricate her hand.

'She said I'd changed. *Me?* Well, of course I've changed, who wouldn't, having to tackle that lot.' He waved his hand again towards the Lloyd's building. 'She said there was no one she could talk to about it, people were clamming up on her, keeping out of her way as though she'd suffered a bereavement or some dreadful disease.'

'I am so sorry, Felix.' Cecily didn't know what else to say. Had these shattering losses changed her? Or Edmund? At least they hadn't taken to the bottle, couldn't afford to. 'Maybe she'll come back when things get better,' she suggested uncertainly.

'She said she got bored of me going on about it all the time. She wanted someone to listen to her thoughts on it. But what else is there to talk about?' he said miserably. 'I'll get straight, you'll see.' His watery eyes stared defiantly at her. 'Don't you give in,' he said, leaning close to her. 'Don't pay another penny.'

'I won't.'

'Maybe . . .' He looked at her a moment. 'Cecily, maybe you could talk to Serena, or rather let her talk to you. I mean, you've been through it, know what it's about. She says she wants to talk to someone other than a damn psychoanalyst who goes on about self-esteem and childhood terrors. Will you help her?'

Cecily felt an enormous wave of sympathy for him. Bluff, over the top, Felix had been devastated more by his losses than she'd realised. Under his armour of bravado was a weak, terrified man. She could see it now in his eyes, in the way his body slumped dejectedly beside her. But what could she do? If Serena had had enough of him, the marriage, how could she persuade her to go back?

'I . . . I'll talk to her, or listen to what she feels, if that would help her understand Lloyd's, but you know, Felix . . .' She paused, thinking if she couldn't get her Edmund back, how could she help with Serena?

'I know, my dear,' he patted her shoulder. 'Your Edmund's gone, fool that he is, and now Serena. You know, we should make a go of it. You and I.' He swayed on his feet.

'I . . . I have a . . . new person in my life.'

'Then you are luckier than me, darling.' He gave her a sad smile and lumbered off. 'Ring her, there's a dear.'

'Ring her.' Felix's voice, once so confident, now pleading with her, echoed in her mind. She wondered how many other women needed to talk to others in the same boat.

'You seem very thoughtful, darling. Anything bothering you?' Jerome said over lunch.

'Sort of. I met a friend and . . .' As she told him, she felt he was not altogether interested.

When she'd finished he said, 'You'd be very good at getting together a group, darling. Just ring one person and you'll probably find a dozen.' He smiled. He seemed preoccupied too. She was about to say something when he spoke again.

'Cecily . . .' he chewed on his lower lip, took her hand and said earnestly, 'I wanted us to lunch as I have something special I want to ask you.'

'Yes?' Her mind was working out how to go about organising a group. She felt a little intimidated by the deluge of emotion she might uncover. But since her fruitless meeting with her agent, and seeing poor, abandoned Felix, she felt she wanted to do something, not just wallow in her own fears and panic. Her thoughts were not entirely selfless, she knew it would help her too, just as it would hopefully help others.

'I . . .' Jerome turned over her hand, moved a little

closer to her. She could feel the warmth of his breath on her cheek. 'Will you marry me, Cecily?' he said in a rush, then seeing her astonished gaze rushed on, 'I love you, we are so happy together. Please let's get married, stop this toing and froing to each other's houses.' He looked so eager, so in love with her, she smiled, leant her head against his, overwhelmed by his feelings, his request. But deep inside herself she knew with sickening pain she could not marry him.

'I . . . Oh, darling, you've taken me quite by surprise.' She pushed the hair off her face, took a deep breath. 'I don't know what to say. I . . .' She looked frantically at the tablecloth as if the answer might be written there.

'Just "yes" will do.'

'I would but . . . not yet,' she said firmly. She couldn't say it's because of Emily, I can't take her on. Instead, she gave him the other reason, one just as important to her. 'I've lost everything in Lloyd's, as you know. I can barely tick over now, and sooner or later they'll come and get the rest. Even if we do win in the courts, it will take for ever. I can't be dependent on you.'

'But, darling—'

'No, Jerome, let me finish. I can't let you pay for me and my children – which probably will happen.' She bit her lip. 'I don't know how much Edmund has lost, but I suspect much more than I have, as he was writing much more. He may earn a good salary, but eventually he, too, may have to pay up. I cannot, will not, expect any man to take me – us – on in these circumstances. I'd be a millstone round your neck, and I don't want anything to ruin our love.' She kissed him. 'Let's stay as we are.'

'Darling, the money's not an issue. I love you, want us to be together.' His eyes were troubled, his mouth turned down in disappointment.

'I want us to stay together, that's why I think marriage is not a good idea – at the moment anyway,' she added, unable to bear the disappointment in his eyes.

He looked down at her hands. 'It's . . . not Emily, is it?'

'No,' she said too fast, then gulped. 'Well, I have to admit I find her difficult, and I know she doesn't like me.'

'She does.' He looked aggrieved.

'Well, not enough. If it was just you and me, Jerome, but the children . . .'

'I even got you a ring,' he said with a sad smile.

'Oh, darling,' She felt dreadful now. Angry with herself for having hurt him, angry with him for putting her in this position with no warning.

Jerome put his hand in his pocket and took out a small blue box and opened it.

'Will you wear it anyway? I brought it especially for you.' He held it out to her.

'Oh, Jerome, I . . . don't know what to say.' Through the blur of the sudden tears, she saw the dark flash of a sapphire with two oblong diamonds either side of it.

'Wear it, for me, for what our love means.' His voice was gentle, tremulous with a hint of sadness. He took her left hand and there shone Edmund's ring, a round diamond surrounded by sapphires.

They both stared at it as if the fire from the stone had mesmerised them. Cecily didn't know what to do. A moment ago she would have taken Jerome's ring, worn it with love and pride because she loved him. But now she realised he meant her to wear it instead of Edmund's, and that she could not do.

'I'll take it back to the jewellers,' he said, his mouth clenched. He put it back in the box and shoved it quickly into his pocket as if it was a shameful thing. 'I'm sorry, I didn't think . . . I should have talked about it with you first.' He took a frantic gulp of his wine, forced a smile.

Cecily put her arms round his neck and cried, the tears hot on her face. She cried for him, for her, for Edmund leaving her, for Felix and the anguish Lloyd's had caused so many lives.

'Hush, darling, it's all right.' He held her close, stroking her back with gentle fingers. 'Forget it, darling. Now, what about this evening?'

'I'll never forget this, never,' she said, blowing her nose. 'God, I must look awful. I'll be back in a minute.' She got up and walked to the loo, defiantly holding herself tall, aware people were looking at her tear-stained face.

This evening, she thought hysterically as she tried to cover the ravages of slug-like eyelids and blotchy cheeks. What excuse could she give this time to get out of being with Emily? The girl had not made lots of friends at school as her father had hoped, nor did she ever want to go and visit her mother at the weekends.

'I must stay and look after you, Dad,' she'd said when Jerome had suggested it once, her eyes challenging Cecily.

Jerome, not seeing this look, or indeed any of the others that flew like poisoned darts behind his back, had obviously been touched by her devotion. Cecily burned to tell him the truth of his daughter's deviousness. Emily did not want her, was doing everything in her power to send her away, but Jerome did not see this. Delighted at having his beloved child with him, pleased that at least her school work had improved, he became bewildered and angry when Cecily tried to talk about it.

'It's been hard for her. I don't expect her mother had much time for her, it's made her resentful of adults. Of course she likes you, you're just imagining things, my darling. You must bring your children round, let them all make friends, then she'll be better,' he'd said impatiently, not wanting to waste their time together with such problems, or admit there might be one.

Her children had still not met Emily. It had been difficult them being away at school, and Cecily was afraid that if Emily hurt her children her own dislike of her would break through the façade of calm friendliness she'd struggled to cultivate. Once broken, it would finish her relationship with Jerome.

'So you'll come round tonight?' Jerome said when she came back from the Ladies.

'I've got to work late. You know the shop's being

redecorated for Christmas. We've got to stack up the shelves ready to open tomorrow. We may be there half the night. Daphne likes everything to look as if it's been laid out for a cover shot for one of the best magazines.' Cecily tried to make a joke of it; knowing she'd be exhausted, confronting Emily would be the last straw.

'But you must come. I'll pick you up.'

'Tomorrow. Why don't you come over for supper tomorrow, or we could go to the cinema?'

'I can't leave—'

'Can't Susan come in?' Susan was 'somebody's secretary' who often stayed over when Jerome went away on business.

'Why can't you come over, Cecily?' His eyes challenged her.

'Jerome . . .' She felt so tired suddenly. 'I can't cope with Emily just now. It's probably my fault. I have so much to worry me at the moment.'

'But, darling . . .' There was an edge of impatience to his voice now.

'Look how she sleeps on your bed whenever I'm there. Or telephones us all night if you're with me and she's with a friend.'

'It's just insecurity, she'll grow out of it.'

'Maybe, but until then I think it better for me not to come round so often when she's there.' She said it quickly as if the words would escape and hide themselves under stones of cowardice in her mind.

He rang her the next day, his voice distant. 'Cecily,

I've got to go to New York tonight, I may be away a week.'

'Shall I take you to the airport?'

'I've got a car coming. I'm flying out with someone else. I love you, Cecily. I'll ring you from New York.'

She could feel his mind leaving her. 'I love you, too. 'Bye, darling, take care.' The phone went dead, and she heard herself saying, 'Come back to me.'

Chapter Twenty

'I don't mind about the money – well, of course I do, dreadfully, but I wouldn't leave him just because of it,' Serena Mayle said, pulling on her cigarette nervously, her foot insistently wiggling up and down.

'I can't leave my husband, he's . . . he's so diminished now,' a middle-aged woman dressed in a faded but once expensive suit, burst out. Then, looking surprised at her own remark, went on, 'He's changed. The old Max without money would have survived but the new one . . .' Her voice petered away.

'We've had to sell our house and most of the furniture. It's been in Michael's family for four hundred years,' a thin, horse-faced woman said painfully, as if each word hurt as she uttered it. 'He feels as if it's his fault, as if he's let the family name down. But he hasn't. However much I tell him it isn't his fault, he won't believe me.'

Cecily sat in her drawing room and listened. The day after Jerome had left, she'd rung Serena. She'd done so driven by the impetus of her idea, and in the hope that

319

it might help the anguish she felt at his leaving like that. If only he hadn't had to leave so suddenly, before she'd had time to make things up to him, to tell him, show him, how she loved him. For she did, surely she did. It was just she couldn't wear his ring instead of Edmund's. Couldn't cope with Emily.

Serena had jumped at her idea of a help line. She'd heard of another woman, Fiona, the horsy-faced one who'd had to sell their stately home. She knew of Barbara who'd admitted Max was difficult to live with. Two others hadn't been able to come, but wanted to another time. Sitting back and watching them, Cecily saw how much good this meeting had done them. At first they'd been awkward and shy, now everyone was explaining how they felt, agreeing, sympathising with each other. There'd even been some laughter. Their own pain and terror was helped by supporting someone else in the same situation. It was as if she had released a dam. At eight thirty to Cecily's relief, they left. She had been growing edgy as time ticked on, she was expecting Stephen and he wouldn't want to sit through all this.

'I can't thank you enough for organising this,' Barbara said, kissing her warmly. 'It hasn't paid our debt, but it's made me feel a hell of a lot better just being able to talk about it with people who really understand.'

'I'm sorry it had to be the evening, but I can't take time off in the day,' Cecily said.

'Of course you can't. I must get a job of sorts too,

though goodness knows who'd pay me to work for them,' Fiona said. 'But your idea of starting this has sparked us off. One of us could have a meeting in the day so that people from the country could come.'

'We could meet at my house, next week, for coffee,' Serena said. 'I've heard of a course for,' she giggled, 'older ladies like us to retrain for a job.'

'Retrain?' Barbara laughed. 'I'll have to start from scratch. I've never done anything paid in my life. Still,' she smiled bravely, 'meeting all of you has inspired me. I could perhaps take in paying guests. I like cooking.'

'There you are,' said Cecily. 'It's an idea.'

'Can . . . can we perhaps swap telephone numbers?' Fiona asked awkwardly. 'Ring each other if we feel down?' She looked ashamed, as if it was a weakness to admit to feeling down.

'Of course, what a good idea,' Serena said, taking some address stickers from her bag and passing them round.

'Thank you, Cecily.' Serena kissed her, staying behind a moment when the others had gone. 'It's been a great help, seeing how the others have suffered and are coping but,' she looked sad, 'I don't know if I can live with Felix on the bottle.'

'Isn't he drinking because you've left him?'

'He started before.' She sighed. 'He was great friends with his agent, rather impressed by him. Thought the sun shone out of his whatsit. Now his trust has been destroyed. He's fighting back – oh, fine words,' she grimaced, 'but words don't pay bills. He's drinking away what little money we have. We'll probably have to take the children away from school. My meagre earnings won't stretch to their fees. He might even lose his job if he carries on as he is.'

Cecily hugged her. 'Oh, Serena, what a mess. I don't know what to do to help. We've all got to rethink our lives.'

'No doubt some people will think that a good thing.' Serena gave her a sour smile. 'The sort of people who think the Queen should move to a flat and Buck House be used for the homeless. But you helped with this evening. It was a brilliant idea of yours. We shouldn't hide away with our problems. I'll organise a coffee morning next week, and maybe one of the others will give one another day.' She smiled. 'See how it will snowball.'

Despite the cold pain of Jerome having left for New York before she could resolve things, Cecily felt a warmth, a sliver of pleasure. Out of this mess she'd achieved something. It might be only tiny, but it was something.

The bell rang. Serena started. 'Oh, someone at the door. Perhaps another distressed Name.'

'It's my brother,' Cecily said, opening the door to see Stephen standing beside his suitcase on the step.

'Hi,' Stephen greeted her with a hug.

'Come in. This is Serena Mayle.' As he shook hands, Cecily saw a sparkle rise in Serena, saw her straighten, smile, a flush on her cheeks, a glow to her eyes. She felt amused, seeing Daniel, remembering the effect he had on women, the soft tone of his voice, the way he looked directly into their eyes as if he knew the secret of their souls. Stephen was exactly the same.

'I won't keep you, Serena. Take care,' she said as they jiggled round each other in the narrow hall.

'Oh, I'm in no rush . . . but, yes. OK, thanks, Cecily.' Smiling, keeping her eyes on Stephen, she left in a fluster.

'Flirt,' Cecily laughed at him.

'Nonsense. She's not my type at all,' Stephen said.

Cecily refrained from telling him how he reminded her of their father, in case it upset him. She shivered as if Daniel had walked past them. Stephen was so like him, not just his looks, but his mannerisms as well. Seeing him flirt, almost automatically, with Serena, he could have been Daniel.

'So where's Lin?' Stephen said, looking round the room as if he expected to see her.

'She's coming tomorrow. Let's ring her. I meant to today but, well, I'll tell you about it later but I had to get these women round.'

'Sounds fascinating. Any more here?'

'Bad luck, no.' She picked up the phone and dialled Linette's number.

'It's me, Lin. Stephen's here. What time are you coming tomorrow?' she asked cheerfully.

There was a long silence before Linette answered in a strained voice, 'I . . . I can't come.'

'What, Lin? Did you say you can't come?' Cecily's voice was sharp with disappointment. Stephen was frowning opposite her. He sprang up and took the receiver from her hand.

'Linny, you've got to come. I'm here, I want to see you.'

Cecily watched his face. It was eager, the small boy who wouldn't take no for an answer, then it clouded over.

'You've got to come, Linny, we're expecting you.' He paused, listened to something she said. 'That's no excuse. Look, I'll come and see you. No, of course I can.' He paused again. 'Why can't I come? I thought you wanted to see me.' His voice was harder now, edged with disappointment.

Cecily put her ear to the receiver, but hearing nothing went to the kitchen and picked up the extension.

'I just can't come. I really can't, not this time. I . . . I'll ring you . . . I'll . . .' Linette sounded agitated, her voice breathless.

'Don't worry about it, Lin,' Cecily broke in, feeling sick with fear. Was she having a complete breakdown? 'We'll talk about it later.' She imagined Richard breathing down her neck, his eyes and the cruel set of his mouth forbidding her to call for help.

'Are you OK? You don't sound it,' Stephen broke in.

'Of course. I . . . I just . . .' Linette's voice was like a moan.

'I want to see you. I won't leave England until I do, Linny,' Stephen said.

There was a long pause, then the receiver was put down at Linette's end. Cecily and Stephen were left listening to each other's breathing.

'Where does she live?' Stephen marched into the kitchen.

'Sussex.'

'Take me there tomorrow. I want to know what's going on.'

Cecily nodded. 'We'll have to do something about her,' she said decisively. Still high on her success of organising her Lloyd's help group, she suddenly felt that wondering what to do about Linette had gone on long enough.

'We'll just see her, talk it through,' Stephen said, his tone like Daniel when he didn't want to be embroiled in an emotional mess.

'We'll take her and the children away from Richard,' Cecily said firmly. 'In fact,' the thought suddenly hit her, 'you could take them with you to America – just for a holiday,' she added quickly seeing the hesitation in his eyes. 'Give her time to think things through away from Richard. Decide what to do.'

'Well, I dunno . . .' It was Daniel. Daniel not wanting to face an emotional outburst with one of his ex-wives or girl friends, Daniel who was generous with his money but not with his time and compassion if he thought there'd be a scene.

Cecily felt a hardness in her. After this evening's tragic revelations of these women's shattered lives she was not going to let Linette become a victim too. 'Yes, you take her with you, Stephen, please. Once she's away from the situation her old strength and spirit will come back but,' she frowned, looked at him awkwardly, 'I . . . I don't know how to pay for the tickets . . .'

'I'll do that, but do you really think—'

'Yes. Do it, please.' She squeezed his arm, saw in his eyes his reluctant acceptance.

'Are you very badly off with this Lloyd's thing?' Stephen said later as they sat together in the small restaurant crowded with scrubbed pine tables and chairs.

'Yes, I am.' She grinned awkwardly. 'I've cut down everywhere I can. I'm afraid to spend anything in case I need something in an emergency, for the children or anything. I took in a lodger,' She laughed, told him about Herr Brehme.

Stephen looked increasingly horrified. 'Let me help you, Cecily. Please. I'd like to. I can easily help, or at least pay for some training so you could get a better job.'

'No thanks, Stephen. I don't want to owe anyone else anything.' She touched his hand. 'I shall manage somehow.'

'You've got the money Daniel left me, haven't you? It was about a hundred thousand pounds. Or has that gone to Lloyd's too?'

'The money he left you? That's yours, you should have it,' she said firmly.

He looked at her intently. 'You did get it, didn't you? I sent it back for you, to the solicitor, via Ronald. I mean, he was dealing with the estate, wasn't he? He sent me a short note with it, enclosing his address.'

Cecily suddenly felt cold. 'Let me get this right, you sent *me* the money that Daddy left for you?'

'Yes. I sent it straight back that same day, with instructions it was to go to you.' He gave her a quizzical look. 'You don't mean . . . you don't think Ronald kept it, do you?'

'This is the first I've heard of it. Oh, Stephen.' She held his hand. 'I dislike him so much I'd believe anything bad about him.'

'I didn't want money, I wanted the castle.' Stephen's mouth went hard, his eyes filled with angry pain. 'Or anyway half of it with you.'

Cecily knew suddenly that she had to tell him now about Daniel and Linette. She looked round the restaurant hurriedly, wondering if it was private enough or if she should wait until they were home again.

'What happened, Cecily?' Stephen went on. 'Did you see the will?'

'I was too upset. Oh, Stephen, it was shattering, his death.' She shivered, remembering the grim-faced young policeman coming to the door. The agony of trying to believe it.

'Did . . .' He looked away, said heavily, 'You didn't have to see him, identify him, did you?'

'No, Edmund wouldn't let me. He and Ronald did that.' The tears came in her throat. When she swallowed she felt she had a stone in her windpipe. 'Afterwards I wished I had seen him, just to say goodbye. Sometimes . . . I know it's mad, but because I didn't see his body, I wonder if he's dead at all.'

Stephen took her hand. 'I thought when I finally heard of his death through my mother that I'd . . . I'd feel free of him. But I didn't. I can't believe he's gone. That's one of the reasons I found it hard to come back. Even now,' he smiled bitterly, 'I wouldn't be at all surprised if he came in here, demanded to know why I wasn't in some team or other.'

'He was too big in our lives, wasn't he? Yet I loved him so, miss him still. But I hate him for what he did to you. You must know that,' she said, sniffing, blowing her nose. 'God, I hate crying in public, my nose goes red.' She took a large gulp of wine.

'But to get back to his will, presumably Edmund saw it.'

'Yes.'

'When was it dated?'

'About ten years before his death, I think.'

Stephen poured out some more wine. 'Could there have been another will, a later one?'

'There could have been. But Stephen,' she took a deep breath, 'I must tell you something. I don't know how you'll take it but—'

'He didn't want me to have it?' His voice was full of angry pain.

'No. Nothing like that.'

'What then? Come on, Cecily, tell me.'

'Gail was blackmailing him.'

'Blackmailing him? Over what?' He looked incredulous.

She was silent a moment, dreading telling him. 'I—'

The waitress, a jolly girl with red hair, breezed up. 'Everything all right? More drinks?'

'Everything's fine, thank you.' Cecily turned back to Stephen. 'I'd rather tell you at home.'

He leant across the table. 'Tell me now.'

She waited a moment, then said, 'You must try to think of Daniel as a man, not as our father for a moment, will you?'

He looked puzzled. 'If you want. Now what happened?'

She dropped her voice so he had to crane forward to hear her words. 'You know how lovely Linette was?'

'Yes.'

'Well, he . . . he wasn't her father of course and he . . .'

Stephen went white. 'Don't tell me he went after Linny?'

'Not how you think. He loved her, not as a dirty old man but—'

'Oh Cecily!' he said so loudly the other diners turned round to stare at them.

'Let's go home,' she pleaded.

'Not until I've got to the bottom of this. You mean he went to bed with her?' His face was thunderous, his mouth clenched with trying to keep his voice down. 'He seduced a girl he'd brought up as his own daughter?'

'It wasn't quite like that.'

'How was it then? Cecily, what sort of a man was he? Seducing every woman – correction, every beautiful woman – he saw. Ruining our childhood, breaking women's hearts and lives, including my mother's and no doubt yours. Then going after his stepdaughter. No wonder she ended up with a man who beats her.' He looked distraught.

Cecily said nothing. Put like that it sounded ugly and brutal. Was it true? 'Linette doesn't see it like that,' she said at last. 'She just feels he spoilt her for any other man, he was so loving, so special.'

Stephen drained his wine glass and poured out some more. 'I think it stinks,' he said. 'And Gail found out and blackmailed him. When did you know this?' he demanded.

'Only a few months ago. Linette told me after I'd seen the bruises Richard put on her.'

'And you never suspected before?'

'No. It happened when I was sent to Paris. And finished, I think, after her abortion, certainly when she married Richard. But that is why Daddy married Gail and left her so much.'

'That abortion! Whose baby was it?' he said savagely. 'Was it our brother or sister?'

'No. Oh, Stephen, don't work yourself up so.' She took his hand. 'She had Michael then, remember. It was his,' she said desperately, determined that the child was not Daniel's. She, too, had wondered if it could be, but she couldn't bear the thought.

'He ruined our lives in so many ways,' Stephen said slowly. 'My God, what damage he did. It goes on for ever.'

'I don't think he was as bad as you think. He did love us, I know he did,' she said gently.

Stephen's mouth clenched and his eyes went dark with jealous pain. 'He always loved his women more than his children – more than me anyway, and because of his lust we've lost everything.'

Cecily sat in silence. She felt so weak knowing it was true and yet not wanting to accept that Daniel had betrayed them so utterly.

Stephen shrugged. 'I wish I knew what made him tick, why he had to inflict such pain on us . . . on me, his own son.'

'I suspect he was jealous of your youth,' Cecily said listlessly. 'He hated the thought of becoming old.'

'I'm going to ring Ronald tomorrow,' Stephen said decisively. 'I'm going to ask to see the will, and ask where my money is, the money I sent to you. I'll buy back the castle, or anyway make him give back your half in exchange for the money, if he's kept it.'

'He's devious, he'll find a way round it. Or only let you have half of it. Do you want to share it with him?'

Stephen smiled with a hint of malice. 'Yes. I'd rather share it with him than let him have it altogether. I shall look into this. But,' he ground his hands together, 'God, Daniel with Linette. How many lives did he ruin?'

'Stephen,' she laid her hand over his as it picked restlessly at the bread on the table, 'try and forgive him.'

'Forgive!' he let out the word like a cry of pain. 'Oh, Cecily, you don't know the half of it.' Then he clamped his mouth shut as if he had said too much.

'Tell me,' she said gently, certain that he was hiding

something from her, a hollow feeling of fear curling inside her.

'No.' He shook his head. 'We've had enough revelations for one night.'

'If there's something you want to tell me, you must,' she insisted, seeing the haunted fear in his eyes again. 'Shall we go home?'

'No, let's have another bottle.' He smiled, clicked his fingers for the waitress.

He's afraid of us being alone, Cecily thought, watching him. It's safe here with the possibility of other people overhearing our conversation providing an excuse not to say too much.

Weary after the emotions of the day, she let it go, knowing in her heart that she was afraid to ask any more.

Chapter Twenty-One

Linette's front door was opened by a stout, red-faced woman in a flowered apron.

'Yes?' She looked enquiringly from one to the other.

'Is Mrs Symonds in? We are her . . .' Cecily decided to keep it simple, 'brother and sister,' she said, smiling cheerfully.

'She's in but she's . . . she's not well. Mr Symonds didn't say you were coming.'

'My brother has just flown over from New York to see her,' Cecily said, shooting a sharp look at Stephen to remind him he was supposed to be helping her.

'Hi. I've just arrived, and we've driven down especially to see her.' Stephen took a step into the house, smiling his attractive smile.

The woman darted back nervously, flushing slightly at his proximity. 'I . . . I . . . don't know . . .'

'We won't stay long,' Stephen grinned, automatically laying on the charm. 'Is she upstairs? Please could you tell her we're here.'

The woman looked anxious, yet also a little in awe of

Stephen. His American accent had become more pronounced, his voice warm, his smile devastating.

Cecily came into the hall too. She tensed herself for a confrontation with Richard, but as he had not appeared she hoped he had left for the office. She looked quickly around her. The door to the drawing room was open, a Hoover stood in the middle of the carpet, a tin of furniture polish draped over with a duster stood on a table.

'I see you're busy.' She smiled towards the Hoover. 'I'm sorry we've disturbed you. Is she in her room? I'll pop up and tell her we're here.' She walked quickly to the stairs and started up them. 'Children at school?' she called down nonchalantly. 'Their father at the office?'

'Yes. The girls get back about four. I give them tea, wait until Mr Symonds gets back,' the woman said, regarding them both with suspicion.

'You must be a treasure, Mrs . . .?' Stephen said in Daniel's rich voice.

The woman went pinker, looked pleased. 'Farmer. Shirley Farmer.'

'Do you work here every day, Shirley? I hope you don't mind me calling you Shirley, it's such a nice name,' Cecily heard him say as she reached Linette's bedroom door.

Linette was lying back on her pillows. Her face was chalk-white, her hair lank. She stared at Cecily as if she was a mirage.

'It's me, Lin.' Cecily fought to hide the shock she felt

at seeing Linette like this. She went up to the bed and took her hand. 'I've brought Stephen to see you.'

'Stephen?' Her eyes stared blankly at her.

Stephen came in. He stood at the end of the bed staring at Linette. He was unable to hide the distress in his face.

'You don't look good, Linny,' he said at last. 'Have you seen a doctor?'

'I'm fine, just run down.' She picked at the bed-clothes, not looking at him. She wore a pale blue night-shirt, its neck high, its sleeves long. Cecily wondered if it covered more bruises. She shuddered. Even after the abortion Linette had pulled round her a defiant ring of tragic resignation, which Cecily had found heartbreaking but had recognised the strength behind it. Now Linette seemed defeated. Cecily knew without any hesitation that they must get her away fast, give her a chance to get her health and strength back.

'I'll say you're rundown,' Stephen said, obviously shocked at this pathetic creature cringing in the bed. 'You need a holiday. Come away with me. I live in New York, I have a holiday house at Long Island. There's plenty of room. Come with me.'

His directness was so like Daniel's, who could never be bothered with scouting round a subject. 'Just put it to them,' he used to say. 'Don't spend hours pussy-footing round the issue. State what you want, what you're going to do, make them say yes or no.'

Cecily was worried about the effect Stephen's direct-ness would have on Linette. She looked anxiously from one to the other. 'Aren't you pleased to see Stephen again?' she said with more cheerfulness than she felt.

'Yes . . . yes, I am.' Linette tried to smile.

'Then come with me,' he said.

'I can't come.'

'Why not?'

'I can't, that's all,' Linette said in a quiet voice, her eyes skittering away from his face, her fingers still agitated, picking at the bedcover.

'Would you like to?' Stephen asked her.

For a split second she looked alert, eager, as if she would suddenly agree. Then she slumped back into inertia again, all energy gone. 'One day perhaps.'

But that look, that tiny spark of enthusiasm was enough to convince Cecily that if they could get Linette away, she would recover.

'We'll leave you to rest, be back in a while,' Cecily said, kissing her, tucking the bedclothes round her. She signalled to Stephen and they went downstairs. Cecily was determined to get more information out of Shirley Farmer.

This was not very fruitful. Shirley was not, as Cecily had wildly assumed, a Grace Poole character, appointed by Richard to guard a mad woman. She was just a simple, good soul who helped out.

'They had nannies, then foreign girls – you know, au pairs, but it was too quiet down here for them. They wanted discos. It's quite a way to a disco from here.' Shirley laughed derisively.

Cecily smiled, but she wondered if Richard's behaviour

had anything to do with the turnover of girls living here. She remembered him boasting jokily once about his attraction to young girls.

'She has a good doctor, I presume,' she said to Shirley.

'Dr Ridges. He's very good. I go to him myself. Don't think much of the other one. She's a woman,' she said as if that was a failing. 'But he's away this week, gone to Paris with his wife.'

'I see.' Cecily suddenly felt she couldn't bear to be in this house another moment. The whole place, done up in beautiful taste – Linette's taste – felt oppressive, like a gilded cage. She wanted to get out into the fresh air, the open sky, to think, to plan how to rescue Linette.

'We'll have a drive round. I want to show my brother the countryside,' she said suddenly, pulling Stephen up from the chair he was slumped in. 'We'll come back later.' She went back upstairs to tell Linette. Stephen followed her.

Cecily sat down on the bed. 'We know what's been happening, Lin. We're going to help you. Take you and the children away to give you space and time to think things out. You do understand, don't you, Lin?' she said earnestly into her fearful eyes. 'You do trust us, don't you?' She wondered if Linette was on some sort of tranquilliser. Or had her spirit become so broken that even escape was too much to cope with?

'I promise you, Linny, everything is going to be all right,' Stephen said valiantly. 'We're going to look after you.'

Linette's eyes darted from one to the other. 'I'm fine

really.' She attempted a smile. 'I just get so tired.'

'Sleep a while, then we'll be back,' Cecily said.

They drove through the rolling countryside, parked the car and walked up the hill to a windmill that stood above the Downs.

As they climbed, Cecily voiced her fears about Linette. Her lethargy worried her and she was beginning to have doubts about packing her off to America with Stephen. She was concerned that the commotion of the journey might trigger a complete breakdown.

'Perhaps we should stay and confront Richard, or try and get her to a doctor,' she said thoughtfully.

'She really does look bad, far worse than I thought she'd be,' Stephen said anxiously. He had been very silent on their drive here, staring out at the countryside as if mesmerised by it.

Cecily stopped walking, feeling a little out of breath. 'Stephen, does your mother really want to be landed with Linette and two children? I mean, if you think you can't cope, say now. You know we can't take them over there and just leave them.' She felt impatient with him suddenly. She was convinced they had to get Linette away from Richard before he completely tipped her over the edge. But would Stephen give her the emotional support she so badly needed? If only she could go with them. There was no way she could keep Linette in London, it would be too easy for Richard to find her, and there was no time to think of somewhere else. New York with Stephen was the only solution at such short notice.

She turned to look at him. He was staring down at

the view, tears pouring down his cheeks.

'Stephen, what is it?' Instinctively, as she would have done when he was a child, she took him in her arms.

'I . . . I just forgot how beautiful England is,' he said, wiping the tears away with the back of his hand.

'There's more to it than that, isn't there?' she said, seeing the anguish in his eyes. 'Is it Linette? It must be a dreadful shock for you seeing her like this when you only remember her as she was, so vital, so lovely.'

He did not answer her, just kept his eyes staring down the hill with its clumps of trees, opening out to the fields and tiny villages below.

'If you don't feel you can take them, we must think of something else,' she said urgently, wondering what on earth they could do instead.

'I can't help. You don't know, can't know . . .' He raked his fingers desperately through his hair. He would not look at her.

She felt impatient again. He was too like Daniel, she thought. He couldn't cope with the emotion of all this. But surely he could tell her he didn't feel he could help, tell her with the sort of charming defiance their father would have used?

'Just tell me why,' she said sharply.

He turned agonised eyes on her. 'I want to help Linny, we *must* help her, get her away, but if you knew, you wouldn't . . . trust me to take them, wouldn't let her . . . and the children go with me.'

'Why ever not?' she said, the pain in his face filling her with panic.

He bit his lip, kicked an imaginary stone at his feet. 'I . . . I was responsible for someone's death,' he burst out, as if expelling poison.

The agony in his face, the brutality of his words, stunned Cecily. She put her hands on his arms, for her own support more than his. 'Tell me,' she said at last. 'You have to tell me now.'

Her legs felt woolly and she sat down heavily on the grass, pulling him with her. She took a deep breath. 'Tell me. Take your time, but tell me everything.'

He would not look at her, but in a monotone began, 'When I got to America I went to Atlanta – I had a friend there from school. Only he wasn't there. I got in with a gang of students, they let me share their room in a motel.' He paused, then said angrily, 'I was lonely, afraid, and they were kind. Then one night some chaps came, boys whose minds had been blown by Vietnam. They had drugs . . .'

Cecily bit her lips, determined not to show any horror, any disapproval.

'I know it was foolish,' he turned on her as if she had reprimanded him, 'but,' he shrugged, 'I got into it. There was a girl, Cathy. She and I had a sort of thing going. One night we went to bed, we were pretty high on drugs, drink. I woke – I don't know when – the window was open, it was cold.' He paused again and she could see the pain eating into him. She took his hand. He held it very tightly.

'I don't know why I left the motel. I just went for a walk, wandered about for, oh, I don't know how long.

When I got back,' he looked at her now, bewildered, like a child, 'they said she was dead, fallen out of the window.'

'But that's not your fault,' Cecily said, desperate to believe it. 'I mean, she could have fallen if she was high on drugs, or thought she could fly – you hear about people doing that.'

'If I had looked for her instead of just leaving, she might have been all right. I was so doped I didn't know what I was doing. I forgot about her. I could even have pushed her out myself,' he said quietly.

'But you didn't! Oh, Stephen, surely you didn't? What did the police say happened? Surely there was an inquest?"

'I ran away,' he said, not looking at her. 'It was all so confusing. They rounded up everyone who was there when they found her, but I wasn't there then. I was out walking,' he repeated as if he was trying to convince her, convince himself. 'But frankly, Cecily, after one of those sessions, no one really remembers who was there and who wasn't. I just got on a Greyhound bus and went to New Jersey.'

'And they never found you?'

'No. I worry about it sometimes, wonder if someone will come and arrest me.' He clutched at her hand.

'Stephen, have you any, even the smallest, suspicion that you might have had something to do with her death?' She spoke calmly but she felt hollow with shock, with the pain of not being there, not being able to shield him from these terrible events.

'All I remember is falling onto the bed with her in my arms. Then waking up because it was cold. But in these states you don't know,' he said wildly, 'you just don't know what weird things you might do.'

'Was the window open when you went to sleep?' Cecily fought to remain calm.

'I don't know.'

Fear and revulsion shot through her, thinking of the sordidness of this world he had inhabited, the waste of his hopes, of the life of the girl. 'So what did you do then?'

'On the journey I had time to think. I just wanted to get away, away not only from Cathy's death, but away from that life.' He shuddered. 'I knew I would die too if I went on like that. I was so afraid I had somehow killed Cathy, and I knew then,' his face was desolate, 'that I could never come home. I thought of the contempt in Daniel's eyes, how he'd almost crow over being proved right about me. For he was right, I was a failure.'

'But you're not now,' she said fiercely, shaking him. 'Somehow you managed to pull yourself round. That must have taken some courage. How did you do it?' Again she felt the agony of not being there to help him.

'One of the boys in the group had been in a clinic outside New York. He told us all about it, and how he'd run away. I checked myself in – I had medical insurance.' He smiled for the first time, a wry smile. 'I made up a bit of a story, they like a challenge.'

'Was it dreadful?' she said gently.

'Yes.' His mouth twisted. 'But . . . anyway it's over. I

married this girl, Beth. She was in there too.' He laughed sourly. 'It was a damn fool thing to do but I got my visa.'

'Oh, Stephen.' She laid her head against his arm. 'I can't bear to think of the torture you went through. Why didn't you let us know? I would have come for you.'

'I was ashamed,' he said quite simply. 'Besides, the psychiatrist was of the view that families screwed you up, they threatened your happiness.' He gave a bitter laugh. 'It took me some years to get over that.'

'You did keep in touch, with cards.'

'Yes. I couldn't quite let you go, and later my mother came out and married Greg, and I got my job.'

'Does she know?'

'No, but Greg does. He's a great man. He . . .' he hesitated, 'he looked into Cathy's death for me. I wanted to put things right. It was assumed she fell out of the window while she was under the influence of drugs and alcohol. Because she was involved with drugs and she didn't have a family, the authorities didn't bother to probe too deeply, just wrote her off. So I'll never know my part in it.'

She hugged him, feeling quite raw inside. 'Can't you accept that might be the truth?'

He smiled, a sad smile that bit deep into her. 'I don't know, but I have learned to live with it, after a fashion, though it often comes back to haunt me.'

They sat, arms round each other, in silence for a while, and then Cecily said, 'But, Stephen, why can't you help Linette?'

He looked at her gravely, his silver-green eyes luminous with unshed tears. 'You asked me earlier if I thought I could cope with Linette. The answer is, I don't know, I'm not sure if I'm capable of helping anybody. I'm good at my job but I haven't been much good with relationships up to now.'

'Oh, Stephen, now you're back with us, your family, you'll feel better. I was thinking of Daddy – how he hated emotions, would dodge out of them whenever he could. I thought for a moment that you were like him, but now I know you're not. This is different, *you* are different.' She looked into his face. 'I know you'll be able to do it. Linette needs you now. You won't let her down.' She smiled at him with an encouragement she did not feel. Yet she knew she trusted him implicitly.

He flushed, as if unused to praise. 'I'm so . . . so happy to be back with you all. I missed the family, the fun we had together. I will help her.' He turned to her, his eyes shining, 'I will. I won't let you down.'

'Of course you won't.' She hugged him, feeling a little of the strain lifting, relieved that she had his support.

'I wonder,' he said, and she could almost see him putting his revelations back into a deep recess inside himself, 'what will happen if her husband finds out. I mean, will he let you snatch his wife and kids and bundle them out of the country? Is he fond of the children? Should we take them away from him?'

'Richard always wanted sons. He blames Linette for having girls. The few times I've seen him with them, he was indifferent to them. But they adore Linette. The children are the reason why she's stayed with Richard, put up with his cruelty. She once said something about him saying she was a bad mother. He's probably terrorised her with some story of saying she's not capable as a mother and he will take them away from her.'

'But you can't just take children away without some sort of proof, legal or medical,' Stephen said.

'Who's to know what medical proof Richard won't come up with? And think what a lot of damage could be done to the girls in the meantime.'

'We must get them away now, today,' Stephen said. 'I leave on Sunday. She could stay with you until then, couldn't she?'

'It gives Richard too much time to find her. They must go sooner.' She chewed her lip, wondering what on earth they could do.

Stephen, fighting with his horror and shock at the situation, suddenly made a decision. 'I'll leave earlier. I have to go into the office tomorrow, but I could leave on Friday.'

'Oh, Stephen, could you? The day after tomorrow? It hardly gives us any time.'

'We'll have to do it. Let's have lunch and make plans. They have passports, I presume.'

'I don't know about the children. Oh, hell, what a nightmare. But we've got to do it, get them away.'

'We will,' Stephen said. 'Somehow we will.'

'Here they come.' Cecily got out of her car. She was

smiling with a cheerfulness she did not feel. She felt exhausted, Stephen's account of his experiences, coupled with getting Linette away, weighing her down. She walked out in front of the green Volvo which slowed down, then stopped. A blonde woman opened the window and grinned uncertainly at her.

'Hello, I'm Cecily Mendelson, Harriet and Chloe's aunt,' she said, peering into the car. 'Hi, girls. I've come to visit you, and brought a new uncle to meet you, Uncle Stephen.'

'Hi, Aunt Cecily,' Harriet said, undoing her seat belt and struggling to get out. Chloe, after a moment's hesitation, followed her example. The two other girls in the car stared at them.

'Don't you want me to drop them at the house?' the woman asked, looking at their car parked in the lane outside the driveway.

'You can if you want to,' Cecily said, 'but we've just been shopping and saw you coming.'

'OK.' The woman turned round to the back of the car. 'Got everything, girls? Homework, lunch boxes?'

'Yes, Mrs Blackton,' they chorused as they scrambled out. Harriet kissed Cecily, Chloe hung back.

'I'll pick you up in the morning then,' Mrs Blackton said, and drove off.

'Why are you here? We haven't seen you for ages,' Harriet said. 'Is that our new uncle? Have you married him instead of Uncle Edmund?' she went on as Stephen got out of the car and came over to them.

'Heck no, I'm your mother's stepbrother.

346

Ex-stepbrother to be precise, and your Aunt Cecily's half-brother.'

'And you're American,' Harriet said admiringly. 'Is he the brother who disappeared?' She looked up at Cecily. A miniature Linette.

'Yes. But now he's back again and come to see you.' Cecily smiled at her. She studied each girl carefully. Chloe had always been quiet, keeping one eye on her sister to see how she reacted to situations. Now she smiled shyly, seemed to be about to say something momentous.

'Have you been to New York?' She reddened with the effort of asking the question.

Stephen squatted down to her level. 'I live there. Would you like to come and visit me there one day?'

Chloe looked anxiously at Harriet who jumped up and down and said, 'Oooh yes. Brilliant. When can we come?'

Stephen stood up, shrugged. 'Whenever you want to.'

'Can Mummy come?' Chloe plucked up her courage again.

'But of course, Mummy must come too.'

'When she's better,' Harriet said.

Cecily's heart turned over, seeing these small girls with their firm little faces and bright eyes. How much did they know? They seemed, as she looked at them now, to be all right, but who knew what nightmares they hid inside. She had to get them away, but the difficulties ahead appalled her.

They all sat round the kitchen table as Shirley

cooked chips and fish fingers. She looked tired. Cecily remarked on it and was treated to a long story about how she wanted to go to the doctor for a check-up for 'her nerves' but had been too occupied here.

'I'll come and sit with Mrs Symonds if you want to go,' Cecily said. 'How about Friday? I could stay until Mr Symonds gets back.' She said it quietly, not wanting the girls to hear, but they were engrossed in the television. If they told Richard, he might suspect something and stay at home. As it was, she was tortured that they'd said too much about visiting Stephen in America, afraid the girls might tell Richard about Stephen's invitation, inadvertently warning him.

'It's only the woman doctor, and a locum, and I don't know the locum,' Shirley said dubiously.

'Women doctors are best, they have to be, to get past the prejudice against them,' Cecily said archly. 'Being a woman she'll understand more about your nerves.'

'She might.' Shirley thought it over. 'But, well, I don't know, Mr Symonds asked particularly—'

'We won't tell him,' Cecily said firmly. 'Men can be . . . well,' she smiled conspiratorially, 'they don't understand how tired we women get running round after them, do they?'

'That they don't. My Cyril says I'm malingering – he can talk. It tires him out to go to the social and get his dole.' She looked affronted.

'You take the whole afternoon off. I'll square it with Mr Symonds when he gets home,' Cecily said, feeling rather sick at what Richard would do to Shirley when he found out. But she couldn't afford to be sentimental, she thought briskly; besides, Shirley looked rather big to beat up. Their priority was to get Linette away. 'Perhaps it would be better not to mention we were here today. I'll ring him later.'

'As you wish.'

Shirley looked a little apprehensive, so Cecily said, 'I know him well, he doesn't like people seeing Linette when she's . . . having one of her turns. I'll ring him later and explain, it'll be better that way.'

'I understand.'

While Shirley was occupied with the cooking and the children with the television, Stephen went into the drawing room to ring his firm's travel agency to get them reservations to New York. When he came back to the kitchen he gave Cecily the thumbs-up sign.

'Why did you do that?' Harriet asked, her attention diverted for a second from the screen.

'Just my way of saying I'm happy,' Stephen said, grinning at Cecily. The last worry left was the passports.

Cecily went upstairs to Linette. She was lying on her back staring at the ceiling. She jumped, her eyes large with fear when she heard Cecily come in. She visibly relaxed when she saw it was her.

Cecily was hit with a wave of fear. Was Friday soon enough? Might Richard injure, even kill her before then? She forced away her panic, and her longing to snatch Linette up, and bundle her and the girls in the car and set off at once. She knew the success of the plan all depended on their staying calm. They must not let

Richard suspect anything. They must get to New York before Richard had a chance to make them wards of court. She sat down on Linette's bed and took one of her agitated hands in hers.

'We must go back to London, Stephen and I, he's got to call in at his office. But we'll be back the day after tomorrow, Friday.'

'That would be lovely.' Linette smiled, the first smile Cecily had seen since they'd come. 'It's wonderful to see Stephen again. Isn't he just like Daniel?'

'He is.' Cecily hugged her. 'Oh Lin, you sound better. Are you on some kind of pills – pills that make you tired?'

'The doctor says I must take them, but I don't like them.' She sighed. 'You never know with doctors, do you? But they do stop me feeling panicky.'

'When do you have to take another one?'

'Richard will give it to me. Shirley gives me one at lunchtime. I think she forgot today.' She looked towards the bathroom. 'I'd better check or Ri—'

'I'll check. Where are they?' Cecily jumped off the bed.

'In the cupboard over the basin in a white plastic box.'

Cecily found a flat box divided into compartments with the days of the week marked on them. In Wednesday there were two pills left. Shirley had forgotten to give her one, and Linette seemed far better without it. Quickly she flushed one down the lavatory, wishing she could throw them all away.

'One left,' she said and before Linette could dispute it she went on, 'where do you keep your passports?'

'In the safe? Why do you want to know?' She looked troubled as if it was an effort to form the words.

'Nothing really. Can you open the safe?'

'Yes. If the key's in Richard's cupboard. Why do you want to know, Cecily?' Linette looked alarmed.

'No reason. Do the girls have their own passports? Miranda and Jamie are still on mine. I've been meaning to get them their own for ages.' Cecily felt unhappy quizzing Linette in this way. She knew she was worrying her, but she couldn't ask the children, or Shirley.

'They were put on mine before our trip to Portugal this summer,' Linette said. 'Richard didn't want them to be, but there was a possibility he might have to come home before me.' She trailed off, looking tired.

Inwardly rejoicing at this news, Cecily went on about her children being on both hers and Edmund's passports. She then chattered about safes and keys, until she winkled out which cupboard Richard's safe key was in. She told Stephen where to look, and when they left for London he had Linette's passport in his pocket.

Before they left, Harriet said, 'When can we come to America?'

'How about the summer?' Stephen said smoothly. 'We'll forget all about it now. In fact,' he paused, then said seriously, 'let's keep this visit a secret, shall we, until the summer. OK?'

'OK,' they chorused, eyes shining with suppressed excitement. Cecily hugged them hard when she said goodbye, worrying all the time that Friday would not be soon enough.

Feeling edgy and crotchety with her anxiety over the rescue, Cecily struggled to remain even-tempered in the shop. She found it difficult to remain patient with one imperious woman who having demanded she gift-wrap one purchase then found something she liked better in another corner of the shop and insisted on taking it instead. Looking up exasperated, Cecily saw Mrs Grant pass the shop outside. She looked so dejected and sad that Cecily made a quick excuse and rushed out.

'Mrs Grant, how are you? I . . .' Then seeing her face, she knew Mrs Grant had too much pride to admit to her losses at Lloyd's. 'How are you?' She forced a smile. 'I'd hoped to see you, I've a group of ladies who meet to talk over . . .' She paused, embarrassed as if she was going to mention a deeply shaming subject. 'Over our losses,' she said firmly. 'They seem to find it some help, talking it over with others in the same boat.'

'Oh . . . well, that's a new idea. But, no thank you. I'm fine, thank you, dear.' Her eyes had lost the merry sparkle they once had. Her sallow skin drooped on her face, her hair was almost white.

'And the family?'

'We're all fine, thank you.' She seemed to take control of herself. She drew herself up, fixed Cecily with a steely gaze as if to say, 'It is vulgar to discuss money. I will bear my shame in silence and with dignity.' And she walked on, leaving Cecily ashamed to have cornered her, admiring her courage.

Later she told Stephen.

'Just like my mother,' he said. 'She knows little of money, would never discuss it. She'd rather starve than admit she's hard up. Poor old thing, but at least you've told her about your group. Maybe after thinking it over she'll ask to join.'

'I hope so. But maybe it won't help everyone. Some people do prefer to bear their troubles on their own,' Cecily said, then seeing his embarrassed look wondered aloud for the hundredth time if they were doing right in trying to rescue Linette. Since he had told her the horrific details of his breakdown there had been a tacit agreement between them not to mention it again.

'Did you get hold of Ronald?' she asked quickly to cover the awkward moment.

'He was very offhand,' he laughed, 'but I could tell I had shocked him. He said he was late for a meeting and would ring me back.'

'And has he?'

Stephen smiled wryly. 'Strangely enough no, he hasn't and whenever I've rung he's been unavailable. But don't worry, I'll get him.'

Cecily nodded. She had to let herself trust Stephen.

At last it was Friday. Cecily, bracing herself to do battle with Richard, convinced that he would be at the house having found out about their visit, was only a little relieved to find he was not. Shirley, with many thanks and more explanations about the state of her nerves, was easily despatched to the doctor and told to enjoy herself for the rest of the afternoon.

Linette was quiet, looking at them anxiously as if not quite certain why they were there. Cecily found a couple of suitcases, opened them on the end of the bed and started to pack for her, asking her what she needed.

'You're not taking me away?' Linette screamed, holding on to the bed, her hands shaking, her eyes wild.

Cecily called for Stephen and held her. But Linette pushed her away. 'I won't go. I'm not ill, I won't go.'

'You and the children are going to America with Stephen. You'll be safe with him,' Cecily said.

'No, no, I can't go.'

'Listen, Lin, you and the girls are coming with me to New York this evening.' Stephen was alarmed at her distress. 'I've got the tickets, look.' He pulled them out of his wallet, opened them, showed her her name and those of the girls. 'You're coming to stay with me and my mother – you remember Fiona? When you feel stronger, you'll be able to decide what to do about Richard.'

Linette stared at him but she did not look convinced. 'It's not a trick . . .?' She looked piteously from one to the other.

'No. We would never trick you, Lin. We're going to take care of you. Take you and the girls on a holiday.' Cecily realised that Richard must have threatened to have her put away. Another monstrous trick of his to keep her here.

'Richard . . .' There was real terror in Linette's voice now.

'I've told Richard,' Stephen lied. He had a letter in his pocket that he was going to leave for him. In no uncertain terms he informed him that he was taking Linette and the girls away to recover from his brutality. If he made any move to get them back he would inform the police of his assaults, and his company.

The doorbell rang, making them all jump. They stayed stock still, staring at each other.

Richard! Cecily thought, or the police to stop them leaving.

She crept to the window, flattening herself against the curtain. To her relief she saw the green Volvo and Chloe getting slowly out of the car, turning back in her methodical way to collect up her belongings.

'The children. I'd forgotten they come back at lunchtime today,' she said in relief and ran down to let them in.

The children were delirious with excitement.

'New York now, today! Not the summer!' Harriet screamed with delight when Cecily told her.

'Is Mummy coming?' Chloe said anxiously. 'She's not better yet.'

'Of course she's coming and she'll get better in New York,' Cecily said to her.

'And Daddy?' Chloe said and the question seemed to hang heavily in the air.

'He can't come, he has too much work at the moment,' Stephen said firmly. 'So we haven't told him. It's a secret, just for us.'

'Oh.' Chloe looked puzzled.

'So we're not to tell him?' Harriet said. 'So he won't know where we are?'

'We're going to surprise him with a postcard from New York,' Stephen told her, exchanging glances with Cecily.

The excitement of going and what to take soon swept away any more questions.

'But who will look after Bramble?' Chloe suddenly wailed, remembering her beloved pony.

'Oh God!' Cecily looked anxiously at Stephen. As the time ticked relentlessly on, she was getting increasingly nervous. What if Richard or a friend called and asked them what they were doing? She had a fearful vision of the police stopping them boarding the plane, Linette being carted off to a mental hospital on Richard's instructions and the girls taken away from her.

'Philippa Archer will have her. She borrows her sometimes. They can't afford their own pony as their father's lost all his money,' Harriet said, trying to jam a huge blue rabbit into her case.

'Let me ring her then,' Cecily said.

Chloe looked dubious. 'She'll have to give her back. We won't be gone long, will we?'

'Of course she'll give her back. Now give me her number.'

Mrs Archer was ecstatic. They would be over by teatime and they would take great care of Bramble. 'My husband's business is going through a sticky patch so we had to sell our pony,' she explained. 'Philippa was so upset but Chloe has been very kind in lending Bramble. How long will Chloe be away?'

Her cheerful, no-nonsense voice made Cecily long to confide in her; instead she said, 'I'll let you know in a day or so. I just thought a break would do them good, and school's not that important at this age.'

'That's true. Is Linette better? Richard says she wasn't too well. I must say I haven't seen her for a while. I should have called round but . . .'

'She's had flu, couldn't shake it off, but she's much better now,' Cecily told her.

When she came back from making the call, there was no sign of Chloe. Keeping their voices down so as not to alarm Linette, they went round the house and the garden calling her.

'I expect she's with Bramble,' Harriet said finally, pulling out all her books from the shelf and trying to squeeze them into an already bursting bag.

As Cecily approached the field she heard Chloe's solemn little voice: 'So we're going to New York with our new uncle, and Philippa's looking after you. Only for a little while, she's not keeping you.'

Cecily felt the tears rise in her throat as she saw the small child cuddle her face into Bramble's woolly neck. She wondered again if they were right in snatching the children and Linette away like this. But then she remembered Linette's body, the cruel marks on her pale skin. What if he began to hit the children too?

'Come on, Chloe,' she said gently. 'We must get going.'

'I'll send you a postcard.' Chloe hugged Bramble who stood patiently and pushed her nose hopefully into Cecily's hand.

Both girls had to be restrained from ringing their friends with the news of their departure, and as their excitement grew, so did Linette's agitation. One minute she would get up to go, the next she would flop down in the chair again, saying she couldn't leave. Stephen began to get rattled.

'Perhaps we should take her to a doctor,' he said anxiously to Cecily.

'No, she'll be fine. Don't give up now, Stephen,' she said briskly. 'You're going to miss the plane if you don't leave now, this minute.'

At that the girls jumped round Linette, pulling at her hands and coat. 'Come on, Mummy, be quick. We can't miss the plane, we can't.'

Just as they got her to the front door, the telephone rang. They all stopped, frozen in horror, and turned back towards it as if the eyes of the caller were on them, daring them to leave.

'I'll go and tell them we're off to New York,' Harriet said importantly.

'No,' Cecily cried. 'It will take too long. Leave it.'

'It's Richard,' Linette said and would have fallen if Stephen hadn't held her.

'Come on,' Cecily said, taking her arm and frog-marching her out of the house. Stephen took the girls' hands and led them out too.

Chloe stopped. ''Bye, Bramble,' she called at the top

of her voice. 'Did you hear her answer?' she asked Stephen.

'I did,' he said quickly. 'I sure did.'

'The lights . . .' Linette turned, tried to get back into the house.

'Leave them on,' Cecily said, shutting the door firmly on the empty house and the still pealing telephone.

Chapter Twenty-Two

'**M**ission almost accomplished.' Stephen hugged Cecily before they went through the departure gates. He looked very young and vulnerable, and she found herself again wondering if she was doing the right thing.

'I do hope so,' she said, expecting to see Richard bearing down on them any minute, demanding his wife and children.

Linette clung to her, her face haunted and anxious. 'I shouldn't be going. Couldn't you come too?'

'No, Lin, not this time. Stephen will look after you.' Cecily's heart felt very full as she prepared herself to leave Linette. She'd have given a lot to go with her. They'd got her this far, but she couldn't bear to think how much longer and tougher Linette's journey to complete health would be. She wished she could be there to help her fight. She thought of Stephen's agonised confession and wondered if it was fair to burden him with this.

'Are you sure you'll be all right, Stephen?' Cecily

asked him quietly when Linette was out of earshot. 'After all, you've taken on quite a lot, two children and, well, I don't know how ill Linette is. She may be teetering on the brink of a breakdown and should be under medical care.'

'Cecily, don't worry about it,' Stephen said firmly. 'I'll be fine. After all, my stepfather's a doctor, he'll know where to go for help if we need it.'

'It's a big responsibility, Stephen. The children are not very old, you know.' In her anxiety she couldn't leave it alone.

'Quit worrying, Cecily.' Then he added fiercely, 'Just because our father walked away from the emotional scenes he created, don't think I will. I won't let Linny down. Especially not after what you told me about our father's treatment of her,' he spat, his silver-green eyes glittering dangerously.

Cecily glanced quickly at Linette to see if she'd heard. 'Forget that, Stephen. Please.'

'Are you kidding? I'll never forget it, or how he laid himself open to blackmail and we lost the castle.'

'We can't think of that now,' she said hurriedly, wishing Daniel had not so complicated their lives. 'You must go. I'm terrified Richard will come before you can get away.' She squeezed his arm, looking into his face and seeing Daniel.

'OK. I hope to be back in London soon.' He glanced at Linette who was standing, staring into space, her children chasing each other round her, squealing with laughter.

'I hope so. It's so good having you back.' She hugged him. 'Thank you for doing this. Without you we couldn't have saved her.' She forced herself to smile though a heavy doom hung about her as if Richard was somewhere hiding there, watching, waiting to pounce on them.

'I'm so glad to be back.' He caught her nervous look, glanced round quickly too. 'I think we're safe. By the time Richard gets home we'll be in the air. But you, Cecily.' He looked anxious. 'What will you do if Richard contacts you? I hate to think of you alone. Is there anyone you can go to? What about Jerome? When is he back?'

'I'll be fine, don't worry about me. You have your hands full as it is.' She ignored the sliver of fear nudging at her. 'Jerome should be back soon.'

'We'd better go, the departure gate's up on the screen. Look, you and your kids must come over. This next summer, whatever happens. Have the trip on me. Come with Jerome.'

'That would be great. I'd love to come with you now, surprise him.' She thought of them all arriving in triumph in New York, though no one else would know of their small triumph, or care that they were there. She thought of turning up in Jerome's room, slipping into his bed beside him, holding his warm body against hers. She sighed heavily. What she wouldn't have given to have him to cuddle up to now.

'I'll call him, try and get him over, before he comes back,' Stephen said.

'Send him home,' she said, holding him close to her, feeling suddenly bereft at his departure. She hugged Linette and the children. She stood alone waving, forcing herself to smile brightly as Stephen, his arm protectively round Linette, the children jumping round them, went from her.

As they disappeared from her sight, she felt distraught, weak with a sense of anti-climax. She went up to see the plane take off, knowing she would not really believe they were safe until she saw the plane depart. As she watched it climbing up into the dark sky, with its lights winking and flashing, rising like a stately bird, she felt an overwhelming yearning to be with them, to share their freedom, freedom from Lloyd's, worry about Jerome and Emily, worry about her children's education, Edmund.

It was then that she cried. Great splashy tears coursed down her cheeks. Ashamed of her weakness, she hid her face and fumbled her way back to her car, empty with loneliness.

She cried all the way back from the airport. Once or twice she had to pull over, put her head in her hands and howl. She kept telling herself how ridiculous and wimpish she was being, but the more she told herself off, the worse she became. At last she realised that in a strange way she was enjoying this outburst. It was as if her problems had been building up like a massive black cloud and, unable to contain any more, had burst forth in this torrent of weeping.

When she finally got home she felt as if she'd been

away weeks instead of just a day. She felt strangely
calm, as if all her tears had loosened the limpet hold of
her pent-up emotions. The house felt huge with emptiness. She wished her children were here, or Jerome. I'll
ring him in a minute, she thought, to cheer herself up,
tell him all about today. She felt hollow with missing
him. With any luck he'd be home this weekend, but the
thought filled her with a mixture of pleasure and agitation. When he came home, Emily came back into her
life.

She picked up the letters that lay scattered on the
mat and without looking at them put them on the
dining room table. She could not face yet another
demand from Lloyd's. She made herself some coffee –
she rarely had wine in the house, now money was so
tight – and wondered what to do.

She felt edgy, deflated and tired after the action of
the day. There were various friends she could ring,
even visit, but as soon as she opened her address book
her energy left her, and she felt she couldn't be bothered with the effort of small talk. She wouldn't dare
mention Linette's flight to anyone. The fear was still
menacing her that if Richard found out where they'd
gone, he'd have the police to meet the plane on its
arrival in New York.

But she could tell Jerome. She got up to get the
number of his hotel in New York. She thought she'd put
it in her diary, but it wasn't there. She began to search
through her papers, dropping them on the floor, impatient that she couldn't find it. She went through to the

dining room where a pile of papers and letters, including today's, lay on the table. She leafed through them. Her heart gave a lurch; there was a letter from Edmund. As she picked it up, all thought of Jerome's number fled. Holding Edmund's letter, she remembered those long years ago when they were newly lovers and had written to each other every day. Where had it gone, that love? His love for her?

'Grow up,' she said to herself out loud. The letter was probably his holiday plans for the children or even, and her heart stung, notice of his marriage to Rowena. She opened it quickly to get it over with. It was a short and to the point.

My dear Cecily,

    I've been hit harder by Lloyd's than I first thought. I am trying to save money where I can and I'm afraid I can no longer pay the full fees of both the schools. I know we have an educational fund, but I can no longer afford to put so much into it each month, so it will realise less.

    Therefore I think it best if Miranda goes to day school, either in London or down here in Kent. I will leave that to you to decide, but I expect you would like to have her with you.

    I have written to her headmistress today to give a term's notice. I hope she will let her leave in January, but if not it will have to be the Easter term.

    I am so sorry about this . . .

Cecily read and reread his words. That he could no longer afford to pay the enormous school fees didn't bother her at all. But she couldn't have Miranda home and not Jamie. It would destroy him if Miranda came home and he did not. Any hope Edmund had of getting him into Eton would be dashed. They must both come home. There were perfectly good schools in London.

She'd ring Edmund at once to discuss it. As she went to the telephone she felt little bubbles of happiness rise in her. At least the Lloyd's disaster had one good side, if the children could come home. Edmund would be relieved, she thought, if she insisted that Miranda could not come home unless Jamie did too. Lots of their friends' children had got into Eton from London schools, and she struggled to list them so she could convince Edmund of her argument.

The telephone rang before she reached it. Still thinking of Edmund and the children, she picked it up, assuming it was him, mentally gearing herself up to persuade him to let them both come home.

'Where's my wife?'

'Oh . . . Richard.' Her heart dropped.

'I come back to an empty house with this bloody note from Stephen, your good-for-nothing bastard brother, saying he's taken her. Where is she?'

'I don't know.' Desperately she tried to think what to say. There were hours before they reached New York, plenty of time for Richard to arrange, if not the police, then some friend to meet them and send them home again.

'I'm coming up to get them. I suppose they're with you.'

'No, they're not here.' The roughness of his voice chafed her with fear. He'd always tried to be charming before when he spoke to her. This was his other side, the side that had beaten Linette. The image of the bruises on her body whirled up the anger in her. 'They're not here, and I will not tell you where they are. They are safe from you, and if you come here, I'll call the police and tell them what you've done to her.'

'Try it.'

'I shall. I saw what you did to her, Richard. Her body was black and blue.'

'It's her word against mine. She's mad, your sister. She did it to herself.' His voice slithered down the line like a snake, making Cecily's flesh creep.

'You're lying.'

'Prove it. She's mentally unstable, just as her mother was.'

'Zara was fine, just vague.'

'Call it vague if you want. She was mad, and so is Linette, which is hardly surprising after what your father did to her,' he retorted and before she could answer, remembering with sickening dread that he knew about it, he said desperately, 'I want my wife and children back, at once.'

'You won't have them,' Cecily said with all the strength she could muster. His words were lies, surely they were lies? For a moment a doubt crept into her mind. She'd seen Linette and her mental state was not good. What if she *had* inflicted those wounds on herself? But could you physically bruise yourself like that, all down your back? She half tried to see how far her own arm would reach. It could be possible, especially if one held something hard in one's hand. But would there be enough strength in one's arm, bent this way, to produce the marks she'd seen?

'I shall get a court order. I can also bring up your father's abuse of her.' His voice was not quite so steady now.

'She was eighteen and it wasn't abuse.' She slammed the receiver down. She was shaking. Could he do that tonight before they landed in New York? Would he know that Stephen lived in New York and had returned there? Would he send police round here or come himself to question her? But almost worse than anything was the thought that Daniel's name would be smeared through the courts.

The telephone rang again. She stared at it as if it was alive and would spring at her. She thought she'd leave it, but her mind was jittery with panic. What if it was one of the children? Or even Stephen saying they hadn't taken off after all or had been diverted? Gingerly she picked it up.

'Hello.'

'Tell me where they are, Cecily, or I'll have you up for kidnap.'

'I won't tell you, Richard, so don't ring me again.'

'I'll get a psychiatrist's report on her. She's not a suitable mother to my children, she—'

'If you ring me again, I'll ring the police myself, now.' Cecily slammed the receiver down on his frenzied threats. Then as quickly picked it up again and laid it on the table, to stop him calling again.

She leant her head on the back of the sofa and shut her eyes. She was trembling, her body felt tense, ready for flight as if he would suddenly appear through a window or batter down the door.

Richard possessed great charm, though Cecily felt there was something sinister behind it. His charm had made her feel anxious instead of flattered, yet only now did she experience the real horror it must have been for Linette. She could still hear his voice, feel it reverberating in her head. Strong, well-aimed threats designed to undermine his victim's confidence. Cecily could imagine him menacing Linette, making her feel guilty and in need of punishment, then turning on that insidious charm, persuading her to feel grateful that he still stayed with her.

She sat a long time and thought about it. The room, outwardly so bright with clear colours on the walls and in the furnishings, had taken on a malevolent air. The familiar scratching of the neighbours on either side of her became noises of an intruder. She yearned for someone to be with her, to laugh at her fears. If Richard was coming, he couldn't be here for at least another hour. Wild thoughts whirled in her head. He might torture her to find out about Linette, she should go and spend the night with a friend. She needed to talk to someone desperately.

She jumped up and searched frantically for Jerome's telephone number. She longed for him with every fibre of her being. He would laugh at her fears, tease her for her ravings. Take her in his arms, use his prowess as a lover to drive away these malingering feelings of foreboding.

Where had she put it? She'd written it on a striped piece of paper taken from the notepad by the telephone and shoved it somewhere safe, she was sure of it. She looked in her diary, her address book, the drawer in the small table by the phone, but it was not there. She'd have to ring Emily.

Quickly, before she could put it off, she dialled her number, praying Susan would answer and give her his number straightaway.

'Hello?' Emily's voice was breathless, excited.

'Emily, it's Cecily Mendelson.'

'Oh, hello.'

Ignoring the sullenness in her tone, Cecily pushed on brightly, 'I hope everything's all right.'

'Why shouldn't it be?'

'No reason. I wondered if I could have your father's telephone number in New York. I seem to have mislaid it.'

'I've just spoken to him, he says he's going to be busy in a meeting for the rest of the day and tomorrow too, and probably the day after that.'

'I know he's busy, Emily, but he must go back to the hotel to sleep sometime. I'd like to leave a message for him, it's very important.'

'I'll see if I've got it. But as he rings me so often I haven't needed to call him.'

'Thank you, that would be kind of you, Emily. Or if you can't find it, ask Susan for it, please,' Cecily said.

'She's having a bath and washing her hair. It always takes her ages.'

'I'll ring her back then, in say half an hour.'

'She'll be in bed by then. She always goes to bed early on Friday nights.'

'Then you will have to find it, Emily. It's very important, and I'm sure you *will* be able to find it,' Cecily insisted, wondering if Emily could guess at her murderous thought of throttling her with the telephone cord.

'Hang on then.' Emily sounded as if she'd been asked to travel the world and face untold dangers to find the number. After about ten minutes she was back. 'I think this is it.'

'It had better be.'

'0101,' Emily started, reading off a list of numbers.

Cecily copied them down, repeating each one out loud as she did so. She then rechecked it with Emily, who said, 'You think I can't read my numbers or something?'

'No, Emily. I just want to be sure *I* haven't made a mistake. Thank you, I'll see you soon.'

'Don't count on it.' Emily hung up.

'Beastly little bitch,' Cecily said to the empty room and dialled the number.

'The Metropolitan Museum,' the woman who

answered the telephone said. 'How may I help you?'

'Is that 212-535-7710?' Cecily asked.

'Sure is. How can I help you?'

Cecily put down the receiver and furiously dialled Emily. She'd had enough of that scheming, jealous child; she'd demand to speak to Susan or go round there herself to get the number, but the line was engaged, and Cecily was sure it would remain so for the rest of the evening. Anger scudded through her, tying her in tight knots. Frantically she searched again for Jerome's number, wondering where on earth she could have put it. She went through her bag, cursing herself, cursing Emily, and when the telephone rang she grabbed it, quite forgetting it might be Richard.

'Darling, at last. Where have you been?'

'Oh Jerome, I've lost your number and I asked Emily and you know what the brat did? She gave me the number of the Metropolitan Museum. She—'

'She must have made a mistake.'

'No, she did not. She's going to ruin us, Jerome. She hates me, is determined that we won't be happy together.'

'Darling, that's not fair.'

All her fears of the day, Edmund's letter, the impossibility of having Miranda home and not Jamie, Linette's escape, Richard's threats and Stephen's harrowing story, exploded from her in an attack on Emily. She hardly knew what she was saying, she felt so furious. She wanted Jerome here with her now, to comfort her, and was angry that he was not. She was afraid that

373

Richard would come while she was alone, and that neither Edmund nor Jerome could help her.

Jerome, knowing nothing of this, listened with mounting horror at her tirade. 'Please, Cecily, stop it. She's my daughter . . .'

But she didn't hear him, or she couldn't stop. Only when she realised that she was talking to a dead line and he'd hung up on her did she halt her flood of complaints. She felt drained, exhausted, knowing she had gone too far. Impossible and manipulative though Emily was, she was just a confused child, and she was Jerome's beloved daughter.

She reached out to ring him straight back to apologise, to explain why she had been so hysterical, and the cold truth hit her like a blow. She still didn't know his number. She slumped back in despair and grief. Without an instant explanation, her words would fester and grow in him, suffocating the love he'd felt for her.

She waited another hour, willing him to ring back. He did not. At last, shaky with fear and despair, she rang Penny who insisted she come round and stay the night.

'It would be wonderful. David is away and I could do with the company. Come for the weekend. Shall I come and fetch you?'

'Goodness, no, I'll be there in a few minutes.'

She threw her night things into a bag, relieved now that she would not be alone, knowing that Penny's cluttered house and cheerful gossip would soothe her anxious mind, make her laugh at her fears. But once she was out of her house in the dark street, she felt vulnerable and afraid, convinced that any moment Richard would come for her, that he was there in the street watching her. He would follow her to Penny's, catch her as she got out of the car. She felt that every shadow hid him, that he was behind the bushes in her neighbours' gardens, ready to grab her.

She ran quickly to the car, and even when she was safely inside she looked fearfully behind the seat in case he was hiding there. But stronger even than this fear was the pain that she'd hurt Jerome. That the wounds she'd inflicted would be too deep to heal.

Chapter Twenty-Three

Cecily congratulated herself on finding a meter so near Harrods. Apart from the fear of being clamped, towed away or giving up any idea of shopping there at all, it was raining, and she did not fancy splashing miles through the streets.

She went in by the side entrance and took the escalator up to the children's department. Miranda wanted a dressing gown for her birthday. It could not be pink, fluffy or with appliquéd animals on it. Having not much else to do that Saturday afternoon, feeling rather in limbo as she was hoping that Jerome would be back today, Cecily thought she'd devote herself to finding one.

Jerome had not rung her back since her disastrous call. She'd rung his house again, determined to get his number and call him back, but the phone had either been engaged or was not answered. She balked at ringing his office, so she waited impatiently for his return, wondering each day if he was back already and did not want to call her.

As she went up the escalator her glance was caught by a man coming down on the other side. He was instantly familiar, and yet a stranger. She turned round to follow his progress, then involuntarily called out, 'Edmund?'

He turned towards her voice as if in a dream.

She called again as the moving staircase took them further apart. 'Edmund?'

Other people looked at her, as did Edmund. Edmund, so pale, so drawn, his hair faded into greyness, stared at her.

'Wait.' She turned to go down, realised by the hostile stare from the woman behind her that she could not.

'Wait, Edmund, please.' She ran up to the top of the escalator, crossed over and went down. He was standing obediently at the bottom. He looked terrible.

'Edmund.' She took him by the arms, holding on to him as if to reassure herself that it really was him and not a ghost. She hadn't heard from him since she'd received his letter last week. She'd tried to telephone, but there'd been no answer from Rowena's house in Kent, and although she'd left messages at his office, he had not rung her back. She'd ended up writing to him.

'You look so ill,' she said. She felt a dreadful fear in the pit of her stomach as she looked at him. 'Is Rowena here?' She looked round as if she would demand to know what she had done to him.

'No. She's at home. I was just getting Louisa's birthday present for her party tomorrow.' He gestured to a bag over his arm.

She linked arms with him, pulled him away from the seething mass of people who poured off the escalator. 'Have you time for a chat? I want to talk about the children. Did you get my letter?'

'Yes, I'm sorry.' Wearily he drew his hand over his forehead, as if he could not bear another complication. 'I've been so busy.'

'Come on, let's go and find somewhere to sit. There's a coffee bar downstairs, isn't there?' He didn't answer so she led him through the men's department and downstairs to the restaurant. To her great relief they found a table in a corner and she pulled him to it.

'Are you not well, Edmund?' she asked again as they sat over their espressos. She almost added, 'You look so old.' There was something so dreadfully faded about him that horrified her. She thought again of cancer, as she had when she'd first seen Linette, but scolded herself that she was being melodramatic. If she went on thinking everyone who looked so dispirited had it, she'd wish it on one of them.

'I'm fine.' His eyes shifted away from her. 'I have a lot to worry about at the moment. I . . . we hope to get away to Rowena's mother for her girls' half-term.'

'That should do you good,' she said without conviction. 'Now, about the children, Edmund. You know we can't bring Miranda home and leave Jamie at boarding school. We could do it the other way round. Despite her grumbling, Miranda's quite happy at Quinton Hall but Jamie's miserable. We both know that.' The words poured out of her, obscuring her concern for his health.

She hoped she didn't sound desperate. Jamie's misery at school, so valiantly borne by him, often reduced her to tears when she spoke of it. She could not make a scene here. Edmund would just get up and walk away; scenes in public, especially somewhere like Harrods where he might see someone he knew, mortified him.

'I think you're exaggerating, Cecily.' His voice was very tired. 'David Sawyer has never said he's unhappy. He's a popular boy, and in the football team.'

'He is not happy, Edmund. He's scared he won't get to Eton, afraid of letting you down, and since you've left us,' she saw him flinch, but she didn't stop, 'he should be at home with one of us, not suffering alone with his worries at school. He might even blossom at a day school, pass his blessed Common Entrance to Eton.'

'It's too late to change him now. He'll not have time to settle in somewhere new and pass the exam.'

'I think he would. I'm not having Miranda home without him. I dread to think what damage that would do to him. Remember Stephen running away from us all, unable to take my father's criticism? Daddy always let Linette and me get away with anything, but he was terribly hard on Stephen. I don't want that to happen to Jamie. It's both children coming home, or neither of them,' she said firmly.

'Cecily, I can't afford it. My losses . . .' His voice trailed off, his eyes haunted with anxiety.

Cecily felt a shot of concern. She put her hand on his arm. 'I understand that, I don't want any more money. I want them *both* home, Edmund. You know I do. Even if this Lloyd's fiasco hadn't happened I'd prefer them to go to day school.' She paused, saw him frown as if he was trying to understand. 'If they were both at day school it would save you much more money, take some of the pressure off you,' she said slowly, as if speaking to someone with small command of the language.

'I have few dreams left.' His voice cracked with emotion. 'I want Jamie to go to Eton. His prep school has the highest percentage of boys going there. I don't think they'd have taken him if they'd thought he wouldn't make it. I can just manage the fees if Miranda goes to day school. Then things must get better. After all, Lloyd's is offering a settlement,' he said desperately. 'Miranda could go back for A levels, or go to one of those international schools abroad and learn languages.'

'I don't hold out much hope for the settlement. Lloyd's can't possibly offer enough, not after what everyone's been through,' Cecily said impatiently. 'But you have a good salary, so maybe you will recoup the money you've lost at Lloyd's. I know I won't on the pittance I earn. But even if you do get your money back, it won't be for years. Jamie must be happy now. Surely that's the most important thing. Let him come home.'

'I want him to stay where he is at the moment. I'll go down and talk to him, explain.'

'He may not understand.' Cecily thought of Stephen and Daniel. Daniel had become cruel in his ambition for his son. She could not bear Edmund to do that to Jamie.

'Edmund, is Eton so important?' she said bitterly, desperately trying to pin him down. 'There are other schools that would suit him better.'

'I want him to go there. It means a lot to me.' His mouth settled into that stubborn line she knew so well. In the early days she'd have kissed it until it softened into laughter or passion. If she hadn't been so anxious about Jamie she might have tried it now.

Instead she opened her mouth to cry, 'But him, what about him? Surely we ought to be thinking about what's best for him, not you, not me.' Suddenly seeing this faded man before her, defeat and hopelessness in his eyes, she was reminded of Linette. She realised that Eton held security for him. It still stood strong against the changing times, a timeless institution not about to self-destruct and spew out dishonour and disregard to those who put their trust in it as other institutions had done. She understood, and she took his hand and stroked it, wanting to put her arms round him and hold him close to her. But she was afraid to in case he jumped up and left her. So she sat there beside him holding his hand.

It helped, knowing and understanding how Edmund was struggling to come to terms with his sense of betrayal over the losses at Lloyd's, but she could not sacrifice Jamie. However good a school Eton was, it would not suit Jamie. He would, for ever, be struggling while others raced forward. Edmund must accept this.

'I know you were happy there, but Jamie is not like you,' she said gently. 'And after all, times have changed, and they no longer just take in the sons of old boys because they are the sons. Let's go down and talk to David Sawyer together, ask him what he really thinks. He's a good headmaster and seems to know each boy very well.'

'He must go to Eton.' Edmund's voice had lost all its fire, he was almost pleading. He looked at her, his eyes beseeching.

Cecily put her arms round him, held him close to her. His body, his scent was so familiar, like a comfortable garment she could never give up. 'Oh Edmund, darling,' she said, the word slipping out before she could stop it. She felt his arms round her, holding her tightly as if he would never let her go. Then they relaxed and the two of them sat there rather ridiculously, awkwardly holding each other.

Suddenly, as if he'd heard a clarion call, he sat up, released her and said briskly, 'I must go, get home for tea.'

'Of course.' She felt cold without him, miserable that he was going away from her, back to Kent and Rowena, to the birthday party of a child who was not his.

'Meet me again, Edmund,' she said gently.

He got up, hovered a moment. 'I . . . well, I'd like to . . . but it's difficult.' He bent down and kissed her. 'Take care, Cecily.' His fingers briefly touched her cheek, his eyes searched into hers, then he was gone, his words echoing in her mind while she tried to decide if they were said in love or regret.

She sat there a long time not wanting to leave the

space where he had been. Together, she thought they could have coped with this Lloyd's business. But it was frightening how badly he was taking it. Perhaps he knew more than she did. He did, after all, go to all the action meetings, whereas she could hardly ever get time off. Perhaps he knew for sure what she only suspected, that there would never be any resolution for the Names who had been ruined.

Yet as she sat there among the shoppers, their bags and their chatter, she knew what it was that had destroyed him. It was the betrayal. He had betrayed their marriage vows by going off with Rowena, yet somehow he did not see it in the same light as betrayal by his peers. He'd been at school with many of the men who worked at Lloyd's, had trusted what they stood for, and he felt they had betrayed him, him and all the others. It was that that he could not take.

She took another sip of her now cold coffee. Edmund was courageous, as were so many of the beleaguered Names. He'd have pulled in his belt, lived in a smaller house, given up holidays, lived in dignity in reduced circumstances, but he could not cope with betrayal.

A sudden coldness gripped her in this warm, bustling place. She tried to shake it off but it would not leave her. She ordered another coffee, but after two sips she left it and wandered as if in a trance back up to the children's department to search for Miranda's dressing gown, the cold feeling inside her following her all the way.

★ ★ ★

'Jerome.' For a split second she stared at him standing on her doorstep as if he was a stranger. The children were home for an exeat and she was expecting Miranda's friend to appear. Then she went into his arms and kissed him. A week had passed since she had expected him back from his trip and this was their first contact since she'd blasted off at him about Emily down the telephone.

He kissed her too, yet she felt his kiss didn't hold his usual warmth. Especially for a lover she had not seen for two weeks.

'I was just passing, I thought I'd ring your bell on the offchance you were in.' He smiled but his smile didn't reach his eyes.

'It's good to see you. Come in. I've got the children here. For once they have the same weekend off.' She wondered why they were being so formal. Why hadn't he rung, said he was coming?

He hesitated. 'I don't want to disturb . . .'

'You won't, they'd like to see you.' She walked back into the house, anxiety picking at her. She sensed that he wanted to see her alone. Well, naturally he'd want to make love to her after not seeing her for so long – wouldn't he? He seemed so distant. She supposed he was hurt, angry about her barrage against Emily, and she hadn't yet apologised. She turned, smiling awkwardly.

'Jerome, I really am sorry about that telephone call. I was . . .' She raked her fingers through her hair.

'Don't worry about that now.'

'I do worry. I couldn't ring you back as I still didn't

have your number. I don't know where I put it. I'd had a terrible day – oh, it's a long story.'

'I saw Linette in New York.' He paused and looked at her almost expectantly.

'How did she look? She sounds so much better.'

He shrugged. 'Fine. Stephen told me all about what happened.'

'So you know what a hell of day it was. Then Richard rang me, threatening me, frightening me,' she added dramatically, hoping for his sympathy, his outrage that she could have been in danger. But there was no sign of it. She pushed on, 'And I so wanted to talk to you but Emily gave me the wrong number. The number of the Met—'

'Mum . . . Oh, hi.' Miranda, crumpled in a large T-shirt, came down the stairs.

'Hello, Miranda,' Jerome said.

'Are you coming with us to Deals? We're going there for lunch.'

'No, I can't today.' He smiled at her.

'Can't you?' Cecily said, suddenly feeling how much she'd missed him. She wanted him there beside her all day. They couldn't make love with the children here, but she could touch him, hear his voice, just be with him.

'I . . . I'm going out with Emily.' He avoided her eyes.

'She could come too,' Miranda said. 'My friend Caroline invited us all. Her family is taking me back to school as Mum can't take Jamie and me back and Daddy can't either, though I'd much rather go back tomorrow and miss double French.' She pulled a horrible face and went into the drawing room. She switched on the television.

'Perhaps you could get dressed first, darling,' Cecily said. 'We'll have to go soon.'

'In a minute. Jamie's not even up yet. He says he feels sick, but it's only 'cos he doesn't want to go back. I told him not to spoil us going out, and to feel sick after lunch.' She flicked the channels back and forth.

'Does he?' Cecily began to feel sick herself. Was Jamie genuinely ill, or was he suffering from school dread earlier in the day than usual? She hovered at the foot of the stairs, torn between going up to him and staying with Jerome.

Jerome guessed her dilemma. 'Go to him, I'll come and see you later.'

'No, stay. Come into the dining room. I haven't seen you for so long, and I do feel awful about what I said about Emily. I wanted to ring you back straightaway but—'

'But you meant it.' His voice was more sad than accusing.

'Yes, I did.' It was best to admit it. She tried to pick out the right words. 'I know I said it at the wrong time, when I was upset about everything. I should have waited until we were together instead of shouting it down the phone across the Atlantic, but she doesn't like me, Jerome. You know she doesn't. She'd deliberately given me the wrong number, so I was feeling very angry.' She looked into his eyes as she said it, feeling suddenly as if she was signing her death warrant. She put her hand on his arm. 'I love you, I miss you. Stay with us today, and tonight. It will work out.' But even as she said it she felt him drawing away from her although he did not move from her touch.

'My first priority is to my daughter. I have decided to put my other . . . relationships on hold for a while. I criticised her mother for having too many boy friends and not giving her enough time, and I seem to be doing the same thing,' he said rather pompously.

'Have you had too many girl friends?' She tried to smile, to joke him out of his mood.

'Not after I met you, you know that.'

'I was only teasing,' she said weakly.

'But I feel until she's older, more settled, that I shouldn't see . . . so much of you.' He frowned, his eyes agonised for a moment, then he took a step away from her. 'I wanted to speak to you more in depth but . . .' His eyes moved towards the drawing room and the noise from the television. 'I know I should have rung, but . . .'

'But Emily wouldn't let you, I suppose.' Cecily knew she sounded bitter, but she couldn't help it. Her instinct was to take him in her arms and hold him, kiss him, persuade him to work round this problem with Emily, but his stilted attitude annoyed her, and so did the way he was taking Emily's side without considering her own.

'I hold you to blame too, Cecily. She's only a child. I was surprised that you, a mother yourself, could say such things to her.'

'What things?'

He looked awkward as if he was about to blaspheme in church. 'That . . . that she was spoilt, a bitch, and if she took after her mother it was no wonder I left her and—'

'*What?*'

'And other things . . . I really didn't think you'd behave like that.' He looked miserable. 'You said you'd call her when I was away and I never thought you'd say such things to her.'

Cecily felt icy cold. 'I did not telephone her at all, except to ask her for your number. Why don't you ask Susan?'

'That's not what Emily said.' Jerome was breathing fast, his eyes bright with injustice and anger.

'And you believe her?' Cecily felt she would faint. It was like the day Edmund told her he loved Rowena, or the day she received her first nightmarish demand from Lloyd's. She swayed, leant against the wall. She couldn't believe it. Jerome couldn't be so taken in, couldn't just take his child's word without questioning it, against her, whom he said he loved, had asked to marry.

'Why shouldn't I? After all, you gave me a taste of it down the phone when I was in New York.'

'I know and I've explained why I said those things. But I'd never say them to her.' Then she wondered if that was true. She'd certainly say a thing or two now if Emily suddenly appeared.

She heard a thump from upstairs as if Jamie was

on his way down. She shot Jerome an appeal. Did he not see that Emily was determined to end their relationship?

'I'm sorry, Cecily.' His face was tight as if he was denying the love they had shared. 'I just can't tell you how . . .' He shrugged helplessly, looking at her with bewilderment as if he couldn't believe he had been so betrayed.

Cecily felt exhausted with defeat. She said nothing for a moment, just let the truth of the scene sink in and take hold of her. She did dislike Emily. Even if Jerome could be persuaded that she had lied about her calls, she would still be there, doing everything she could to destroy their relationship. It was finished, she realised with hollow pain. One way or the other, it was over.

'I did not call her. I did not say those things, she is lying to you about that. But she's won. She wants you to herself, not to share you with any other woman. So,' she shrugged wearily, 'I concede defeat.'

'Cecily . . .' He took a step closer to her.

'It's true, and one day you'll find out. But that's how it is and I haven't the strength with everything else that's going on at the moment to cope with it.' She went out of the room and to the stairs, her heart almost breaking.

'Jamie,' she called, 'are you all right? Get dressed, we're going out soon.'

Then she went into the drawing room where Miranda was lolling on the sofa watching the television. She marched up to it and switched it off. 'Go and get dressed, we'll never get to the restaurant at this rate.'

'Oh, Mum, I was watching that,' Miranda howled.

'It was rubbish. No wonder you never do well at school if you fill your brain with this drivel all the time. Go and get dressed.'

'No. I'm watching this. I don't want to go to Deals anyway. I hate Caroline Parker, she—'

'Tough, we're going,' Cecily said and, snatching out the plug of the television, she picked up a pair of scissors from the table and cut the cable.

'Mum, you can't!' Miranda wailed, furious yet amazed at Cecily's act of vandalism.

'I can and I will, now go and get dressed. Please, darling.' She felt near tears now, furious and ashamed of herself for taking out the anger she felt for Emily on Miranda. But seeing her slumped there in front of that appalling television show reminded her of Emily. That apathetic stance she had, that sullen exhaustion whenever she asked her to do anything. She stared miserably at her daughter who shrugged and left the room.

'Mum's gone mad,' she heard her say to Jerome. 'She's cut the plug off the television.' Then she heard her stump upstairs calling to Jamie and telling him the same thing.

Jerome came into the room. Cecily would not look at him. Now she had lost her temper in his hearing it would be another nail in her coffin. Well, she told herself without conviction, who wants a lover who only listens to one side of the story, his malicious daughter's?

'Go then,' she said keeping her back to him. 'I can't stand goodbyes, just go.'

'But, Cecily—'

'I don't want to hear any more.' She pulled round her all the self-respect and dignity she could muster. 'It was wonderful before she spoilt it, but now it is over. Please go.'

She could sense him hovering, but she would not turn round. She needed every ounce of her self-control not to throw herself in his arms and beg him to stay.

'Goodbye then.'

She heard him move out into the hall and to the front door. Not until she heard the door close behind him and his steps fade away up the road did she allow herself to cry.

Part IV

Chapter Twenty-Four

'So I'm going to sell the castle. It's a dump, your father just let it go. It needs a fortune spending on it.'

'I think it will stand firm for a few more years.' Even as she said it, Cecily knew there was no point arguing with Ronald. He owned the castle, he could do what he liked with it. She couldn't stop him.

'The farmer next door might buy it though not at a good enough price. I was too generous with you, Cecily.'

'Well, I've no money left to give you, Lloyd's has seen to that.'

'I wasn't asking you for money.'

'Ronald, about money, what . . .' She stopped suddenly. Stephen had told her he would deal with Daniel's £100,000 that he sent back to her via Ronald.

'If you should see him at some social gathering, don't even hint you know anything about it,' Stephen warned when they'd discussed it again. 'Let me find out about it before he can cover his tracks, then I can get him.'

The way he said it, the menacing look in his eyes,

convinced Cecily that Stephen was determined to get back at him, not only for this but for all the mischief he had caused since the day he shot the seal at Dunnet Point.

Remembering this, and hoping Ronald did not suspect what she'd almost said, she got up, walked over to the drinks tray and offered him another drink.

'No thanks.' He shot her an evil look. He was more solid now than he had been in his youth, his hair had a strange black sheen to it as if it was dyed. He seemed even more sinister to her now than he had before.

'I don't know why you came to tell me you were selling it,' she said hurriedly to hide her disquiet. 'You haven't been in touch with me since you bought it. You know there's nothing I can do or say about it.' She glared at him with dislike. It made her sick just to think of him living in the castle, looking out at the sea, walking on the moors, especially if the money Stephen had sent back could have prevented him having it.

Ronald stood in the middle of her drawing room, legs apart, a whisky in his hand. She wondered if he'd come to taunt her with his plans.

'I just wondered if you know much about planning up there.'

'No. You can go and ask though. You're not trying to turn it into a theme park, are you?' Her remark was sarcastic, then seeing his expression she said incredulously, 'You can't! Even you couldn't think of something so awful.'

'I can't afford to be sentimental, Cecily. This is business. Quite a few people go to John O'Groats and the Orkneys. I could offer them something else. I wondered if you knew anyone on the council – wait.' He thrust out his hand holding the whisky glass, to fend off her words. 'I'd make it worth your while.'

Cecily stared at him open-mouthed. She couldn't believe what she was hearing. 'You mean you'd pay me to try and get round someone in the Caithness planning department so you can build a theme park on that lovely piece of coastline? You must be mad.'

'Not quite like that.' He tried to laugh.

'How like then?'

'If I knew what could or could not be built there, I would know who to approach to sell it to. There's no money in land for farming these days. I thought of finding a developer or even doing it myself, after all I am in the business.' His smile was smug. 'It may not be a theme park exactly, but a hypermarket or a leisure centre . . .'

She jerked up as if she'd been given an electric shock. 'No, Ronald, I shall do nothing to help you. If I can stop you I will but—'

'My dear Cecily, you can do nothing. I was just giving you the chance to make a little cash, but if you don't want it . . .' He threw the last of the whisky down his throat and plonked down his glass.

She stared at him, not really sure what he had hoped she would do. She knew some of the more influential people up there, it was true, had known them since she was a child. Then it dawned on her. 'They don't like you up there, do they? That's why you've come to me. You hoped I would somehow smooth over your atrocious plans. Well, you're wrong, I shall do nothing to help you.'

'I thought you needed money.'

'I need my own money,' she said coldly, staring at him intently.

'Cecily, darling.' The endearment was a sneer. 'You can't afford to be so choosy. The news about Lloyd's does not look good for you. They've offered this settlement, then changed the amount again, but it looks as if it will be accepted by the majority of the Names. Then you can't go to court, you'll have to get on with it.' His fleshy lips curved in a semblance of a smile. 'What do you have? You're out in the cold, no one's going to bother with small fry like you.'

His words struck a chill in her. She thought of the years ahead, skimping and saving just to live, Lloyd's taking everything she possessed, even beyond the grave.

Outwardly no one would guess that she possessed nothing. She lived in a small but beautiful house, wore clothes that still looked good, ran a car, but it was all an illusion, and bit by bit it was being eroded. In the end she would have to go bankrupt; at least then she hoped she would be free of Lloyd's hold.

Lloyd's had now made a £900 million offer. Provided the Names dropped litigation, a quarter to a third would be knocked off their supposed bill. Cecily had laughed when she'd got the offer. 'How generous they've been. I only owe three-quarters of a million now,' she'd said to Edmund on the telephone. Some of her group of women, now swelled to over twenty, had been dismissive of the terms too, though one or two longed for a settlement to put an end to their nightmare.

'I don't know.' Edmund sounded dispirited. 'But if we do accept, it will be the end of years of court cases, and the possibility of losing even more on a legal technicality.'

'I'm going on fighting,' she'd said firmly. 'What they've offered makes no difference to me.'

'I'd pay you cash, put it in some secret account for you.' Ronald was pushing on, seeing her reflective mood as she thought over her conversation with Edmund.

'No,' she said. 'Whatever happens, however much they take me for, I'll not take your money. I took it once for the castle and I've regretted it ever since. I should have tried to find another way to pay back the bank. I just panicked, owing all that much. I was a fool to act so fast.'

'I'm giving you one last chance. You'll be a fool again if you turn it down. They'd listen to you up there. Just tell them you need the money from selling the site, persuade them that it could attract more tourists, more business to that part of Scotland.' His mouth was tightening now, his eyes hard as they glared at her. 'Nearly three hundred thousand tourists passed through last year so—'

'I've said no, so leave—' she said bluntly.

'What about your children? Are they to suffer because of your damn pride? I hear Edmund's lost a fortune, and now he's got this woman, there will be none from that quarter.'

'Money isn't everything.'

'Maybe, but none is nothing, sweetie, believe me. Are you prepared to send your children to some inner-city comprehensive, live in some hovel?'

'It might not come to that.'

'Want to bet?' Ronald laughed roughly. 'My dear Cecily, spoilt, sheltered little Cecily, you're going to have to face up to the harsh world outside your privileged haven. I was thinking of giving you quite a sizeable sum if I sold the castle well. It would protect you from all that.'

'Get out!' she shouted, stung by his remarks, knowing they were true, afraid that in her anger she'd taunt him about Stephen's missing money. 'We will cope somehow. There's nothing wrong with state schools. We'll live in the country – somehow we'll survive.' Her eyes narrowed with hatred for him. To spite him, she was determined to survive. Whatever Lloyd's did to her, she and her children would come through. If they had to live in a hovel, they would do so with dignity and get some fun out of it. The rats of the world would not see her suffer. 'Now go, and don't come back.' She marched out of the room and yanked open the front door.

'You'll regret this,' he said coldly.

'I hate dishonesty . . . I wouldn't feel comfortable with this . . . this deal.'

'What do you mean?' he asked quickly, a dull red colour rising in his face.

'Just go.' She resisted temptation to push him out into the street. She took a deep breath. He would never know how hard it was to turn down his offer of money. Recently she'd realised with sickening pain that she'd have to sell some of her good pieces of furniture, to pay for the action groups. Christie's were coming to value them in a few days.

'You never liked Mother and me, did you? You and Linette, you always thought you were so superior, and your father too, he treated my mother abominably.' His bitterness made him more revolting. There was so much resentment burning in him, Cecily realised.

'You never gave us cause to like you,' she said acidly. 'Remember the seal?' She was tempted to add the time he squashed himself against her in the attic, but she didn't in case it encouraged him to try it again.

'How sentimental you are, Cecily. What's one seal when children are dying every day of cruelty?'

She ignored this remark, worrying now that he might say something about Daniel and Linette. It seemed extraordinary that he didn't know. But if he did know, surely he would use it against her. Perhaps Gail had been so ashamed of herself blackmailing Daniel that she had not told her son.

'Don't come crying to me when you're on the streets,' he spat. Cecily almost expected him to add, 'where you belong.'

'I'll do without your help, thank you,' she said firmly.

401

'Goodbye, Ronald.' She flattened herself against the wall so he should not touch her as he passed. He slipped past her like a snake, going to a gleaming dark Mercedes that was double-parked outside. As the interior light went on Cecily caught a glimpse of an over-made-up, red-haired woman in a fur coat sitting in the driver's seat.

As the car slid away, Cecily shut the door and went back to her drawing room.

'Oh, Daddy, what did you do to us?' she shouted angrily at his photograph on the table in front of her. 'It's you that's lost me the castle. Now what will it be turned into.' She realised now that she'd never blamed Linette. Had she really been seduced, all innocent and trusting? Or had she known exactly what he was after? The thought sobered her. Had they both betrayed her?

She ground her hands together. If Ronald would sell the castle to someone pleasant, another family to grow up there as they had done, she might feel differently, not let these bitter feelings distort her mind. But to turn it into some vulgar theme park, or hypermarket – surely he was taunting her, surely he wouldn't get permission for such a thing. But money, as he'd said, was money, and there were people who'd be quite happy to see the whole of Britain covered in tarmac and hideous shopping warehouses.

She rang some of her friends in Caithness. They were all horrified, though not surprised, at her news.

'He's just the sort that would do it,' John Forbes, an old friend of Daniel's, said. 'I'll look into it. Thanks for the warning. It's not the same without all of you.'

She was still sitting and brooding on the unpleasant scene with Ronald when Miranda came back from a day out with friends. It was half-term.

'I'm going to have no friends at the new school,' she said petulantly, throwing herself down on a chair. 'I wish I didn't have to leave Quinton Hall.'

'Darling, Daddy and I have been over this so often with you. Besides, you do have friends. Sophie Garland is there and Kate Pickford and I'm sure Belinda—'

'They're not my friends.'

'They were when you were little. You'll soon catch up with them again.' Cecily felt so drained after her scene with Ronald she couldn't drum up much enthusiasm for Miranda's social life. The last weekend exeat they'd had a dreadful scene taking Jamie back. However she and Edmund had explained it to him, he felt utterly betrayed by them.

'Miranda doesn't even want to change schools, why can't she stay and me come home?'

'I've explained, Daddy wants you to go to Eton, he thinks you'll be happy there, that it will be a great advantage in your life. School shapes your whole life. You may not think it now, but the time you have there . . .' Even as she said it, the words felt empty. If you weren't happy and couldn't grow and flourish somewhere, it could do lasting harm, not good.

She'd had endless telephone conversations with Edmund over it. She'd asked to meet him but he'd been away or busy. All the time he'd been incredibly distant about it, until she decided she'd have to go down to Kent one weekend, Rowena or no, and fight to have Jamie home.

It had been difficult getting Miranda into a good London day school. In the end she had to stay at her boarding school another two terms as the school they liked would not have space until September. Cecily had offered to help pay her fees, knowing she would have to sacrifice yet more furniture, and her jewellery too, but Edmund had refused.

'I'll deal with it,' he'd said abruptly. 'Pay out while I still can.'

He'd rung off then, leaving her feeling deflated. Whenever she mentioned Lloyd's or money he'd clam up. The Names had been given until Valentine's Day to decide. The view in the newspapers was that there would be a majority vote in favour of the settlement, despite the conditions involved.

Without Jerome, Cecily felt very bleak. Her empty bed yawned huge and lonely.

Once she thought she saw him coming out of a restaurant in Knightsbridge. It was late at night and she was coming home alone from a dinner party. She slowed her car, opened the window, wanting just to call out to him, to hear his voice again. But he walked quickly away up a dark street, and she was not sure it was him after all.

'Oh, Jerome,' she sighed in desolation. 'Why didn't we try harder? Why did I let you go?'

She hadn't tried to replace him. Other men she found

wanting and, she admitted to herself, she wondered how she could embark on an affair when Miranda was living at home all the time. Miranda was thirteen now and beginning to become critical. Cecily prayed she would not be another Emily.

'I don't know why you and Jerome broke up, he was nice,' Miranda said. 'Charlotte Wain's mother has lots of rich boy friends and they give her masses of presents.'

'Jerome was not like that.'

'He might've been. We didn't see him enough. Why don't you go out with someone richer? Someone who'd give us money so we needn't sell our best things.' She'd been furious when Cecily had told her that some of the furniture would have to go.

'I don't want to, Miranda. Let's drop it, shall we?' She was wearied by Miranda's cross-examination of her love life. It convinced her further that it would be a nightmare if she did indulge in another affair. Not that she'd met anyone she'd remotely like to have an affair with.

The telephone rang and Miranda pounced on it. 'Hi, all the way from America. I wish I was there. I hope we're coming this summer, but it all depends on Lloyd's,' Miranda said. 'It all depends on Lloyd's' had become a catchphrase in their household. 'You know I'm moving schools? I'm going to day school. I shall be so tired, parties every night . . .'

'Not while you're living here, there won't be.' Cecily took the receiver out of her hand. 'Hello.'

'Cecily, it's me. How are you?'

'Lin! How are you? You sound great.'

'I feel wonderful. Stephen's been marvellous, got me some help. I feel much more positive.' She laughed. 'He's got in touch with solicitors in London, everything. I'm going for a divorce, it's the only way.'

'I think you're right. But will you live out there?' Bitter after her meeting with Ronald, she suddenly didn't want to see Linette just at the moment.

'No, I'll be back in a month or so. I must get the girls back to school. But I've decided to move to London, find somewhere tiny, near you – if I can get my money back from Richard, that is, but Stephen . . .' she paused. 'I don't know what he's done or said, but he seems to think he can get most of it back.'

'I'll look round and see what's on the market,' Cecily said as cheerfully as she could.

'Are there any houses going in your street?'

'Not that I know of at the moment.' She didn't add that soon her own might be up for sale. Her financial situation was becoming so bad she might have to sell the house and move to a flat. She swallowed this new pain and said with forced brightness, 'I'm so glad you're better. Stephen's come up trumps after all. I was afraid he was too much like Daddy over emotional things.'

'He is. You've no idea how like Daniel he is.' She laughed, making Cecily suddenly wonder if they, too would end up in bed. Linette rushed on, 'Fiona and her husband Greg have been marvellous too, so supportive.'

'I wish Stephen would come here and sort out Ronald,' Cecily said, ignoring the painful suspicions that haunted her, that Linette had been as much to blame for her seduction as Daniel. She told her of his plans for selling the castle.

'The creep. What did he think you were going to do? Bribe everyone to let him build his monstrosity? But he can't, Cecily, he really can't. What can we do?'

'I don't know. I've warned people up there, but the castle's no longer mine, I can't do anything. You know I would if I could.'

'What a creep he was. Remember the seal?' Cecily could feel her anger down the line.

'I saw him with a woman in a fur coat the other night. I don't think it was a seal.'

'Good thing I wasn't there, I'd have skinned her. You know Stephen's pretty sure Ronald's made off with the money he sent back for you.'

'Can he prove it?' Cecily said.

'He's doing his best. Daniel's solicitor has retired, but they are looking into it.'

'You know how long that can take,' Cecily laughed.

'Don't let Ronald turn the castle into a Scottish Disney,' Linette said. 'I couldn't bear it after all the wonderful summers we had there.'

'Don't remind me,' Cecily said through gritted teeth, wishing she could confront Linette with her part in their losing the castle and feeling guilty for doing so.

'I think Daddy and Rowena are going to break up,'

Miranda announced as they shared a pizza for supper.

'What do you mean?' Cecily stared at her. This was the first she'd heard of it.

'He never talks, or eats much. Just sits and worries. She gets quite cross.' Miranda crammed her mouth full.

'Wait until you've finished your mouthful.' Cecily felt a tiny prick of hope. She knew Miranda, like Emily, jumped to peculiar conclusions, but Edmund had never married Rowena and that was strange. They were both now divorced, so why did they not marry? Had their love gone sour and – she hardly dared think this – would he come back to them?

'At the weekend he just sat in his chair. I tried to talk to him, but it took ages to get through. Philippa Evan's father tried to go back to her mother but she wouldn't have him. Would you take Daddy back? If he was sorry and would never do it again?' She fixed Cecily with her eyes, the same clear eyes as Edmund had, tomato sauce from the pizza on her chin.

'I don't think it's come to that,' Cecily said. 'Maybe he was tired, or ill.'

'Rowena was cross all the time.'

'I thought you had a nice weekend.' They hadn't talked much since she'd been home. She'd spent the weekend with Edmund, he'd dropped her back, without coming in, as was usual these days. Then she'd spent today with a friend so Cecily could work. Tomorrow evening she went back to school.

'I did. Friends of the girls took us out. We went

408

swimming and to the cinema.'

'So Daddy didn't take you?'

'No, he sat in his chair.'

'I see.' Cecily decided not to ask any more questions. If Miranda had been out so much of the time she wouldn't have seen how long Edmund stayed in his chair. He was probably very busy all weekend but just happened to be in his chair when she was there.

Cecily popped home in her lunch hour to let in the man from Christie's to value her furniture. He was a good-looking young man, but she wouldn't have cared if he'd been a gorilla; she felt as if she was selling her children. But there was nothing for it, money was pouring out like a flood now. She dared not stop paying to the action groups in case, when it came to court, she would be excluded from any payout they might be awarded. Her losses came to nearly one million pounds. A million pounds, she'd thought, remembering how when they were children a million had seemed like all the money they'd ever need to live an extravagant life. Now, although she'd never had it, she'd lost it.

Yet another letter had come from Lloyd's explaining that if she didn't pay, or at least come in and discuss how she would pay, a writ would be served on her. The fear she had felt at this had been overwhelming. It made her realise how helpless she was against such a vast institution.

She went to one of Serena's meetings. The other women there put on a show of defiance, of bravado, but Cecily felt that, underneath, their courage was failing.

Others had had letters like hers. There were more stories of houses and possessions sold, of middle-aged and untrained women floundering about in the job market. She left feeling almost more depressed.

The man from Christie's looked round at her furniture. 'That's a very pretty cabinet,' he said, indicating the black and gold Chinese cabinet Daniel had given her for her twenty-first birthday.

'I don't want to sell that.'

'It's the best bit you've got. That table's nice.' He noted everything down, breaking her heart a little more each time as she pointed out the few pieces he could put in the sale. I must earn more money, she thought desperately, find some way to keep the rest. But she knew in her heart that however much she earned, Lloyd's would come for it.

Cecily worked hard all that week, staying late in the evenings helping Daphne restock the shelves and clean out the stockroom. There was nothing else to do, and she could not bear to be at home to see the empty spaces where her furniture once stood. She felt weighed down with a sort of apathy, and wanted only to stay in her safe environment.

Valentine's Day came and to the newspapers' surprise the majority of the Names threw out Lloyd's offer. The Chairman expressed regret, there were dire warnings of the horrors of litigation, but Cecily felt elated. Rough though the way ahead might be, over seventeen thousand Names were prepared to fight on.

She rang Edmund to crow over this, but his office

said he was away on business. She wished she could tell Jerome. Instead she rang up all the ladies on the help line, and suggested a celebration.

'Oh no, dear,' Barbara said sadly, 'I'm not celebrating. I hoped they'd settle. Now it looks like it won't be settled in my lifetime, and I'm so sick of it all.' She sounded so low, Cecily was concerned. She rang Serena who had not taken Felix back but had found a new lease of life with this group, helping them all she could.

'I know, Barbara's been very down lately. Just worn out by it. I think she needs professional help. I'll see to it,' she said briskly. Cecily could see her eagerly planning how to help her. Serena had been wonderful coping with the other women, but she could not cope with her own husband's problems, brought on by the same cause.

It came to Jamie's Sunday out. Edmund, whom she'd at last contacted, sounded strange when she tried to arrange when he would see him.

'I can't see him, not at the moment.'

'Why? Will you be away?'

'No. I'll see him another time.' He'd rung off and she'd felt the old anxiety rise up in her. Then she thought he was afraid to see Jamie in case there was a scene about him staying at boarding school.

Jamie looked as if he had shrunk. He was certainly not growing and Cecily felt sore with anguish. He'd have to leave the school, he couldn't stay there. He seemed resigned, like a person in prison. She looked

411

round for the headmaster and saw him with some
parents.

'Hang on a minute, darling, I just want a word with
Mr Sawyer.'

'Why, Mum? What do you want to say? Dad came
down last week, he saw him.'

'He didn't tell me.'

Jamie stared ahead. 'He came down to see about me
going to Eton. He took me out to the Little Chef for tea
and bought me tons of sweets.'

'We were meant to be coming down together, Jamie. I
wish he'd told me.' She felt annoyed that Edmund had
not rung her, asked her to come with him. Seeing the
parents leaving the headmaster, she got out of the car.

'Mr Sawyer.' She smiled as she went towards him. He
was a large, ungainly man with a florid face. The boys
loved him.

'Why, Mrs Mendelson.' He took her hand in his
heavy-boned one. 'How are you?'

'I'm fine, thank you. I'm . . . I'm worried about Jamie.
He looks so pale and thin and—'

'I know. There are a lot of coughs and colds about at
this time of the year. He had a nasty one last week. He
needs feeding up. I'm sure you'll be doing that today.'
He smiled kindly at her. He was used to mothers'
concern.

'I'm more worried about his education. My . . . my
ex-husband came down this week, I understand. I wish
he'd told me, but—'

'Mrs Mendelson, it's a difficult time for the boys,

coming up to Common Entrance. Jamie is a worrier. It is also difficult . . .' he coughed, cleared his throat, may have blushed under his red skin, 'when homes break up. But he has a good brain, he must just apply it better. I told your . . . er . . . Mr Mendelson, we must not make hasty decisions. We'll see how the rest of this term goes, then we'll decide what, em, further education will suit him best.'

'So Eton—'

'Mrs Mendelson,' he held up one of his large hands, 'I said we'd make no hasty decisions. Enjoy your day with him, it looks like being a sunny one.' He smiled and then turned to another parent who was hovering beside him.

Jamie said nothing when she got back into the car. She talked to him most of the way back, telling him about Linette, amusing stories about her work, Miranda. But he only grunted or answered in such a stilted, polite way, her heart nearly broke.

This formal child, she thought, is my son and yet we cannot talk and laugh together as we should. She took him to one of his favourite hamburger joints for lunch, but he barely ate. Then to the Launch Pad in the Science Museum, another favourite place, and all the time the clock ticked on.

At five o'clock, an hour before they were due to leave, he lay on the sofa while she packed up things for him, knowing she'd never buy him all these things if he lived at home all the time. Guilt, she thought drily, is expensive.

413

'Jamie, it's not long till the holidays now,' she said, dreading the painful drive back.

'I think it's for ever,' he said, and closed his eyes. He had the face of an old man.

She sat down beside him and put her hand on his forehead to stroke away his hair. It was boiling hot.

'Jamie, don't you feel well?'

'No.' He didn't open his eyes.

'I'll get the thermometer,' she said, knowing that whatever it said she would keep him here tonight.

His temperature was 101. She tucked him up in bed and rang the school.

'There's a lot of it about, poor chap,' said the matron. 'Let us know how he gets on.'

'Thank you.' She put down the phone. They were a decent lot at his school. If only Edmund didn't expect so much of him, he might have been happy.

The phone rang again.

'Cecily, it's Rowena.'

'Rowena?'

'Yes. I'm sorry to ring, but I don't know what to do. It's Edmund.'

'What's happened to him?' A tiny bubble of hope rose in her. Had their affair finished? Did he want to come back to her?

'He's most odd, so quiet. I don't know what to do. It's this Lloyd's business, he . . .'

Cecily now felt annoyed. Was Rowena getting tired of him because he'd lost his money? Edmund had told her she wanted another child, marriage too, no doubt, both expensive things that Edmund could not now afford.

'We're all battling on, it's not easy for any of us,' Cecily said briskly, thinking of her furniture. 'I know a marvellous old lady who's doing bed and breakfasts to help meet her losses. I'm hoping to do the same. People are taking all sorts of jobs that they'd never have dreamt of taking before, just fighting back, any way they can.'

'I know, Cecily,' Rowena sounded desperate, 'but he's not coping. He's given up. He—'

'What can I do? I don't live with him,' Cecily said impatiently. If Edmund was with her, they would pull through together.

'I want you to come down. I'm sorry, Cecily, I know it's a cheek after . . . everything. But please, I'm worried about him. If you could talk to him . . . Come down tomorrow.'

'I can't, Jamie's ill. He's got a temperature. Nothing serious, but I must keep him at home for a day or two.'

'I really do need you, Cecily. The doctor's given him some pills but—'

'Pills? What pills? They won't bring our money back.' Edmund never took pills, never went near a doctor if he could help it. How could Rowena let him sink so far?

'For depression.'

'Let me speak to him now,' Cecily said. Depression. Edmund used to laugh at such a word. Self-indulgence, he called it.

'No, he's asleep, that's why I'm ringing.'

'But it's only seven o'clock.'

'I know.'

'I'll come when I can, Rowena. Get him to ring me when he wakes up. Tell him Jamie's at home, maybe he'd like to talk to him tomorrow.'

When she'd put the receiver down she was thoughtful. It was quite unlike Rowena to ring and ask for help like that. But then no one else knew Edmund as she did. Was Rowena just fed up with his change of mood? Miranda had said she was cross all weekend. Possibly she was bored rigid with this Lloyd's business, and who could blame her? They all were. Maybe she wanted to sound off at someone who knew what she was going through. Perhaps she should join their group, talk to others in the same boat. Cecily smiled ironically.

But her call made Cecily feel uneasy. Had the strain of the Lloyd's losses really made Edmund ill? He'd looked terrible when she'd last seen him. But he must buck up and fight back, she thought, feeling like snatching up the telephone and telling him to do so at once. But what if Rowena was handing him back to her? Would she take him? Deep down inside she knew the answer. Whatever he'd done, however much he'd hurt her, she would take him back. After all, she did still love him. She sat for a long time thinking about it, trying to ignore the little flame of hope that burned in her. She went upstairs to Jamie, happy he was at home.

Chapter Twenty-Five

It was not so bad taking Jamie back in daylight. After two days at home he seemed to have filled out a bit and went back with a stoic cheerfulness that almost broke Cecily's heart.

She arrived at work mid-morning. She walked into the shop smiling.

'Here I am. The traffic wasn't too bad so I'm earlier than I thought.'

There was a silence, an icy chill as she entered. Daphne looked agitated. Gilly stifled a gasp, clamped her hand to her mouth, her eyes jumping from Daphne to Cecily in tortured anxiety.

'What is it?' Cecily felt as if her stomach was filled with stones. Was Daphne going to sack her? Explain nicely that really she needed someone more reliable who didn't have ill children, long lunch hours with lovers, and stepsisters who had to be rescued from violent husbands.

'Cecily, my dear . . .' Daphne wrung her hands, her made-up face working. 'Look, can we go downstairs? I have some bad news . . .'

Something had happened to Miranda, or to Jamie, although he'd seemed fine when she'd dropped him. Maybe he'd been seriously ill after all and had collapsed. She felt faint, as if all her strength was draining out through her feet. 'The children . . .'

'No, dear. It's not the children. Let's go downstairs.' Daphne took her arm gently as if she was an invalid and led her to the stairs going down to the basement. Cecily heard Gilly make a sound like a sob. She stopped, stood firm.

'Please tell me. Is it my mother? Linette? Has Richard found her? Beaten her up again?'

'No, it's none of them. But come downstairs, we don't want to be disturbed by a customer.' Daphne went firmly on ahead and Cecily was forced to follow her.

'My dear,' Daphne looked as if she would burst into tears, 'there is no easy way to tell you, but your . . . Edmund is dead.'

'Dead?' The word was alien to her. 'Dead? I don't understand. When? How?'

'This morning. He . . .' Daphne cleared her throat, gave a little gasp. 'I'm afraid, my dear, he . . . shot himself.' Tears fell from her made-up eyes, making rivulets down her beige cheeks. Cecily watched transfixed for a moment. She'd never seen Daphne's face, or her composure, collapse so. She felt she was struggling through a mist, cloying as a spider's web, which any moment would clear like waking from a dream.

She shook her head as if to dislodge the words that

were now embedding themselves into her consciousness.

'Shot himself? An accident. He must have been cleaning his gun and it went off. Is that what happened?' The words were stiff, difficult to form. 'How do you know about it?' Her voice was frantic now. 'Are you sure?'

'A man . . . Giles . . . I don't remember his other name, I wrote it down. He said he was Rowena's brother.'

'Makin, Giles Makin,' Cecily said helpfully as if by getting the answer right, the story would not be true.

'He rang . . . he was staying there. He found him. My dear, I just don't know what to say.' Daphne came up to her and quite unlike herself gave Cecily an awkward hug. 'Is there anyone I can ring, to be with you?'

'My children.' Cecily thought of that brave little boy she'd just dropped off at school, walking away from her, his back stiff, determined not to show his unhappiness. She thought of Miranda, just changing from a child into a woman. How they both adored Edmund.

'My children,' she cried out with anguish. 'Get me my children.'

For a few moments she was hysterical, the pain of the grief tearing great chunks out of her. She was aware of voices, concerned, kind, and then a cup of hot, sweet tea was put to her lips and she heard Gilly say, 'Try and drink this, it will help.' She drank, felt it running down her throat with her tears. Although she knew something terrible had happened to Edmund, she still couldn't grasp it.

After a while she felt calmer.

'What should I do?' she said to Daphne who was sat beside her. 'I must get to the children.'

'When you feel up to it, I'd ring Giles. I have the number. Is there anyone who could fetch the children?'

'I will . . . I must do that.'

'Then you must find someone to go with you. You can't go alone,' Daphne said firmly. 'I'll come with you if you'd like me to.'

'That's sweet of you, but you have the shop. I'll ring Penny – she's Miranda's godmother, she'll know what to do.' Cecily felt detached from her body, as if she was mechanical and running on auto pilot.

'First ring Giles,' Daphne said. 'Do you feel up to it?'

'I must.' Still she didn't really believe it. Edmund dead? And in such a way. She rang him. Giles's voice was brusque as if giving orders. She remembered he'd been in the army.

'I'm sorry, Cecily. It happened this morning. Rowena had taken the children to school. I found him in the garage. Shot himself in the head. I'm sorry.'

She could imagine him telling army parents and wives the cold, brutal facts of a loved one's death. But then she thought, however you tell it, such news is always stark and cruel.

'Was it an accident?' she heard herself asking.

'No, Cecily.' His voice was gentler now. 'I'm afraid not.'

'Why?'

'Look, do you want to come down? I know it's a damn difficult business, but Rowena is very cut up and—'

'I'll come. I've got to tell the children, they're at school, but I'll come. I don't know what to do.'

'Have you someone close to the children who could collect them? Or go with you tomorrow after you've been here? I'd tell their head teachers today, though.'

'Yes. I'll see you later then.' She rang off, stupefied with grief.

She rang Penny who came straight round and took her home. It was Penny who rang the children's schools and she who bundled Cecily into the car to drive her to Kent.

'Haven't you other things to do?' Cecily said at last as they trailed through the traffic.

'Nothing that can't wait. I'm so sorry, Cecily. It's a terrible thing.'

'I should have gone to see him. Rowena did ask me to, but Jamie was ill . . .' The guilt was like a jagged weapon sawing inside her.

'You may not have been able to do anything. If he was that depressed . . . Did he leave a note?'

'I don't know. But I know why he died. It was Lloyd's. He felt so betrayed. I know it was that.' She thought back to the last time she had seen him. 'Take care, Cecily,' he'd said, looking so drawn and pale.

'It wasn't because he'd felt he'd made a mistake, leaving you and the children?'

'No. He loved Rowena, he wouldn't have left us if he hadn't. He loved me too.' She smiled. 'If he hadn't been so correct he'd probably have liked to set up home with both of us.'

They arrived at Rowena's house. Edmund and Rowena had both bought it when they had moved in together, but Cecily thought of it as Rowena's house. In the drive was a police car, a Volvo and a black van.

Penny shuddered when she saw the van and parked as far away from it as possible. Cecily didn't seem to notice it. She was thinking, why do we rush to people when they have died? It's too late. Do we rush in case we can stop them, catch the last of their spirit before they go?

Giles came out of the house and strode towards them. He opened her door. 'Cecily, my dear Cecily.' He helped her out as if she was infirm, and kissed her. 'Dreadful business. I'm so sorry.'

'This is Penny Young.' She gestured towards Penny.

'Good to see you. Let's go in. Rowena's inside.'

Numb, Cecily allowed herself to be led in. Rowena, she thought, do I want to see her? Is she not in some way responsible for this? She wanted to stop, to wait awhile and get her bearings, but it was as if she was on a conveyor belt, moving ever forward.

Rowena, her face swollen and blotched with tears, was slumped on a sofa. A policewoman and another man sat with her. Cecily had not thought what she would say, how she would cope with this meeting. She only knew she had an overwhelming desire to be where Edmund was.

'Oh Cecily . . .' Rowena crumpled again in sobs.

The policewoman offered tea, and the man walked over to her and shook her hand. 'I'm Simon Oats, the family doctor. Come and sit down. This must be such a shock for you.'

'Where's Edmund?' Cecily said. 'I want to see him.'

There was a cry from Rowena, a gasp from someone else.

'No,' said Giles. 'You really can't, Cecily. Believe me, it would upset you too much.' He came over to her and hovered awkwardly in front of her. 'Rowena hasn't seen him. Better not.' He couldn't meet her eyes.

'I want to say goodbye to him,' she said, feeling how unreal this all was. She looked round the room. It was overdone in chintz with borders in plain colours, and bows. Far too 'pretty' for a country house. There was nothing of Edmund here. He didn't belong here. How could he be dead here?'

'I know, my dear,' the doctor took over. 'But in cases like these it's better not. Remember the good times you had.'

'I would just like to hold his hand,' Cecily insisted. She couldn't understand why they were being so difficult. Edmund was her husband; whatever the courts had decided and whatever Rowena thought, he was her husband, the father of her children.

She felt rather than saw them exchange glances.

'You mustn't . . . it's horrible . . . he's shot,' Rowena gasped. 'I haven't seen him. I don't want to.'

'I want to touch him, just once more,' Cecily said, feeling like a child whom no one understood. 'I'll accept it better then.' She looked at the doctor. He had kind eyes.

He smiled and put his hand on her arm. 'If you insist, you can see the body but not the face. That's not the Edmund you must remember. Wait here a minute.'

'She can't,' Rowena cried. 'She can't see him.'

Giles went to her and Cecily walked away to the large window and looked over the garden. She'd often wondered what their house was like. She still couldn't see Edmund here, it was far too fussy and elaborate. She found herself wondering how many metres of chintz they'd needed, and what on earth it must have cost. The doctor came back into the room.

'If you're sure?' He looked at Cecily.

'I'm sure.' She followed him outside and over to the garage. She felt as if she was somehow outside her body, drugged or asleep. She was glad the doctor was beside her. He felt real, alive and reassuring. Her breath was coming fast, and once he stopped her and asked if she really did want to see Edmund.

'Take a few deep, slow breaths,' he said.

He stopped by the black van. Inside was a plain box; the lid had been removed and a form covered with a blanket lay in it. It wasn't Edmund, it was nothing like Edmund. Yet when she saw his hand with the signet ring on the little finger, she knew it was him. She stretched out and touched it. It was cold and stiff.

She held his hand, not looking at the shape that belonged to it. She looked at her feet in their neat patent shoes, the gold chains on the front. She moved her hand over Edmund's as if willing it to warm up, to curl over hers. She felt the hard edge of the ring.

Suddenly she knew she had to have it. Take it from him and carry it always. She glanced back at it. His fingers seemed so thin. She glanced at the doctor who was pretending to be studying the garden.

She moved her body in front of Edmund's, surreptitiously keeping the doctor in her sights. She eased the ring off and held it in her hand. Then the pain hit her; holding Edmund's ring in her hand seemed the final proof that he was dead, that he really was gone from her for ever. She thrust the ring into her coat pocket.

'Why?' she heard her voice cry out. She turned away from the shape in the box that was Edmund, back into the winter sunshine of the day. 'Why did he do it?' She felt cold, she stumbled, but the doctor caught her, led her to a garden bench and eased her onto it.

'He was very depressed, his financial situation was troubling him. His losses at Lloyd's seemed to mount up with no redress, and then when the settlement was refused, there seemed to be no end. He became . . .' He paused. 'Well, he became rather irrational about it. Worry does that to some people.'

'Did he leave a note?'

'Not much of one. Just "I'm sorry".'

'What will I tell the children?' Cecily felt she would never leave this garden seat, just sit here until the end of her life, waiting for Edmund.

'How old are they?'

'Thirteen and almost twelve.'

'I think it is always better to tell them the truth, but make them realise it's not their fault in any way.

Children, as well as adults, torture themselves so with guilt. Anxiety can be like a cancer, eating into a person's courage, their reason, until all their resources are gone and they see no other way out but death.'

'I'll remember that.' She gave him a ghost of a smile. 'Rowena asked me to come and see him, but my child was ill and—'

Simon Oats put his hand on her arm. 'Whatever you do, don't reproach yourself. I could have put him in hospital, but I didn't think he'd do this. In some cases, depression caused by divorce or . . . bereavement, people learn to open a new chapter in their lives. But in this case, the demands for money kept on coming. When the Names refused the offer, I suppose it seemed to him that there would be no end to it. Short of incarcerating him with no access to the Lloyd's situation, I don't see that there was anything we could have done.'

'It was the betrayal. He felt betrayed by his peers,' Cecily said. 'He was rather old-fashioned, perhaps naive that way. He never thought such men would betray their Names. Had he lost the money honestly he would have made the best of it, somehow coped with it. I know he would.' It suddenly seemed important to her to clear Edmund's last act with this man. She did not want him to think Edmund was a coward, had deserted at the first sign of trouble.

'I know.' Simon Oats patted her arm. 'I have other patients with the same worries. Quite a lot live round here.' His mouth twisted with anguish. 'I don't know about the financial amounts involved, but the emotional dues are enormous. Divorce, illness, impotence, job loss as people can't work properly any more. Decent, cheerful, courageous people I've known for years, have hardly ever seen in my surgery, now broken by this.' He shook his head. 'I know it's cold comfort, my dear, but Edmund is not the only one to be driven to this. I fear there will be more deaths before this year is out.'

Cecily put her hand over his. 'It must be difficult for you not being able to help them. Thank you for trying with Edmund.'

He squeezed her hand and she saw there were tears in his eyes. Before she could say anything, Penny came over to them, keeping her eyes firmly away from the black van.

'How are you?' she said.

Cecily was jolted back to reality. 'We must go now. Go to the children,' she said and got up.

'Take it easy,' Simon Oats advised, concern in his face. 'Would you like me to give you anything?'

Cecily turned to him. 'Only if it will bring Edmund back. There.' She smiled sadly. 'You know no pill will do that. I can't be drugged now, I have the children to support.' She took Penny's arm, it was reassuring in its solid tweed. 'I won't go back in, please say goodbye for me.'

'I will. Take care of yourself,' Simon Oats said gently.

'Cecily . . .' Rowena appeared at the front door; Giles was with her.

Cecily swore inwardly. She couldn't bear to see Rowena again. She wanted to leave this alien place, take Edmund's spirit back with her, hold it close away from this house, this woman.

'I'm going now.' She almost ran towards the car, feeling suffocated by this place. 'I must fetch the children.'

'You have his children. I have nothing,' Rowena wailed, tears gushing from her eyes.

'Come inside, Row, come on.' Giles looked embarrassed and tried to manoeuvre her inside. The doctor came swiftly towards them.

'I wanted his child, but he wouldn't give me one. I have nothing . . . *nothing*,' she screamed.

'You go, we'll look after her,' Simon Oats said, touching Cecily gently on her arm as he passed her.

'Come on,' Penny said and pulled her towards the car.

'That bloody Lloyd's killed him. Took all his money so I couldn't have his child and killed him. Do you hear, killed him!' Rowena screamed at Cecily as if she was responsible, her face distorted with grief.

'Tell that to the Chairman,' Cecily said quietly and went with Penny to the car.

'That must have been terrible for you. She could have waited,' Penny said as they drove off.

'It's true though,' Cecily said quietly. 'He's not the first to take his own life because of Lloyd's, and Simon Oats doesn't think he'll be the last.'

'Where does it leave you? This Lloyd's business.'

'I don't know. My money's going fast, mainly on the action groups. But that means nothing now . . .' Her voice trailed away. She stared out of the window at the passing landscape. 'Somehow,' she said with more strength than she felt, 'I'll have to fight on, for the children's sake, now that Edmund has . . .' Her voice broke in a sob, and Penny had to stop the car to take her in her arms and hold her while she wept uncontrollably.

Linette came over from New York to be with Cecily in those terrible weeks after Edmund's death. It was a time of numbing, bewildering pain and desolation. Linette, her health and confidence restored, did her best to guide Cecily and the children through it, helping in all sorts of practical ways in the home.

One afternoon the telephone rang and Linette, as had become her habit, answered it. Cecily never spoke on the phone now. She showed no interest in the call and when Linette had finished she said, 'Cecily, that was rather strange.'

'Oh?'

'You remember . . . well, darling, I don't want to upset you further, but I think it's important.' She looked at her anxiously, and when Cecily made no answer she continued, 'You know that Daniel spent his last night with a woman?'

Cecily nodded wearily.

'That was her, she feels dreadfully guilty and all that, but she's got Daniel's briefcase. Remember that old battered thing he had?'

'Yes.' Cecily perked up a little. 'He had it through the war.'

'Apparently he left it behind that night. She was married at the time and she hid it at the back of some cupboard from her husband. Then when Daniel was killed she felt so guilty and she didn't know what to do with it, so she did nothing. Forgot all about it. Now she's moving house and she's come across it again. She got your number from one of Daniel's friends. Her nephew's bringing it round tomorrow. That's all right, isn't it?'

'S'pose so.' Cecily didn't care. She seemed quite unable to come to grips with life at all. It was two weeks now since the funeral. That terrible day. Rowena had seemed to be drugged and Cecily had not known where to sit, until Giles had led her, Linette and the children to the front pew on the other side to Rowena and her daughters and parents. Everyone had treated her as the widow, though Cecily hadn't noticed it, being so occupied with the children and her own grief.

'Even the vicar thought you were the real widow,' Linette said afterwards.

'I am,' Cecily had said. 'He never married Rowena.'

It was not until Linette appeared from answering the door with Daniel's briefcase in one hand and his coat in the other that Cecily remembered about the phone call the previous day. The sight of the familiar case, so much a part of Daniel, made her gasp as if he himself had come back.

She held out her hand for it and the coat and Linette gave them to her. The coat still smelled of him; it was faint now, but unmistakable, and she nearly swooned with wanting him back.

'Oh, Lin,' she said brokenly, 'how I wish he was here to support us all now.'

Linette took her in her arms. 'I'll take them away. I'm sorry, it was thoughtless of me to bring you more memories.'

'No, don't.' She ran her hands over the battered leather of the case, tried to open it, but it was locked. 'It makes me sad, but somehow,' she gave a watery smile, 'strong too. As if he is somehow here, willing me to be strong.'

'Maybe the keys are in the coat pocket.' Linette turned the coat over and looked in both of them. 'No. I wonder what's in it? Shall we try and open it?' She looked excited, like a child wanting to know a secret.

'I bet there's nothing in it but love letters,' Cecily said, pushing it away. 'I don't want to know, Lin, it would kill me to read his love letters now, when my love is dead.' A tear splashed onto her hand.

'OK, I'll move it, put it over on that chair,' Linette said, picking it up and putting it there. 'I'll hang his coat in the cupboard, shall I? Until you decide what to do with it.'

'Thanks.' Cecily slumped back, defeated by her grief.

But strangely, the arrival of Daniel's things helped her return to life. She felt he was close to her, urging her to pick up the reins again, and although she still refused Linette's offer of taking the case to a locksmith to open it for her, she slowly and carefully began to live again.

'Why can't *we* go to America? Is it because we have no money?' Miranda said peevishly in the car on the way back from dropping Linette at the airport.

'No. I just don't feel like going at the moment. Maybe we'll go in the summer.'

'I feel like going,' Miranda said. 'I could have gone with her.'

'We will all go another time.' Cecily didn't like the selfishness that was invading Miranda. It reminded her of Emily.

'Did Daddy die because he couldn't afford to send me to Eton?' Jamie suddenly burst out through clenched lips that evening.

'Oh, darling, of course not.' Cecily took him in her arms and held his thin, shaking body to her. 'It was nothing to do with Eton. I explained it to you. Shall I again?'

She had explained it to them many times, but when she saw Jamie's tight little face she was sure he did not believe her.

'If we have no money,' Miranda said, flicking from one television channel to another, 'then we'll have to go to a state school, won't we?' She looked accusingly at Cecily.

'Not yet anyway.' Cecily could see Jamie was listening with every fibre of his body. 'We had an insurance and if you both go to day schools,' she emphasised the word 'both' and saw Jamie visibly relax, 'you can hopefully stay until at least GCSE, then we'll see. Don't let's worry about that yet.'

'Day school? But Daddy said . . .' Jamie tailed off.

'I know, darling. But things have changed. We must all live together here, and find schools in London. I've a list somewhere, Penny or someone got me one. We ought to look at it.' She got up and picked up the huge pile of letters that had been gathering dust on the table. Linette had gone through some of them for her, but she had kept putting them off. Now that Linette had left she must take charge of her life again.

She found the list and gave it to Jamie to study. She opened a few letters from friends, then came to one from Jerome. The postmark and stamp were from America.

She felt a little lurch to her heart as she recognised his handwriting, but dismissed it, and opened it quickly.

My Dear,

No one has invented words to cover such a time, such a sadness for you.

I knew you always loved him, so this must hit you very hard. I met Linette just as she was leaving New York to go to you and she told me all about it.

Let me know if there is anything I can do,

My deepest thoughts,

Jerome.

She folded the letter carefully and put it in her pocket and mechanically went through the others.

The last one was a letter of condolence from Edmund's underwriter at Lloyd's. With a cry of anger and pain she tore it up and flung it on the floor, jumped up and stamped and ground it into the carpet.

'Whatever's the matter, Mum?' Miranda looked up mildly from the television screen.

'Bloody murderers,' Cecily shouted, throwing the pieces of the letter to the other side of the room. She flung herself down again and explained it to them, her breath coming fast and angry.

'Mum,' Jamie said when she'd finished, carefully putting aside the list of schools, 'I'd better try and go to Eton, as Daddy wanted me to.'

He could not understand why she cried so, biting back the words that, unless he got a scholarship, they could never afford it now.

Chapter Twenty-Six

It was May, the light pure and clean, the flowers and leaves bursting through. Cecily pottered in her tiny London garden and thought longingly of Caithness.

It sat there always, like a bird on her shoulder. It was madness to keep thinking of it, yearning for it now she could no longer go there, knowing that being there would ease her tortured thoughts.

Ronald had tried repeatedly to ring her, but she'd put the telephone down, not wanting, in her present weakness, to hear if he had turned the castle and its wild grounds into some vulgar monstrosity. She didn't even know if he'd returned the money Daniel had left Stephen, nor did she care. She knew she was being protected by Stephen and Linette from any dramas in that direction, and for that she was grateful.

She found a school for Jamie, but like the one she'd found for Miranda, there was only a place in September, so for the moment they went to a small co-ed in Barnes. To her relief they found the work easy and made a few friends. But on the days their grief became too much to bear she let them stay at home, telling herself that in September they'd all pull themselves together, start afresh.

'I'd love to go to the castle in Caithness,' she said to the children one evening as they ate supper. 'I really miss it, don't you?'

'Let's go then,' Miranda said. 'We can break in. You know, by that shaky door by the back scullery. No one will know.'

'We can't, darling. Besides, I don't know if Ronald has sold it. It might be a theme park by now.'

'Then we can have a go on that. But he couldn't have built it already. Could he?'

'Let's go and see.' Jamie put down his fork. 'Just go and look. No one can stop us looking.'

'No, they can't,' Cecily agreed. The thought was irresistible.

'We can stay in a hotel, or if we haven't enough money someone will have us to stay,' Jamie said.

Cecily smiled at him. He was growing now, his face less taut, but she still heard him crying out for Edmund in his sleep.

Edmund's death enveloped her like a heavy cloak. Sometimes she struggled through the folds and was almost light-headed. At other times the bitter cruelty of his passing hit her like a sledgehammer. Her emotions swooped from raw guilt at not guessing his deep anguish, not saving him, and anger at his leaving them to the yawning emptiness of bereavement, knowing she would not see him again.

She had written to the Chairman of Lloyd's and told him that she had overpaid their debts. 'My husband's life is worth a thousand times the whole of your losses,' she wrote. 'Do not ask me for more. The debt is now yours, and you will never be able to repay it.' He had written back, polite, deeply sorry, and she had thrown it away. She had not wanted a letter from him, but she had wanted him to know that as far as she was concerned, her debt was paid, though the knowledge that a writ, like a bat of doom, might arrive any moment pierced her with claws she could not shake off.

She could go to Lloyd's, cap in hand, and ask for help. They had their own bankruptcy scheme and were said to be willing to help the destroyed Names. But she couldn't bring herself to go, to ask for charity from the very people who had ruined her life. The first of the court cases had started, but it would go on a long time. There was a feeling that everyone was waiting for the outcome, so for a moment the pressure from Lloyd's had eased, but her financial problems had not. She knew she would have to sell the house and move somewhere smaller. She had not told the children yet, not wanting to burden them further.

'I think I'll ring someone up first, to see if the castle's still there,' she said to Jamie and Miranda. 'I don't want to go back if it's a theme park or a hypermarket.'

She got on to Molly Eskine who ran an art gallery nearby.

'We're thinking of you, it's so nice to hear from you,' Molly started, getting rid at once of the embarrassment of mentioning Edmund's death.

'Has Ronald sold the castle?' Cecily asked, relieved Molly had not gone on about Edmund. She found it very difficult to cope with. The way in which he had died made the subject such an awkward wedge between otherwise caring people.

'Not that I know of. He's not been here these last months. I saw Jane Drew in Wick last week. She's thinking of leaving, can't stand him. There's a new laird at Kinhavie.' She mentioned the vast estate that bordered the land of the old castle. 'Old Jock's dead, did you know?'

'No, I'm sorry, but he was ninety, wasn't he?'

'At least. His nephew died last year, so this new heir is a cousin. He's looking for staff.'

'So she'll go there?'

'She's thinking of it. He's very rich, but he'll need to be, the place is a ruin. But getting back to Ronald,' Molly went on, 'his friends are so rude. They treat people up here as if they are inferior or mentally deficient. And they run up bills. Oh my dear, it was a sad day when you left us.'

'I had no choice. I had to pay back the bank.'

'I know. Well, it's no good looking back,' Molly said heartily. 'But we all miss you and of course dear Daniel.'

'I wondered what had happened to the castle, if it was still there.'

'It was yesterday,' Molly laughed. 'I don't think he'll do anything until the summer. Jane Drew wasn't expecting him, but then, as she said, he's apt to just turn up without warning.'

'Is it a theme park?' Jamie asked when she got off the telephone.

'No, not yet.'

'Is Ronald there?' Miranda stuffed half a banana into her mouth.

'Darling, do you have to eat like that?' Cecily couldn't help saying. She often wondered if Miranda would become a well-mannered woman. At the moment it was difficult to believe she ever would.

'Is he there?' Miranda repeated as soon as the banana would let her.

'No. He hasn't been there for a while. Not many southerners like it up there in the winter.'

'Then we must go.'

'Do let's, Mum, please. We can break in through that door and camp.'

'Squat. Can't squatters stay in somewhere if it's empty?' Miranda said.

Cecily looked from one eager face to the other. Their eyes were shining and it was the first time since Edmund's death that they had been excited about something. The castle wasn't hers any more, she had no right to it, and yet . . . It was as if that wide luminous sky was lighting up the room. She could almost taste the salt in the breeze coming off the sea, hear the haunting cry of the sea gulls as they whirled round the ruin, ducking and swooping for food. It would be the last time they would go there, before Ronald destroyed it. She'd regret it for the rest of her life if she didn't go once more.

'I don't know,' she began but the children could see from her expression that they had won her over.

'We must go. Too bad about school. We know all the work anyway,' Miranda said. 'Let's go tomorrow, before Ronald pulls it down.'

'Yes, tomorrow. We can go tomorrow, can't we?' Jamie said, his face holding more hope than Cecily had seen for years.

'I don't know about tomorrow, I have to tell Daphne – I mean she's been so kind.'

'She said that girl could help till she went to university in the autumn and we don't have to go to our new schools till September so what's stopping us?' Miranda said with a touch of impatience.

Daphne had been more than kind. Cecily had struggled in to work when she could and one morning Daphne had said to her, 'Look, my dear, I know this is hell for you, but I may have a solution. A friend of mine's daughter is at a loose end until she goes to Bristol in October. I could take her on until you feel up to it. Give yourself time with the children, to come to terms with things. How are you for money?'

'I've sold some furniture, I have a little for now,' Cecily said. Part of the money from the furniture she'd put aside to pay for a course to get her a better job, but now she had this yearning for Scotland, for those wide, limitless skies. She'd spend it to go there. The course would have to wait.

Her mother had offered to lend her money, but she'd refused, determined to go on being independent as long as she could. Cynthia and Gerald had not come over for the funeral.

'I can't stand them, especially when they're young people. That bloody Lloyd's,' Cynthia said. 'But you and the children come here. I'll pay for your tickets, stay as long as you want.'

'I might do, later, thanks,' Cecily had promised.

'I'll talk it over with Daphne tomorrow,' Cecily said now. 'Maybe we'll go at the weekend.'

'Not tomorrow?' Jamie pleaded, the light going out of his eyes.

Cecily hugged him. 'Not tomorrow, but in a day or so.'

'So we have to go to school tomorrow?' Miranda said sourly. 'That means I have to do my history. Please can't we go tomorrow?'

'No,' Cecily laughed. She suddenly felt lighter as if the weight of Edmund's death had shifted, letting her breathe.

They went on the Saturday, setting off early in the morning by car. At the last moment Cecily put in Daniel's briefcase. She hadn't opened it yet, she still couldn't face it, but just the sight of it brought back powerful memories of him, and she needed it to keep her courage up. She told a few close friends and Daphne where they could be contacted if necessary. 'Not if it's Lloyd's though,' she said firmly. 'They can wait.'

She rang Linette and Stephen, leaving a message on their answerphone.

They spent the weekend with friends on the border
then drove on up. Despite her anxiety at what she'd
find, Cecily found her heart lifting as she drove. The
summer had burst forth all at once, the yellow gorse
glowed from the hedgerows, new leaves shimmered on
the trees, highlighted by the sun.

'Are we going to drive up to the door, or hide the car
and sneak in?' Jamie said.

'I should have rung Mrs Drew,' Cecily said. Now they
were so near she felt sick with apprehension. She had
not rung Jane Drew for the simple reason that she did
not want to hear that Ronald was there. She could not
have driven all this way knowing he was there. She
wanted to stand one more time in the grounds beside
the castle, even if she could not go in. She couldn't even
do that if Ronald was there.

'Let's just ring the bell,' Miranda said. 'Like visitors.
If Ronald is there we could pretend we'd left something
behind.'

Various other ideas, some more fantastic than others, such as Jamie's idea to wait until after dark then
with grappling irons and ropes get onto the roof and
take up permanent residence in the attics, were put
forward until, by now almost mechanically, Cecily
drove in through the gates and up the drive.

There were no other cars outside the castle. The children jumped out and Miranda ran to the door and pulled
the iron bell handle. The door opened almost immediately and Jane Drew looked at them incredulously.

'Cecily! Miranda and Jamie.' Her mouth dropped

open, her hand shot up to cover it, the other went to her heart as if to stop it flying from her breast.

'Can we come in? Is Ronald here?' Jamie said.

'Jane, forgive us. We just wanted to come. We can stay in the bed and breakfast in Keiss.'

'You can't, she's shut it for redecoration. You must stay here. Oh, it's all right, *he's* not here,' she added darkly.

'We can't . . . I mean it's not mine and . . .'

'We were going to break in and squat,' Jamie said.

'Not really.' Cecily smiled awkwardly. 'We just wanted to come and didn't really think.'

'This is your home. Whatever legal jargon's taken place, this is your home,' Jane Drew said firmly. 'Of course you must stay. It's been empty for months. There's no harm in you staying here. I was just cleaning the hall when you rang the bell. I was thinking what a pity it is, cleaning for no one. But now you're here . . .' Her faded face broke open with a smile. 'Stay for a while, for old time's sake.'

Under the wide skies, the bunched clouds tipped with pink, gold and grey, the rugged earth sprouting rich, new grass and wild flowers, Cecily felt the peace come back to her. It was like touching base with the true meaning of life. Gone was the rush and bustle of London, and with it the tangled thoughts that tortured her nights. Edmund's signet ring encircled her finger and every so often she'd touch it and wish he had not left them the way he had. But in that soft yet savage light she felt the healing start in her soul. As she watched her children's cheeks become rosy, their eyes shine, she thought, we will survive, somehow we will make our lives whole again.

Shopping in Thurso a week later Cecily saw Molly Eskine. She was standing on the pavement talking to a tall, brown-haired man.

'My dear Cecily, I heard a rumour you were here,' she greeted her.

'I was going to ring you but . . .'

'I understand, my dear. Meet the new laird from Kinhavie, Andrew McEwen. Cecily Mendelson, true owner of the castle.'

'I'm so glad to meet you at last. I've been hearing terrible stories of theme parks, roller coasters. I do hope they're not true.' His voice was rich and held a hint of laughter.

Cecily felt her hand being clasped in a firm handshake and looked up into the open face of a man in his mid-forties. His grey eyes looked straight into hers. She was struck by a haunting sadness deep in them, but his full mouth smiled in pleasure.

'Not if I can help it, but it's . . .' She paused, looked again into his congenial face, finding her eyes drawn to it, wondering about the touch of sadness in his expression. 'It's not mine any more. I'm only trespassing.'

He laughed. 'We'll do our best to stop him building anything outrageous there. Call on me if you need me.' He smiled, said goodbye to them both and strode away up the hill.

Molly, watching her gaze, said, 'Who'd have thought wizened old Jock would have had such an heir. He's only a cousin, so I suppose there needn't be much likeness. But he's a great improvement, very popular around here, especially with the lasses.'

'He's not married?'

'Not at the moment,' Molly laughed. She linked her arm through Cecily's. 'In a fairy story, my dear, you'd marry him and live happily ever after, keeping an eye on your castle from his estate.'

'Oh Molly, what nonsense,' Cecily smiled. 'But I feel I have an ally in him. He'll fight against Ronald's ghastly plans.'

'That he will.'

Cecily wrote to Linette and Stephen, telling them with mischievous glee of their trespassing. 'I force myself not to think of what might be here next year, though the new Laird of Kinhavie won't put up with any eyesores,' she wrote. 'I just think of today. I wish you would all come and trespass too, have a summer like we did when we were children.'

Miranda and Jamie took up riding again and spent much of their day at the riding stables. One morning after she'd dropped them, Cecily took her art things and went down to the beach to paint. She hadn't painted for years and now in this lull in her life decided to start again.

The sea had eaten great chunks out of the land. She sat on one of its tooth marks in the soil and started to sketch the sweep of the sea, the jagged lines of shingle left bare by the outgoing tide. She worked hard, wishing she could capture the light. She felt rather than heard someone approach her.

'Hello, Cecily.'

She looked up in surprise. 'Jerome.'

'I was told I'd find you here. Am I disturbing you?' His eyes flickered to her work then back to her face.

'I . . . I can't believe it.' She squinted at him through the pale sun, her breathing constricted, her heart pounding. 'Why are you here?'

His eyes, rich brown like chestnuts, stayed on her face. He was more lined, she thought, but he looked good in his blue sweater and jeans. She looked incredulously at him, as if she'd somehow conjured him up and he would just as quickly disappear. She felt a pang of sadness at what she'd lost.

He saw her expression and said, 'Cecily, forgive me. I had to come to see how you were, after Edmund's death.'

'It's a long way to come.'

He smiled, sat down beside her, yet far enough away not to touch her. 'I tried to ring you, went to your house, then to the shop. They told me you were here. I flew up this morning. Dropped my things at the hotel in Wick and came here. Your housekeeper told me you were on the beach.'

Cecily pretended to study her work. She liked the feel of him beside her, but her heart wept.

'I wanted to say I was sorry about how we parted. I accused you of things you didn't do. I've learnt more about the wiles of teenage girls since.' He gave her a swift, contrite smile. 'I've been meaning to contact you for ages but I've been away on business and I didn't like to intrude on your grief. Then yesterday morning I thought, I can't go on putting it off. She can only show me the door. So here I am.'

'I couldn't cope with Emily,' Cecily said straight out. 'I know she's had a bad time, but I couldn't cope with her behaviour. I didn't say those things to her but—'

'I know now that you didn't.' He raked his fingers through his hair. 'I'm . . . I'm so sorry I accused you of it. I should have known you wouldn't say such things. I'm sorry.' He looked so contrite she stretched her hand out to him, but he didn't seem to see it.

'I found it very difficult having her with me suddenly. I felt guilty about my marriage break-up, devastating her life. I overcompensated, I know that now.'

'None of us knows how to be a parent,' Cecily said, letting her hand rest on the grass beside her.

'Too true.' He laughed. 'But I missed you. I knew . . . well, I knew you really only loved Edmund but . . .'

'How did you know?' Her voice was quiet.

'The way you talked of him, the way your eyes still looked hurt by him. Oh Cecily, I'm so sorry it ended as it did. It must have been hell for you.' Impulsively he leant over and snatched her hand up from the grass. Seeing the signet ring gleaming in the sun, he stared at it as if it was a barrier between them. 'My poor Cecily.'

'It was dreadful. He was driven to it by Lloyd's. I wish I could have helped him, convinced him that it didn't matter, that Lloyd's was not worth a hair of his head, certainly not his life.'

'They have a lot to answer for.'

'Jerome, do you think they know what they've done?' Her face was twisted in agony. 'Do you think they thought of the destruction they were causing in people's lives? It's not just the money, it's the betrayal, the dishonesty.'

He gently stroked her hand with his fingers. 'Greedy people don't think of others. And somehow that beating of their breasts, and their saying they didn't know all this would happen seems doubly sick now.'

'More than thirty people have committed suicide already,' she said. 'But still they do not care. It is a good thing Edmund never married Rowena. Suicide invalidates the estate protection plan and any money he had left would have been taken from her. They go on trying to squeeze money from the widows of those they have killed. It's shameless.'

'What will you do?' Jerome said gently.

'I've got the children into good day schools for September.'

'And your job?'

'Daphne's been so kind and kept my job open, but I'll have to train for something that will make more money. I'll have to sell the house too, buy something smaller.'

'You have such guts. I admire that in you.'

There was warmth in his eyes and she wanted so much to hold him, to feel his arms encircle her, feel the comfort of his body against hers. But she dared not touch him, in case he rejected her. He had come, no doubt spurred by Edmund's tragic death, to apologise. But Emily was surely still with him, and they had no future together while she was there.

'I must go and get the children,' she said briskly, pulling away her hand and packing up her paints. 'They're at the riding stables, but I feel they get under Karen's feet while she's trying to muck out and cope with her own children.' She got up and began to climb up to the garden.

'How long are you here?' She threw the words over her shoulder.

'I don't know.' He watched her carefully. 'I've been working awfully hard, travelling a lot. I felt I owed myself a few days off.'

For the rest of the day they kept on safe subjects. She heard that Linette had a new love in her life, 'a charming man, quite besotted with her'.

The children accepted Jerome without question. He bought them a kite and they flew it in the garden above the sea. Cecily, seeing them together, realised how much they needed a male figure in their lives. But there was Emily, and she would wreck it all.

'Stay for supper,' she said. 'It's not much, Mrs Drew has gone to her daughter's for the evening. I'm cooking spaghetti.'

'I'd love to. Thanks.' His eyes caught hers, and she read the unmistakable invitation. She turned away biting her lip, not knowing how to tell him that she did

not want to be his lover again while Emily was still
with him.

The children were tired after all the fresh air and
they went to bed quite soon after supper.

'May I stay?' Jerome said when she came back to the
drawing room from tucking them in.

Cecily looked out at the silver and black sea, the
moon weaving its light between the waves. Unconsciously she fingered Edmund's signet ring, a habit
she hardly knew she had when she was indecisive or
troubled about something.

'Not tonight,' she said, keeping her eyes on the shim-
mering water.

'I understand,' he said, and without saying anything
more, left her. She heard his steps going down the
wooden staircase to the hall. She yearned to run after
him, to catch him in her arms and hold him again, but
she stood there, staring out at the black and silver sea,
and let him go.

She stayed for a long time looking out at the sea, the
dark shape of the ruin silhouetted against the slowly
pulsating water. Why had Jerome come? Was it to salve
his conscience after he'd wrongly accused her of being
unkind to Emily? Or did he really love her and want
her back? He had fitted in to this day perfectly, but this
was a magical place, a place outside real life. If they
could stay here for always, then it would work between
them.

She heard the surge of a car come up the drive, saw
the lights cut the corner of the castle, heard the crunch

of gravel as it stopped. He'd come back. Not content with her answer, he'd come back. She smiled.

She heard the front door open and slam, pounding feet two steps a time on the stairs. She waited by the window, a smile of welcome for him on her lips.

Ronald burst into the room.

Chapter Twenty-Seven

'What the bloody hell are you doing here?' There was spittle on Ronald's lips, his face was flushed, his breath came fast. 'I found out you were here from that shop you work at. I came at once. You're trespassing. I'll get the police on you.' He lurched towards her menacingly.

For a moment, Cecily was transfixed. Her body, a second ago relaxed, open to Jerome's touch, took a moment to adjust to this brutal intrusion, for though by rights it was his castle, she felt he was the intruder, not her.

'It no longer belongs to you and you've fucked it up with the council, getting your friends to work against me.' He was close to her now, spit hit her face. She wiped it off disgustedly, jumping back from him.

'Stop shouting. You'll wake the children.'

'I'll shout if I want. Your family always thought themselves so bloody superior to everyone else, taking what they wanted. I gave you money for this . . . this dump, but you come back and live here as if it's yours.

I'm not having it.' He waved his clenched fist at her. 'Do you hear me? Get out now, or I'll call the police.'

'I'll go in the morning, the children are asleep now.' She stood firm, trying to control the terror coiling inside her. Was he going to hit her? Beat her senseless in his anger?

'You will go now. Where's Jane? I suppose she's in on this. I'll dismiss her for a start.'

'It's not her fault. It's entirely mine. I know I shouldn't be here, I'm sorry.' The apology sounded like an insult. She moved away from him, nearer the door. If he attempted to hit her she'd snatch up that marble lamp and hit him back. Her fingers itched to pick it up now, hold it as a weapon to protect herself. 'I just wanted to come back one more time, to try and come to terms with Edmund's death,' she said defiantly.

She saw a look of contempt cross his face. For a second she thought he was going to make some remark about Edmund's cowardice. She said bitterly, 'I know I should have asked you, but you would have refused to let me come, wouldn't you?'

'You bet I would.'

'I'll go in the morning.' She turned to leave him.

'You will go now.'

'The children—'

'I said now.'

'Mum.' Jamie's voice came from the top of the stairs. 'Who's shouting?'

Any idea she had of begging Ronald to let them stay for the night evaporated. The children couldn't possibly

454

stay here with Ronald in this mood. She must take them away at once.

'Ronald has come back,' she said briskly. 'He's in a very bad mood and we must leave.' She went up the stairs to him. 'Wake up Miranda, and pack quickly.'

There was a loud clink and a curse as Ronald helped himself to a drink. Jamie looked scared. 'We must go to . . .' As he hesitated, pain in his eyes, Cecily knew he'd been about to say 'Daddy'. 'Jerome,' he said, looking at her steadfastly with Edmund's eyes. 'He will look after us.'

'Yes, you're right.' She hugged him, feeling his small body trembling against her. 'Don't worry, Ronald's just bad-tempered. He's driven miles,' she said, trying to sound as if it was a perfectly natural reaction. 'Hurry now, I'll come and help you.'

In fifteen minutes she had them dressed, in the car, their luggage haphazard in the back. Then she remembered that she'd left Daniel's briefcase in the wardrobe in her bedroom. She ran back upstairs and fetched it.

As she reached the landing outside the drawing room Ronald came out. He stared at her angrily then, seeing the case, blanched and lunged at it, trying to grab it out of her hands.

'What are you doing? Leave it alone!' She clung to it, her fingers sore with the force of wrenching it back.

'Give it to me.'

'No. Ronald, let me go.'

He grabbed the case with both hands, pulling desperately at it, as if his life depended upon it. She could see

the veins standing out like ropes on his temple, his
teeth gritted with effort. Why was he in such a frenzy
for it? she thought in panic, holding onto it with all her
strength but feeling it easing from her grasp.

'Leave it, it's not yours, it's Daddy's!' she screamed,
stamping on his foot. He let go with a curse, his eyes
alight with anger, his mouth snarling obscenities. She
ran to the top of the stairs but he was after her.

'Give me that case!' he yelled. But she kicked out and
tore down the stairs, tripping on the last step, almost
crashing to the floor. He came heavily after her. She
ran through the front door, slammed it behind her,
jumped into the car, flinging the briefcase on the floor.

'What is it?' Jamie said fearfully.

'It's Uncle Ronald, he's going to kill us,' Miranda
screamed as Ronald lurched out of the door and threw
himself at the car.

Fighting to remain calm, her fingers trembling,
Cecily started the engine, praying it wouldn't stall.

'Lock the doors,' she ordered the children. 'Quickly.'

They jumped up, falling over each other to do so.
Ronald flung himself at the car door, pulling at it,
screaming at them. Cecily jammed her foot on the
accelerator. The car jerked forward and he fell on the
gravel. She didn't look back until she was outside
Jerome's hotel in Wick.

They stumbled into the hotel, Cecily dishevelled and
dazed, clutching the children and Daniel's case as if
Ronald would be there waiting to snatch them away.
She had a sudden fit of panic. What if Jerome wasn't

there? Had he gone off to find more amusing company? She thought quickly of her friends; the Eskines or the Forbes would help her, but it meant getting back into the car and driving on. She didn't know the people who owned this hotel, but there must be room for them, just for tonight.

'Will Ronald come and get the case?' Miranda asked, trembling. Cecily had told them about the struggle, unable to keep the fear from her voice.

'No. I don't know why he wants it. It's as if he's gone mad, but he won't have it,' she said with more determination than she felt. She looked down at it. She must get it opened tonight, break the locks if necessary, to see what it was he was so desperate to find. She cursed herself for being so feeble about opening it before.

They passed the bar and saw Jerome talking to the landlord. Cecily felt a wave of relief. His face lit up, then creased in concern when he saw the state she was in and the children.

'Whatever's happened?'

'Horrible old Ronald's come and chucked us out,' Miranda said.

'He tried to hurt Mummy, he wanted her case,' Jamie said.

'Are you all right?' Jerome looked anxiously at Cecily, taking her arm and leading her to a chair. Betty, the landlord's wife, came out from behind the bar, concern fighting with curiosity on her face.

'Whatever is it? You look as if you've been in a fight. Shall I call the police?'

'No, I'm fine.' Cecily forced herself to smile. Being safe with Jerome relaxed her defences. She felt immeasurably tired, but she couldn't give up yet.

'I thought it best if we came to you,' Jamie said, standing there, not very tall, but straight and trusting. Cecily's heart lurched. Was Jamie transferring his trust from Edmund to Jerome? He didn't know how much he was asking.

'You were absolutely right. Well done, Jamie,' Jerome said, putting his hand on Jamie's shoulder. Cecily felt she would cry.

'Let's find you rooms,' Jerome said, 'then see what we do in the morning. There is space, isn't there?' he asked Betty.

'Yes, we have two rooms left. One's only small, mind. But don't you think I should call—'

'No thank you, they just need to sleep,' Jerome said firmly, helping Cecily up and shepherding them all upstairs.

'Ronald won't come here, will he?' Jamie asked as Cecily, feeling like a robot on auto drive, tucked him in.

'No, of course not,' Jerome answered quickly, looking at Cecily. 'I'm here to see he won't.' He smiled at them.

'He's drunk and he'll murder us,' Miranda said. 'I think we should call the police.'

'Don't worry, he won't hurt you,' Jerome said firmly, taking Cecily's arm and leading her from the room. 'Mummy looks asleep on her feet, let me find her room.'

Jerome took Cecily to her bed despite her protests. 'I must open this before I sleep. Ronald wants it. It belongs to my father. I should have opened it ages ago when I first got it, but I couldn't face it. I'm sure it's only love letters and old bills, but . . .' She swayed on her feet and Jerome put his arms round her. She let herself lie against him a moment, savouring the comfort of his body.

'I'll get it open for you. You lie down, I promise I won't let it out of my sight.' He gently released her onto the bed.

'Would you?' She felt so tired, so distant from it all. Deep inside she felt the pain of being thrown out by Ronald. It wasn't her castle, but if only he'd let her stay, just one more night. She lay back, shut her eyes and let the yawning abyss of despair engulf her. She had nothing left. She would have to sell the house in London to survive, buy something tiny in another area. If they didn't win the cases against Lloyd's, what then? For one terrible, black moment she felt as if she stood over the same yawning abyss as Edmund had. There seemed no hope.

'I may have to break the locks,' she heard Jerome say. 'I'll just go down and see if Tom, the landlord, has any tools. Will you be all right? I'll come straight back.'

'Don't let Ronald have it.' She half sat up as if to grab it from him. Jerome came back to her.

'No one will have it, I promise you. I won't be long.' He laid his hand on her hair a moment, then he left her. As he closed the door behind him, she felt utterly alone. 'Oh Edmund,' she moaned despairingly at the flowered walls. 'Why did you go?'

She woke some hours later. It was morning and Jerome was sitting on a chair by the window watching her.

'Sleep well?'

'Yes. The children?' She struggled to get up.

'Eating an enormous breakfast with the new Laird of Kinhavie.'

'In his house?'

'No, he's here downstairs. Tom introduced us and the children are telling him about Ronald.' He laughed.

'The briefcase!' she cried, pushing back the bed-clothes to jump out and find it.

Jerome picked up some papers from the table, came over and sat on her bed. 'This was in it,' he said handing it to her. 'There are some other papers as well – a sealed letter to Stephen, bills and such.' He smiled. 'It's a will.'

'A will?' She stared at it, the words jumping like black spiders on the page.

'It's dated a few months before your father's death. Didn't you tell me he died in late 'eighty-eight.' He pointed out the date. 'It leaves the castle to you and to Stephen.'

'Not to Gail?' She looked up at him incredulously.

'No. Look.' Jerome showed her, putting his other arm round her shoulders. 'He obviously changed his mind, decided that you should have it, despite everything. It just never got to the solicitors.'

Cecily let his words sink in, then she said sadly, 'But Ronald bought my half off me, and most of that money's gone to Lloyd's one way and another. He now shares it with Stephen.'

'I think everything needs to be properly investigated,' Jerome said. 'You must ring Stephen, tell him about this. This makes the other will invalid.'

Cecily stared at the will a long time. She felt the warmth of Jerome's body beside her on the bed. It was pleasant to be so near to him again. He held her close.

'Come back to me,' he said. 'I miss you so much.'

For a moment she said nothing, fighting with her emotions. It was so good being here with him again. His body, his scent so familiar, so loved, so missed. But she did not want to burden him with her problems, be a millstone round his neck, destroying his love for her. And she didn't want to take on Emily. 'I don't know what to do,' she said slowly. 'I'll have to sell the house. I wish . . . I wish I could stay here. I feel more able to cope up here.' She leant her head against him.

'I'll look after you. All of you.' He kissed her, caressing her gently. 'Don't let Lloyd's ruin us being together. Life is too short, darling. We'll be all right together.'

'Emily . . .'

'She'll be fine. She wants to go to a school in Switzerland to do her A levels. I know more how to handle her now, and she's making friends, isn't so possessive.' He pulled her closer to him. 'I'm so sorry about . . .' He paused, sighed. 'I shouldn't have believed the things she said about you.' He sat up, looked helplessly into her face. 'I just overreacted, never thought she'd tell such lies. I must say it gave me a terrible shock to know she could behave like that. Will you ever forgive me?'

'Of course.' She smiled at him. 'She was probably afraid of losing you.'

'Oh, darling, I missed you.' He kissed her, his lips urgent on hers, her throat, her breasts, his hands on her nightdress, lifting it from her.

'I don't know what to do.' She felt too agitated to make love. She kissed him quickly, disentangling herself from his embrace, jumping out of bed. 'What time is it in New York? I must ring Stephen. You said there was a letter.'

'Let him sleep a little longer. Stay here with me.' He tried to pull her back.

'I'm sorry, Jerome, I feel I must do something. Find out the truth about the castle, about Ronald. Please understand.'

'All right,' he sighed, 'if you promise we'll go to bed early tonight. Or better still have a long siesta.'

'I promise,' she laughed, 'if I've got hold of Stephen by then.'

'I'll track him to the ends of the world,' he grinned, then looked more serious. 'Cecily, why must you sell your house in London? If that's not too intrusive a question.'

'I can't make ends meet,' she said with an attempt at a brave smile, turning away as she dressed. 'I'm paying out to the action groups – as you know, one case is being heard at the moment. I hope it goes in our favour, but it's too late for me, I think. My only way of getting more money is to move to somewhere smaller.'

'I could lend—'

'No, thanks. I must work it out for myself. I've heard that if I put money – in this case money from the house – into a trust fund for the children it may be safe from Lloyd's clutches. I shall also use some to train myself for a better job.'

'But you'll live in London?'

'I don't know.' She couldn't meet his eyes, glimpsing the longing for her there.

'So you've got it all worked out?' There was a tinge of sadness mixed with the admiration in his voice.

'Not really, but I must.' She looked at him gravely. 'Edmund couldn't fight any more. There was more at stake for him. He couldn't cope with the betrayal of people he thought were his friends, his own kind. But I must fight on, for the children, give them the best life I can.'

'Let me help you.' His voice was gentle, he stretched out his hand and took hers. 'I want to help you.'

'Thank you, Jerome, thank you for being here when we needed you. Thank you for coming back.' She held his hand, looking at him with love.

He pulled her close to him, down on his knee. 'I love you.' He put his arms round her, and they sat close together for a moment. She was the first to break the silence.

'When can I ring Stephen? I can't wait to tell him. Should I open the letter? What do you think?'

'Give him another hour. Tell him then.' He stroked her back. 'We have time to make love.' His eyes were liquid with desire, his breath warm on her skin. She yearned to get on, find out what treachery Ronald had committed, but suddenly she wanted to please Jerome, give him what he asked. She kissed his mouth, moulding her body into his.

'That was wonderful, any hope of an encore?' Jerome said later, kissing her again.

'No, sorry, not now.' She laughed, kissed him quickly and jumped out of bed. 'We must get on, goodness knows what the children are up to.' She bathed, dressed and ran downstairs, not waiting for Jerome. In the dining room she saw the children sprawled at a corner table, laughing at something Andrew McEwen had said.

'Mum, he's got a pony and cart and we can borrow it whenever we want,' Jamie said, his eyes shining.

'Oh, that's kind but . . .' Cecily smiled at Andrew, who stood up and offered her his chair. 'We'll be going south soon.'

'I've heard about that monster at the castle,' Andrew said. 'If you'd come to me, I'd have shot him.'

'We were fine. Jerome was here and—'

'We've got to get rid of him. He's ruining the land. Spoiling my shoot,' Andrew said. 'He and his friends have caused a lot of trouble round here, owing money and such. Is there no way we can get him out?'

'I don't think so. But . . .' Cecily paused. This was private business.

Andrew saw her hesitation and smiled. There was that same sorrow in his eyes she'd seen when she'd first met him. She felt a surge of compassion, and felt that Andrew McEwen could be trusted. 'Jerome's found a will, a later one.' She told him and the children what was in it.

'Then the castle's ours and we can live here for always,' Jamie cried.

'And I can ride every day,' Miranda chimed in.

Andrew was grave. 'I don't know what to say. If he knew there was another, later will, he'll be in trouble. I've got a top-rate lawyer. If you'd allow me, I could put it in his hands.'

'Thank you, but first I must ring my brother in New York. It's really his castle now.'

'Of course.' He got up from the table. 'You know where to find me if you need me, any time.' He smiled at her. "Bye, Jamie and Miranda, come over when you want.'

'We will, thanks,' Jamie answered, catching a look from Cecily.

'When are we going riding? We'll be late if we don't go soon,' Miranda said.

'I'll take you,' Jerome said, coming over to them. 'I've a few business calls to make, then I'll take you.'

'Don't worry, I'll go,' Cecily said, taking his hand. 'I feel a need to get out in the fresh air.'

'If you're sure.' He squeezed her hand, looked into her eyes. 'Come back,' he said quietly as the children drifted away.

'I ought to return to London. I've nowhere to stay here now.'

'You stay here with me. I've got another week. Please, Cecily. Let's just be together, let things go as they will.' He put her hand to his cheek, then his lips. 'I love you.'

She kissed him. 'I love you.' The words came easily. She jumped up from the table. 'I want to wake up Stephen, tell him about the will!'

'I'm coming right now,' Stephen said. 'I'll get that bastard. You know he did take that money Daniel left me. He made out some rubbish about a trust fund.'

'But how did he get round the solicitor?'

'God knows, but I'll find out. He must have used my money to buy you out.'

'Oh, and there's this letter too, addressed to you from Daddy.'

There was a silence, she could almost feel him digesting this. 'What does it say?' he said at last.

'I haven't read it.'

'Read it to me.'

'Are you sure? I could send it.'

'Read it.'

She opened it, feeling a sudden rush of emotion as she saw the page of Daniel's writing. She swallowed, flicked her eyes down the page, then began.

My dear Stephen,

    I know I've been a lousy father. I loved you so much yet somehow I always ended up hurting you. I made a mess of my life and yours, all of you children, breaking up your homes so often. I was too arrogant and selfish to admit this, but I became afraid that you would ruin your life and the lives of those you loved, as I had, so I picked away at your faults, taking the anger I held against myself out on you. I see all that now.

I understand why you ran away. I chased you away, so I can only blame myself. You'll never know how much I wanted to find you, see you again and explain, but I knew I might start on you again, destroy the life you had built up for yourself, so after a while I kept away.

I leave the castle to you and Cecily as you both loved it so. I'd like to think of you all there with your own children.

Try not to hate me too much,

D.

There was a long silence, broken only by them both weeping. Cecily pulled herself together first.

'Then the castle's doubly yours,' Cecily said, 'as Ronald took your money.'

'I want you to have it, Cecily. How can I live in it? My life is here. Of course I'll come for the summers.' He laughed. 'But I can't live in it all the time. But you and the children can.' There was another silence, then he said quietly, 'So Daniel loved me after all, wanted us to both share the castle.' His voice trembled.

'I knew he always loved you. The tragedy was he couldn't tell you, but now he has, in the only way he could. Do you think Ronald knew he'd changed the will?' Cecily thought back. The only will seen after Daniel's death must have been the one written after Gail had blackmailed him. Somehow Ronald must have found out about it, been frantically looking for it so he could destroy it.

'Maybe Daniel told Ronald, then died before he could take the will to the solicitor. You know Daniel, he thought death was for other people,' Stephen said. 'Listen, Cecily, I'll be there as soon as I can. Yes, I'll find the hotel. Thank God Jerome's there with you. Stay clear of Ronald until I can get to him.'

'What did he say?' Jerome asked her when she came back downstairs.

'He's coming straight over.' She smiled.

'As king of the castle?' Jerome laughed.

'He wants me to live in it.'

'To live in it always?' Jamie asked, his face alight.

'Then I can have a pony,' Miranda said. 'Brill, to live here always.'

'I haven't decided.' Cecily was aware of Jerome's sudden stillness. 'I've found you both schools in London and—'

'There are schools here,' Jamie said. 'The Laird of Kinhavie has a son my age. He's with his grandparents at the moment, but he's going to school here.'

'I didn't know he was married,' Cecily said.

'His wife died,' Miranda said. 'She had cancer. Then Jock died and his nephew. He hadn't expected to be laird, but he's pleased he is. Betty told us when she gave us our breakfast.'

'She is rather a gossip,' Jerome said in Cecily's ear. 'Goodness knows what stories will be going around about us.'

'Let's go riding, we're going to be late,' Miranda said, 'and Karen won't think we're coming and let someone else ride Velvet.' She pulled Jamie towards the door.

'Will you come too?' Cecily turned to Jerome. 'I won't be long, I can leave them a few hours.'

'I've some calls I must make. I'll wait for you here and guard the will.' He bent forward and kissed her, dropped his hand on her shoulder in a caress, before leaving the room.

Cecily drove the children to the riding school; they chattered all the way, exhausting her with their questions.

'I have not made up my mind what is best for us,' she said firmly. 'Wait until Stephen gets here.'

The hotel was small and dark and Cecily gave in to her urge to linger awhile on the moors. The sky, cut with long smudges of cloud, soared above her, on and on, stretching away for ever, merging into the sea that shimmered ahead. As she walked, trying to sort out her raging emotions, reach a solution for their lives, she gradually felt the peace seep into her, the power and the strength of the land healing her, renewing her spirit.

She'd lost Edmund, truly lost him. He had 'gone before', as the vicar had said at the funeral. But she felt closer to him here, felt more at peace at his passing than she had before.

Ahead in the distance she could see the castle, white against the sea. Relief poured over her. Daniel had not forgotten Stephen. Lloyd's could not get it from her if it was in Stephen's name. Joy, a feeling of elation, flooded her suddenly. Standing here looking down on the castle that had been the catalyst of her life, the keeper of so many memories, holding so many of the most important scenes in her life, she felt close to them all again. Daniel with his charm, his winning ways with women, Edmund whom she loved still. She felt the living spirits too, Linette and Stephen, their childhood somehow running into Miranda and Jamie's, and Jerome, who'd come to find her. She stood there letting them ebb in and out of her thoughts, wondering where she would be next year, what Lloyd's would have reduced her to. Whether there was a writ waiting for her in London.

Then on the wind as if he was beside her, she remembered something Daniel had once said to her. 'The best revenge is to live well.'

She would stay here, the decision was suddenly clear. Laughter and the power of life surged through her, making her feel invincible. 'I will,' she laughed to the wind. 'I will live well.'